COLD RED

Chris Ryan was born in Newcastle. In 1984 he joined 22 SAS. After completing the year-long Alpine Guides Course, he was the troop guide for B Squadron Mountain Troop. He completed three tours with the anti-terrorist team, serving as an assaulter, sniper and finally Sniper Team Commander.

Chris was part of the SAS eight-man team chosen for the famous Bravo Two Zero mission during the 1991 Gulf War. He was the only member of the unit to escape from Iraq, where three of his colleagues were killed and four captured, for which he was awarded the Military Medal. Chris wrote about his experiences in his book *The One That Got Away*, which became an immediate bestseller. Since then he has written over fifty books and presented a number of very successful TV programmes.

To hear more about Chris Ryan's books, sign up to his Readers' Club at bit.ly/ChrisRyanClub

You can also follow him on social media:
Twitter: @exSASChrisRyan
Instagram: @exsaschrisryan
Facebook: ChrisRyanBooks

Also by Chris Ryan

Manhunter
Outcast

COLD RED

CHRIS RYAN

ZAFFRE

First published in the UK in 2023 by
ZAFFRE
An imprint of Bonnier Books UK
4th Floor, Victoria House, Bloomsbury Square, London, WC1B 4DA
Owned by Bonnier Books
Sveavägen 56, Stockholm, Sweden

A CIP catalogue record for this book is
available from the British Library.

Hardback ISBN: 978-1-80418-260-4
Trade paperback ISBN: 978-1-80418-261-1

Also available as an ebook and an audiobook

1 3 5 7 9 10 8 6 4 2

Typeset by IDSUK (Data Connection) Ltd
Printed and bound in Great Britain by Clays Ltd, Elcograf S.p.A.

Zaffre is an imprint of Bonnier Books UK
www.bonnierbooks.co.uk

This book is dedicated to the fallen soldiers of Ukraine

One

Ruslan Masutov sat in the gloom of the underground shelter, a pair of bulky headphones clamped over his ears, watching the live feed on the laptop screen. Nearby, the other three guys on the team checked their weapons one more time. They had spent the past four days living in the cramped space below ground, eating cold rations and taking turns to monitor the radio channel, waiting for the signal.

They were ready.

Masutov was the commander. He was a big bear of a guy, with a thick beard and a nose that looked as if someone had taken a sledgehammer to it. A tattered bush hat stained with dirt and sweat crowned his slab-like head. The hat had once belonged to an Australian, a volunteer in the Ukrainian Foreign Legion. Masutov and his colleagues had captured the man during a raid on a village a few miles outside Kharkiv. They had dragged the prisoner into an abandoned shack, stripped him naked, and bound his hands and feet with rope. Then they had taken out their rage on him.

For two sickening days the Australian had held out against his torturers. Eventually, even Masutov found himself revolted by the injuries they had inflicted on the man. When another soldier had produced a pair of box cutters, Masutov had drawn his pistol and shot the Australian in the head. What he guessed they called a mercy killing. Later, they had burned the corpse in the yard. Masutov had orders to destroy any evidence of their crime, but he'd kept hold of the bush hat. Like a souvenir. A reminder. He had worn it ever since.

Like Masutov, the other soldiers in his team were ethnic Chechens. Sungaev and Arsanov had served under Masutov in Syria, and before that in Crimea. Both were dependable warriors, level-headed and calm under pressure. At twenty-three, Islamov was the youngest of the four and the newest recruit to the Akhmat Battalion. He was pale-faced and slender, with a scraggly joke of a beard and short buzz-cut hair.

All of them were dressed in standard-issue army fatigues, with Chechen flags stitched onto their shoulder patches. On their arms they wore black-and-orange striped cloths, the colours of the St George ribbon, worn by all loyal supporters of the cause. The ribbon symbolised Russian military prowess.

Islamov, the youngster, sat apart from the rest of the team and stared vacantly at the wall, his left leg hammering rapidly. The guy was shitting bricks. Which was understandable, thought Masutov. In less than thirty minutes, if everything went to plan, they would all be dead.

Five days ago, as the battle for Balanivka raged in the streets, Masutov and his comrades had been taken to one side by their commanding officer and told they had been chosen for a special mission. One that would earn them great glory among their brothers and lead to the eventual defeat of the fascist enemy. But it would also require them to make the ultimate sacrifice, their CO had added gravely.

The men had readily agreed. Partly because they were loyal soldiers. But also because they knew they had no choice. They had families back home. The CO had explained in painstaking detail the many terrible things that would happen to them if they refused to carry out their mission. It was a no-brainer. They were all agreed on that point. Better that they would die so that others might live. As an added incentive the CO had promised that their loved ones would be looked after, once they had completed their mission. Mother Russia always took care of her own.

The following day, as the shattered remnants of the Russian forces began pulling back from the town, Masutov and the other guys had covertly taken up their positions in the shelter in a lightly wooded area twenty metres due east of the main square. The shelter itself was essentially a massive hole four metres deep, excavated by a mechanical digger, buttressed on all sides with an inch-thick steel frame in the shape of a 'T' and covered with a waterproof membrane. The whole area had then been backfilled to ground level with eighteen inches of soil; a layer of fallen leaves on top obscured the patch of disturbed earth.

The shelter had everything the Chechens needed to survive for several days. A camouflaged filter system ensured a steady supply of fresh air from above ground. Battery operated LED lights were set up at points around the shelter. A coaxial cable ran from the hatch opening to an aerial in the upper branches of the nearest tree, providing an encrypted comms link with the surveillance team, while a concealed high-resolution camera gave them a live feed of the target location to the west. There was a shitter on the left arm of the 'T' and a storage area for rations, kit and bottled water opposite. There was a row of stretcher beds on the longer side of the shelter, a makeshift table and seating area at the back constructed from ration packs.

Masutov and Sungaev were both packing AK-47 assault rifles. Islamov and Arsanov each had an AK-12. Which was essentially an upgraded version of the Soviet-era AK-74 rifle, chambered for the same 5.45 x 39 mm round. Each man had also been issued with a belt of RGN hand grenades. Basic hardware. Capable of getting the job done, but fundamentally low-grade kit. Nothing unnecessarily expensive. Nothing their superiors would regret not being able to recover from the attack. Which in itself hinted at the doomed nature of their mission.

Four days ago, in the pale light of the predawn, a few hours before the last Russians abandoned the town, Masutov and his men had been sealed inside their hideout.

Then they had settled down to wait.

In the West, they called them stay-behind shelters. NATO troops had built shitloads of them along border with East Germany during the Cold War, anticipating the day when vast Russian tank columns would sweep across the Fulda Gap. The rationale behind such shelters was simple. While conventional forces were retreating, Special Forces units would crawl into the shelters and wait until the enemy had advanced beyond their position. Then they would carry out stay-behind operations, sabotaging factories, supply lines and communication systems.

Soviet troops had stumbled upon a few of these structures during their regular patrols along the East German border. Moscow had been so impressed with the idea that they had decided to copy it. Kremlin agents had consequently set up an improvised network of shelters across Germany, France and elsewhere. One guy in Masutov's battalion once claimed he had helped to dig a hideout in a field in Lincolnshire.

The Chechens were under strict orders to stick to a hard routine in the shelter. Which meant pissing and shitting in plastic bags, eating only cold food, no smoking or raised voices. No phones. Nothing that would give them away to any clearance patrols that might be lurking in the area.

They took turns stagging on, one man monitoring the video feed and the radio channel. After six hours he stood down and the next guy took over. Sungaev and Arsanov passed the time reading books, napping and doing sets of press-ups and stomach crunches. Anything to take their minds off the attack.

Islamov sat in a corner of the shelter and kept to himself. The kid was scared. Masutov knew the signs. He'd seen it in the faces of other young warriors in the moments before a firefight. Fear of death, partly. But also fear of letting your brothers down. Masutov tried to think of some words of comfort. Something to boost the kid's morale. Nothing came to mind. He gave up and refocused on the laptop.

For the past three days they had watched their comrades' retreat unfolding on the screen. They had seen exhausted men scrambling back from their defensive positions, some badly wounded; others had ditched their equipment in the desperate rush to escape. For a short while the streets had been almost deserted. Then there had been a sudden flurry of activity. Columns racing in from multiple directions, soldiers riding on top of armoured vehicles, cheering and waving blue-and-yellow flags.

Ukrainians.

The fascist infantry had followed close behind, sweeping through the buildings overlooking the square, searching for any hiding enemies. A few men had posed for selfies in front of a wrecked tank. Gradually, civilians emerged from ruined buildings to embrace their liberators or beg for food.

Masutov had watched and felt the anger burning in his veins.

He was a proud soldier. He had volunteered for the battalion because it paid well, and because killing was all he knew. But the war he found himself in had not been the one he had been hoping to fight.

Equipment was faulty or missing. Supplies were constantly scarce. Leadership was non-existent. Masutov's unit had suffered some appalling reverses. The enemy had proved unexpectedly stubborn. Morale had plummeted. A few weeks ago, they had been given a new task: shooting conscripted Russian convicts who tried to flee the battlefield. Anyone who refused the order was shot themselves. The situation was a giant clusterfuck.

Although he would never admit such a thing to his brothers, Masutov had begun to privately question the wisdom of those making the big decisions in Moscow. At times, he wondered whether they could even win. He figured it would need something extraordinary to change their fortunes. A high-stakes gamble. All or nothing.

What the Americans called a Hail Mary pass.

For the first seventy hours, he had been sceptical of their chances of success. It seemed like a long shot. How could they be certain that the target would even show up? At best it had to be a calculated guess. And there was something else to consider. If the target failed to appear, the mission would have to be aborted. No choice. In which case Masutov and his colleagues wouldn't have to die launching a suicidal attack. Which was undeniably a good thing. But which also meant they would be on their own, miles from safe territory, in an area teeming with enemy troops. They would have a decision to make. Surrender to the Ukrainian fascists, make a run for it, or remain in the shelter in the hope that their comrades would come to their rescue?

Like any good soldier, Masutov had closed his mind to these questions. He'd kept his attention solely on the mission. Watching and waiting. But after seventy-two hours he was prepared to accept defeat. The target was nowhere to be seen. He wasn't going to turn up. Someone further up the food chain had fucked up. He resigned himself to aborting the op.

And then, thirty minutes ago, everything had changed.

Masutov had been on stag when he had seen the movement on the laptop screen. A small crowd gathering on the western side of the square, sixty metres from the shelter. Men and women dressed in civvies. Young people, mostly. Armed with an array of video cameras and tripods, boom mics and smartphones.

Journalists.

Masutov had counted at least thirty of them. They had been shepherded into position by a group of Ukrainian soldiers. Cameramen had checked angles and lighting; sound guys had tested their mics. Assistants unspooled cables. Everybody was gearing up for the main event.

The mission was on.

As soon as Masutov had caught sight of the cameras, he'd felt a quickening in his chest. He had swiftly alerted his men. *Get your shit together. We're on.*

This is really happening.

Now they waited in tense silence. The last moments of their lives. Arsanov swigged from a plastic bottle of water. Sungaev closed his eyes and muttered a prayer. Islamov tapped his foot nervously. Masutov craved a cigarette.

A voice came over the radio. 'Have you got eyes on the camera crews?'

'Yes. We're watching them now,' Masutov said. 'Have they left yet?'

There was a long pause.

Then the voice came back.

'Not yet. Any minute now. We'll let you know when the target is on the way. Just make sure you're ready.'

The voice clicked off. The channel went silent again. Masutov tried to ignore the tension he was feeling in his guts and checked his shitty watch. Ten o'clock in the morning.

Almost time.

* * *

'This is a fucking bad idea, mate,' Carl Hedges said.

Sergeant Luke Carter looked round at his mucker. The two SAS men were sitting at a table in the corner of a large tented area seven miles due west of Balanivka. Nearby, a crowd of Ukrainian soldiers stood mingling and drinking brews, while others scoffed down plates of hot food served up by the slop jockeys at a make-shift canteen point. Beyond the tent there was an ammunition dump, a bunch of forty-five-gallon steel drums and a cluster of armoured vehicles parked on a wide patch of dirt close to the road-side. Further away, fields of sugar beet and potato crops stretched towards the horizon, pockmarked with clumps of trees and a few ramshackle hovels. Clouds the colour of wet cement smothered the sky, threatening rain.

The laager point had served as a forward operating base for the Ukrainian troops during the recent struggle to retake Balanivka. A staging post, to ferry manpower and weaponry to the frontline. The battle had raged for weeks. Territory had been taken, then lost again. Like something out of the Great War. Until three days ago, when there had been an unexpected breakthrough. The Russian soldiers had suddenly withdrawn from the town to a heavily defended point some twenty miles due east. Balanivka had been abandoned. It was in Ukrainian hands once more.

The recapture of the president's birthplace had been a symbolic victory for his administration. Now he intended to crown the achievement with a speech to the world's media in front of the town hall.

Which was why Carter and Hedges found themselves in the wasteland of eastern Ukraine, three hundred miles from Kyiv.

Luke Carter was the leader of the four-man Regiment team attached to the presidential bodyguard. For the past few months Carter and his three colleagues had been guiding the Ukrainians, advising them and making sure there were no weak points in the president's security arrangements. All four lads were with The Wing, the covert unit within 22 SAS that worked hand-in-glove with Five and Six. Prospective recruits to The Wing had to undergo positive vetting before they could be admitted to the Regiment's inner sanctum. Every aspect of their lives was put under the microscope, every weakness assessed. Only those who had passed were trusted to safeguard the president.

The SAS had been the obvious choice for the job. A rotation of lads from E Squadron had spent the past eight years operating in Ukraine, covertly training up local forces to battle Russian irregulars in the east, while preparing for the day when Moscow might try to take another bite out of the country. They had the experience and the reputation, for few other SF units could match the Regiment when it came to the art of bodyguarding. The

Hereford pioneers had practically written the manual on close protection tactics back in the day.

The president had resisted the suggestion at first. He felt it was bad PR to appear on national TV imploring his countrymen to resist the invaders at all costs, while being guarded by a bunch of foreign soldiers. But his NATO allies were insistent. Too much was at stake, they had said. They had invested huge sums in supporting the fight against the Kremlin. Billions had been spent on arms and equipment; training packages had been established; the intelligence services in Washington and London had launched propaganda campaigns to undermine the enemy. The loss of Ukraine's commander-in-chief would be a devastating blow to their efforts.

Therefore, a compromise had been reached. The SAS would direct their Ukrainian counterparts, but they would remain discreetly out of shot when the cameras started rolling.

The president's visit to Balanivka was a closely guarded secret. Outside of his inner circle, only a handful of people were aware of his intention to travel to the newly liberated town. Earlier that morning the president, his most trusted advisors, his sixteen-strong Ukrainian bodyguard team and his four SAS advisors had flown by helicopter from Kyiv to the laager point. Meanwhile, an advance party of two SAS soldiers and a pair of Ukrainians had gone ahead to prepare the site. As soon as they gave the all-clear, Carter and the others would head straight for the town square.

In-and-out job, thought Carter.

Five minutes from start to finish. Dismount, meet some of the town's liberators, deliver the speech, then return to the FOB and get back on the chopper to Kyiv.

At least, that's the plan.

'Did you hear me, fella?' Hedges went on his melodic Welsh accent. 'I said—'

'I know,' Carter replied irritably. 'You don't like the mission.' He sighed. 'I told you already, there's fuck all we can do about it.'

Hedges shook his head. 'It ain't right. We're taking a big risk. Fuck me, it's only been three days since them Russians were kicked out.'

'It's nothing to do with us. We're here to do a job. That's it.'

'I don't give a toss,' Hedges replied sharply. 'Someone should have a word with the guy. If he gets plugged by some sniper today, we'll be the ones getting it in the neck from the head shed.'

Carter glanced at the other SAS man. Hedges was built like a bodybuilder, with arms like snooker balls stuffed into a pair of socks and legs as wide as V2 rockets. A lot of the lads at Hereford had interests outside the business of soldiering. Some were into history, others preferred rugby, or getting pissed with the lads. But not Hedges. The bloke only cared about two things: door-kicking, and fitness. At camp he spent most of his free time in the gym, busting out sets of deadlifts and squats and guzzling protein shakes.

But he also had a foul temper. The kind that could ignite at the slightest provocation. Particularly on days when he couldn't train or control his diet.

Such as today.

Carter shrugged. He said, 'At least he's got some balls on him. Coming out here to deliver a speech. Can you really see any of our lot in Westminster doing the same?'

Hedges snorted. 'It's unnecessary. We're indulging the bloke. This is a fucking ego trip.'

Luke Carter gritted his teeth and looked away. There was no point arguing with Hedges when he was in this sort of mood. He could try explaining that the president hadn't made the trip to massage his ego – that he was in fact here as an act of defiance intended to boost the flagging morale of his troops, while at the same time getting under the skin of his nemesis in the Kremlin in an attempt to frustrate him. Goad him into making mistakes. But it wouldn't make a difference, Carter knew. Hedges wasn't the type of Blade who saw the bigger picture. He didn't give a shit about anything beyond his own narrow pursuits.

Carter said, 'We'll be exposed for a few minutes, mate. No more.'

Hedges fumed through his nostrils. 'Let's hope the others have properly searched the area. Otherwise we're gonna be shafted.'

Carter mentally rehearsed the plan they had drawn up before leaving Kyiv. The advance party was tasked with clearing the site ahead of the president's visit. Buildings had to be searched for sniper teams. Routes in and out of the square checked for obstacles and booby traps. The journalists had to be directed into place, their cameras and other equipment inspected to make sure nothing had been tampered with. Meanwhile US signallers would monitor the airwaves for any signs of Russian transmissions or mobile activity.

Once they were given the green light, Carter would notify the president and the commander of his BG team. Then the party would make the short drive to the centre of town, several kilometres due east of their location.

They were taking no chances. The president was going to be dangerously exposed while he was in Balanivka.

Hedges is right about that much.

Screw this one up, and our heads will roll.

A moment later, a voice squawked in Carter's earpiece.

'We're all set up here,' Josh Bowman said.

Bowman was in charge of the advance party clearing the square. A true East End lad, born and raised in Barking, Bowman was one of the older Blades in 22 SAS, one of a dying breed, a highly capable operator and a Regiment enigma.

Everyone at Hereford had heard the story of how Albanian mobsters had murdered Bowman's wife and daughter during his time as an undercover police officer. Later, Bowman had joined the army before applying for Selection. Then, for two years, he had disappeared from the camp without a word of explanation. There had been rumours that he'd transferred to the Cell, the ultra-secretive unit within the SAS.

'We've got the shot ready,' Bowman continued over the comms. 'It's a good vantage point. Church and town hall in the background, as your man requested. Flag has been raised above the building. We're on the left side of the statue as you approach from the west. One of the Ukrainians will meet you at the dismounting point. It's a fifteen-metre walk from there to the spot where the president will give his speech. Clear line of sight, so the cameras can swing round to catch a shot of him walking towards them.'

'Fuck me, he sounds like James Cameron on set,' Hedges muttered. 'He'll be giving an Oscar speech next.'

Carter tapped his pressel switch and spoke into his throat mic. 'Any dead spots in the vicinity?'

'Negative. We've gone through the place with a fine-tooth comb. It's clear.'

'What about them local soldiers, mate?'

'They're all here,' Bowman said. 'Three men and three women from the force that liberated the town, plus their CO. They think they're here for a flag-raising ceremony, nothing more,' he added.

'Roger that,' Carter said. 'We'll let you know once we're en route.'

'Better make it quick, fella. Before Tyler scares off what's left of the local talent.'

'Cockney bastard,' another voice hissed over the comms.

Tyler Dunk was the second SAS man on the advance party, a massive guy from the Black Country with pitted skin and a face that should come with a trigger warning. He was also the scruffiest bloke in the Regiment. The kind of guy who could look shabby in a Savile Row suit.

'Tell the commander we're leaving now,' Carter said to Hedges. 'Get his men organised. I'll inform the mark.'

'Roger that.'

Carter rose to his feet and marched briskly across the tent to a tall, broad-shouldered guy dressed in a pair of beige khakis and an olive-green T-shirt, reading through a paper copy of a speech.

'Sir,' Carter began.

Artem Voloshyn, the President of Ukraine, looked up at him. 'Yes?'

'They're ready for you, sir.'

'Now? We go now?' the portly figure standing next to Voloshyn asked. Andrii Kravets, the president's press officer, was a sweaty guy, dark-haired and unshaven, his round face framed by a pair of oversized glasses. His paunch bulged beneath his crinkled shirt.

'That's right,' Carter said. He nodded at Voloshyn. 'Me and Sergeant Hedges will ride with you both in the main vehicle, sir.'

'And my bodyguards?'

'Major Lysenko and Sergeant Tatarin will travel with us,' said Carter. 'The rest will go in the support vehicles. Just remember—'

'Five minutes, no more. Yes, I know.' Voloshyn smiled again. 'You have one thing in common with my press officer, Sergeant. You both tire of the sound of my voice, I think.'

Carter grinned.

He turned and led Voloshyn and Kravets towards the other side of the tent, where the sixteen Ukrainian bodyguards were hastily assembling under Hedges' angry glare. Two men stood next to the thickset Welshman. Major Lysenko, the commander of the presidential bodyguard team, was a serious-looking guy with arched eyebrows and heavily lidded eyes. At his side was Sergeant Tatarin, his 2iC, a lantern-jawed soldier with a neatly stubbled beard and a permanent frown. Carter approached and cocked his head at Lysenko.

'Are your lads ready, Major?' he asked.

Lysenko nodded. 'Yes. All good.'

'We'll be travelling with the president in the Mastiff,' Carter said. 'Once we arrive on site, we'll wait until the rest of the guys

13

have debussed and taken up their respective positions around the square. The president doesn't leave that wagon until we've established a ring of steel around him. If there's any trouble, we'll call off the event and head back here on one of the designated routes. Is that clear?'

Lysenko shared a knowing glance with his 2iC. The two of them hated taking orders from a Regiment man and made little attempt to hide it. A pride thing, maybe. They were the cream of the Ukrainian crop. Voloshyn's most dedicated soldiers. They felt his presence sent a message about their inability to protect their chief.

If I was in their boots, I'd probably feel the same way.

But Carter didn't really care about hurting Lysenko's feelings. As far as he was concerned, they had a job to do. If that meant a few bruised egos, so be it.

'Sure,' Lysenko replied coldly. 'We understand.'

Carter nodded. 'Get a fucking move on.'

Lysenko bellowed an order at his men. At once the other fourteen lads snatched up their weaponry and kit, left the tent and hurried towards the armoured vehicles.

Carter and Hedges were wearing the same uniform as the Ukrainians: army fatigues, plate armour, personal radio systems and swept-back ballistic helmets. In addition, the two Hereford operators had olive-green face coverings over their noses and mouths. They were required to disguise themselves at all times while on ops in Ukraine, since the presence of SAS personnel was politically sensitive. If they were accidentally caught on camera and identified by Russian intelligence, it would trigger a diplomatic shitstorm.

Both Carter and Hedges were also equipped with dual net comms systems, allowing them to rapidly switch channels and communicate back to Hereford on an encrypted line, without having to worry about anyone else on the team listening in.

Which made sense on several levels. Although they were firm allies, there was a limit to how much int Whitehall was willing to share with the Ukrainians.

They were going in with a serious amount of hardware. Carter and his colleagues were packing suppressed L119A2 assault rifles, manufactured by Colt Canada and based on the old Diemaco C8. Which was essentially a Canadian variant of the M4 carbine. Whereas the Ukrainians were equipped with the standard M4. The same weapon, more or less, minus the suppressor and a few other niche features. Each soldier also had four spare thirty-round clips of 5.56 NATO brass in their front vest pouches, plus holstered Glock semi-automatic pistols as their secondary firearms, and a strip of brightly coloured blue tape around their left leg.

The ribbons were a vital part of their uniform, identifying them as friendly forces. Some time ago, the Russians had begun impersonating Ukrainian troops by wearing matching strips of blue cloth around their right arms. In response, the Ukrainian high command had begun issuing new orders each day, stipulating where soldiers should display their ribbons. One day they might be told to strap them around their left arms; the next day they might be required to tie them on their right leg. It was a pain in the arse, but a necessary safeguard against Russian forces trying to pass themselves off as the good guys. And a powerful reminder, thought Carter.

The enemy was cornered and desperate. Their early hopes of a stunning victory had evaporated. Now they found themselves on the back foot, suffering from a catastrophic drop in morale and increasing discontent back home. From now on, they would increasingly resort to dirty tactics in an attempt to claw back the initiative.

We'll need eyes in the backs of our heads today.

They started at a quick pace towards the row of vehicles parked along the dirt patch, a hundred metres away. A rough track ran from the wagons to the main road to the north. Carter and Hedges led the way, followed by Major Lysenko and his subordinate, Sergeant Tatarin, marching either side of the president. The rest of the Ukrainians on the BG team followed close behind, the muddied ground squelching and sucking under the trample of their boots.

Carter, Hedges, Kravets, Lysenko and Tatarin made directly for a Mastiff patrol vehicle. A heavily armoured six-wheeler, equipped with a mounted Browning .50 cal and a 40 mm grenade launcher. Whitehall had supplied a number of them to Ukraine since the start of the war. The Mastiff was a big beast, offering maximum protection for the occupants if they blundered into any IEDs en route to the town.

Carter vaulted into the back of the Mastiff and dropped into one of the fold-down seats fitted along the sides of the main cabin. Major Lysenko, Kravets and Voloshyn planted themselves on the seats opposite, while Tatarin and Hedges made for the front cab, the Ukrainian sergeant taking the wheel and the Welshman depositing himself in the shotgun seat. Another Ukrainian filed past Carter and made for the hatch further forward, taking the gunner's spot situated between the front and main cabs.

From outside, came the dull thud of doors slamming shut as the other thirteen Ukrainians piled into a pair of Bushmaster mobility vehicles. Seven guys would travel in the lead wagon, with the other six following at the rear of the convoy. If they ran into an ambush on the way, the front and rear vehicles would put down fire, giving the guys in the Mastiff a chance to escape.

Lysenko wrenched the rear door shut and yelled out to Tatarin that they were sealed inside. Several voices flared up over the comms, talking in a stream of guttural Ukrainian. The guys in the Bushmasters, Carter presumed, confirming that they were also ready.

Sergeant Tatarin gunned the ignition. The Mastiff lurched forward along the track, following one of the Bushmasters as it headed for the main road.

Thirty seconds later, they were rolling towards Balanivka.

* * *

Seven miles to the east, the voice came back over the radio.

'Target is on the move. They just left.'

Masutov sat up and felt the breath hitch in his throat. *This is it*, he thought. *It's really happening.*

'How many?' he asked.

'Sixteen,' the voice said. 'Three vehicles in total. Target is in the middle vehicle.'

He didn't know how they were able to monitor such a highly guarded figure. Didn't ask. Such things were above his pay grade. He assumed there was a drone. Eyes in the sky. One of the advanced new reconnaissance models the Kremlin had deployed in Ukraine, maybe. Sweeping several thousand metres above the ground. Tracking the presidential convoy as it bowled towards its destination.

The voice said, 'Remember the plan. Go in hard and fast. The first thirty seconds are everything.'

'Yes,' Masutov said. 'I remember.'

'Don't fuck this one up. Think of your families.'

The voice clicked off again.

* * *

The wagons rolled through the devastated outskirts of the town. Not that Carter could see any of it. There were no windows in the back of the Mastiff. Just a confined space with a tangle of thick cables hanging from the sides and a set of metal toolboxes stored beneath the seats.

Carter searched the president's face for any sign of anxiety or tension but saw none. The guy looked almost supernaturally calm. Kravets sat to the right of his boss, beads of sweat studding his pale brow.

Carter felt a stab of unease in his chest. The same feeling he'd had when he had first been told about the president's desire to travel to Balanivka.

He tried to reassure himself that the chances of an attack this morning were minimal. Every inch of the main square and the surrounding area had been thoroughly swept by the advance party. Signals teams at the NSA and GCHQ had done their jobs and had come up empty. Not a whiff of Russian comms activity in the town.

But the anxiety kept gnawing away at him.

We're taking a big risk, Hedges had said. *It's unnecessary.*

Carter wondered whether he should have tried harder to dissuade Voloshyn. He could have suggested delaying the event by a few days, giving them a chance to send in a second clearance team. Make sure they hadn't missed anything first time round.

Never go in half-cocked.

The unwritten credo of the Regiment. Rushing into things without the proper planning was how mistakes got made. Men had died in the past because of planning failures.

But Carter hadn't argued. Instead, he had simply nodded along and agreed to the job. Figured it wasn't his place to kick up a fuss. He was a soldier, after all, not a political strategist.

My brother wouldn't have stayed quiet, he told himself.

Luke had always looked up to his older brother. Respected him. Jamie was the reason he'd wanted to become a soldier in the first place. The pair of them had been in each other's pockets as kids. Growing up in a rough estate in Northumberland, with a violent alcoholic for a father, sticking together had been the only way to survive. Jamie had defended his little brother on those dark nights when the old man staggered through the front door, breath reeking of whiskey, ready to fly into a rage at the slightest provocation.

Once, during one of their frequent arguments, their father had grabbed a kitchen knife and lunged at their mother. Jamie had knocked the weapon out of his hand and beaten him senseless. Luke had been twelve years old at the time, but even now, he could still vividly recall the sight of his father lying on the kitchen floor, pawing at his shattered nose, blood oozing out of his mouth. Jamie had paid dearly for that incident, although the old man never laid a finger on their mother again.

Luke didn't have a father as a role model. But he had his older brother. And so when Jamie had joined 22 SAS, Luke had been determined to follow in his footsteps. Four years after joining the Paras he'd passed Selection.

Since then, their careers had taken very different paths.

Luke was a soldier's soldier. A team player. One of the lads, respected by everyone, not a guy who picked sides or peddled agendas. He didn't question orders or rub people the wrong way. He did what he was told, kept his head down, and paid no attention to the bear pit of Regiment politics. He had joined the SAS to fight. Why waste energy on the other stuff?

Some guys applied for Selection thinking they would be going to a unit where everything was straight down the line. Then they got there and realised it wasn't. The Regiment was like any other unit in that respect. There were glory hunters who awarded themselves gongs they didn't deserve; careerists who paid more attention to their promotion prospects than the business of soldiering; arse-kissers who worked their way up the greasy pole by befriending the right people. Luke had never let any of it bother him. There were tossers and backstabbers in every walk of life. Best not to take any notice of them.

But Jamie felt differently. He was genetically programmed not to take crap from anyone. He refused to turn a blind eye to the institutional bullshit that came with the territory at Hereford.

That attitude had made life difficult for him. He'd made enemies. Lots of them. Too many to stay out of trouble. His reputation as a brilliant soldier had protected him for a while, but eventually he'd slipped up. Then the wolves had pounced.

Now Jamie was a pariah, seeing out his army contract on glorified gardening leave, while Luke was running ops with The Wing.

Luke didn't know how to feel about that. He loved his brother. After cancer took their mother, Jamie was the only family he had left. Luke knew how much being in the SAS mattered to him; he would have given anything to get Jamie out of purgatory. But he was powerless to help. He knew how the system worked. Once you crossed the head shed, there was no way back. Not unless you had friends in seriously high places.

And Jamie doesn't have any of those.

Luke shrugged off this depressing train of thought as the Mastiff hurtled through the streets.

All we've got to do is survive the next ten minutes, he reminded himself. *A quick routine in front of the cameras, then we're straight back to the safety of the base.*

In and out. Job done.

The Mastiff made a series of quick turns, then dropped its speed. Two minutes later, they jerked to a halt. The engine cut out, and then Hedges's voice sparked up in Carter's earpiece. 'We're here, mate. We've got sight of the square.'

Carter said into his throat mic, 'Josh, is everyone in position?'

'In position,' came the reply from Bowman. 'We're ready to roll.'

Carter swung his gaze towards Lysenko. 'Major, tell your men to get out and await further orders. Drivers are to stay where they are, plus the gunner,' he added, indicating the soldier standing forward of them at the turret hatch, manning the top-mounted Browning .50 cal.

'OK.'

Lysenko shouted over the comms, ordering the soldiers in the two Bushmasters to debus. Carter tipped his head at Voloshyn and Kravets in turn and said, 'Wait here. Don't move until I give the signal that it's safe to leave the vehicle.'

Carter released his safety harness, rose to a low crouch, wrenched open the rear door and dropped down from the back of the vehicle, his rifle fixed to his sling. Lysenko followed, closing the door to the main cab behind him, while Hedges circled round from the front cab. Close by, the other soldiers had already dismounted from the Bushmasters and formed up in a tight grouping.

Carter stretched to his full height and glanced round, orientating himself. Back in Kyiv he had spent hours consulting satellite imagery and maps of the town. The convoy had stopped on the southern side of the square. North of their position was the square itself. Which was essentially a pin-neat garden studded with trees and flower beds. Paved avenues led towards a marble pedestal in the centre, surmounted with a bronze statue of a medieval warrior on horseback, brandishing a spear and shield.

There was a small wooded area twenty metres or so to the east of the square. A playground to the west, next to a row of bombed-out storefronts. All around, Carter saw signs of the recent battle for the town. The twisted metal carcasses of several Russian vehicles littered the roads; the pavements were strewn with debris, broken glass, shrapnel, pools of dried blood and bits of hastily abandoned kit.

To the north of the square stood the town hall: a three-storey pastel-coloured edifice with a Ukrainian flag draped from a brass pole protruding over the entrance. Next to it was a whitewashed church with a slate-clad spire. Further away, Carter caught sight of the blackened husks of several derelict apartment blocks and offices.

A mass of journalists had assembled close to the centre of the square, partially screened behind a thicket of trees and bushes. Bowman and Dunk stood beside them, clearly identifiable by their face coverings and the suppressed L119A2 rifles slung across their fronts. Half a dozen paces away, near the bronze statue, seven Ukrainian soldiers – infantrymen and women – waited patiently for the ceremony to begin.

Carter swung round to face Major Lysenko.

'Post two of your men on that corner,' he said, stabbing a finger at a crossroads fifty metres upstream from their position, on the north-west corner of the square. 'I want two guys watching the road at our six o'clock, two more facing the junction to the north-east, and two more on the street to the south-east. The gunner will keep an eye on the side street directly to the south of our position. Questions?'

Lysenko shook his head and started barking orders to his men. The four teams quickly split up, sprinting towards their respective postings, while the gunner on the Mastiff wheeled the turret round to face the side street ten metres to the south of the convoy. Between them, they would cover the main approaches to and from the square.

As soon as Major Lysenko had confirmed that the soldiers were in position, Carter yanked open the Mastiff door and said, 'OK, sir. We're ready for you now.'

Voloshyn slapped his hands on his thighs, rose to his feet and clambered out of the Mastiff. Carter directed him towards the reporters fifteen metres to the north, while Kravets walked immediately behind his boss, his face drained of colour, eyes darting anxiously left and right. As Lysenko and another bodyguard marched alongside their president, the throng of cameras and smartphones swivelled towards them. Poised to capture the moment as Voloshyn walked up the avenue.

Carter got back on the comms and said, 'How far have we got to be from the mark to stay out of the shot?'

'Move three metres to your left,' Tyler Dunk said in his slow Brummie drawl. 'That should do it.'

Carter and Hedges shifted to the side of the president, stepping away from him, until Dunk came back on the net and said, 'That's it. You're out of the shot now.'

'Good job you ain't accompanying the mark, Tyler,' Bowman cut in. 'You'd break them cameras if your mug was on show today.'

'Fuck off, Josh.'

Voloshyn strode purposefully towards the crowd waiting for him in the square. Carter and Hedges quick-walked in the same direction, staying several paces from the president. When the footage was broadcast on the news that evening, it would show Voloshyn in the company of his loyal bodyguards; no one watching at home would ever know that the Ukrainians had a group of SAS lads accompanying them every step of the way.

The cameras tracked Voloshyn as he made straight for the line of soldiers. The heroic defenders of Balanivka.

One of them, an officer in a camo-pattern field cap, stepped forward and stiffly saluted his commander-in-chief. Voloshyn smiled broadly, and the two men pumped hands as the cameras clicked and whirred frenetically. Dunk and Bowman stood next to the line of Ukrainian soldiers, giving their backs to the media as they scanned the area.

The guy in the field cap exchanged a few words with the president, gesturing towards several gutted buildings overlooking the square. Describing the atrocities inflicted on the town by the invaders, Carter supposed. Mass artillery bombardment. Scorched earth. Conscripts fed remorselessly into the meat grinder of the Russian army. More or less the same tactics they had used on the Eastern Front eighty years before. But less effective now.

Voloshyn listened and nodded sombrely. Then the officer introduced him to the line of soldiers standing at his side. Liberators of the ancestral home of their beloved president. Voloshyn was a class act. That much was clear from the way he worked the audience. He shook each soldier's hand in turn, smiling genially, sharing a few words and posing for selfies. The Ukrainians clearly adored him. The most popular guy in his country's history, probably. There was only one other person in Ukraine who even came close to that level of adoration.

Kravets tried to hurry his boss along. The PR man was obviously desperate to get back to the relative safety of Kyiv as quickly as possible, Carter thought. But Voloshyn refused to be rushed. He took his time. Which was all part of the performance, Carter guessed. He was sending a clear message to the ruling cartel in Moscow. Showing them he wasn't afraid. That he could walk freely through the streets of a town only a few miles from Russian-held territory, without fear of attack.

The president smiled for a photograph with the last soldier, and then Lysenko hastily ushered him towards a patch of ground marked by a pair of sticks driven into the soil. The sticks had been placed by the advance party and indicated the spot where the president would make his live address to the cameras. From that position, the press corps would be able to get a shot of Voloshyn with the bullet-scarred town hall and church in the background to the north.

Voloshyn cleared his throat and turned to address the cameras, flanked by his merry men.

'Today, we celebrate a historic moment in our country's history,' he began, speaking in faintly accented English. Another part of his charm offensive, Carter realised. Making sure that his words would be disseminated as widely as possible in the global media. Getting his message across. Something Voloshyn had excelled at since the war had begun.

'My people come from this land,' he went on. 'My father worked the soil here, and his father before him. This earth is in my blood. It does not belong to President Zhirkov, or any of his cronies in the Kremlin. They have not worked this land, or fought for it, or died defending it. No. It belongs to the people who live here, whose

24

ancestors toiled here for generations. So does eastern Ukraine. So does Kherson. So does Crimea.'

Carter swept his eyes across the square. Scanning for any sign of a threat. He saw the two Ukrainians at the crossroads to the northeast. The other teams were watching the adjoining roads from their positions on the corners of the square. The gunner atop the Mastiff trained the .50 cal on the side street to the south.

Half a dozen paces away, Bowman and Dunk continued observing the ground to the north, monitoring the town hall and church.

Hedges and Lysenko kept their eyes on the crowd.

Kravets dabbed his sweaty brow with a handkerchief.

Voloshyn continued, 'But this fight – this is not just a fight for Ukraine. No. This is a struggle for the soul of Western civilisation. The whole world once tried to appease our enemies. Now they understand that evil cannot be negotiated with, it cannot be placated. Some people forgot this. They did not realise that the most important values – you must be willing to fight for them. To die for them. It is up to our soldiers, in this land, to keep alive the flame of freedom. Every town we recapture, every Russian force driven back to the east, is a victory for all peoples of the West.

'The Russians try to take what is not theirs. They kill our people, bomb our cities. They threaten to destroy our nuclear power plants. They declare their intention to wipe us from the earth. It does not matter. We will drive them back. The victory here at Balanivka is only the first step on a long road. Today is the beginning of the end of the invaders' illegal occupation—'

Then Carter heard the gunshots.

Several of them.

Coming from the west.

Carter's nine o'clock.

In the next moment, he heard the shrieking din of bullets hammering against metal. He looked south just in time to see the gunner on the Mastiff jerking wildly as a round caught him square in the face. Three more bullets missed their target, ricocheting off the turret housing and the .50 cal in a flurry of glowing sparks.

'Contact! Contact!' Bowman roared over the net. 'Rounds coming in!'

Carter swung round, looking towards the patch of woodland on the far side of the square. He saw four figures in army fatigues breaking clear of the treeline, less than forty metres from his position. Packing assault rifles.

Pissing bullets as they dashed towards the throng of reporters.

Dunk, Hedges and Bowman had turned to look in the same direction. So had Major Lysenko and the rest of the faces in the crowd. For a second they stood frozen with shock and indecision.

Then all hell broke loose.

Panic instantly spread through the crowd. People started fleeing in every direction, screaming in terror and racing for cover behind the base of the statue and the surrounding greenery. A soundman chucked aside his boom mic and sprinted towards the armoured vehicles. He made it no more than four or five metres when a torrent of hot lead struck him in the lower back and sent him tumbling to the ground.

Dunk and Hedges broke forward to engage the enemy. Bowman and Lysenko dropped to their knees beside the statue, putting down rounds to cover their advance. The two soldiers on the far corner of the square realised what was happening and abandoned their post, charging south towards the attackers. The two nearest assaulters whipped round to face them and let rip, cutting both the Ukrainians down.

More rounds spattered the blacktop as two more Ukrainians raced up the street from the south-east corner, M4 barrels flaming. The assaulters dived for cover behind the burned-out shell of a truck before the Ukrainians could put the drop on them.

Carter sprang into action. Not an active decision. More of an instinctive reaction in the lizard part of his brain. The product of

26

millions of years of evolution, sharpened by the thousands of hours of hard training in the Regiment.

Priority number one.

Secure the mark.

Get him to safety.

The crowd had rapidly dispersed. Several bodies littered the ground close to the spot where Voloshyn had been delivering his speech. Carter saw a blonde woman in a puffer jacket, her legs and stomach stitched with bullets, her shattered camera lying beside her. Kravets was sprawled lifelessly on the ground nearby. The lower half of his face had been blown off.

Amid the chaos, Carter spotted the president hurrying in the direction of the town hall. Away from the safety of the convoy. Carter yelled at him to stop, but the guy didn't appear to have heard him and carried on running. Sensory deprivation. His threat levels were in the red zone. Carter had seen it happen to people in the thick of a firefight. Adrenaline overload. Some people lost control of their senses. Some sort of chemical imbalance. They stopped thinking rationally.

Carter broke into a run, darting across the open ground as rounds fizzed through the air around him, ignoring the despairing cries of wounded civilians begging for help. He couldn't worry about them now. The life of the president was more important than anything else. Unpleasant, maybe. But that didn't make it any less true.

Carter quickened his pace and caught up with the president in half a dozen strides. He thrust out an arm, grabbed hold of the guy by his bicep.

'This way!' Carter shouted, indicating the Mastiff on the southern side of the square. 'Now!'

He dragged the president towards the convoy forty metres to the south. At his nine o'clock, two of the assaulters were slumped on the blacktop beside the truck, bodies riddled with holes. The remaining two gunmen were crouching next to a bus shelter. Dunk and Hedges were pinning them down with suppressive fire, while Lysenko and the other Ukrainians broke forward. By now the rest of the soldiers had rushed across the green to join the fighting. Fire-and-move tactics. The enemy shooters were hopelessly out-numbered. In a matter of moments, they would be cut down.

Ten or twelve seconds had passed since the start of the attack.

Carter hastened on.

A small voice at the back of his head wondered why the Russians had staged such a futile assault. Four guys against sixteen trained soldiers and their SAS advisors. The enemy didn't stand a chance.

So why the fuck are they attacking us?

Something isn't right.

As Carter manhandled the president towards the Mastiff, he noticed a sudden blur of movement in his peripheral vision. Coming from his three o'clock. Due west of the square.

Forty metres away.

Carter stopped and looked past his shoulder.

Then he saw them.

Three figures, crawling out of a manhole in the middle of the road.

Running straight towards him.

All three of them wore the same basic uniform as the gunmen to the east. Except none of these guys was carrying a weapon. All three had bulky vests strapped to their fronts – and suddenly Carter understood.

These guys aren't shooters.

They're suicide bombers.

Distraction. A simple tactic. But effective. The gunmen to the east were the cannon fodder. Drawing attention towards them so their mates could sneak up on the president and send him over to the Otherworld.

'Fuck's sake,' he growled at Voloshyn. 'Hurry up.'

He hurried on towards the convoy, but the next time he glanced back he saw that the bombers had closed on them, fists clenched tight around their detonators. The belts were designed to trigger as soon as the wearer released his thumb from the detonator switch. Voluntarily or otherwise. A failsafe. In case anyone tried to neutralise the attacker. Shoot the guy, his hand would instinctively go limp – and the belt would detonate.

The bombers were less than thirty metres behind them now.

Forty metres to the Mastiff.

We're too far away, Carter realised grimly. *We'll never make it.*

A simple question of time and distance. The three guys in the suicide squad had no bulky armour or weaponry to slow them down. They were gaining ground fast. They would close on Carter long before he could bundle Voloshyn into the back of the wagon.

The kill radius of a typical suicide vest was around ten metres, Carter knew. Could be more. Depended on how much explosive material the wearer had strapped to their front.

Carter had a matter of seconds before the nearest bomber drew within range.

He made an instant decision.

Carter stopped in his tracks, spun round and threw Voloshyn to the ground, pinning him down with his full body weight. Partly to shield him from any fragmentation. But also to stop him from running away in a blind panic. In the confusion of the firefight, there was a chance that the guy might blunder straight into the path of the onrushing bombers.

'Enemy at the rear!' Carter yelled. 'Suicide vests! They've got fucking vests on!'

Carter kept the president pinned down with one arm and tore his Glock semi-automatic from his thigh holster.

In the corner of his vision, towards the east, the Ukrainian soldiers were still plugging away at the gunmen behind the bus shelter. Hedges and Dunk were there too. None of them seemed to have heard Carter.

The nearest bomber was no more than twenty metres away when he lined up the Glock with his central mass and fired. Two rounds of nine-milli Parabellum flamed out of the pistol barrel in quick succession. The first bullet nailed the fucker in the crotch, shredding his balls. The second struck him in the face, shattering his lower jaw. The bomber spasmed as if Doctor Frankenstein had thrown a switch and reanimated him. He tumbled forward, and then there was an earth-shattering boom as the vest detonated, vaporising the guy. Instant cremation.

The other bombers ran on past their atomised mate.

Carter hastily swung the Glock across. Lined up the next target. The second bomber was fifteen metres from the president. Carter loosed off four rounds, drilling the bastard in the shoulder and neck, giving him a one-way ticket to Paradise.

The bomber fell away a moment before the detonator activated. The fragmentation from the blast swept over Carter in a furious roar, nicking his flesh. He felt a burning pain in his right hand and released his grip on the Glock and dropped his gaze. A piece of shrapnel had embedded itself deep in his palm.

Then he looked up again and felt his stomach drop.

The third bomber was danger close. Ten metres away. He had veered to one side of his comrades and bore down on Carter at an angle, fist clamped tight around his switch.

Ready to detonate.

Carter knew he was out of luck. His gun hand was in rag order. He had no time to snatch up the Glock with his one good hand and drop the target. In another couple of seconds the bomber would be right on top of him. Killing range.

We're fucked.

The rapid crack of a rifle erupted at his three o'clock. The bomber jerked and tumbled backwards, as if he'd slammed into a clothesline. Carter pressed himself flat against Voloshyn as the bomber's vest exploded. The heat from the bomb blast fanned outwards, flinging a wave of shit over him.

The gunfire on the other side of the square quickly ceased. Carter lifted his head and saw Bowman at his one o'clock, his rifle raised and trained on the spot where the bomber had been standing a moment before. There was nothing left of him now except a black-scarred patch of earth and a few scraps of burned clothing. The guy had vanished. Like a magician performing a trick act live on stage.

Several metres away, the bomber's severed head had landed in a bed of peonies and carnations, mouth agape in an expression of dumb surprise. Carter climbed to his feet, relief coursing through his bloodstream.

He looked towards the eastern side of the square. Dust gritted his eyes, his teeth and gums. The remaining two attackers were lying in a tangle of limbs and broken glass next to the bus shelter. Dunk, Hedges and several of the Ukrainians were moving towards the woodland beyond the square. Flushing out any more enemies that might be lurking in the immediate vicinity. The other four Ukrainian soldiers were jogging back over to deal with the maimed civilians.

Carter patted the president down, checking for injuries. The guy had sustained a few grazes and cuts to his hands, and he was badly shaken, but otherwise he seemed unharmed.

'Are you OK, sir?' he asked. 'Does anything hurt?'

Voloshyn winced and said, 'I feel like I've got crushed ribs after you sat on me. Otherwise, I'm OK.'

He smiled weakly, then coughed again and winced in pain. Nearby, Bowman was shouting at a pair of Ukrainian soldiers across the square and pointing at the manhole.

'Post some grenades in that drain! Fucking now!'

The two men promptly set off in the direction Bowman had indicated. One of them ripped a grenade from his belt, chucked it through the opening and shrank back. There was a pause, followed

31

by a deafening boom, and a plume of smoke belched out of the hole. A moment later, the two men edged forward and emptied several bursts from their M4s into the drain mouth. Any enemies down there would have been shredded to bits.

Carter slung an arm around the president and helped him to his feet. He looked round at Bowman and said, 'Tell the drivers to get the vehicles going. We're leaving.'

'Roger that, Luke.'

Bowman set off at a quick trot towards the convoy, hollering at the drivers. Standard operating procedure. Extract the mark. The immediate priority. Gather everyone together and evacuate the area.

At his side, Voloshyn was staring numbly at the carnage. Dead bodies, spent rounds, gleaming pools of blood.

Carter said, softly, 'Sir, we've got to get you out of here. Right now.'

The president started to protest. 'My people. I can't . . . I can't leave them.'

'There's no time, sir.' He started hauling Voloshyn away. 'We've got to go.'

There was a strong possibility that the Russians would stick a missile in the area once they realised the attack had failed. Carter decided against sharing this thought with the president.

Just then he heard a voice calling out from the direction of the statue. Carter looked over and saw a young woman in a blouse, her back against the pedestal, her left hand staunching the flow of blood from a wound to her right arm. She said something in Ukrainian to Voloshyn. Carter couldn't understand a word of it. But whatever she said had a powerful effect on him. Tears welled in his eyes; his lower lip quivered. He swallowed hard, then turned and paced reluctantly towards the Mastiff.

Carter, moving alongside him, spoke urgently into his throat mic. Updating the rest of the team on the president's status and the failed attack by the suicide bombers.

'Is everybody all right? Anyone down?'

Above the ringing noise in his ears, Carter heard a hoarse Brummie voice crackling over the comms. 'Me and Carl are fine,' said Dunk.

'Major?'

Lysenko said, 'We have three men down. Repeat, three men down. All enemies neutralised.' He paused. 'They're Chechens.'

Carter said, 'How the fuck did we miss them? We swept the place clean.'

Dunk said, 'There's a stay-behind shelter out here. Pissing distance from the square. Professional job. Looks like they were on hard routine.'

Carter felt something shift in his stomach.

Christ, he thought. *They must have been hiding down there for days.*

'Everyone back to the RV,' he said over the net. 'We're getting the fuck out of Dodge.'

Bowman stood beside the wagon, visually scanning the streets behind them. Carter guided Voloshyn towards the rear of the Mastiff, yanked open the door and helped the president up the steps. Voloshyn staggered inside and collapsed onto the nearest seat. In the dim light of the main cab, Carter saw the slack form of the gunner crumpled beneath the hatchway. His face was a messy gout of blood and bone.

'Wait here,' Carter ordered the president.

He stepped back from the cab and saw Bowman staring at him.

'Jesus. What the fuck just happened?' he asked in a low voice.

Carter said, quietly, 'It was a set-up. They knew we were coming.'

'But – how?'

'I don't know. But they wouldn't have gone to the hassle of building a stay-behind shelter unless they knew the president was going to show his face here. Doesn't make any sense.'

Bowman rubbed his jaw. 'Maybe it was pure luck. They might have left a few blokes behind hoping that Voloshyn would turn up.' He shrugged. 'This is his hometown. They must have figured there was a decent chance he'd make an appearance.'

'Maybe.'

But Carter wasn't convinced.

The way those Chechens came at us, it took some serious planning, he thought. *They set it up so they could draw the Ukrainians onto them. Buy some time for the bombers to have a free run at the president.*

Thirty seconds.

That's all they would have needed.

The rest of the BG team scrambled back towards the convoy. The Ukrainian soldiers moved hurriedly across the square, collecting the bodies of their dead comrades, while Carter filed a report with the radio operator at the forward mounting base.

'We've had a contact,' he said. He forced himself to speak slowly to make himself understood to the Ukrainian operator. 'Repeat, we've had a contact. We'll be coming back on route bravo. Repeat, route bravo. Get a reception party ready and get the bird turning. We'll be with you in figures twenty.'

'Is the mark injured?'

'He's fine, but we've got three men down and multiple civilian casualties. We need paramedics and reinforcements to throw up a cordon and secure the area.' Something else occurred to him. 'Get someone to seize all the cameras and phones from the journalists. No leaked recordings. We can't let anyone know this happened.'

The Ukrainian soldiers finished bundling the last bodies into the backs of the Bushmasters and jogged over to their respective wagons. Major Lysenko, Hedges and Dunk clambered after Bowman into the Mastiff cabin.

As Carter started to follow them, a guy in a hoodie called out in a pleading tone of voice. Not Ukrainian. But an accented English voice. American, or Canadian, perhaps. He stopped and glanced at the man. He was kneeling on the ground beneath an oak tree, cradling a grey-haired woman in a suit. Blood gushed down the man's face from a wound to his scalp. His shirt was drenched red.

'Don't leave us,' the guy in the hoodie cried. 'Please, don't!'

'Help is coming,' Carter told him. 'Stay here. Paramedics are on the way.'

Then he swung up into the cabin and pulled the door shut behind him. He took the empty seat opposite the president, while Lysenko got on the comms and instructed the drivers to get moving.

A few seconds later, they were pulling away from the square. Back towards the relative safety of the FOB.

'Fuck me, that was close,' Hedges said.

Nobody replied.

Bowman nodded at Carter's gun hand and said, 'You'll need to get that cleaned up before it gets infected.'

Carter looked down at his blood-lacquered hand. In the mad rush to bug out of the town, he'd quite forgotten about his wound. Adrenaline had numbed the pain, dialling it down to a dull, constant throb. Nature's painkiller. The jagged piece of shrapnel had buried an inch or so deep in his palm. A painful injury, but nothing that would keep him out of action for long.

'What did that woman say to you back there?' Carter asked the president. 'Sir?'

Voloshyn had been staring at the floor. He looked up and blinked rapidly, as if snapping out of a trance state.

'She begged me to leave her – to save myself,' he said, his voice choked with emotion. 'She said I needed to live. So that Ukraine could survive. Even if it meant—'

He broke off and looked away, his eyes rimmed with tears.

Carter sat back and fell silent. A troubling thought picking at his skull.

For security purposes, only a handful of individuals had been informed about Voloshyn's visit to Balanivka. Major Lysenko, his 2iC Tatarin, the SAS protection team and his inner circle of advisors. Maybe a dozen people in total. People with impeccable credentials, their backgrounds thoroughly vetted by the intelligence agencies. Each of them had demonstrated their unstinting loyalty to their leader.

So how the fuck did the Chechens know where to find us? Carter wondered.

But he already knew the answer.

Someone had told them about the president's movements, he realised. Tipped them off. The only explanation for the attack. Which could only mean one thing.

We've been betrayed.

Two

Seventeen hundred miles away, at exactly ten o'clock in the morning, Warrant Officer Second Class Steve Duncan swept into the blandly furnished briefing room on the first floor at SAS headquarters. The fourteen lads sitting on the rows of cheap chairs waited in silence as the commander of Air Troop, G Squadron made directly for the lectern, his massive arms swinging at his sides, fists the size of wrecking balls. Alongside him marched a slightly younger guy in his late thirties, greyhound-lean and rugged-faced, dressed in a pair of black jeans, plaid shirt and Timberlands, with mussed brown hair that showed the first shoots of grey at the edges.

Warrant Officer Jamie Carter, one-time hero of the Regiment and now a Hereford exile, stopped next to Duncan behind the lectern and felt a tingle of anticipation.

Six months ago, the head shed had turned Carter into an outcast. They had banished him from his squadron, turfed him out on long-term leave and left him to rot. His reward for single-handedly preventing a conspiracy involving rogue elements within the CIA, an ex-Regiment legend and a plot to smuggle suitcase nukes to Taiwan. He should have received a gong for his actions. Instead, the top brass had scolded him and delivered a stark warning. *Tell anyone about this, and we'll crucify you.*

For the first time in his life, Carter had kept his mouth shut. He took the terms on offer and walked out of the camp gates the same day. The smart choice. He knew they weren't bluffing. Either he agreed to play along, or he was facing extradition to the US on a murder charge. Execution of a CIA fixer. A sentence of twenty years to life behind bars in some hellhole prison.

Since then Carter had been kicking his heels. Enforced furlough. His days had been spent on life admin and honing his fitness, going on punishing runs through the hills near his modest home. Keeping himself sharp for the day when his skills would be needed again.

With one eye on his future, he had reached out to a few mates on the private Circuit. Old Hereford hands who had left to set themselves up in the trade. Over drinks he'd sounded them out about contract work. He'd assumed, perhaps naively, that a soldier with his track record would not be short of offers. But he had quickly discovered that the world had moved on. The younger guys in the Regiment had degrees and online courses in security management. They were fluent in cyber security, corporate espionage, money laundering. Skills Carter lacked.

Employers didn't want mercenary warriors. They had no use for trained killers. They wanted technicians.

In his darkest moments, Carter regretted not leaving the Regiment sooner. He had been a young Blade during the wars in the Middle East, back when Uncle Sam had been hell-bent on forging democracies in Baghdad and Kabul, with the Federal Reserve footing the bill. Some of the lads at Hereford, spying an opportunity to make their fortunes, had left the Regiment early and set themselves up as private military contractors on the Circuit. There had been stories of guys later selling their businesses for tens of millions of dollars.

Carter had missed out on the gold rush. He'd stayed on in the Regiment. A foolish decision, in retrospect. Now his prospects looked bleak. He had no specialist qualifications: no one gave you an MBA for intervening to stop a deadly terrorist attack. The best he could hope for was a contract with one of the oil companies. Steady work, but dull. Not the kind of career he had envisaged for himself after leaving Hereford. But better than nothing. Better than a kick in the teeth.

He had eighteen months left. Eighteen months on the sidelines, keeping himself busy and collecting his Special Forces pay. Then he'd leave the camp for the last time and try his luck on Civvy Street.

But then three days ago, everything had changed.

Carter had received a call out of the blue from the Regiment CO, Peter Hardcastle, summoning Carter to his office.

He'd arrived at the meeting the next morning fully expecting to be told that he was being sacked. The final nail in the coffin of his career as a Blade. Instead, to his astonishment, Hardcastle had offered him a lifeline. A transfer to G Squadron.

Now, suddenly, Carter was back in from the cold.

Ready to go back to doing what he did best.

Soldiering.

Silence fell like a curtain over the room as Duncan prepared to speak.

'Right, lads, before we get down to business, we've got a new face in the Troop,' he said matter-of-factly, his voice carrying a trace of his tough Glaswegian roots.

Duncan was feared and respected in equal measure. A legend of the Regiment, he was also something of a closed book. Not someone who engaged in chit-chat or went out on the lash at the end of training. Carter had seen Duncan from time to time at one of the local watering holes in Hereford, sitting alone and sipping a Diet Coke, but you had the sense he was watching everyone out of the corner of his eye.

He gestured towards Carter and continued. 'I'm sure you all know Geordie. No doubt you're wondering what he's doing here. Turns out D Squadron have had enough of him after he fucked up on his last op, so they've dumped him on us.'

Most of the soldiers chuckled heartily, but one guy at the back stared coldly at Carter, his face taut with barely concealed hostility.

Eddie Rigg, a veteran Blade, had long greasy hair, a straggly beard and sleeves of elaborate tattoos inked down both of his arms. With his dark jeans, black boots and Metallica T-shirt he had the look of a biker. All that was missing was the leather jacket.

Next to him sat a thickset Fijian. Sekovi 'Sek' Vonolagi was the descendant of Regiment royalty. His father and uncle had both served in the Royal Green Jackets before joining 22 SAS. Sek's father had fought at the Battle of Mirbat in Oman in the 1970s; his uncle had taken part in the Iranian Embassy Siege and later saw action in the Falklands. No one had been surprised when Sek had followed in their footsteps by passing Selection. A fearless warrior, he had only two interests outside the Regiment: rugby, and family. Physically he was a beast, bull-necked and thick-muscled, as wide as he was tall. His T-shirt looked as if it had been shrink-wrapped around his biceps.

'You gonna teach us something we don't know, Geordie?' Sek said. He grinned.

'Yeah, how to royally piss off the head shed,' replied a squat figure sitting on the front row.

Carter looked at the man who had spoken. At first glance, Brad Hickey looked more like a Southern redneck than an SAS soldier. He wore a bright-red baseball cap, chewed tobacco and had a tattoo on his right arm of a coiled rattlesnake above the words DON'T TREAD ON ME. Hickey had spent a couple of years going out on joint ops with the lads in Delta Force and SEAL Team Six, and the experience had turned him into a massive American SF fanboy.

Carter smiled wearily. He knew what these lads were thinking.

They think I've been sent here as a punishment, to piss me off.

Everyone knew his hard-luck story. How he had been shafted by the bosses in the wake of the Tajikistan op. By posting him to G Squadron they were taking him out of his comfort zone. Hoping to get a reaction from him. Provoke him into kicking up a fuss. Something that would give the powers-that-be an excuse to sack him.

40

'That's enough,' Duncan said. He turned to Carter. 'Welcome to Air Troop, Geordie. I'm sure you'll get to know everyone very well over the next few weeks. Have a seat.'

Carter nodded and took an empty chair on the front row, wedging himself between Hickey and Tom Farrell, a softly spoken Ulsterman with a shock of red hair and a neatly trimmed beard. Farrell was one of the longest-serving men in the Regiment, with a wife and four kids. He rarely said much, but he was quick-witted and had a sense of humour as dry as a bag of bones.

Duncan looked towards two men sitting beside the lectern. Carter recognised them both from previous jobs. The younger man was Lyndon Grist, a tall, bookish int officer attached to 22 SAS from the Intelligence Corps. Grist served as the interlink between Hereford and the security services and had responsibility for preparing target packs for the team. Next to him sat Christopher Smallwood, the Regiment ops officer, a career Rupert in his late thirties with a receding hairline, arched eyebrows and a severe manner.

'Fellas. Over to you,' Duncan said.

Lyndon Grist, the int officer, got up and circled round to the lectern, while Duncan stood to one side. Grist coughed to clear his throat and then addressed the men.

'Gentlemen, this mission is a hard arrest on foreign soil. I'll run through the background target pack we've got from Six, take any questions, and then hand over to Steve.'

Grist paused and tapped keys on a laptop. A moment later a photograph flashed up on one of the massive screens mounted on the rear wall behind the lectern. Carter found himself looking at a puffy-faced figure with silvery hair, a grey-flecked beard and slitted eyes framed by a pair of rimless glasses. A pinkish scar shaped like a sickle curved down from the corner of his left eye.

Grist said, 'Your target is this man. Denis Viktorovich Gorchakov. Russian national, born in what used to be Leningrad. Fifty-three years old. Started out running a catering firm before he moved to Moscow. According to the int we have from Six, Denis Gorchakov is one of Russia's most powerful figures. For the past twenty years he's made a fortune working as the accountant for several high-profile oligarchs. He's also rumoured to be the president's personal banker.'

'Fuck me, he must be worth a few quid,' said Sek.

Grist said, 'Six believes that Gorchakov is one of Russia's richest men. They estimate that his personal wealth is somewhere in the ballpark of three billion.'

Farrell whistled. 'Tell you what, Brad. With that much wonga, even a thick bastard like you might stand a chance of getting laid.'

That prompted a few hearty chuckles from the others. Hickey glared at him. 'I get my fair share of action, mate. The women can't get enough of this.' He pointed to his crotch.

'They're hardly dating you on account of your towering intellect, are they, now?' Farrell joked. Laughter spread throughout the briefing room as the others joined in.

Sek snorted and said, 'Even if this Russian fella is minted, he's not likely to be flaunting it. His kind never do. Money will be securely hidden in a Swiss bank.'

Duncan smiled. 'Nothing is secure in this world, Eddie. Not anymore. You should know that.'

'Gorchakov is extremely paranoid,' Grist cut in. 'Comes with the territory when you handle money for the likes of the Russian president. He knew that one day his enemies would come looking for him.

'A few years ago, he started buying up diamonds, works of art, gold bullion. Anything he could readily liquidate if he needed to make an emergency getaway.'

Duncan said, 'Basically, our man is sitting on a ton of transportable wealth. Stuff he'd want to keep close to hand. Probably got it hidden in a safe somewhere in one of his properties.'

'What's the interest in this guy?' asked Farrell. 'Someone in Whitehall needs some help fiddling their expenses, like?'

Grist said, 'Gorchakov has spent his career investing stolen funds on behalf of his bosses. Which means he knows all the Kremlin's dirty financial secrets. Where the president's cash is hidden. What assets he owns, where the money came from, who got a slice of the action. Illegal activities, criminal networks, corrupt dealings. Obviously, what he knows is of considerable interest to Vauxhall.'

Sek stroked his jaw thoughtfully. 'Are we sure this guy is the president's personal banker? Last I heard, he was one of the bloke's harshest critics. He's always on TV slagging him off.'

Grist said, 'Six believes that's an act. A smokescreen, designed to conceal the true nature of his relationship with the president.'

Duncan smiled thinly. 'Typical Kremlin tactics. Misdirection. Make it look like your mates are working for the other side. That way, no one will suspect them of doing your dirty work for you.'

'Got to hand it to the Russians,' Farrell said. 'They're crafty. Even if they are a bunch of murderous bastards.'

Grist nodded and ran a hand through his thinning hair. 'Vauxhall had their suspicions about Gorchakov. They knew he was close to the president, but they couldn't be sure.

'But then Gorchakov started making public statements against the president. Which raised a couple of questions. Why wasn't the Kremlin trying to silence him? Where did all his wealth come from? The more Six looked into it, the more they were sure that this guy was the president's money manager.

'For the past several months, Gorchakov has been living under the radar in Poland. The official story is that he fled Moscow after the president turned against him. In fact, Six believes that the Russian president deliberately organised the move in order to protect Gorchakov.'

Hickey creased his brow. 'But if Gorchakov is the president's banker, surely he'd want to keep him close?'

Grist shook his head. 'The president has a growing number of enemies inside the Kremlin,' he explained. 'People who would like to get hold of Gorchakov. Have a conversation with him. It's in his interest to keep him well away from Moscow.'

Duncan said, 'There is mounting internal opposition to the president. The war in Ukraine has weakened his position and his enemies smell blood. Senior Kremlin officials are now openly discussing how to get rid of him.'

'What has that got to do with our man?' asked Hickey.

'Three days ago, Six received credible int that the FSB is planning to snatch Gorchakov from his bolthole in Poland. The working theory is that they're going to torture him into giving up his secrets, then deliver an ultimatum to the president: stand down, or you'll lose everything.

'In light of this development, Vauxhall has sanctioned an operation to lift Gorchakov and extradite him to London. That's where you lads come in.'

Carter said, 'What's the target location?'

Grist signalled to Duncan. The latter leaned over and worked one of the laptop keyboards. A series of images promptly flashed up on the wall-mounted screens behind the lectern. Carter saw a low-resolution satellite shot of a large rectangular compound surrounded by a perimeter fence, set in a sprawling landscape of dense woodland. There was a street view of the same location; another screen displayed a photograph of what looked like an identical building.

Grist said, 'Gorchakov owns four properties in Poland. Scattered throughout the countryside. All built in remote areas. All built to the exact same specs, using the same materials. Same carpet, furniture, gardens. Same everything.'

'Bit fucking extreme,' remarked Sek.

'Maybe he's got a condition,' Hickey suggested. 'OCD, or some shit.'

'Bad enough to build the same gaff four times?' Sek looked sceptical.

'Could be,' Farrell said. 'I knew one lad who did close protection for a Greek shipping magnate. Billionaire. Had mansions all over the world. He reckoned this fella had the same suits, watches and shoes at every house. He'd get himself measured up for a Savile Row suit, then order five of 'em and send one to each place.'

'Which one is Gorchakov staying at now?' asked Carter.

'None of them. Right now, he's out of the country. Last seen in Geneva. Dealing with clients, we think.'

Sek wrinkled his brow. 'Then how do we know which mansion to target?'

'We don't,' Grist replied. 'At least, not yet. But we believe that Gorchakov is due to fly back to Poland imminently.'

'Are you sure?'

Grist nodded. 'Gorchakov makes frequent trips to Geneva, once every couple of months to meet with clients. Usually follows the same routine. He flies in on his private jet, stays in the presidential suite at the Grafton Hotel for six nights before heading home. In the meantime, we're monitoring activity on his accounts. Soon as that goes silent, we know that he's finished his business and is heading back. At which point we'll track the flight path of his private jet. The destination will indicate which property Gorchakov will be staying at in Poland.'

'What's the green light for the arrest?' asked Carter.

'You'll wait until we have official confirmation that Gorchakov is at his residence. Which will come from our friends at Cheltenham. They'll be monitoring internet and phone activity at all four locations. As soon as he logs onto a computer, uses his phone or the landline, we'll know about it. Then you'll fly in and snatch the target.'

'That's hardly ideal. We're not gonna have much notice.'

Grist shifted his weight and shrugged. 'Can't be helped. We can't do anything that might alert Gorchakov. If he realises he's being watched, he'll get spooked, and there's a very good chance he'll go underground.'

'What about bodyguards?' asked Farrell in his soft Belfast brogue.

'Eight guys on the BG team. Gorchakov never travels anywhere without them. When they're cutting around on the roads, he rides in a Rolls-Royce Phantom with his bodyguards in a couple of G Wagons, front and rear.'

'Polish?'

'Russian. Ex-Spetsnaz, so they're capable enough. Armed, of course.'

'Do we know their routine?'

'According to our source, four of them patrol the grounds when the big boss is staying over for the night. Another two guys posted at the gatehouse at all times. We can assume two more will be inside the building, guarding the principal or taking a nap.'

Carter said, 'Who's the source?'

'One of the maids. She was sacked several months ago and sought asylum in the UK. Came to Six's attention when she listed her previous employer on a job application.'

'Why would she dob in her old boss?'

'It's a personal thing. She claims Gorchakov treats his staff like shit. Sixteen-hour shifts, dirty accommodation, no running water or electricity. Some of the girls were regularly abused.'

Farrell said, 'We should be locking the bastard up, not giving him a new life on the taxpayer's dime.'

'Haven't you heard, Tom? Crime pays.' Sek grinned. A ripple of laughter spread through the room.

Grist said, 'The maid's information is solid. We can trust her.'

'Has he got any local protection? Polish police, security forces, anything like that?' Carter asked.

'Not as far as we're aware, no. Gorchakov prefers to rely on men he knows he can trust.'

'Anyone else in the house?' asked Sek. 'Wife and kids?'

Grist shook his head firmly. 'Gorchakov's family is still in Russia. The president has kept them there as collateral. To make sure Gorchakov doesn't get any ideas. The only other occupants are the household staff.'

'Does he have a strongroom?'

Carter glanced over his shoulder. The question came from Eddie Rigg. The bike fanatic with the long beard. Rigg had been quiet so far during the briefing, but now he seemed to be staring at the images on the screens with a keen interest.

'Good question,' said Duncan. He looked towards Grist. 'Lyndon?'

Grist said, 'As far as we gather, yes. The maid has confirmed that there's a strongroom on the second floor of each property. Gorchakov mainly uses them to store his loot. They're glorified safes.'

'Specs?' Sek asked.

'We're looking into that as we speak.'

Rigg said, 'We'll need to know everything about those rooms before we fly out. Thickness of the walls, type of door, whether there's plumbing and electricity inside.'

'And what kind of locking system the guy uses,' Sek added.

Carter glanced at him. 'What difference does that make?'

'We're just covering all the bases, Geordie. Don't want any nasty surprises when we get inside, do we?'

Carter stared at him but said nothing.

Duncan said, 'Once we've secured the target, we'll hand him over to Six. They'll subject him to an enhanced interrogation and find out what he knows.'

'Then we'll get the beers in,' Farrell added.

Hickey stared at him with raised eyebrows. 'Sure you should be drinking at your age, Tom? Jesus, you're so old you were probably on the fucking Ark.'

'I'll buy you a bloody shandy, you wanker.'

Farrell and Hickey both laughed easily. But Carter wasn't tuned in. He was puzzling over something.

'Why the big fuss over this bloke?' he asked. 'Why does Six give two shits about some Russian accountant buying up a load of country piles and yachts for his boss?'

The int officer turned towards Smallwood. The ops man said, 'Gorchakov is the fixer to the Russian elite. He's the guy who arranged the purchase of the president's superyacht and his palace on the Black Sea coast. Billions of dollars in assets. The propaganda value of British officers seizing the president's prize yacht will be immense. It'll embarrass him. Make him look weak in front of his own people.'

'It might also concentrate minds inside the Kremlin,' Grist added. 'The president's remaining backers might start to reconsider their positions if they think their assets are at risk.'

'What if the target resists arrest?' Carter wondered.

Smallwood met his gaze evenly. He said, 'Six wants Gorchakov alive. No ifs, no fucking buts. If the principal resists, do whatever it takes to suppress him. But make sure you bring him back while he's still drawing breath. Or you can forget about a career in this squadron, Geordie.'

* * *

A short time later, Grist wrapped up the intelligence briefing. Then Duncan stepped forward and announced that they were taking a short break. Grist and Smallwood left the room, while Carter, Rigg and the rest of the Troop drifted towards a table near the back. Plates of sandwiches had been laid out, along with a load of snacks and fresh fruit, and stainless-steel urns filled with coffee and tea. Carter fixed himself a brew, grabbed a ham and cheese sandwich and chatted with a few of the other guys. There was the usual Hereford small talk. The guys swapped rumours about Blades who had left the unit recently. The jobs they had landed, the money they were supposedly making. A retired veteran from the Gulf War had recently killed himself. Sek moaned about how he'd have to miss a rugby match at Twickenham the following week. Hickey bored everyone senseless about his recent trip to Florida to meet up with his new besties from

Delta. They were going to go into business together one day, Hickey said. Running their own training packages. Hickey had big plans for his life after the Regiment. He was going to make a new life for himself in the US, apparently. Sell up his terraced house, buy up a condo in Tampa and get rich. He couldn't wait.

Rigg stared at Carter from across the room. A look in his eyes as cold as liquid nitrogen. Carter wondered what he had done to piss the bloke off. Maybe nothing. Maybe Rigg just didn't like him.

That happened sometimes at Hereford. You were living in a close-knit world, spending your time in small patrol-sized units, surrounded by a bunch of lads with strong personalities. Sometimes people simply didn't get along.

But still. It seemed fucking weird.

Twenty minutes later, Duncan marched back into the room with Grist and Smallwood. The men of Air Troop returned to their chairs for the operational briefing. Which covered logistics, times, locations, equipment. Everything they needed to know before planning the assault in detail.

'Mounting-up point will be at Ramstein Air Base in Germany,' Duncan said. 'Once we land, there will be a planning briefing. Then it's a case of waiting for confirmation that Gorchakov is on site. Once we get the green light, we're straight on the Black Hawks.'

Hickey said, 'Time to target?'

'Anything from forty minutes to two hours, depending on which property you'll be assaulting. Refuelling en route at a friendly base in western Poland.'

'What are the rules of engagement?' Farrell asked.

'Neutralise any BGs who attempt to return fire, secure the rest and get in and out of there as quickly as possible.'

Smallwood coughed and said, 'Six is very keen for this mission to go smoothly. We don't want to find ourselves in a position where we need to explain to our Polish friends what's happened. Or, God forbid, risk a blue-on-blue with the local police.'

'You'll also be going in sterile,' Duncan said. 'That means stand-ard uniforms. No badges or insignia. Nothing that might identify you. That goes for you, especially,' he added, glaring at Hickey.

'Me?' Hickey affected an innocent look. 'What the fuck have I done, chief?'

'Them badges you wear. That stupid challenge coin you carry round – the one with the winged dagger on it. That shite might be acceptable in the Land of the Free, but as long as you're in my Troop, son, you'll leave that crap in your locker.'

Carter said, 'When do we fly out?'

'Two days from now,' Duncan replied. 'A few days before Gor-chakov is due to finish his meetings with his clients in Geneva. We leave at 0600 hours on the dot. Chopper to Brize Norton, then we'll cross-deck for onward flight to Germany.'

The meeting continued throughout the early afternoon. There was a long discussion about the kit they'd need for the job. Explo-sives, rifles, cutting devices. Then Duncan left the room. He returned two minutes later with a guy from 18 Signals. Jacob Moody was a combat communicator with the look of a triathlete, slim and wiry. He walked the team through the tech they would be using on the op. Comms kit, eavesdropping, drones, cameras. There would be a direct link from Ramstein to GCHQ at Cheltenham throughout the mission, Moody said, providing the guys with up-to-the-minute information on any goings-on at the stronghold. Moody would also accompany the team to Germany so they could deal with any technical glitches before mounting up.

In addition, each soldier would swap the SIM card on his phone for a local one prior to their departure. Some time ago, Whitehall had discovered that Kremlin agents had been covertly position-ing Pineapple Wi-Fi devices around the base at Credenhill. The Pineapples were small, mass-produced units that allowed hackers to stealthily glean personal information from anyone who logged onto a public Wi-Fi network.

The Russians were rumoured to have installed Pineapples at several other locations: Cheltenham, Vauxhall, the SBS camp at Poole. In theory, they could use the data scraped from the phones to identify and track British personnel operating in Ukraine. As a result, changing SIM cards was now part of standard operating procedure for all Regiment men on overseas ops.

Once Moody had finished the tech brief, Duncan stepped forward.

'OK, fellas. I think that's all the basics covered for now. If anything else comes up before we fly out, I'll let you know.

'In the meantime, sort out your kit and weaponry. Any other questions?' He looked round the room, then nodded. 'Good. Then I suggest you get a move on. We leave in two days.'

Three

At two o'clock the following afternoon, Jamie Carter and the rest of the team reported to the G Squadron hangar located at one end of the camp at Credenhill. The cavernous space was a hive of activity as the soldiers checked and packed their equipment ahead of their flight to Ramstein the next morning. Glock pistols and L119A2 rifles were broken down into their individual components and cleaned to make sure they were in good working order. Ballistic helmets, aviator gloves, knee pads and elbow pads and tactical plate carriers were packed into army backpacks. Also carried by each man: tourniquets and shell dressings, suppressors for their primary weapons, night sights, rail-mounted red-dot sights, flashbangs, L2 grenades, smoke grenades, several pairs of plasticuffs, and five spare clips of ammo: 5.56 x 45 mm NATO rounds for the L119A2s, nine-milli brass for the Glock semi-automatics.

In one corner of the hangar, Eddie Rigg was checking over a hydraulic jig. Which was a four-foot-long pole with a pair of metal sleeves at one end which expanded when inserted in the slight gap between frame and door. The resulting force pushed everything outward, allowing the operator to easily wrench the door away from the surrounding frame. A vital piece of kit for any Method of Entry team.

At a nearby table, Sek was assembling a stack of shaped charges for blowing open doors and windows. The burly Fijian worked methodically, connecting strips of det cord to cigarette-packet sized lumps of C4 explosive. Both the cord and the C4 were rigged up to lengths of thin electrical wire. There were rolls of double-sided black tape on the table, plus two dozen Claymore clacker firing devices used to detonate the charges.

Close by, Hickey tested a metal detector. The kind of thing used to detect landmines, shaped like a garden strimmer, with a bulky main operating unit and a telescopic rod attached to a search-head at the other end. Hickey, chewing his Skoal tobacco, disassembled the detector and started packing the separate parts into the carry case.

While Carter checked his weaponry, he caught sight of Farrell handling a thermal lance. The lance was a nifty tool, a man-portable pressurised cylinder filled with oxygen, rigged up to a length of cutting cable. A favourite of UK SF teams. Ideal for slicing through steel doors or when you needed to hack through metal bars on a window in a matter of seconds.

Two additional thermal lances rested on the floor.

Farrell noticed Carter watching him and looked up. 'Something wrong, Geordie? Or are you just admiring my good looks?'

'What are we taking them things for?' Carter indicated the thermal lances.

'Backup, son. In case we need to cut the principal out of the strongroom.' He patted the cylinder and grinned broadly, revealing a set of crooked yellow teeth. 'Or do I need to explain room entry procedures to you?'

Before Carter could reply, Duncan set down his Glock and marched over. 'There a problem, Geordie?'

Carter said, 'Why do we need three lances? One is more than enough for the job.'

'No harm in preparing for the worst, is there? Better than winging it like your old mates in D Squadron.'

Carter tensed his muscles. Farrell and Duncan shared a laugh.

'I've never needed three lances to make a hard arrest,' Carter said evenly. 'Or a metal detector.'

Duncan shrugged. 'We do things differently in G Squadron,' he said.

'I'm starting to realise that.'

Duncan stepped towards him, dropping his voice to a low growl. 'What are you trying to say, mate?'

Carter pointed to the pile of explosives Sek had been putting together. He said, 'There's got to be twenty framed charges over there. Our guys never used more than two or three on house assault. This looks more like we're planning a bank raid than a hard arrest. And what the fuck do we need a metal detector for?'

Something glinted in Duncan's eyes. 'In case you've forgotten, we're under orders to retrieve any int the target has got stored in his gaff. Laptops, phones, hard drives. Them Russians are all the same. Slippery bastards. He might try and stash his hardware somewhere when he hears us crashing through the front door.'

Carter shook his head fiercely. 'We don't need all this kit. We'll be weighed down.'

The team leader shot him a filthy glare. 'Listen, here, you thick bastard,' he said frostily. 'Me and the lads have been kicking in doors for the past six years. We've done shitloads of busts in Iraq, Afghanistan. We know what we're doing. So don't tell us how to do our fucking jobs. All right?'

Carter met the Scot's gaze, his jaw set firm. Around the hangar the other twelve guys had stopped what they were doing and looked towards him. Like schoolkids anticipating a scrap. The logical part of his brain told him not to argue the point.

You've been in G Squadron for five minutes, the voice cautioned. *This is your one chance to salvage your career.*

Don't screw it up.

'It's your call, Steve,' he muttered.

'Aye. It bloody well is.'

Duncan eyeballed him for a moment longer. Then he wheeled round and walked away.

The other lads went back to work; Carter turned his attention to his kit. But he couldn't shake the seed of doubt that had been forming in his head since the briefing.

It was true that every squadron had their own way of doing things. Contrary to the popular image of the Regiment in the media, standard operating procedures varied from team to team. Knowledge gained in the field was passed down from one group to the next by the veteran NCOs: the men who formed the spiritual backbone of the SAS. The best soldiers adapted to the situation in front of them. It wasn't unusual to find subtle differences in the ways that each squadron tackled a problem.

So maybe it was nothing, Carter told himself. Maybe Duncan and his guys were just covering all the bases.

But maybe not.

Half an hour later, the men finished packing their kit. They stowed their ops baggage in a secure area, ready to snatch up and load onto the Chinook the next morning. Then they left the hangar, passing the helipad as they made for the car park a short distance away, chatting and joking.

As Carter started in the same direction, Duncan called out to him. He turned and saw the bluff Scot strolling over.

'No hard feelings, Geordie?'

Carter made a face. 'Jesus, Steve. I ain't a fucking snowflake.'

Duncan relaxed his features into a warm smile. He jerked a thumb in the direction of the hangar. 'Look, I know all that kit might look a bit excessive. But we just like to make sure we're not going in half-cocked. You know how it is.'

'It's fine,' Carter said.

There was a pause of silence as Duncan regarded the younger man. Then he said, quietly, 'I know why you're here, mate. I've heard all the stories on the grapevine.'

Carter said nothing.

Duncan continued, 'The way the head shed shafted you after that siege in Mali is fucking disgraceful. They should have given you a medal for what you did out there.'

Carter shrugged. 'It is what it is.'

Duncan cleared his throat and said, 'Me and the lads are going to RV at the White Horse later on. Get a few beers in. Sort of a Troop tradition the night before we head out on an op. We'll be there from eight o'clock, if you're interested.'

Carter thought: *These guys are meant to be professionals. Instead, they're spending the night before a mission out on the lash.* But he decided against saying anything. He'd already got off to a bad start with his new colleagues.

That tongue of yours has got you in plenty of trouble in the past.

'You're welcome to tag along,' Duncan went on. 'But don't feel like you've got to come or anything. I know it's not really your bag, Geordie.'

He smiled, but there was something peculiar about his tone, Carter sensed. An implication that his presence would not be entirely appreciated at the Troop's pre-op piss-up.

Carter didn't take it personally. He'd been a Blade for long enough to know the score. He was damaged goods. A cautionary tale. One minute you were flavour of the month with the head shed, the hero of the Regiment. Then you weren't, for whatever reason, and suddenly everyone else wanted to steer clear of you. He'd seen it happen to guys in the past. Good soldiers whose careers had suffered because they had pissed off the higher-ups.

Carter had no interest in going out on the lash. There had been a time, once, when he had enjoyed that side of Regiment life. Bonding with his muckers over several pints, getting into scraps with the locals outside the kebab shop after closing time. But then he'd had a wake-up call. One of the veterans had taken Carter under his wing. Showed him the importance of dedicating himself to being an elite operator. Nowadays, Carter was something of a loner. He preferred his own company to getting hammered with a few idiots in some grungy pub.

'Thanks,' he said. 'But I'll take a rain check. Got some life admin to sort out.'

'Course, Geordie. No worries.' Duncan slapped him cheerfully on the shoulder. 'See you bright and early tomorrow, son.'

Duncan turned and beat a path towards his slate-grey Range Rover. Rigg and Hickey made for their Harley-Davidsons. The two lads were both massively into their motorbikes, always discussing new customised stuff for the Harleys or flicking through copies of *MCN*.

Carter gave his back to the others and folded himself behind the wheel of his Volvo S90. He was looking forward to a quiet evening at home. A walk across the hills, perhaps, then a few hours reading before he got his head down. He had a biography of Alexander the Great he was keen to finish. Better than sitting in a boozer all night, listening to Hickey, Rigg and the rest of the lads in Air Troop talking shite.

He gunned the engine and steered out of the car park.

Twelve minutes later, Carter reached his home a couple of kilometres outside Credenhill. He eased the Volvo to a halt at the end of the gravel driveway, climbed out and started for the front door.

He was about to shove the key in the lock when his phone buzzed.

Carter took out his phone and peered at the screen. *No Caller ID.* He stepped back from the door, swiped a finger across the scuffed glass to answer.

A gruff voice on the other end said, 'Geordie, it's Phil Greening.'

Carter froze.

Major Phil Greening was the 2iC of the Regiment, a hard-as-nails old sweat from G Squadron with twenty years of service under his belt. It was unusual for an ex-ranker to reach the upper echelons of the SAS; as such, he commanded total respect among his peers. But he wasn't the sort of bloke who checked in for a casual chat. Whatever Greening wanted with him, it had to be bad news.

What the fuck have I done now?

'Listen, Geordie, I need to speak with you.'

Not a request. But a demand. Carter sighed through gritted teeth.

'Sure. When?'

'Tonight. The King's Arms near Madley. Seven o'clock. We'll grab a pint and I'll explain everything then.'

'Why? What's this about?'

'I can't say right now. Not on the phone. Just make sure you're there tonight. Got it?'

'Roger that.'

'And Geordie?'

'Yes?'

'Don't mention this to anyone else.'

* * *

The King's Arms was an old-school boozer housed in a crumbling red-brick structure six miles outside Hereford. The place had seen better days, and better decades too. The paintwork was peeling; dirty net curtains were drawn over the windows. A sign outside promised 'good food and cold beer'. Which was setting the bar pretty low, in Carter's opinion. He left his Volvo in the car park and paced briskly towards the entrance. Seven o'clock in the evening. Dusk was encroaching on the landscape. In the distance, a ribbon of leaden cloud stretched across the horizon.

Carter knew he was in the shit. No other reason why Greening had reached out to him directly.

I don't know what I've done wrong this time, he thought.

But it seems I can't set foot in camp these days without pissing someone off.

He took a deep breath and stepped inside the bar.

The decor looked like something out of a documentary about the Kray twins. Cigarette burns on the frayed carpet, velvet-padded stools, dark wood panelling and chipped furniture. A stench of stale beer hung in the air, so thick you could probably get hammered on it. A flatscreen TV fixed to one wall showed the rugby highlights. A handful of punters sat at the bar. Old men with bloated faces and packets of rolling baccy, sipping cheap beers while they scanned the betting tips in the redtops.

How the owners stayed in business was a mystery to Carter, up there with the Bermuda Triangle and the appeal of social media.

Carter scanned the faces of the drinkers and caught sight of Greening at a table at the back, sipping a pint of Guinness. Two people were sitting opposite Greening, their backs to Carter. A man and a woman.

Carter beelined for the table and wondered what the fuck was going on.

Greening rose to greet him. The Regiment 2iC was crisply dressed in a Barbour jacket, polo shirt, dark jeans and desert boots. His hair was the texture of steel filaments; his bushy eyebrows slanted downward at an angle so that they formed a distinctive 'V' above the bridge of his nose. He was in good shape for his age, trim and honed. The skin was pulled so tight over his face it looked like it might snap.

'Geordie. Thanks for joining us,' Greening said. They shook hands.

'This is Alex Maitland,' he continued, gesturing towards the woman. 'She's with Five.'

Carter looked the MI5 officer up and down. A black woman in her mid-thirties, with scraped-back brown hair and a high-cheekboned face angling down towards blood-red lips. She wore flared trousers and blazer over a plain white work shirt. From a mid-range high-street chain, probably. A salary as a Five officer wouldn't stretch to anything more luxurious. She had a delicate manner, but Carter sensed there was an underlying steeliness to her. As if she had been built from some seemingly fragile but unbreakable material.

'Pleased to meet you,' Maitland said in a voice that could have come from anywhere in the Home Counties.

Greening waved a hand at the guy next to Maitland. A flabby white bloke in a bin-liner suit. He looked about a decade older than Maitland, and about fifty kilos heavier. A few wispy strands of greying hair were raked over his otherwise balding pate.

'Mark Sutton,' Greening said by way of introduction. 'From our friends over at the National Crime Agency. Mark is with the Organised Crime Command. Mark, this is Geordie.'

Sutton nodded a greeting. 'All right, fella?'

Carter blanked him and looked questioningly at Greening. 'What the fuck is going on, Phil?'

'Take a seat, Geordie. Get you a drink? Beer? Coke?'

Carter shook his head. 'I'm fine.'

'Suit yourself.'

Carter took the empty chair next to the Regiment major and racked his brains, trying to figure out what he could have possibly done to draw the ire of the security services and the police.

Greening set his Guinness down. Rested his meaty hands in his lap.

'How are you finding life in G Squadron?' he asked.

'Fine,' Carter replied impatiently. 'But I've only been there about five minutes.'

In the tail of his eye, he noticed both Maitland and Sutton watching him closely.

'And the other lads? You're getting on well with them?'

'I guess so. What's this about, Phil?'

Carter had a visceral dislike of polite chat. He preferred to drop the bullshit and get straight to the point.

Maitland said, 'Have you heard of a group calling themselves the Steel Reapers?'

'Doesn't ring any bells. Why?'

'It's a motorcycle club, operating within the SAS,' Maitland said. 'Membership is restricted to serving soldiers. It's a small group. No more than a couple of dozen members.'

'Including several of your new friends in Air Troop,' Greening put in. 'We know that Steve Duncan and Eddie Rigg are definitely part of the club. Possibly Brad Hickey. Along with several other lads. Duncan is one of the founding members, actually.'

'Good for him.'

Maitland said, 'The Reapers are run like a proper bikers' club. There's a sergeant of arms. A president. A clubhouse. New prospects have to swear an oath before they get badged. And they don't ever discuss their activities with outsiders. Sort of like the Freemasons. Which is why you've never heard of them.'

'They might sound like a crap heavy metal band,' said Sutton. 'But don't be fooled. They're a dangerous bunch of lads.'

Carter glanced at the NCA officer. He had the deflated look of a guy who had never made it higher than the lower rungs of his profession and knew it was all downhill from now on. He quickly decided that Maitland was the more senior of the two. A young woman on the up. A future director general at Thames House, possibly.

'How so?' Carter asked.

Maitland said, 'We have reason to believe that the Reapers are involved with known criminal elements operating inside the UK. Specifically, a motorcycle club with suspected links to organised crime. They call themselves the Blood Kings.'

Carter tensed. A hollow feeling spread through his chest. 'Doing what?'

'Fencing stolen goods,' Sutton said. 'That's one aspect of it. But it's possible that they might be caught up in a bunch of other stuff, too. Drug trafficking, extortion. Murder.'

'Jesus Christ.'

He knew that some of the guys at Hereford were mad about their motorbikes, and there had been rumours that several of them had formed an unofficial club. Carter had always assumed they spent their downtime fixing up their vintage two-wheelers and cutting around country lanes in their bike leathers. But he'd never imagined that they would be associating with organised crime figures.

He shook his head. 'Are you sure about this?'

'We have a source in the Kings,' Sutton responded. 'In the Plymouth chapter. A UC.'

Greening said, 'A UC is—'

'I know what it means. You've got an undercover cop on the inside. Go on.'

Sutton cleared his throat and said, 'Our UC tipped us off about a big deal the Kings had lined up.'

'What kind of deal?'

'Cash, in exchange for ammunition. Specifically, six hundred rounds of 9 x 19 mm Parabellum.'

'Obviously, the scale of the deal sounded alarm bells,' Maitland said. 'A typical street-level sale might involve twenty or thirty rounds at most. Often a lot less. Getting hold of that much ammunition is beyond the reach of most ordinary criminals.'

Sutton said, 'We put surveillance on the sellers. Had our people track them from the RV.'

'And?'

'They tailed the sellers all the way back here. To Credenhill.'

'Shit.'

Greening coughed and said, 'Of course, we don't know the full extent of the relationship. Could just be one or two bad apples in the Troop. Perhaps they allowed themselves to get mixed up with the wrong crowd. Happened before, unfortunately.'

Maitland gave him a look and said, 'The Kings are notorious. They're active on the continent, and in North America too. Several of their members are wanted in connection with crimes ranging from kidnapping to manslaughter. You don't strike up a casual friendship with these guys. Not without knowing who they are, and what they do for a living.'

'Plus, there's the money,' Sutton added.

Carter crinkled his brow. 'What money?'

'Duncan and his biker buddies snapped up a place a few miles up the road from the camp. About a year ago. They've paid for all the building work in cash. Tens of thousands of pounds.'

Carter shrugged. 'Maybe Steve won the lottery. Or came into a tidy inheritance.'

Sutton stared at him.

Maitland said, 'Cards on the table. Your friends are up to their necks in trouble.'

'They're not my mates. Christ, it's not even my squadron.'

'That's as maybe. But we have evidence of SAS personnel conspiring to sell stolen ammunition to the Kings, and large unexplained sums of cash, and we know that the Reapers have a pre-existing relationship with the Plymouth chapter. Which is deeply concerning on several levels. It raises the question of what the soldiers are getting in return.'

'You think they're selling more than ammo?'

'We're dealing with highly skilled soldiers with years of Special Forces training. Flogging stolen equipment is bad, obviously, but it's not the only service they have to offer. For all we know, they might be instructing the Kings. Teaching them surveillance tactics. Weapons training. Eavesdropping techniques. Helping to plan the murders of rivals. Maybe even executing them.'

'Pure speculation, of course,' Greening cut in. 'The truth is, we simply don't know.'

'How long has this been going on?' Carter asked.

Sutton said, 'We think it goes back to Iraq. At the time, Duncan and some of the veterans in Air Troop were suspected of looting valuables when they were going out on raids each night. Jewellery. Gold bars. Cash. Weapons. Trinkets. Anything they could take with them that might fetch a good price on the black market.'

Carter considered. He'd taken part in loads of door-kicking ops in Iraq. Back when the Regiment had been going toe to toe with terrorist cells in the country. Each night his strike team had gone out on multiple raids, swooping in to lift one suspect before piling straight back into the chopper to execute the next mission. Counter-insurgency on steroids. Some of the targets had been high-ranking figures under the old regime and had enriched themselves accordingly. Carter had never personally witnessed anyone on his team taking a five-finger discount from the buildings they'd busted.

But then again, he hadn't paid much attention to his mates. He had been too busy trying to stay alive.

'Smuggling the loot back to Hereford would have been easy enough,' Sutton carried on. 'They might have hidden it in their baggage. Or in the vehicles. But the big problem these days is banking the money. You can't stroll into your local Lloyds and pay in two hundred grand in cash, not without HMRC taking a keen interest in your affairs. That's where the Kings came in.'

Maitland said, 'We could never prove anything. But we think Duncan was the original point of contact. He and the Plymouth chapter president go way back, according to the UC.'

Carter said, 'What about the dough? If the lads are bent, they'll have stashed the money somewhere. So where is it?'

Sutton squirmed. 'We're not entirely sure.'

'Have you checked the squadron fund?'

Each SAS squadron, Carter knew, had its own individual fund for organising stuff like Christmas parties and refurbishments. Most of the money came from petty fines and donations.

'We have,' Maitland said. 'It's clean. Three grand plus change in it. Ditto the clock tower fund.'

'So where's the cash?'

'Could be anywhere. Maybe the Reapers used the biker crew's accountants to launder it for them. Might be hidden offshore. Or they might have stored it somewhere until it's safe to retrieve. Could be sitting in a storage unit in a field in Shropshire, for all we know.'

Sutton said, 'Obviously, if we knew where to find the money, we wouldn't be sitting here now.'

'What's any of this got to do with me?' Carter asked.

Maitland said, 'This is a delicate situation. But the guys in the Reapers are a close-knit bunch. Oath-bound never to betray their brother members. Which means we're fumbling in the dark. We need to know how deep this thing really goes.'

'Assuming the UC's claims are true,' Greening said.

'Our guy has never let us down in the past,' Sutton said, bluntly.

'The point is, we need to get in front of this thing,' Maitland said. 'Establish what's actually going on. That means finding out who is involved with the Kings, the exact nature of their relationship, any other illegal activity they're potentially caught up in.'

Sutton said, 'That's where you come in, pal.'

'We want you to keep a close eye on the other men in your Troop,' Maitland explained. 'Watch what they're doing. Who they're fraternising with. Anything that might help us better understand what's going on.'

A cynical laugh escaped Carter's throat. 'Sorry, love. You're asking the wrong person. I ain't a snitch.'

Maitland narrowed her eyes. 'This isn't about being a grass. You're looking at this through the wrong end of the telescope. We're asking you to help expose a potential criminal conspiracy right at the heart of the SAS.'

'By spying on my own kind.'

Greening shifted uncomfortably. 'I know it's far from ideal, Geordie. I don't like it any more than you. But the Regiment's reputation is at stake. If this got out, it would ruin us.'

Carter laughed bitterly. 'The Regiment? What did you lot ever do for me? All them years I put in, putting my balls on the line, and you bastards threw me on the scrapheap.'

'That wasn't my decision.'

A realisation suddenly dawned on Carter. He felt the blood boiling in his veins.

'That's why you transferred me to G Squadron, isn't it? So you could strong-arm me into being a plant.'

Greening smiled apologetically. 'We had no choice. We couldn't approach any of the guys in the Troop, or anyone else in G Squadron, because we didn't know if we could trust them. It had to be an outsider.'

'I've read your file,' Maitland interjected. 'You're the perfect candidate for the job. Someone with a deep sense of bitterness and enmity over the way they've been treated by their superiors. A divorcee who lives alone and struggles to make his monthly maintenance payments. Who knows? It might even encourage Duncan to bring you into his confidence, if he thinks you're desperate enough to turn to crime.'

'Jesus, don't go overboard with the compliments.'

Greening said, 'There is something else we can offer you. Something that might be of interest.'

Carter looked at him. Waited for the major to go on.

'How would you feel about becoming the new squadron sergeant major for G Squadron, Geordie?'

'They already have one.'

'For now. But – assuming the intelligence picture is accurate – once this is over he'll fall on his sword.'

'Even if he isn't directly involved?'

'The fact is, two of his men have been caught flogging ammunition to an organised crime group on his watch. That's grounds for dismissal alone.' He grinned. 'Do this for us, and you could be the new SSM.'

'What if you're wrong? What if it's more than just a couple of bad apples?'

Greening snorted. 'Assuming that these men are, in fact, guilty, they will be punished accordingly. They'll regret the day they set foot inside the camp.'

Carter fell silent and stared out of the grimy window. He struggled to believe what he was hearing. There had always been a few shifty characters in the ranks at Hereford, soldiers who had dabbled in crime for one reason or another. The worst offenders were usually weeded out before they could do any reputational damage. But what Maitland and Sutton were describing was something much more serious.

If they were right, G Squadron was rotten to the core.

He didn't give a toss about the stolen goods. Others had done much worse in the past and got away with it. The head shed had form when it came to sweeping the ugly stuff under the rug. None of his business.

But rubbing shoulders with a bunch of drug dealers and killers was a different matter.

Greening was right, he realised. If word got out that Britain's elite soldiers were profiting from organised crime, that might sound the death knell for the Regiment.

There would be a public outcry. Ministers would inevitably demand blood – never mind that they were only able to enjoy their flat whites and craft beers because men like Carter – hard men, from the roughest parts of Britain, places the rest of the country had forgotten about – were willing to get their hands dirty.

'The Regiment has taken a battering in public lately,' Greening said. 'No way we'd survive if this leaked to the public. You realise that, don't you?'

Carter thought about his younger brother.

Luke had followed him into the SAS after joining the Paras as a nineteen-year-old. He was one of the good guys, a keen soldier with a bright future ahead of him in the Regiment.

Are you really going to let a few corrupt idiots destroy Luke's career?

'Fuck it,' he said. 'I'm in.'

'Good man,' Greening muttered as he patted Carter on the back. 'This is a good thing you're doing, Geordie. The CO won't forget this.'

'Tell him to thank me later,' Carter growled. He nodded at Maitland. 'I'm guessing you lot are running this show. Not Tony Soprano here,' he added, gesturing towards Sutton.

Maitland said, 'This is a joint operation between Five and the NCA. But it's been agreed that we will take the lead on this one. Given the . . . security implications.'

Carter nodded. 'What do you want me to do?'

'For now, nothing. You'll carry on as normal, but keep your eyes peeled and your ear close to the ground. If you see anything suspicious, you are to report to us.'

'How long for?'

'As long as it takes. Until we have sufficient evidence to understand how deep this thing goes.'

'What about surveillance?'

Sutton said, 'We've had bugs in their homes for weeks. Car tracking. The guys at Cheltenham have been monitoring phone and internet activity. Ever since we learned about the ammo deal.'

'And?'

'And nothing. It's a dead end. No one has said or done anything incriminating. All they do is talk about rugby, beer and sex.'

'They're probably using burner phones,' Maitland said. 'That's our assumption. If some of them are in deep with the Blood Kings, they'd want to cover their tracks.'

'Of course, these guys will have done their anti-surveillance training,' Greening said. 'They won't be making any amateur mistakes. If, indeed, they have anything to hide.'

Maitland looked Carter hard in the eye. 'This is a dangerous undertaking. I can't stress that enough. If Duncan and his friends find out you're a plant, there's no telling what they might do.'

Carter laughed. 'I'm a big lad. I can look after myself.'

'I'm serious. Don't take any unnecessary risks. Don't do anything out of character, anything that might draw attention.'

'Save your breath. I've worked for your people in the past. I know the drill.'

Maitland stared at him. She said, 'This is our best chance of exposing the Reapers. But if we slip up – if they have even the faintest suspicion that we're onto them – they'll cease their activities. Our hopes of putting a stop to them will go up in smoke.'

'Any questions?' Greening asked.

'How do I contact you?'

The major motioned to Maitland. She dipped a hand into her jacket pocket and fished out a miniature phone no bigger than a thumb drive, with a grey plastic case and a tiny keypad below a postage-stamp-sized display.

Maitland handed him the mini phone and a USB charger. The device fitted snugly in the palm of his hand and weighed no more than a pound coin.

She said, 'Keep this on you at all times. The battery only lasts for ten hours, so it's best to keep it switched off and check in once a day for any messages. There's a SIM card installed with a single number in the address book. Text me if you need to request an urgent meeting. The phone runs on the old 2G network. Most carriers still operate the frequency, so you shouldn't have any problems getting a signal.'

Carter pocketed the phone and charger. 'Do you seriously think the lads in G Squadron are bent?'

Maitland considered the question. Then she said, 'Ask yourself this. If they're prepared to sell ammunition to known criminal entities – bullets that may very well be used to murder civilians, or a police officer – what else might they be willing to do?'

Carter said nothing.

He thought about the metal detector he'd seen back at the squadron hangar. Six hours ago. Back when he had been getting ready for a routine hard arrest. Looking forward to a new start in G Squadron.

He thought, too, about the thermal lances. The hydraulic jack.

The big stack of explosives.

The questions they had been asking at the briefing. Their interest in the Russian's strongroom.

More like a bank raid than a hard arrest.

'Remember,' Maitland said. 'Watch your back. I'm serious. If you find yourself in trouble, we won't be able to help you.'

Four

Ten hours later, in the bleary grey light before dawn, the fourteen men of Air Troop RV'd back at the squadron hangar. Grist and Moody joined the team as they lugged their army baggage from the storage racks over to the Chinook waiting for them on the nearby helipad. The morning was damp and cold, and Carter could see his breath misting as he approached the rear of the chopper. He climbed the hydraulic loading ramp to the main cargo hold, passed the loadie and took his place next to the other soldiers on the webbing seats, his rucksack secured between his legs. At the far end of the cabin, he could see the glowing lights of the cockpit panels as the two pilots went through the usual pre-flight check, while the steady drone of the turboshaft engines filled the hold, mingling with the *whump-whump* of the front- and rear-mounted rotor blades.

Carter sat quietly in the dimly lit cabin, anxiety stirring in his guts.

He had spent a restless night replaying his meeting with Greening, Maitland and Sutton, weighing up various scenarios and processing the intelligence – or rather, the int they had chosen to share with him. He had to assume they were holding some stuff back. Five's way of doing business, in his experience. They shared only the information they needed to – only what they considered essential to the success of the mission.

With the stolen ammunition sale, the security service had enough evidence to nail a couple of guys in the Troop. If their instincts were right, Duncan, Rigg, Hickey and the rest were embroiled with a band of violent criminals. Maybe they were selling guns. Maybe they were even killing guys who had crossed the Blood Kings in the past, or owed them money.

It's possible that they might be caught up in a bunch of other stuff, Sutton had said. *Drug trafficking.*

Extortion.

Murder.

Carter decided he had two big problems. The most immediate concern was the risk of discovery. He would have to tread carefully. If he tried befriending Steve Duncan and the other members of the Reapers, they would become suspicious. Which could be fatal.

Best to bide my time, Carter thought. *Wait for an opportunity to present itself.*

Which brought him to the second problem.

There was a risk that the top brass might turn him into a scape-goat. Suppose he found nothing damning. In that case, the head shed could use his report to cover themselves if the shit ever hit the fan.

Don't look at us, they would protest. *We ordered an investigation into these allegations. Blame our plant. He failed to do his job. Geordie Carter let us down.*

There was a chance that he was being set up to fail. Those who made it to the top of the Regimental pyramid were politically ruthless. They wouldn't hesitate to shaft someone else if it meant saving their own arses. Even an ex-ranker and Hereford legend like Phil Greening.

But he was sure of one thing. There would be zero chance of the guys going to jail. The Regiment hated airing its dirty laundry in public. Moreover, Whitehall would be desperate to avoid the ugly spectacle of serving SAS men taking the stand at the Old Bailey. Duncan and the others would be dealt with behind closed doors, he guessed, dismissed from the Regiment on some bullshit pretext. Losing an army radio, or some other minor breach of protocol.

The last soldiers boarded the Chinook. The loadmaster signalled to the pilots, the rear ramp raised to the closed position, entomb-ing the passengers in the cabin. The blades increased to a deafening scream, and there was a sudden lurch as the chopper lifted off the ground. A few minutes later, they were pitching forward across the dawn landscape.

*   *   *

The ride to the RAF base at Brize Norton took twenty minutes. The engine dialled down to a dull whir, the ramp lowered, the men piled out of the Chinook, and there was a swift transfer to an A400M Atlas military transport aircraft waiting for them on the tarmac stand. A slick-looking airlifter, with propellors shaped like scimitars. The replacement for the old Hercules C-130. Faster than the Herc, able to carry a much heavier cargo across a greater range. But not much more comfortable, from a passenger's point of view. There was a row of canvas seats fixed to either side of the fuselage, a loadmaster's station, some luggage racks, and not much else.

They were buckled up and in the air in less than five minutes. A smooth operation, every part of the machinery running like clockwork. The British military at its finest. There were times when Carter could look past the bullshit and take pride in being a soldier. But increasingly, he found himself at odds with the institution. He hated the office politics and the cronyism, the shameless opportunism.

Maybe I'm better off out of it, he thought. *Perhaps it's time to jack it in. Tell the bastards I'm not interested in selling out my mates and quit Hereford for good.*

Carter had given his life to the Regiment. In return, they had shafted him. Turned him into an outcast.

In his naivety, he had assumed that being a committed soldier would protect him from his enemies inside Hereford. He had been wrong. He'd learned the hard way that only those prepared to play the game thrived in the snake-pit of Regimental politics. He'd seen officers writing up their own citations during ops in Iraq, painting themselves in the best possible light to ensure they received a medal at the end of it. He'd seen one Rupert putting a couple of rounds in a severely wounded insurgent during a Baghdad house raid, so that he could claim the credit for slotting the guy. Junior officers had led their teams on pointless missions in the hunt for glory, recklessly endangering the lives of good men.

His brother had found it much easier to adapt to life in the SAS. But Luke had always been an easy-going kid. At school, he had been universally popular in a way that had eluded Jamie. Luke's friendly nature and no-nonsense attitude had allowed him to flourish at Hereford without getting sucked into the political vortex that chewed up and spat out so many capable soldiers.

Jamie Carter hadn't been so fortunate. His few friends had cautioned him. Told him to look the other way. He'd ignored their advice and called out those who put their own interests ahead of the unit. He had been paying the price for it ever since.

Now he'd reached the endgame. The last days of his career as a Blade.

But as much as he hated some aspects of the Regiment, he dreaded having to leave. He remembered the advice he'd been given by an old colleague in D Squadron.

When you're in the Regiment, you're a hero, the guy had said. *Everyone wants a piece of you.*

But when you leave, you're a nobody. All of a sudden, no one gives a shit about you anymore.

Fifty-nine minutes later, they touched down in Germany.

Ramstein Air Base had been built in the early days of the Cold War on an area of swampland on the western side of the Rhine. The previous year it had been the stopover point to process the mass exodus of refugees from Afghanistan. Now it functioned as the forward operating base for US and UK SF missions in Ukraine. On the main tarmac apron, teams were directing armoured vehicles and pallets of equipment onto the back of a pair of waiting Hercules C-130 transport craft. Other planes were being refuelled or attended to by teams of mechanics. The relentless grind of the military machine. In the distance, scraps of mist clung to the peaks of low wooded hills.

A short, grizzled-looking soldier in his fifties greeted them. He looked like a private school rugby teacher. Short dark hair, hands like a pair of JCB buckets. Face with more cracks in it than a code-breaking manual. Sergeant Major Mike Beattie was one of the Regiment lifers. Twenty-plus years of service. Probably earned his winged dagger beret back in the days of the Black Death. Carter had seen him around the camp a few times in the past, dishing out bollockings to the young crows. He had been dispatched to Ramstein on a two-year posting as the local coordinator, overseeing the day-to-day operation of the Reg contingent.

Beattie swaggered over, carrying himself like he owned the place. Which he did, in a way. 'All right, fellas. Good flight?'

'Yeah, cracking,' Farrell deadpanned. 'Top quality service. I'm never flying business class again.'

Beattie stared at him, not getting the joke, then nodded at Duncan.

'We've got you set up inside.' He flapped a hand in the direction of a massive hangar situated on the far side of the apron. 'This way. I'll give you the grand tour.'

He started towards the hangar at a brisk pace. Carter, Farrell and the rest of the men in Air Troop hefted up their rucksacks and followed him across the rain-greased tarmac. They swept past the duty guard and stepped inside a space as big as a football pitch, divided into several areas. On the left side of the hangar a bunch of prefabricated modular units had been stacked on top of one another, like Lego bricks. Stairs led from the ground floor to a series of heavy-duty gantries providing access to the upper tier.

'Doss block,' Beatie said. 'Ablutions in the unit next door. Hangar is fully secure. Guards on duty twenty-four-seven. No fucker gets in here without the proper clearance.'

75

He pointed towards a row of windowless steel-framed units on the far side of the hangar.

'Planning section. Soundproofed, with secured locks on the doors. You're in Briefing Room Four. Here. You'll need this.' Beattie plucked out a white plastic key card from his pocket and passed it to Duncan. 'The card only works on the door to your allocated room.'

'What about the Scaleys?' asked Duncan.

The sergeant major gestured towards several units in another part of the hangar. 'Signallers are set up over there. Their kit is rigged up to satellites and radio antennas. Encrypted comms with GCHQ.'

Beattie indicated the other areas of the hangar. There was a cookhouse, a makeshift gym with free weights and treadmills, a kitchen, a cordoned-off space for storing kit, and a breakout area where guys could grab a brew and watch the news on the pancake-flat TV. Plus a separate accommodation block for the air crews.

The place was a whirlwind of activity. Dozens of Regiment operators went about their business, scoffing down food in the canteen, busting out sets on the bench presses or packing kit. A few sat around chatting or watching films on their laptops. Carter noticed some familiar faces from D Squadron among them. His old team. None of them paid the new arrivals any attention. Everyone minded their own business. Which was as it should be.

'I'm based off-site,' Beattie said. 'But there's a permanent staff here at all times. Clerks, plus the guards. If you can't get hold of me, they should be able to help you. Any questions?'

'Where can we grab a pint later?' asked Farrell.

'Nowhere. The rest of the base is strictly off-limits. You're not to leave the hangar under any circumstances.'

Duncan said, 'We're on a fifteen-minute standby anyway. The beers will have to wait till we're back home.'

Hickey chewed on his baccy and grinned. 'Guess you'll have to stick to the orange juice for now, Tom.'

Farrell shot him a savage look. 'Shouldn't you be hanging out with the Delta lads in the next hangar, swapping QAnon theories?'

'Fuck off.'

Sek puffed out his cheeks. 'Let's hope they're showing the rugger on the telly, boys. Otherwise, we're gonna have to pass the time listening to more of Tom's crap jokes.'

'Right, you lot,' Duncan said. 'Drop your bags and grab some scran. We'll RV in the briefing room in an hour.'

Five

At exactly ten o'clock, the team filed into the shipping-container-sized unit that would function as their base of operations during their stay at Ramstein. There was a long table in the middle of the room ringed by twenty chairs, and more hardware than a branch of Currys. There were laptops and tablets, a secure landline, several mobile devices, a tangle of hosepipe-thick black coax cables. Four computer screens so big they could double up as snooker tables.

The guys took their respective places. All fourteen men from Air Troop were present, plus Moody, the communicator from 18 Signals who had travelled with them from Hereford, and Lyndon Grist, the Regiment int officer. Between them they would coordinate the surveillance and eavesdropping during the operation to snatch Denis Gorchakov. The ops officer, Smallwood, had stayed behind in Hereford but would oversee the operation remotely.

Duncan kicked off proceedings.

'First things first, we'll have to draw up immediate action plans. One for each stronghold,' he began.

'The fuck do we need to do that for, chief?' Hickey questioned. 'The layouts are all the same, aren't they? One plan's all we need.'

Duncan shook his head. 'The approaches will be different. Getaway routes. Flight paths. All of that malarkey. There will be subtle but important variations in the plans. Look, I know it's a royal fucking pain in the arse, but that's the way it is.'

'What about the building designs? Have we got blueprints?'

Duncan said, 'Our friends at Six pinged them over a while ago. Architectural diagrams, mapping and so on.'

'Satellite imagery?'

'On its way from the Americans. Taking some time to get it ready, as always, but should be with us in a few hours. There's a team of suits at Vauxhall working to supply us with more information as and when they receive it.'

'We'll need to know every single thing about them buildings,' said Farrell. 'Thickness of the glass on the windows, locking systems, panic buttons. The works.'

Duncan said, 'Desk jockeys are already on it. They're checking the latest footage to see how the strongholds illuminated at night, too, so we'll know where to find the dead ground when we fly in.'

Hickey took off his baseball cap, mussed his matted hair and placed it back on his head again. 'What's the deal with the assault, chief?'

'We'll split into two teams,' said Duncan. 'An assault team will make the hard arrest. Second team will establish a cordon outside the stronghold. Six lads to guard the outside. Eight on the assault group.'

Carter wrinkled his brow. 'That's a bit fucking much. We should divide them teams equally. Seven lads on each.'

A harsh look flashed in Duncan's pale eyes. 'Are you questioning my judgement?'

Carter shrugged his shoulders and said, 'I just don't see why we need so many guys inside. That int we've got suggests the bulk of the BGs will be patrolling the grounds. That's where the firefight will be. If there is one.'

Duncan shot him a look that could cut through a block of ice. 'This is the way we're doing it. End of.'

Carter started to argue his point, then cut himself short. Duncan returned his piercing gaze to the other lads and carried on outlining the plan.

'Both groups will go in by chopper and debus right on top of the target,' he said. 'The lads on the assault team will breach the stronghold at the designated entry points and go in to make the hard arrest. Meanwhile, the cordon team will set up a defensive perimeter in the ground and deal with any guards in the vicinity. If they surrender, secure them with plasticuffs. If they show any signs of force, you have authorisation to neutralise them.

'I'll be leading the assault group into the stronghold,' Duncan went on. 'Geordie, you're 2iC, so that means you're in charge of the cordon. Try not to fuck this one up, eh?'

Polite laughter rippled through the room. Carter stared at him, his muscles tensed with anger. Duncan stared back, daring Carter to defy him.

'That all right with you, Geordie? Or have you got a problem with that as well?'

Carter pursed his lips. He knew that Duncan was deliberately giving him the shitty end of the stick by putting him on the perimeter instead of the assault force. But there was no point contesting the decision, he told himself. Partly because it was sound tactics to keep your commanding officer and your deputy on different teams. That way, if one group of lads ran into trouble, the 2iC would be instantly available to take command.

Besides, if he tried angling for a place on the assault team, some of his colleagues might start to question his motives. He remembered Maitland's warning, back at the King's Arms.

Don't take any unnecessary risks, she had said.

Don't do anything out of character, anything that might draw attention.

'No, mate,' he replied. 'That works for me.'

Farrell feigned a look of surprise. 'Fuck me sideways. Geordie Carter not questioning orders. That's a first. I don't know about the rest of you, but I'll need a double Jameson's after that.'

The men seated either side of Carter erupted into laughter, easing the tension in the room. The noise subsided, and then Duncan pointed to a detailed map of Poland on one of the screens.

He said, 'Once we have confirmation of the target location, we'll board the Black Hawks and head across the border, stopping to refuel here, at Gornika Air Base.' He tapped a finger, indicating a spot in western Poland, a few miles due east of the German border. 'The base is manned by a detachment of RAF personnel, so they'll be expecting us. Then it's straight back in the air and on to target.'

Farrell said, 'What about the return trip?'

'Same routine.'

'Where are the strongholds, exactly?' asked Rigg.

'The nearest one is twenty minutes by bird from Gornika. That's Stronghold Alpha. Delta is the furthest. Fifty-five minutes from the FOB to the target. Once we're on site, we'll secure the area, apprehend the target and scour the place for int. We'll need to conduct a full sweep from top to bottom. Grab everything we can get our hands on.'

'Maybe we should just break into all of them houses,' Sek joked. 'Make sure we don't miss out on any valuable int.'

'Yeah. A *thorough* sweep,' Hickey chuckled. He winked at the big Fijian. The pair of them exchanged a knowing look and grinned, as if they were in on a private joke.

The team proceeded to discuss detailed planning for each stronghold. They covered Actions On, establishing what to do if the choppers went down, marking emergency RVs and rallying points. They studied the grounds of each compound, looking for ideal landing zones, measuring how far the assault group would have to run from the Black Hawks to the target. They checked and noted down the distances to the nearest police stations in the area, and the locations of any friendly forces.

'What if someone raises the alarm?' Sek asked. 'Two of the homes are only a few minutes from the local police stations. They might rock up before we have a chance to get out.'

Moody said, 'One of you will be carrying a barrage jammer. Works like the countermeasures Chevrolet in the US presidential

81

motorcade. As soon as you activate it, anyone in the area trying to use a phone or computer will find that the signal has dropped. That'll stop anyone from putting in a call to the Polish police.'

They went through the rest of the plan. When they had finished, they walked through it again, so that everyone understood what they were doing.

Carter was impressed with the way the lads applied themselves. They were switched on. Dedicated soldiers. He found it hard to imagine that they were caught up in anything seriously dodgy. One or two of them, perhaps. But that was no different to any of the other squadrons.

Perhaps they allowed themselves to get mixed up with the wrong crowd, Greening had said.

It's happened before.

Which was true enough. He'd known some shady characters during his time in D Squadron. Guys who had been caught with their hands in the till. That sort of activity had been going on for almost as long as the SAS had been in existence.

Could these guys really be corrupt? Carter asked himself.

He honestly didn't know.

They took a short break, and then they turned their attention to the house assault. Rooms were mapped out. Floors allocated to different members of the attack team. They looked at entry and exit points, breaching methods, identified the most likely hiding spots for the target. They wanted to leave nothing to chance. Once they landed they were going to be on the clock. They couldn't afford to get bogged down dealing with unexpected problems.

At the same time, Farrell and Sek examined the plans for dead spots. The pair of them stared at the layout of the basement with puckered brows.

'What the fuck is that?' Sek wondered out loud, tapping a finger against a boxed-in area.

Farrell squinted at it. 'Void for a chimney, maybe.'

'Can't be,' Sek replied. 'It's only on this floor. Nothing above it. Or below.'

'Well, it sure as shit ain't the plant room. That's over to the right, fella.'

Sek grinned. 'Mark it up? Point of interest?'

'Aye. Definitely,' Farrell replied, lips parting into a crafty smile.

A short time later, Rigg said, 'What's the craic with the strong-rooms?'

'That's a question for Lyndon,' Duncan replied. He nodded at Grist. 'Well?'

'Six has been looking into it,' Grist said. 'They've obtained the plans from the company that installed the rooms. Same specs at all four homes. Emergency power supply, plumbing and ventilation. Reinforced steel door. Biometric locking system.'

'Walls?'

'Galvanised metal. Six inches thick.'

'Easier to cut our way through the door,' mused Hickey. 'If we have to.'

'Panic button?' asked Rigg.

Grist nodded. 'As far as we know, all the rooms have a secure connection to the local police station.'

'Response time?' asked Rigg.

'Between seven and twelve minutes. Depending on the distance from each station to the relevant compound.'

'Any other hiding spots that aren't on the blueprints? Hidden doors? Safes?'

'Not to our knowledge. We've walked through the layout with the maid. She's adamant that Gorchakov hasn't made any structural changes to the buildings since they were constructed. But it's possible that he might have a secret hiding place his household staff don't know about.'

Carter had been poring over the architectural plans while the others had been talking. He looked up and said, 'Those strong-rooms are all the way up on the third floor.'

Rigg looked towards him. 'Yeah, so?'

'There's nothing else of interest up there, according to these drawings. Just some storage areas and spare rooms. All the main living and sleeping quarters are on the lower floors.'

'What's your point, Geordie?'

Carter said, 'The target will be closer to the ground floor exits than the strongroom. It's more likely he'll leg it in that direction. Why would he head to the third floor? He'd be trapping himself.'

'No, mate,' Tek cut in. He nodded at the satellite imagery on the screens. 'There's nothing for miles near any of the compounds. Arse-end of nowhere. Where would he go?'

'There's the garage,' Carter pointed out. 'He's got a fleet of classic cars stored at each compound. He could easily jump in one of them and make a getaway.'

'He might. But he wouldn't get very far, as long as you lot out-side do your fucking job.'

Carter said, tetchily, 'It's a waste of time focusing on the strong-room. He's not going to be hiding in there.'

Rigg stared at him, face contorted with anger.

'Since when were you the expert on making hard arrests? Last time I checked, you spent the last six months out on your arse, twiddling your thumbs while us lot were doing the business.'

Carter glowered at him. He opened his mouth to reply, but then Duncan came between them, acting the role of peacemaker, his hands raised in a placatory gesture.

'Easy, fellas,' he said, breaking the silence. 'Calm down, the pair of you. We're all on the same team here. Geordie, I know you're keen to do a good job and make an impression, seeing as you're with the big boys now.'

Duncan grinned.

'We've got one chance at nabbing the target,' the Scotsman continued. 'But if we're too busy sniping at each other we'll get nowhere. Focus on your individual responsibilities, and let's make sure we bring that bastard home with us. Then we can get the beers in and celebrate.'

*　*　*

The briefing continued throughout the rest of the afternoon. Moody updated them on the eavesdropping and surveillance ops. They had a team monitoring Gorchakov's luxury jet, he said. Which at that moment was sitting on the ground in a private hangar at Geneva airport. They had specialists monitoring the chatter on the accounts held by the Russian. New satellite images were periodically down-loaded to their laptops. Nothing was being left to chance.

Rigg and Sek kept circling back round to the strongrooms. They wanted to know how long it would take to exit each building from that room. How long to cut through the door with the thermal lance. The manufacturer of the biometric locking systems. What they were likely to find inside. They were very interested in those rooms, down to the tiniest detail.

Carter wondered about that.

He thought again about the thermal lances. The framed charges, the metal detector.

He thought, too, about Duncan's decision to stick him on the cordon team. Maybe it wasn't a tactical move. Maybe there was another reason for wanting to keep him outside the stronghold.

But he had nothing concrete. No hard evidence of wrongdoing. No smoking gun.

In the late afternoon Duncan called an end to the briefing. They left the secure unit and spent a short time organising their kit. Helmets, breaching devices and plate armour were dumped in the taped-off area at the rear of the hangar, ready to snatch up at a moment's notice. Along with several collapsible North Face rucksacks.

'What do we need them for?' Carter asked Duncan.

'Why the fuck do you think?' Duncan snapped. 'To scoop up any int we come across, you daft prick.'

A short time later they made their way over to the cookhouse and scoffed down the greasy portions of food served up by the slop jockeys. Then it was a question of waiting until they got the heads-up from the signallers. Which could come at any time, Moody had told them. Could be an hour or two. Could be a couple of days. Impossible to tell.

Several of the lads from the other Reg teams mingled with the new arrivals. Carter caught up with a couple of old mates from D Squadron. Conversation was strictly superficial. No one asked why he had been transferred to G Squadron, or what his new Troop was doing at Ramstein. None of their business. And they had their own workloads to tackle. They didn't give away any details about their ops, but Carter could take a guess. Training packages, teaching the Ukrainians how to fight, how to handle specific weaponry. Close-protection jobs for high-profile officials. His own brother had been posted to Kyiv some months back. Had probably passed through Ramstein on his way east, Carter guessed.

He watched the rolling news on the TV in the breakout area. There was a lot of stuff on the economy. Inflation was going up. Sterling was going down. Energy bills were going to cost more than the Apollo space programme. There was some stuff about the US elections, and the spectre of a comeback by the former president. The war in Ukraine had been pushed down the agenda. War fatigue. People could only tolerate hearing about mass death and destruction for so long before they tuned out.

There was a short item about an attack on a military installation in Crimea. Dozens of Russian soldiers had been killed, vehicles obliterated. No one had claimed credit for the explosions. But the direction of travel was clear. The momentum was with Ukraine's forces. The Russians were retreating. Ceding territory. Abandoning conquered towns. The pro-Kremlin mayor of one eastern city had been shot dead in the street.

The newsroom cut away to an official ceremony in Kyiv. The Ukrainian president was awarding a medal to one of his generals. Voloshyn was decked out in his trademark military shirt and khakis. The general was in standard uniform. He was lean and slender, with hair the colour of wood ash and a face that looked as if someone had chiselled it out of a block of granite. His nostrils were so wide you could plough snow with them. An eyepatch covered his left socket.

The two men shook hands and smiled for the cameras, and then the commander made a short speech to the gathered dignitaries. The caption at the bottom of the screen gave his name as General Viktor Koltrov.

'Our soldiers are doing something no one else thought possible,' the dubbed voice translated into English. 'They have made a stand against tyranny and oppression. They have shown that they are willing to fight – to die – for their freedom. All the world should remember this.

'When the invader sought to crush us, when others predicted disaster and defeat, our warriors refused to cower. They met the enemy head-on, with courage and determination. Now we are forging a new chapter in our glorious history.'

The general looked straight into the camera as he continued.

'Soon, the day will come when the last Russian tank is driven back across the border. This evil will not win. The toil and sacrifice of our soldiers will not be in vain, my friends. We will achieve total victory, so that the soil runs thick with the blood of the dead occupiers. Glory to Ukraine!'

General Koltrov punched the air, drawing a raucous cheer from the audience. There was something in the way he carried himself that reminded Carter of a hawk.

'Wish we had someone like that running the show back home,' Farrell remarked.

Carter looked round at him in surprise. 'Who? This bloke?'

'Sure. Why not?' Farrell tipped his head at the figure with the eyepatch. 'Koltrov is the real deal, so they say. Liberator of Kharkiv. A proper commander. Not like them pricks we've got in the head shed.'

Carter snorted his contempt. 'He's a Rupert. They're all the same, mate. In it for themselves.'

Farrell shrugged. 'At least he's not conducting the war from behind the safety of a desk. You've got to give him credit for that.'

'Doing his job doesn't make him a hero.'

'Maybe not. But how many of our generals would do the same thing, if they were in his boots? Ask yourself that.'

'Fair enough,' Carter conceded. 'But it doesn't make a scrap of difference what this guy does. It'll come down to the guys on the ground, at the tip of the spear, and the quality of training and kit. Like it always does. Ruperts don't win wars.'

'They can sure as shit lose 'em, though.'

Carter laughed. 'True.'

Farrell said, 'You mark my words. This guy is going places. They say he's in line to be the next president.'

'Not if this thing goes nuclear. There won't be a country to rule over then.'

Farrell puffed his cheeks and exhaled. 'Jesus, you're a depressing bastard sometimes. Thought you Geordies were supposed to be all about the banter.'

Carter laughed drily. 'You've been watching too many reality shows, mate. We don't all eat at Greggs, either.'

The hours ticked by. The team spent most of their time in the briefing room, continually refining the plan as a steady stream of information flowed in from Vauxhall, Cheltenham and Washington. When they weren't fine-tuning the house assault, they dossed in their bunks or streamed TV shows on Netflix. Hickey beasted himself on the weights. Sek watched the rugby and gulped down gargantuan quantities of coffee. Duncan sat in a corner with Beattie, the pair of them chatting in muted voices. Carter buried himself in a new history of the Vietnam War.

The men were used to the routine. Waiting was ingrained into their DNA. One of the first things you learned when soldiering in 22 SAS. You had to be prepared to sometimes lie in an OP for days on end, living on cold rations and staying mentally alert, watching for an enemy that might never show. A few days in a hangar, with a cosy bed, warm food and entertainment wasn't exactly a hardship.

Thirty-seven hours after they had arrived at Ramstein, Duncan summoned the Troop back to Briefing Room Four. Moody and Grist were sitting at one end of the table, amid a clutter of laptops, computer cables, notepads and paper coffee cups. Like students pulling an all-nighter.

'We just got word from Cheltenham,' Grist said. 'Gorchakov's jet took off from Geneva half an hour ago.'

'What's the flight path?' asked Rigg.

'They're bound for a private airfield at Sobotka. Which is equi-distant between strongholds Bravo and Delta.'

'So he could be heading to either one of those places,' Rigg said.

'Correct.'

'How long until we know for sure?' asked Sek.

'The jet is due to land at Sobotka in an hour. Eleven o'clock local time. Once he gets in, we'll have to wait until he logs on or uses the landline before we know which stronghold to hit.'

Moody said, 'There's no mobile coverage at either location. So we can be fairly sure he'll be leaving a digital footprint shortly after he's through the front door. Even if it's just to check his email.'

Carter looked at the map on one of the big screens. Bravo and Delta strongholds were both situated in Lower Silesia. The south-western corner of Poland.

Bravo was twenty kilometres due south of the airfield at Sobotka. Delta was about the same distance to the east. Nothing to suggest Gorchakov would favour one site over the other.

A fifty-fifty call. Like a coin toss.

Duncan said, 'Get some rest. Could be a while before we get confirmation. The Scaleys will wake you as soon as they have more news.'

Some of the guys returned to their bunks in the accommodation block. Most didn't sleep. The mood among them had subtly changed. Action was imminent. Any moment now, they would get the signal to go in. Months of planning would come down to a few minutes on the ground, kicking in doors and getting the job done. Carter knocked back black coffee and tried to concentrate on his book. He was reading about the Battle of Dien Bien Phu. Fourteen thousand French soldiers against eighty thousand revolutionaries under Ho Chi Minh. The last days of French Indochina.

Eleven o'clock came and went.

Three hours later, the call went up from Moody and the men assembled once more in the harshly lit briefing room. Moody looked like he hadn't slept in a month. Grist paced up and down the room, his phone clamped to his ear, talking in a low voice to the person on the other end of the line. The last soldiers filed inside, Duncan shut the door, and then Grist terminated the call and said, 'We've just had the green light from Vauxhall.'

'Where's the target at?' asked Duncan.

'Site Bravo,' Grist said. 'South of Sobotka.'

'We're sure?'

Moody nodded. 'GCHQ has a match on Gorchakov's voice. He's made multiple calls from the landline. Plus we have internet activity from three different devices at the same location. Phone, TV, computer.'

'At two o'clock in the morning?' Hickey pulled a face. 'What's the guy doing, watching porn?'

'He's a money man,' Grist explained. 'They're slaves to the stock markets. Probably monitoring his investments in Hong Kong.'

Duncan levered himself out of his chair and said, 'Right, lads. The mission is go. Grab your kit. We're moving out immediately.'

Six

The journey east took them a little over two hours, through a pitch-black landscape studded with clusters of apricot light. Like constellations in a night sky. Duncan, Carter, Rigg and Sek rode on one of the UH-60 Black Hawks. Hickey, Farrell and the rest of the Troop were close behind in the second chopper. Both Moody and Grist had stayed behind at Ramstein to remotely coordinate the intelligence and comms sides of the op with Six and GCHQ, feeding through any new information to the men in Air Troop as and when they received it.

The soldiers were packing all the necessary kit for a door-kicking op: suppressed LL19A2s, ballistic helmets, plate hangers, pistols and grenades, NVGs, personal radios. The designated entry teams had their specialist breaching equipment: shaped charges, thermal lances, hydraulic jigs. Each man also carried a series of scribbled notes, indicating the direction to the compound from the landing zone at all four sites, so they wouldn't have to waste precious seconds orientating themselves when they hit the ground.

There was a brief stopover at Gornika to refuel the Black Hawks. To avoid suspicion the local Polish commanders had been told that the guys were taking part in a training mission in support of Ukrainian troops. The birds were on the ground for less than five minutes. Then they were back in the air and racing south towards site Bravo. A distance of approximately 150 kilometres from Gornika. Forty-five minutes to target.

We'll be dropping out of the Black Hawk at around five o'clock in the morning, Carter calculated.

Then we'll give Gorchakov the wake-up call of his life.

They screamed south across the predawn terrain in near darkness. The lights inside the cabin had been turned off; both pilots and the loadie had switched to their NVGs. So had the assault team. They would keep their NVGs lowered until they were almost on top of the target location; if the grounds were suitably well illuminated, they would flip up their goggles and switch to their natural night vision instead.

As they closed in on the target, Carter checked his rifle one last time. Making sure he had a round in the snout, ready to discharge as soon as he dropped out of the Black Hawk. He did the same for his holstered Glock. The pre-assault routine. Like a football player in the dressing room before a big game. Then he looked up and noticed the others. Rigg and Farrell were inspecting the lances. Sek was sorting out his lock-picking kit. Hickey popped a wad of chewing tobacco into his mouth, gripping his metal detector tightly.

No one paid any attention to their weapons. They seemed more preoccupied with their breaching gear. Which struck Carter as odd.

Rule number one when you were going into a potential firefight: double-check your hardware. No Blade wanted to get the dreaded dead man's click when the enemy was bearing down on them from twenty metres away. But these guys were apparently more concerned with their door jigs and shaped charges than the chances of suffering a stoppage.

At four thirty in the morning, Duncan announced they would have to make an unscheduled stop. Traffic had been detected at Site Delta. Someone was using the landline. Vauxhall had ordered them to wait until they had looked into it. There was a possibility that the target had left Bravo and made the short trip east to the Delta stronghold. The pilots set down the Black Hawks in a field several miles due north of Sobotka while the team waited in tense silence for further updates.

Time slowed to a crawl. Five minutes passed. Then six. Then seven. Then Moody came back over the comms and confirmed that the target was definitely at Bravo. The activity at Delta was a false alarm, he said. Apparently, the gardener had been using the landline to call his wife.

Twenty minutes later, as the first fiery streaks of daylight glowed near the horizon, the pilot's voice crackled over the comms channel. 'Five minutes out.'

The men waited.

Hickey chewed his wad of tobacco aggressively.

Sek checked his shaped charges.

'Three minutes out,' the pilot said.

In the gathering dawn, a thousand metres below, Carter could see the barren Polish countryside. A sprawl of stubbled fields, farmhouses and woodland.

'One minute out,' the pilot said. And then: 'Outside of the house is lit up.'

'Don't worry about that,' Duncan replied. 'Just get us onto the target.'

The men flipped their NVGs up. No need to use them on the op, not with the grounds lit up like a Christmas tree. They would only need their goggles if the power was cut during the raid and the estate was plunged into darkness.

The loadmaster stood beside the side door, scanning the gloom below and communicating with the pilots as the Black Hawk began its swift descent. There was a sudden jolt as the landing gears touched the ground, and then the loadie gave the signal and the passengers snatched up their kit and spilled out of the side of the chopper.

Carter pushed forward and swept his eyes across the ground, the grass swishing beneath the downwash. They had landed right on top of the designated LZ in the palatial gardens at the front of Gorchakov's estate. Fifty metres to the north stood the mansion itself, a three-storey mock-Georgian structure with a porticoed entrance topped with an ornate pediment and pointed roof turrets projecting from the corners. Like something out of a fairy tale. The lights were on in several of the ground-floor windows, but the upper storeys were pitch-black.

A paved central avenue ran from the gated entrance to a carriage circle with a pair of Mercedes-Benz G-Class wagons parked at the nine and three o'clock positions and a Rolls-Royce Phantom at the twelve. Left of the avenue was a domed pavilion overlooking a pond filled with water lilies. Further away, thirty metres or so from the main building, Carter spied a single-storey timber-framed garage with a pitched slate roof, four parking bays and a log store. Three of the bays were closed. There was a pristine-condition Aston Martin DB5 in the fourth bay. A million dollars' worth of classic automobile. A service road led from the garage towards a smaller, separate entrance on the western side of the property.

To the east was a tennis court and a large garden dotted with exotic trees and statues. The whole area was illuminated by scores of security lights along both sides of the avenue. Like strip lights on a runway.

The layout was instantly familiar to Carter. He had spent hours studying every square inch of the Russian's properties, committing the details to memory. Directions, distances. Dead ground. The benefit of intensive preparation. One of the things that separated elite SF from everyone else.

The second Black Hawk had touched down twenty metres away, on the western side of the central avenue. Both choppers would keep their blades turning and their engines burning throughout the operation. Ready to take off again the instant the teams reboarded.

Duncan's booming voice fizzled over the net, rallying the assault group to his position beside the second chopper. As they hurried towards the main entrance, Carter, Sek, Farrell and the three other guys on the cordon team took up their pre-designated positions. Farrell and Matt Scowcroft, a short, cocky Essex lad, broke west, towards the pavilion. Carter and Sek focused their attention on the gatehouse at the front of the estate, fifty metres due south. The two other members of the cordon group, Jarrod Vokes and Kevin Redzic, had responsibility for clearing the ground to the east. The tennis court and the garden.

Eight guys on the BG team, Carter reminded himself.

Gorchakov never travels anywhere without them.

Thirty metres away, the gatehouse door crashed open.

Two figures barrelled out of the structure. Musclebound heavies stuffed into tight-fitting dark suits. One of the guys had a shaven head; his colleague sported a red goatee and wore a pair of pearly white trainers.

Both were gripping AK-12 assault rifles.

'Drop your weapons!' Carter shouted. 'Now!'

The heavies ignored him.

That was their first mistake.

And their last.

The man with the goatee was a couple of paces ahead of his bald-headed mate. Twenty-five metres from Carter and Sek. He caught sight of the soldiers spilling out of the two Black Hawks and started bringing up his AK. A sound idea, in theory. Neutralise the nearest threat. But terrible in practice. Because Carter was already aiming at him.

Carter lined up the L119A2 with the guard's trunk. Which was immense, anatomically speaking. All that work Goatee had done in the gym, honing his pecs and abs had provided Carter with an ample target. Like taking aim at King Kong at point-blank range.

He squeezed the trigger twice. Rounds whistled out of the muzzle. Spent jackets sprung out of the ejector port. The rounds smacked into Goatee in the midriff, stitching him in the guts. He groaned and folded at the waist, and Carter emptied a third shot, plugging the guard in the head on the way down. He was dead before he hit the ground.

Carter swivelled towards the bald-headed guard as he charged forward and brought up his AK-12. Baldy had the same idea as his dead friend. Kill the invaders. He had no intention of changing his plan, clearly. Too late in the game. He was already committed. Better to plough on and hope for the best.

Carter double-tapped the onrushing heavy with surgical precision. Two rounds thudded into his chest, giving him a matching pair of lung punctures. The third struck a few inches higher, catching him in the neck. He made some sort of grotesque gurgling sound and crumpled to the ground in a tangle of lifeless limbs.

Two guards down.

Six to go.

Two of the heavies would be inside the building, Carter knew. Protecting the target.

Which left four more guards patrolling the grounds.

Assuming the maid's information was accurate. There was always the chance she might be wrong. Or Gorchakov might have bolstered his security detail in recent weeks. Any number of reasons for the sudden change in the BG routine.

We'll find out soon enough.

A muffled explosion rumbled across the estate, barely audible above the blast of the choppers, as the assault group detonated one of their shaped charges. Carter glanced over his shoulder, spotted the telltale cloud of acrid smoke spewing out of the breached entrance to the stronghold, fifty metres north of his position. He saw the glass shards from the blown-out windows, glinting in the glow of the exterior security lights.

The assault team charged through the front door, a chorus of voices relaying information over the net as they systematically began to clear their designated floors.

Five seconds had passed since the start of the op.

Carter heard Farrell screaming over the comms: 'Lose them! Lose the weapons!'

He snapped round to his right. Ten metres away, Farrell and the Essex boy, Scowcroft, were advancing to engage a couple of suited guards rushing over from the western side of the estate. One of the BGs had ignored the threat and aimed his AK at the two SAS men. A gout of flame spewed out of his muzzle, illuminating the gloom as he fired a quick burst at Farrell. The rounds whipped past the Ulsterman, missing him and slapping into a statue at his four o'clock.

In the next beat there was a weak *ka-ka* as Farrell fired twice. The guard on the left toppled backwards, arms pinwheeling, like an acrobat falling from a circus tightrope. He fell into the pond, splashing down amid the water lilies.

The fourth guard froze, stricken with indecision. A perfectly natural reaction. His confidence had been dented. He had just seen three of his friends get cut down. Doubts were beginning to seep into his mind. Should he stick to the original plan or make a run for it? Literally a life-or-death decision.

The guard went for a third option. Not flight or fight. But surrender. He tossed aside his weapon and raised his arms so high he looked like a televangelist praising Jesus.

'On the fucking ground!' Farrell yelled, keeping his rifle aimed at the heavy. 'Stay where you are!'

The guard sank to his knees while Scowcroft scampered forward and ripped out a pair of plasticuffs from his side pocket. He shoved the Russian face-down on the grass, roughly pinned his arms behind his back and slapped the restraints around his wrists.

To the east, a short distance from the tennis court, another pair of guards had thrown in the towel. They lay on their fronts ten metres from Vokes, the young soldier from East Hull bellowing at them to stay still while Redzic rushed forward to cuff them.

Through the ground-floor windows, Carter saw a series of blinding white bursts of light as the assault team chucked flashbangs into the various rooms. Lights were flicking on in the upper-floor windows; in others he spotted the torch beams from their rifles cutting through the darkness.

He hastened over to Farrell and Scowcroft and dropped to a knee beside the plasticuffed guard. He grabbed a fistful of lank hair and lifted the Russian's head.

'How many others in the house?' Carter shouted above the incessant whir of the choppers.

The guard hesitated. Carter shoved the rifle barrel hard against the guy's cheek.

'How fucking many?'

'Two,' the Russian replied. 'Two inside.'

Carter released his grip. The guard's head sagged, his cheek slapping against the paving as Carter got on the comms channel.

'Steve, we've got three BGs down, three others secured,' he reported to Duncan. 'Cordon is set. Watch your back. There are two guards in the house, possibly more.'

There was a pause of two or three seconds, accompanied by several bursts of gunfire. Then Duncan said, 'Roger that. We've already sorted them. Two guards. They're both down.' He sounded slightly out of breath.

Christ, that was quick, Carter thought.

These guys don't fuck around.

'Any sign of the target?'

'Not yet. Wait out, Geordie.'

Carter glanced at the other guys on the cordon team. Farrell and Scowcroft were keeping watch over the three plasticuffed guards. Vokes, Redzic and Sek scanned the grounds in every direction. Observing the entrance to the stronghold, the gardens east and west of the avenue, the road beyond the wrought-iron gate.

Watching for threats.

They weren't expecting more trouble from within the estate. They were thirty seconds into the op. The grounds were quiet and still after the initial fury of the firefight. No sign of any more guards.

Their main task now was to prevent anyone else from entering or leaving the building. There was always the possibility that Gorchakov might give the assault group the slip and make a run for it through the front door. Or reinforcements might rock up at the front gate to try and rescue their boss.

Or the police.

The sounds of the suppressed weapons wouldn't have carried far, Carter knew, but someone in the vicinity might have heard the burst from the AK-12. The barrage jammer should have knocked out the phone masts in the immediate area, but there was always the chance that the equipment hadn't functioned properly. Murphy's Law. If it can go wrong, it will.

We're six miles from the nearest town, Carter reminded himself. *Six miles from the nearest police station.*

If someone makes the call, we'll only have a few minutes to bug out before the plod get here.

He looked back again at the mansion. Flashes and torch beams periodically flared up in the unlit windows, allowing Carter to track the other team's progress as they worked their way systematically through each floor. Speed and aggression, combined with forward momentum. A textbook Regiment building attack. The kind of thing they had practised countless times before at the Killing House.

At some point he noticed that one of the second-floor rooms had caught fire. The blaze spread rapidly, engulfing the curtains, shrouding them in bright orange flames. Smoke billowed out of the window.

Then Carter's eye was drawn to something on the other side of the building. A window on the far right of the third floor. The hallway leading to the strongroom. Through the glass he saw orange sparks flying off the wall as the assaulters began cutting their way inside with the thermal lance.

How the fuck has the accountant managed to lock himself in there? Carter wondered. Gorchakov would have had to race upstairs, hurry down the corridor and seal himself inside the room in double-quick time.

Carter watched and waited.

After a short time the third-floor window went dark again.

They've cut through the door.

They're inside.

He kept staring at the window outside the strongroom. Waiting for Duncan to come back on the comms and announce that they had acquired the target.

Instead, there was dead silence.

A moment later, a voice hissed in his ear.

Not Duncan. Not the assault group.

Moody. The signaller. Monitoring the op from the signals room at Ramstein, four hundred miles away.

'Geordie, someone has triggered the panic button inside the stronghold. That thing goes straight through to the police station, mate. You need to get out of there immediately.'

'What happened to the fucking jammer?'

'That only works on certain frequencies,' Moody explained. 'Panic alarm must be on a different channel.'

'How long have we got?'

'Officers will be on your coordinates in figures seven or eight minutes.'

'Roger that. Steve, what's your situation?'

No answer.

Carter tried again. 'Steve? Have you got the target yet?'

Seconds passed. Still nothing.

'Target acquired,' Duncan replied at last. 'We've got him, Geordie.'

'Bring him outside. Cops are on their way.'

Duncan said, firmly, 'Stay where you are. We're conducting a search for technical materials. We'll be out in figures five. Wait out, Geordie.'

'Shit,' Carter muttered under his breath.

We're cutting it close.

Too close.

He hurried over to Farrell and Scowcroft, dropped down beside the nearest plasticuffed guard and rooted through his pockets. He pulled out a vape stick, a slim leather wallet, a pack of chewing gum, a smartphone with a cracked display. Some coins. A load of other crap.

'The car keys,' he growled. 'Where are they?'

The bodyguard tipped his head at the guy next to him. A mean-looking son of a bitch with a widow's peak of black hair and a bristly moustache. Carter scooted round to the guy and started patting him down. In the front pocket he found what he was looking for. A small chrome key fob with the Benz motif engraved on the front.

'What the fuck are you doing?' Sek asked.

He was speaking over the net. Easier than trying to have a conversation with a pair of helicopter engines roaring nearby.

'We need to block the entrance,' Carter said. 'Slow down the cops. Wait here and watch the approaches.'

He shot to his feet and wheeled away, sprinting towards the two G-Wagons parked in front of the mansion. He tapped the unlock button; the lights flared on the vehicle on the west side of the carriage circle. A pimped-up version of the standard G-Class, with a grey matte finish, rear spoiler, double exhaust and run-flat wheels.

Carter ran over to the side of the wagon, his heart pounding furiously. He tore the driver's door open and slid behind the wheel. The boy-racer theme continued on the inside of the wagon. There was a lot of gold trim on show. A lot of black leather and embossed badging.

The door clunked shut. Carter punched the stop-start button, upshifted into Drive and stamped on the accelerator. Meat Loaf blared out of the speaker grilles as Carter steered counter-clockwise around the circle and bowled south along the main avenue, the engine belting out its machine-like roar as he sped towards the front gate. A few moments before impact, he slammed on the brakes and wrestled the wheel hard to the right; the tyres squealed in protest, the G-Wagon lurched and rocked before it came to a halt side-on with the wrought-iron gate, blocking the entrance. Carter cut the engine, pocketed the key fob, leaped out of the vehicle and jogged back over to the cordon team some sixty metres away.

'You two,' he said, looking at Vokes and Redzic in turn. He motioned towards the gate. 'Get over there and watch the entrance. Anyone shows up, put some suppressive fire down. Move it.'

The two soldiers sprinted down the main avenue at once. The front gate was the main access point to the estate. If the cops arrived before the assault group had exited the stronghold, the makeshift roadblock would buy them a few extra seconds to make good their escape. Not much. But better than nothing.

We're on the clock now.

The stopwatch inside Carter's head told him that four minutes had elapsed since the op had gone noisy. Six minutes until the police rolled up at the front gate. By now the fire on the second floor had spread to the neighbouring room. In a few more minutes the upper storeys would be a raging inferno.

He tried raising Duncan again to warn him about the blaze. Got nothing. He tried Rigg and Hickey, the other five assaulters. He got the same result every time.

No response.

Carter broke off and reached out to the other guys on the cordon team. 'Sek, Tom. Have you got comms inside?'

Sek and Farrell glanced at one another. Then Sek shook his head. 'No, mate. Net's gone quiet as a dog's fart.'

'Must have a radio jammer inside,' Farrell said. 'Only explanation.'

Carter started to reply.

Then he noticed a shadowy blur in the periphery of his vision.

He snapped his gaze towards the left of the mansion, tracking the movement. His ten o'clock. The dimly illuminated stretch of ground between the stronghold and the timber-framed garage. Seventy metres away, a stout, silver-haired figure in a dark jacket hurried out of the side of the building. At this distance, in the thin dawn light, he was too far away to properly identify. Not the right build for a bodyguard. A VIP, maybe. A guest. Or a client. Someone getting the five-star treatment from the accountant. Therefore a person of interest. He carried a leather satchel over his shoulder and moved in a lopsided gait as he hastened towards the garage.

Towards the vintage cars.

Carter instantly grasped his intention. *He's making a run for it.* Get to the garage, fire up one of the motors. Escape via the smaller gated entrance on the west side of the compound.

Carter glanced back at Farrell, Sek and Scowcroft. They hadn't seen the silver-haired figure fleeing from the house. Scowcroft was still standing behind the guards while Sek and Farrell kept a close eye on the front of the stronghold. They were obsessed with that entry point. They seemed more interested in what was happening inside than the surrounding area.

The silver-haired guy in the suit was twenty metres from the garage now.

Closing fast.

'Movement, extreme left,' Carter yelled over the thunderous din of the choppers. 'There's a runner. Going to engage now.'

He broke into a mad dash across the grass and raced past the pavilion and the lead-riddled bodyguard floating among the water lilies. Lungs burning with the effort as he sprinted towards the garage to intercept the guy before he could leg it from the estate.

The man in the suit had almost reached the Aston Martin. He was less than half a dozen paces to the car. Carter quickened his stride, running for all he was worth. The guy stopped beside the driver's side door, fumbled in his pockets, dropped a set of car keys – Carter saw the glint of metal in the glow of the security lights – and stooped down to pick them up.

'Stop there!' Carter shouted. 'Move and I'll blow your head off!'

The guy automatically froze. He stayed bent at the waist, his back to Carter, as if he had stooped to examine a rare species of butterfly.

'On your knees! Drop the satchel!'

The man did as he was told. He set down the satchel and slowly lowered himself to his knees, his hands still raised. Carter swept forward and shoved him face-down on the asphalt. The guy moaned and protested in a foreign tongue as Carter pressed his full weight down on his lower back, pinning him to the ground while he fished out a pair of tri-fold plasticuffs from his pocket. He slid the loops over the guy's hands and cinched them tight, drawing a sharp cry of pain as the material dug into the soft flesh of his wrists.

'Let me go,' he begged in harshly accented English. 'Please.'

Carter stood up and rolled the man onto his back. He dug out his utility torch, flashed it in his face.

And did a double take.

He was looking at Denis Gorchakov.

Seven

Carter stared at the Russian for a long cold beat. His mind was racing. He felt as if someone had just punched him in the breadbasket. He took in the salt-and-pepper beard, the narrow slitted eyes, the jowly cheeks. The sickle-shaped scar below his left eye. The grey hair.

It's definitely him, Carter thought.

This is Gorchakov.

So who the fuck had the assault team arrested?

'Let me go,' Gorchakov said nervously. The Russian had a look of fear and desperation in his eyes. 'Please. I can pay. I have – money.'

'Shut the fuck up.'

A moment later, Sek came sprinting over from the direction of the estate. He caught up with Carter, glanced at the target lying on his back, and stopped mid-stride as if he'd walked into an invisible wall.

'What the fuck?' He shook his head. 'Is that—'

'Yeah,' Carter said. 'It's him.'

'I thought the lads had made the arrest?'

'So did I.'

'Then what the fuck is he doing here?'

I don't know, Carter thought to himself.

'Check the bag,' he shouted.

Sek bent down and reached for the satchel. It was some sort of designer brand, Carter noted. Brown leather with a suede trim, a cross-body strap and a polished clasp. The Fijian flipped it open. Peeked inside.

'He's got a couple of laptops in here,' he shouted back. 'Disk drives. Phones. Some documents. Loads of crap. No money, though,' he added with a hint of disappointment.

Carter pointed the barrel of his L119A2 at a spot between the Russian's eyes. 'How the fuck did you escape?'

Gorchakov licked his lips. He looked shit-scared. His eyes were as wide as lampshades. Sweat beaded his brow. His mouth opened and closed in terror.

'Tell me,' Carter growled.

The Russian replied in a panicked voice. 'There's a . . . a body double. Inside. He surrendered – to your friends.'

'That's who they arrested?'

Gorchakov nodded quickly. 'Don't shoot me, please. I give you money. Anything—'

'Shut up.'

Carter thought: *Body double.*

This guy must be more paranoid than we thought.

He tried raising Duncan again. 'Steve? Are you there?'

For a moment, he got nothing.

Then Duncan said, 'I can hear you. We're having some signal issues over here. What's going on?'

Carter told him about Gorchakov legging it out of the building. The body double. Duncan listened in silence and then said, 'How do we know your guy isn't the double?'

'Check your man,' Carter said. 'Check for the scarring under his eye.'

Duncan went quiet again for a couple of beats.

'No scarring on our guy,' he said. 'He's the double, all right.'

'Crafty fucker must have left his double inside while he did a runner,' Sek said. 'Almost worked, too.'

'We're taking him back to the chopper now,' Carter said over the comms channel. 'Hard arrest has been made. Exit the building now.'

'Roger that. We'll be out in a few minutes. Still checking for hardware.'

'No need,' Carter said. 'Target was carrying a load of hardware with him. Get out of there, mate.'

Duncan was interrupted by a muffled boom over the comms.

One of the assaulters has just set off an explosive charge, Carter realised.

They're opening something up in there.

Duncan said, 'The Russian might have left some vital stuff behind. We're doing a thorough sweep of all floors of the house. Out in figures two.'

'There's no time,' Carter snapped. 'Cops are on their way, for fuck's sake.'

Nothing.

Carter tried again, but he got the same dead silence he'd heard before.

Fuck it.

'Come on,' he said to Sek. 'Give us a hand.'

They grabbed hold of Gorchakov by his biceps and hauled him upright. It was like lifting a skip bag filled with rubble. The guy must have weighed north of twenty stone. Carter slung the satchel over his shoulder. Then they frogmarched the Russian towards the cordon team. He staggered along between his captors, moaning softly and making all sorts of wild promises. By now Carter guessed that six or seven minutes had passed since the start of the op.

Three minutes until the cops arrived on the scene.

He was halfway towards the front of the estate when Farrell came rushing over. The Ulsterman nodded approvingly at Carter.

'Nice work,' he said into his throat mic. 'Can't believe he almost managed to sneak out.'

'Have you got comms with the lads inside?' Carter asked. 'I can't get hold of them.'

'Same for us. Just went dead. No answer.'

'Shit.'

'Get a move on,' Sek said, breathing hard. 'Get him on the chopper.'

The three of them carried on towards the nearest Black Hawk, moving as fast as they could manage while carting along twenty-stone-plus of sweaty Russian.

Farrell kept glancing back at the house. The guy looked nervy. *Anxious for his mates to bug out in time,* thought Carter.

Or maybe he had something else on his mind.

As they neared the chopper he noticed the glow of police sirens on the horizon. Some two miles due south. A long chain of them. Red and blue neon bursts flashing and popping in the grainy half-light. Getting larger as they raced towards the estate.

Carter figured they had two minutes before the cops reached the front gate. *Two minutes until we're completely surrounded.*

He looked over at the stronghold. There was still no sign of anyone on the assault team emerging from the front door, and he wondered what the fuck was taking them so long.

In another dozen paces they had reached the side of the chopper. Sek bundled Gorchakov into the cabin and strapped him into one of the canvas seats. Then Carter felt a hard shove in his back. He stumbled forwards; before he could recover, a pair of hands dragged him bodily into the Black Hawk. Farrell clambered in after Carter and pulled a black hood over Gorchakov's head, while Sek hollered an order at the loadie. The latter signalled to the pilots to take off immediately.

'The fuck are you doing?' Carter shouted above the thunderous roar of the engines.

Sek said, 'We're getting out of here. Back to base. Orders from the assault group.'

'What about the other lads?'

'They'll be right behind us,' Farrell said. 'Out of there any minute.'

'But that's breaking SOPs.'

Sek said, 'The target is the priority. We need to get him back to base before the cops show up.'

Before Carter could protest further there was a sudden lurch as the chopper lifted off the ground. He dropped into the nearest seat, Gorchakov's leather satchel on his lap. Rage simmering in his blood.

It was against all standard procedures to leave your mates behind during a mission. All kinds of stuff could go wrong. The assault team might find themselves in a firefight with the police, or the chopper might crash on take-off. In which case they would be in the shit, alone, with no way out.

If anything happens to them, we'll have blood on our hands.

As the chopper climbed higher, he caught sight of Duncan and the rest of the assault group streaming out of the stronghold. Each soldier was shouldering a bulky-looking rucksack in addition to their regular kit, Carter noted. Some of them seemed to be struggling under the weight of their loads as they hustled towards the second Black Hawk.

Scowcroft, Redzic and Vokes swiftly abandoned their respective positions and raced over to board the chopper with the assaulters, leaving the cuffed guards behind.

Further south, the loose chain of police cars sped towards the entrance. They were a minute or so out, Carter guessed, and he felt a slight pang of relief. It would be a close-run thing, but the assaulters would make it out with moments to spare.

To the north, the fire on the second floor had spread rapidly. The whole eastern wing of the building was now wreathed in flame; tendrils of noxious smoke eddied up from the turret, tarring the pallid sky.

The mansion disappeared from view as the Black Hawk banked sharply to the right before levelling out. The loadmaster had a short discussion with one of the pilots through the boom mic attached to his headset. A look of surprise and bemusement flashed across his face. Then he shrugged and returned to his station.

'What was that about?' Carter shouted above the noise.

'Message from the other pilots,' the loadie replied. 'They're gonna zigzag around and create a distraction. In case the police start taking shots at us. They'll expose themselves to any incoming flak. Give us time to get to safety.'

The chopper quickly gained airspeed. Far below, the wood-studded hills and ploughed fields scrolled past in a steadily increasing blur as the Black Hawk raced away from the stronghold.

Heading towards the air base at Gornika.

* * *

They stopped briefly at Gornika to refuel. While they waited, Carter told the loadie to check in with the pilots on the other Black Hawk. He wanted to make sure the assault group had managed to get clear of the stronghold.

The loadie came back a few minutes later to make his report. The second heli had successfully evaded the police without taking any hits, he said. No casualties from the main assault. They were running behind the first chopper but would catch up with them for the post-op debrief in Germany.

A few minutes later, they took off again and continued west towards Ramstein. The same route as the outward journey, but in reverse.

Gorchakov stayed silent during the journey, breathing erratically through the hood. The Russian was having to adjust to a whole new reality. An hour ago he had been the president's banker. One of the most powerful players in the Kremlin. Now he was a prisoner. There would be no more private jets or lavish holidays, no more tooling around in his prized Aston Martin.

His new life – the one Six would give him in exchange for his int – was going to be a lot less glamorous. A new identity, a semi-detached house in some dreary town in Wiltshire, a monthly retainer. Enough to keep him in beer and ciggies, but not much else. Probably the occasional trip to Vauxhall to brief his handlers on the financial dealings of some minor player in the Russian political elite. There were worse fates. But Carter doubted that Gorchakov would see it that way. He would be swapping the corridors of power for suburban anonymity.

They landed at Ramstein shortly after eight o'clock in the morning. A full six hours since they had left the air base. The pilots skilfully brought the bird down a short distance from the Regiment hangar. The engine reduced to a low whine, the loadie gave the thumbs up, and then Farrell and Sek hefted the shell-shocked Russian to his feet and manhandled him out of the side door.

Dawn had fully broken now. Rods of sunlight broke through the clouds, burning up the last shreds of morning mist. Carter followed the others out of the chopper and paused a few paces from the fuselage. Searching the sky for the other Black Hawk.

Nothing.

No sign of the chopper.

Carter was trying to make sense of the assault, mentally logging details ahead of his next meeting with Maitland, Sutton and Greening. He thought about the explosions inside the mansion. The comms cutting out.

Sek was calling out to him from across the tarmac stand. 'This way, Geordie. Reception party is waiting for us inside. Let's give them the big prize. Come on.'

Carter put the lid on the dark thoughts in his head and hurried away from the Black Hawk.

He caught up with Farrell, Sek and Gorchakov as they reached the hangar entrance. They manhandled the hooded Russian past the sentries and escorted him towards a separate interrogation cell located towards the rear of the structure. Two shadowy-looking figures stood outside the prefab container, waiting to receive Gorchakov. A pasty-looking man in a plain suit, and a dark-haired woman in a grey jacket and pencil skirt and oversized glasses. Both of them had that air of arrogance, suspicion and insecurity shared by all those who worked in the security services. Carter guessed they were the Six officers.

Lyndon Grist, the Regiment int officer, was standing next to Mr and Mrs Bland. Carter glanced round, but there was no sign of Mike Beattie, the sergeant major running the show at Ramstein, which surprised him. Attending to business with one of the other SAS teams operating out of the hangar, he assumed.

They handed the Russian over to the Six officers. Carter gave them the satchel Gorchakov had been carrying and said, 'Here. Forensics will want to take a look at this stuff.'

Mr Bland accepted the satchel without replying and handed it to Mrs Bland. As they marched Gorchakov away to a holding cell, Grist stepped forward and grinned.

'Good work, guys,' he said. Then the smile dropped from his face. 'Where's the other lot?'

Sek rubbed the back of his neck as he explained how the assaulters had been delayed by their attempts to create a distraction.

'How far behind are they?' asked Grist.

'No more than a couple of minutes,' Carter said. 'They bugged out of the stronghold right behind us. Should get here any moment.'

Grist said, gravely, 'That was a ballsy move. Drawing enemy fire away from the target. Duncan's call, I presume?'

'I think so,' Carter replied.

Grist nodded again. 'Good man. I expect he'll be up for a medal.'

Sek said, 'If anyone deserves a gong, it should be Geordie. He's the one who apprehended the target. If it wasn't for him, the guy might have done a runner.'

'Is that so?' The int officer eyed Carter with something approaching admiration. 'Five minutes in G Squadron and you're already making a name for yourself. You surprise me, Geordie Carter. At this rate you'll be OC by the end of the year.'

'Right, let's do the post-op debrief,' Farrell suggested.

'What, now?' Carter looked at him with raised eyebrows. 'What's the big hurry?'

'Just makes sense to do it right away.' Farrell shrugged. 'Get that shite over with, like.'

Carter shook his head angrily. 'We should wait for the rest of the lads to come in. None of us was on the assault team,' he pointed out. 'We need their version of events.'

Sek said, 'What difference does it make? We all know what happened. There's no big fucking mystery.'

A stony silence hung in the air. Carter stood glowering at him. Then Grist coughed and said, 'I agree with Geordie. Better to wait and do it properly once everyone is present.'

'Fuck it, then,' Farrell muttered.

As they waited by the side of the hangar, Carter glanced sidelong at Farrell and Sek, his mind working overtime. He wondered why they had been so keen to do the debrief right away. They seemed in a big hurry to leave Ramstein. He had the distinct impression they wanted to get out of there as quickly as possible.

He shook his head again. Everything was happening very fast. Too fast for Carter's liking. As if it had all been carefully planned beforehand. Like a military operation within a military operation.

A cold feeling spread like a chill across the nape of his neck. The old familiar sensation, prickling his skin, telling him that something was seriously wrong.

Two minutes later, the familiar whirring of an approaching chopper carried across the grey-blanketed sky.

Carter saw the second Black Hawk approaching from the east. Nose pitched slightly forward, rotor blades beating the air. It came in low and hovered in the air for a beat before it slowly descended towards a cluster of hangars on the far side of the tarmac stand. Virtually the other side of the air base from Carter's vantage point.

'What are those idiots doing? They're landing in the wrong place.'

Farrell didn't reply. Carter tried raising the assaulters on the comms to find out what was happening. He got the same dead silence he'd encountered back at the stronghold.

The bird disappeared from sight behind the hangar.

Sixty seconds passed. Then the chopper lifted into view again and hopped over to the Regiment hangar before landing on the apron a short distance from the other Black Hawk. The soldiers dismounted from the side door, laughing and joking with one another. The assault group, plus Scowcroft, Redzic and Vokes. The other half of the cordon team.

Duncan swaggered towards the hangar at the front of the group, looking chuffed to bits. Carter had seen that look before, on the faces of other lads at the end of an op. The look of a true warrior, satisfied with his handiwork.

As they drew nearer, Carter noticed that some of the assaulters' clothes were torn and scorched in places. A few of them had sustained grazes and cuts during the attack, but otherwise they seemed to be in good nick. Then Carter noticed something else, too.

Their rucksacks were missing.

All but one.

Duncan strolled straight over to Carter and thumped him heartily on the shoulder. 'All right, fella?' He grinned. 'What's wrong with you? Got a face like you've been dick-slapped.'

'What the fuck happened back there?' Carter snapped. 'Why didn't we fly back together?'

Duncan laughed it off. 'We were late getting out of the building, you twat. Wrapped up searching for technical goodies. Thought it was best to get the target out of harm's way.'

'That wasn't the plan.'

'The plan changed. You know how it is.'

Carter stared daggers at him, the blood pounding between his temples. 'No. I fucking don't. Mate.'

Duncan relaxed his features into an easy smile. 'Chill out, for fuck's sake. The plan worked, didn't it? Job done.'

'What the fuck was that about?' Carter said, changing the subject. 'Landing on the other side of the airfield.'

Duncan raised his hands in a placatory gesture.

'Don't look at me. Blame that useless pilot. Dickhead got the wrong LZ. Landed us all the way over on the other side of the base. Had to tell him to hop back over here.'

Carter watched the Air Troop leader with a growing sense of unease. He knew that Duncan was lying. The RAF pilots used on SF ops were the best in the business. There was no way they would make such an amateur mistake.

'Get on with the debrief,' Grist announced. 'Geordie, Steve, Sek. We'll run through everything in the usual room. Shouldn't take long.'

'Let's bloody hope not,' Duncan replied under his breath.

Grist didn't appear to have heard him. 'The rest of you can have a well-deserved rest,' he said. 'Pack your kit, fix a brew and put your feet up, gents. You've earned it. We're heading back to Hereford at two o'clock this afternoon.'

* * *

A short while later, Carter, Duncan, Sek and Grist gathered in the briefing room. Grist sat on one side of the table next to Moody, with the three soldiers lined up opposite. Several items had been arranged on the table between them. Gorchakov's luxury satchel, a North Face rucksack with the contents laid out on the polished walnut. A battered laptop that looked as if it predated the invention of the wheel, a couple of basic-looking burner phones, three Manila folders stuffed with printed-out documents, some legal pads and a stack of paperwork.

Carter ran his eyes over the meagre haul and felt a pressure building inside his head, pushing against the backs of his eyeballs.

He wasn't thinking about the hardware in front of him. He was wondering what had happened to the other bags. And what was inside them.

Grist kicked off the debrief. 'Let's get straight down to it, lads. Talk me through what happened.'

'Insertion was fine,' Duncan said. 'Entry to the stronghold wasn't a problem. Explosive charge on the door to gain access. All the kit was in good working order.'

Carter sat bolt upright. He said, 'That's not true. The radios were out of order. Comms were down for three to four minutes total. Two separate occasions.'

Moody knitted his brow. 'That's the first I've heard of it.' He looked towards Sek and Duncan. 'Is that true?'

'Geordie's right. We lost comms once or twice during the raid,' Duncan said. 'We figured it might be a radio jammer – seeing as the target has invested in a premium security package at his gaff.'

'No.' Moody shook his head determinedly. 'That can't be it. If the signal was jammed it wouldn't have dropped in and out like that.'

'So what happened?' asked Carter.

'Could be a faulty radio,' Sek suggested. 'Those new sets have been playing up since we started using them. Load of crap. Better off with the old kit, if you ask me.'

Moody made a doubtful noise and pointed at Carter's personal radio. 'Let me have a look at that.'

Carter detached the radio and passed it to Moody. The signaller examined it delicately, like a jeweller assessing a precious stone, or an archaeologist examining a priceless artefact. He pushed various buttons and twisted dials, then handed it back to Carter.

'Looks all right to me,' he said. His brow heavily puckered as he puzzled over the problem. 'Doesn't make sense. One or two radios might break down, but loads of them? At the same time? Highly improbable.'

'What are you saying?' Grist asked.

Moody didn't answer. Instead, he turned to Sek and Duncan and said, 'Did anyone switch channels during the raid? By mistake, perhaps?'

Duncan and Sek looked at one another. They looked back at Moody. Shook their heads.

'Not as far as we know,' Sek said. 'We just had the same issue as Geordie. The net went quiet, then it came back. Then it happened again. Just like he said.'

Moody shrugged and looked irritated, as if he found the explanation unsatisfactory. 'I'll take a closer look into it back home. See if there's some other reason for the kit playing up.'

'Go on, Steve. Let's hear the rest of it,' Grist said.

Duncan said, 'We cleared the building and apprehended the target. Or at least, we thought we did. Unbeknown to us, the target had a body double. While we were restraining the wrong guy, the real target did an exit right and tried to make an escape. Thankfully, Geordie was on hand to make the hard arrest following correct identification. It's thanks to him that the mission was successful.'

'So I've heard. Continue.'

'Subsequent to making the arrest, we scoured the place for intelligence. We searched high and low, but this was all we could find.'

Duncan waved a hand at the meagre haul of hardware and documents on the table.

'Not forgetting the satchel the target had on him, of course,' Grist added.

'Aye. That too.'

'But you were in there for almost ten minutes,' Carter said. 'I heard you lot blasting your way through the place room by room. It can't have taken you that long to check for int.'

Duncan stared at him with flat eyes. 'Like I said. We were doing a detailed sweep of the house. Every nook and cranny had to be cleared.'

'What about the strongroom?'

'Same deal. Emptier than a Tube carriage in a pandemic. Target must have relocated all his loot. Maybe he was worried about the Russians coming after him and decided to stash his wealth somewhere off the grid.'

'Explains the body double,' Sek said. 'He'd only do that if he was worried about being taken out.'

Grist said, 'Six will send in a team to check the other properties, naturally. See if he's hidden anything else.'

Duncan continued his narrative. 'After completing our search, we exited the property and boarded the helis. As per my instructions, our pilots zigzagged around the property to draw any fire away from the target.'

'Did the police engage?'

'Negative. We were out of range before they could open fire.'

'Any casualties?'

Duncan folded his thick arms across his chest. 'Two of the guys suffered some light burns from the explosive charges. Brady twisted his ankle clearing the basement. That's it. Nothing serious.'

'Any equipment left on site? Anything that might identify you?'

'No.'

'Any enemies killed on site?'

'Two bodyguards inside the stronghold.'

'And outside?'

'Three enemies clipped,' Carter said. 'Three more BGs surrendered. We disarmed and restrained them and left them in front of the building.'

'Good job we had Geordie on the cordon team,' Duncan remarked. 'Listen, if you're planning on writing anyone up for a citation, it should be him. Saved the day.'

Carter said, frostily, 'Cut the bullshit, Steve.'

'Calm down, lad. You did well. What's the fucking problem?'

'I don't need a gong. I ain't interested.'

'Steve's trying to do you a favour, you moody cunt,' Sek said. 'No need to get arsey about it.'

Carter bit back on his anger and looked away. He had a nose for bullshit, and at that moment the briefing room stank of it. Duncan was laying it on thick, bigging up Carter in an attempt to deflect the attention back to him. Making Grist focus on his heroics, rather than the question marks surrounding the op.

He turned to the int officer and said, 'What's the deal with the Polish authorities? They must know about the raid by now, what with the cops being alerted.'

'That's being sorted out through diplomatic channels. There won't be any noise from them. Would have been a different story if any of the officers had been injured.'

'And the target?'

'He'll be stuck on a private jet in the next hour or so. Six will take him to a black site for an enhanced interrogation. Find out what he knows. Then they'll take him to a safe house. As for the hardware, Six will have their forensic guys strip everything for data. Go through it with a fine-tooth comb.'

Grist paused and drummed his fingers on the table.

'We did find something else, though. Something – unexpected.'

He leaned across the table and reached for the satchel. Popped the clasp, unzipped an internal storage pocket and pulled out a small velvet drawstring pouch. While the others looked on curiously, Grist tugged on both ends of the drawstring and tipped the contents onto the table. A shower of diamonds spilled out of the bag. Each one perfectly round and about the size of a penny coin. Carter counted twenty of them. Gleaming beneath the stark glow of the panel lights.

Sek stared at the diamonds, his mouth hanging open in shock.

'Jesus,' he gasped. 'Look at that, will you.'

'Five carat diamonds,' Grist explained. 'Gorchakov's maid told us that he had a stash of them. Used to carry them with him wherever he went. His getaway fund, we presume.'

'Fuck me.'

Carter did a quick mental calculation. The going rate for a five-carat diamond varied considerably, depending on the cut, colour and clarity. But say a minimum of a hundred thousand dollars for the lower quality stuff. With an upper limit of half a million for the premium cuts.

He was looking at perhaps two million bucks' worth of diamond.

He glanced sidelong at Duncan. The Scotsman was staring at the rocks intently. Then he lifted his gaze to Sek. An accusing expression flashed across his face.

Grist fired off a few more questions before he wrapped up the debrief. They filed out of the unit, and Carter hauled his weary body over to the canteen to grab a brew while Sek and Duncan walked over to the far side of the hangar and disappeared through a plain door. Carter watched them, questions boring like drill bits in the sides of his skull.

Where were they going?

What the fuck are they up to now?

'Something on your mind, mate?'

Carter looked round. Farrell was sitting at one of the tables and helping himself to a plate of biscuits.

'No, mate. It's nothing.'

'Cheer up.' The Ulsterman popped another biscuit into his mouth. 'We got the job done, didn't we? Not every day we nab a Russian billionaire.'

'No. Guess not.'

He grinned and wiped his mouth with the back of his hand. 'You know what your problem is, Geordie? You don't know how to relax. Too highly strung. Need to let your hair down once in a while. Know what I'm saying?'

121

'Maybe.'

Carter poured a cup of black coffee and wandered over to the breakout area. He wasn't in the mood for chatting shit, so he turned his mind back to the debrief. He thought about what Moody had said about the comms issues.

Not a problem with the radios.

Not a jammer.

There could only be one other plausible reason for the comms dropping out during the raid, Carter thought to himself. And in that moment, as the realisation sucker-punched him, he felt a cold tingle of fear crawling down his spine.

Because then he grasped the appalling truth. It was right there in front of him. Staring him in the face.

I hope I'm wrong, Carter thought to himself.

But if I'm right, this could destroy the Regiment.

Eight

The Troop returned to Hereford at four o'clock in the afternoon. The CO and the ops officer were there to greet them and congratulate them on a job well done. Then it was back to the mind-numbing routine of training and waiting on standby for the next mission. Duncan ordered the team to meet the next day at the squadron hangar to unpack their kit. There was a heated discussion about where they would go for beers that evening, and who was buying the first round. Everyone seemed to be in fine spirits. There were plenty of smiles and laughs and a lot of good-natured piss-taking. The World Cup-winning team, arriving back home to a heroes' welcome.

Carter took a rain check on the celebrations and drove straight home from camp. He changed into his civvies, had a scrub and a shave, cracked open a bottle of supermarket-brand beer from the fridge, fired up the wood burner. Then he retrieved the mini phone he'd secreted in his survival pack. Carter powered up the device, navigated the crude menu system and tapped out a new text message on the micro-sized keypad:

Need to meet. ASAP.

He hit Send.

He placed the mini phone on the side table, sipped his crap lager and flicked on the TV while he waited for a response. He spent several minutes pointlessly scrolling through the streaming sites, found nothing but junk, and settled on the news. On which the general theme seemed to be Britain's gradual slide into the sea. House prices were going up. A mid-terrace in London now cost more than the GDP of Botswana. The next generation were never going to be able to afford a house. Climate change was killing humanity. The rich were pulling up the drawbridge.

Same old story, Carter thought. *The people in charge make a fucking mess. Then they shuffle off stage and leave it to everyone else to pick up the bill.*

There was a story about the ongoing counteroffensive in Ukraine. Russian forces were engaged in fighting dangerously close to the nuclear power station at Holovika, in the south-east of the country. The largest station in Europe. Ukrainian forces had recently reconquered the area ahead of a renewed push towards Kherson. They were making rapid progress, the report said. Gaining ground at an astonishing rate. Even the Ukrainians seemed surprised by their success. The Russians were being driven back towards the Dnieper.

The local Russian commander appeared in front of the media, threatening to bomb Holovika unless the Ukrainians withdrew from the area. The power lines connecting the plant to the national grid had been damaged in the recent Russian shelling, the report claimed. Engineers were having to rely on diesel generators until they got the power up and running again.

The camera cut to a NATO summit meeting in Berlin. The fresh-faced US Secretary of State stood behind a lectern, flanked by the US and NATO flags as he addressed the camera directly.

'Let me be absolutely clear,' the secretary said in his smooth Californian accent. 'The president takes any threat of nuclear escalation extremely seriously. Any attempt to destroy civilian nuclear infrastructure, or the deployment of strategic nuclear weapons against Ukraine, will result in swift and firm retaliation from this administration, the likes of which the world will not have seen before. We strongly advise Russia to resist a potentially destructive escalation of hostilities, and call for the establishment of a protected zone around Holovika as a matter of international urgency.'

Carter's phone buzzed with an incoming message from Maitland. He scooped up the device, clicked it open. Frowned at the tiny screen:

Tomorrow. 1700. Same place.

He was about to turn the phone off when another text came through:

Did you find anything?

On the TV, the news had moved on to other world events. Famine in Bangladesh, sabre-rattling over Taiwan, a fraught general election in Italy. He stuck it on mute.

He wrote:

You were right. It's not just a few bad apples.

* * *

Major Phil Greening sat at his kitchen table and stared at the burner phone, wrestling with his conscience.

He had a decision to make.

The most difficult of his career.

Make-or-break time.

There was a Golden Virginia tobacco tin next to the burner, filled with disposable SIM cards. If Greening needed to reach out to his contact, for whatever reason, he had to first insert a fresh SIM in the phone, then dial the number he had committed to memory, taking care to properly dispose of the card afterwards. Crushing it and flushing the debris down the toilet was the preferred way of doing this, he understood. He had also been told only to make a call in the event of an emergency.

Think of it as a fire alarm, they had told him. *Don't break the glass unless it's an emergency.*

Greening was immensely proud of what he'd achieved in his Regimental career. Few rankers ever made it as high as second-in-command of the SAS. He had succeeded through a mixture of determination, ability, making the right friends, and, yes, a large dollop of good fortune. But there were times when he yearned for his old life as a raw recruit in G Squadron.

Times like now.

He had known about the goings-on in his old squadron for a while. When he'd first been alerted to the problem, Greening had decided to let it slide. That had been his first mistake. He had tried to rationalise the issue. After all, the Regiment historically attracted risk-takers. Gamblers. Non-conformists. Guys who often acted as if the normal rules didn't apply to them. The vast majority of soldiers in 22 SAS were honest, hard-working, decent lads. But one or two sometimes strayed into criminality.

He remembered some of the stories doing the rounds at Hereford twenty years ago. Whispered tales of SAS legends who had cooked the books while training up foreign militias, inflating the numbers of soldiers and pocketing the difference in supplies and money. Soldiers who had looted buildings during raids, stripping them bare.

It happened. Unpleasant, but a fact of life. And no one got hurt. What they called a victimless crime.

Greening had tried to keep his hands clean. He didn't approve of the actions of some of the men under his command, but he'd learned to quietly tolerate them. As long as they were doing the business, and nothing got out of hand, he was prepared to look the other way.

But then Steve Duncan and his colleagues had gone feral.

The problems had started soon after Iraq. That was when the Steel Reapers had started hanging out with the Blood Kings on a regular basis. Things had quickly escalated after that. Greening had been forced to cover for his men. He had worked his whole life to avoid trouble, and now, at the very pinnacle of his career, he was having to lie to protect a group of guys who were in too deep with a criminal gang. Good soldiers, he reminded himself, first-class operators, some of whom he had taken through Selection himself.

He should have intervened at that point. Taken Duncan aside and read him the Riot Act. Threatened to shop them to the CO unless they got their act together. Instead, Greening had simply carried on as normal, hoping that things would blow over, telling himself that the lads would see sense eventually.

That had been his second mistake.

Now Greening found himself in an impossible position.

And he was running out of time.

Way he saw it, he had two possible courses of action.

Option one: he could choose to say nothing. Allow the investigation to run its course, and risk exposing the actions of the guys in Air Troop. As it inevitably would. Geordie Carter was many things, but he was nobody's fool. And the Reapers had started to get sloppy. Things would come to light. Inevitable. Greening was looking at a scandal that could destroy the reputation of not just G Squadron but the whole of 22 SAS.

Or he could make the call. Save his old squadron – and the Regiment – from humiliation.

If he acted, he would virtually guarantee that the investigation would hit a dead end. There would be some disappointment at Thames House and Scotland Yard, but the higher-ups at Whitehall would breathe a collective sigh of relief. They hated it when outsiders shone a light on the inner workings of the Regiment, for fear of what they might find.

It would mean ruining the life of a good soldier, Greening reminded himself. But the sacrifice was surely worth it. The future of the Regiment was on the line.

Therefore, not really a choice at all.

Greening knew what to do. In truth, he had already made up his mind when he'd climbed out of bed that morning. Since then, he had been stalling for time. Trying to delay the thing he knew must be done, even as the thought of it shamed and appalled him.

Mistakes made, coming back to haunt him.

He took a swig of Famous Grouse, steeling himself.

Then he picked up the phone and punched in the number.

It rang three times before a scratchy voice on the other end answered.

'Yes?'

'Steve, it's Phil. Listen, we have—'

'I told you not to call this number,' Duncan interrupted.

'This is an emergency. There's something you need to know.'

There was a bout of cold silence.

'Go on,' Duncan said.

'You're being watched. They're onto you.'

The line went silent again.

'Police?'

'Among others. Our friends north of the Thames, too.'

Then Duncan said, 'How?'

'There's a plant,' Greening said. 'In your Troop.'

'Who?'

Greening hesitated. He was about to get his hands dirty again. An unfortunate turn of events. His own fault. But he wasn't going to make a third mistake.

'I'm not doing this for you,' he said. 'I'm doing this for the sake of the Regiment. Just so you understand.'

'Phil?'

'Yes?'

'Give me a name.'

Greening told him. The line went quiet for several beats. Long enough for Greening to wonder if he'd lost signal.

'Steve? You there?'
'Leave it with us. We'll take care of it.'
'How?'
'Better you don't know.'

Nine

Exactly thirteen minutes before the meeting, Carter stepped outside his front door. Home was a two-bedroom cottage set on the fringes of an isolated village, a few miles west of Credenhill. The place had been a dump when he'd bought it four years ago – all he could afford after his divorce and the maintenance payments. Carter had rebuilt it from the ground up with the help of his brother. Walls had been replastered. Fences erected, floors sanded, brickwork repointed, roof tiles replaced, guttering cleaned, paving relaid, doors rehung. The knackered old garage with the asbestos roof had been demolished; in its place stood a tall timber structure with an office set in the eaves.

His ex-wife was a psychotherapist now. Which probably said something about their relationship.

Carter crossed the gravel and approached his Volvo. He was intensely aware that he was about to destroy the careers of several Blades. He didn't know how he felt about that. He couldn't care less about the looting. Morally wrong, perhaps, but no worse than the rich bastards in the Establishment, fiddling their expenses or handing out contracts to their mates in exchange for a lucrative slice of the action.

Far as he could tell, the only difference was that Duncan and his mates had been caught red-handed.

He realised something else, too.

My own career is finished after this.

Carter had hoped that his transfer to G Squadron would signal a fresh start. An opportunity to start over again. Redeem himself. Now he saw with terrible clarity that the Regiment had only brought him back to serve a purpose. Once the investigation was over, they would almost certainly want rid of him. He was a liability. The other guys in G Squadron – the ones who hadn't been dealing with the Blood Kings – would view him as a snitch. No one would want to go near him. Greening's promise to make him squadron sergeant major was bullshit.

They'll retain me for as long as they need me. Then chuck me on the scrapheap. The Hereford way.

He slid behind the wheel. Fired the engine and stopped at the edge of the main road. Looked left, then right. A Harley-Davidson came roaring into view, the unmistakeable roar of its engine cutting across the air. It whizzed past the Volvo and disappeared from sight as it swerved round the next bend in the road.

Idiots, Carter thought to himself. There were tons of bikers in the area these days. Tooling around the countryside, causing accidents and irritating the locals with their noise and litter.

He pulled out of his front drive and motored south towards Madley. Twelve minutes later, he rolled into the car park on the eastern side of the King's Arms. At five o'clock on a Thursday afternoon, the area was quiet. There was a nursery school on the other side of the potholed road. A service station and an Indian takeaway further east, next to a dilapidated bus stop. Further along, a row of crumbling red-brick terraces and a clutter of newbuilds.

A white Mercedes-Benz Sprinter van had carelessly parked on the edge of the junction directly west of the pub. Thereby blocking the view of anyone trying to turn onto the main road. Delivery driver. Area was full of them. Barrelling down the roads, criss-crossing the same streets multiple times each day, blocking driveways and side streets.

He pushed through the door and stepped into the pub. He counted a dozen or so customers scattered around the joint. In one corner, a shaven-headed bloke in a hoodie pumped coins into a fruit machine. A couple of fake-tanned young women sat at a table drinking cocktails. A huge guy at the bar was drinking alone, his thick arms and neck inked with richly detailed tattoos. Further along, an old-timer in a flat cap admired the tits on the woman behind the bar. Carter had seen more life in a petri dish.

Cost of living, maybe, Carter mused. Cheaper to drink own-brand beers at home than down the local. But also lonelier, and bleaker.

He found Maitland and the others at the back of the bar. Sutton sat in the middle of the trio, attired in the same bin-liner suit he'd worn at the first meeting. Greening to his left. Maitland to his right, smartly dressed in a single-breasted jacket, silk blouse and a dark pencil skirt. Her lips were glossed a deep shade of purple. The opposite end of the spectrum from Sutton, fashion-wise. The kind of person who could wear frayed hand-me-downs and still look like a million bucks.

Greening stood up to greet him and gestured to the empty stool. Carter parked himself on the padded velvet, declined the offer of a drink, and the others listened patiently while he talked them through the raid in Poland. Sutton took frequent swigs from his pint glass of Coke. Maitland left her sparkling water untouched. Greening didn't have a drink, Carter noted. The 2iC occasionally interrupted him, seeking clarification on some minor detail or confirming the chronology of events. Like a detective questioning a key witness to a crime. He seemed agitated, constantly checking his watch and shifting his weight.

Carter finished his report. Sutton stared at his empty pint glass. Maitland bit her lower lip, a slight frown creasing her otherwise smooth complexion. Greening took out his phone, glanced at it, then laced his hands together and looked levelly at Carter.

He said, 'Let me see if I've got this straight. You're saying that the whole of Air Troop is corrupt. Yes?'

'Not everyone. One or two of the guys might be sound. But the majority of them are in on it.'

'You're sure?'

'As sure as I can be.'

'But you have no definitive proof. No smoking gun.'

Greening spread his hands in front of him, like a poker player revealing a dud hand.

'That's right,' Carter said.

'Then how can you be so certain? I don't mean to piss all over your story, Geordie, but there's nothing concrete here. Just a load of hearsay and suspicion.'

'No. It's a lot more than that.'

'How do you mean?' Maitland asked.

'They went overboard on the kit front. I personally saw them packing three thermal lances. For a hard arrest. That's unheard of, in my experience. They took a metal detector, too. When I asked why they were bringing it, they fobbed me off with some bollocks about needing to search for hidden tech.'

'Maybe they were being cautious,' Sutton said.

Carter gave him a look. He said, 'Then there's the time they took clearing the house. They were tearing that place apart, blowing their way into various rooms.'

'Searching for hardware, maybe,' Sutton suggested. 'Like Duncan said.'

Carter shook his head. 'I've done house clearances. Hundreds of them. This wasn't like any job I've been on. It was – different.'

'In what way?'

'They knew the police were en route, and they still insisted on searching the house for several minutes. That was reckless. Could have ended up with us in a firefight with the cops.'

'Poor tactical judgement, no doubt,' Greening agreed. 'But it doesn't definitively point to anything more sinister.'

Carter said, 'There's more.'

'We're listening, Geordie.'

'There were problems with the comms. The net went silent, on two separate occasions during the raid. At first I figured it might have been a technical problem with the radios, but the signallers ruled that out. They told me they tested the devices and didn't find anything wrong with them.'

'Then why did the radios stop working?'

'They didn't,' Carter said. 'The other guys had switched channels during the mission. They were communicating on a different frequency so I couldn't listen in.'

'You're sure?'

Carter said, 'The comms dropped while the guys on the assault team were clearing the stronghold. That can't be a coincidence. If they were searching for loot inside the house, they'd need a way of talking to one another privately. Establish what they'd found and where.'

'Could they even do that?' Sutton asked. 'Change channels, I mean?'

'Easily enough, aye. Get everyone to set their radios to the new channel before flying out. Whenever the guys need to talk in private, they just switch frequencies, then jump back on the main net when they're finished. That's how I'd do it.'

'But you didn't actually hear them talking about any of this stuff?'

'No.'

'This is all just pure speculation. You have no idea what they were saying.'

Carter eyed the overweight NCA man. 'I didn't need to hear them, mate. There's only one reason why they'd want to cut me out of the chatter, and it wasn't to talk about the fucking weather.'

'Go on,' Maitland said. 'Please.'

Carter thought for a beat. 'They had rucksacks. The assault group guys. They were carrying them when they left the house. Eight in total. But when they got off the chopper, the rucksacks were gone.'

Maitland searched his face. 'Any idea what happened to them?'

'I can do better than that.'

He told her about the second Black Hawk landing on the wrong side of the air base at Ramstein. How it had been out of sight behind another set of hangars for several minutes. He mentioned Duncan's piss-poor excuse for the cock-up. Pilot error.

'You didn't believe him?' Sutton asked.

'Course not.' Carter snorted. 'No RAF would make that sort of mistake. Never in a million years.'

Maitland said, 'You're suggesting they landed in the wrong place deliberately?'

'They needed a place to unload the backpacks before they returned to the hangar. Too risky. Someone might have taken a peek inside. If I was in their boots, I'd do the same thing. Give the pilot a slice of the action and get them to set down away from the rest of the team.'

'But they'd need someone on the ground for that,' Greening pointed out. 'To help unload the stuff and bus it over to the aircraft.'

Carter nodded and said, 'I think Mike Beattie is in on it.'

'Mike? Jesus.' Greening wore a look as if someone had taken a dump on his front lawn. 'Based on what evidence? Or is this another one of your bloody hunches?'

Carter said, 'Beattie should have been there to receive us when we returned. But he was out of sight the whole time. He's in charge of logistics at Ramstein, so he's ideally placed to coordinate the transfer. And I saw him talking with Duncan before the operation. Furtive, like.'

'Doesn't mean anything. They could have been reminiscing about the good old days. Discussing the price of petrol. Anything.'

'I know what I saw,' Carter said tetchily.

'But that's just it,' Sutton pointed out. 'You didn't actually see the transfer taking place, did you?'

'No.'

'Did you even get sight of the contents of the bags?'

'No.'

'What else?' asked Maitland.

'That's it.' Carter shrugged. 'That's everything.'

Sutton looked disappointed. Greening checked his phone again.

Maitland said, 'This is all very promising.'

'But?'

'It's a long way from being conclusive. Personally, I'm going to need a lot more in order to escalate this thing.'

'I agree,' Greening said. 'The careers of Regiment men are on the line here. I want to be absolutely certain of their guilt before we take any action we might regret. I suggest we hold off until we have gleaned more concrete information.'

Carter felt the rage rising in his throat. 'I'm taking a major fucking risk. Some of the lads are already giving me funny looks. If I start prying too hard, they'll realise something is up.'

'We're not asking you to,' Maitland said coolly. 'Just keep doing what you're doing. Let's see where this takes us.'

'Good plan,' Sutton chipped in. 'They're bound to stick their snouts in the trough again soon.'

'Besides, you were the hero of the mission,' Greening pointed out. 'From the sounds of it you're well on the way to earning their confidence. Keep this up, and they're bound to bring you on board.'

'I ain't doing anything illegal.'

'No, Phil's right,' Sutton said. 'This is good for us. If you're invited to join the group, it'll mean we can definitively identify those parties involved with the Kings.'

'Good for *you*,' Carter corrected. 'Not me.'

Maitland said, 'One thing I don't understand.'

'What's that?'

'I can't get my head around why Duncan and his friends weren't more careful to cover their tracks. They must have known how it would look to you – that you'd know something was off.'

He nodded and said, 'I think they were using the raid as a test. They wanted to see how I'd react. To see if I was OK with what was going on. Like being on probation, I guess.'

'They were assessing a potential recruit.'

'Not just that. I think they were worried about infiltration.'

Sutton said, 'We've been over this already. They know your background. Your . . . issues with authority. They've got no reason to suspect you of being a plant.'

'Doesn't matter. These guys are playing for high stakes. One wrong move, their careers are in the shitter and they're looking at a long stretch picking up the soap at Wormwood Scrubs.'

Maitland stared hard at him. 'Did they suspect anything?'

'I don't think so. That's why I kicked up a fuss about the stunts they were pulling. I had no choice. If I didn't look surprised, they would have smelled a rat.'

'Let's hope you're right,' Sutton said. 'For all our sakes.'

Maitland called an end to the meeting. They agreed to RV again nine days later, at a new location to be confirmed closer to the date. She wished Carter luck and told him to be careful. Sutton wandered off to field a call on his phone. Carter stood up, grabbed his Belstaff leather jacket and shaped to leave. At the bar, the thickset guy with the extravagant tattoos caught Carter's eye for a moment before he downed the rest of his pint, slid off his stool and made for the door.

Greening placed a hand on Carter's shoulder.

'Good work,' he said. 'I mean it. This is a fine thing you're doing. We all appreciate the dangers of this mission.'

He gave a bitter laugh. 'Nah, you really don't. It's not your head on the block if this thing goes tits up, is it?'

Carter didn't wait for a reply. He gave his back to Greening and headed for the entrance, feeling angrier than he'd felt for a very long time.

*　*　*

There were two gang members in the Sprinter, an older guy and a young prospect. The older man had a thick whitish beard shaped like an upside-down spear tip and pinhole eyes surrounded by an avalanche of weathered flesh. By far the biggest thing about him was his chest. It was huge. Gargantuan. A freak of nature. Fifty-nine inches at its widest point. His name was Jimmy Naismith, but everyone knew him as Big Daddy.

He was the driver.

The guy in the front passenger seat was nineteen years younger. With his leather waistcoat and tattoos, Conor Ward looked the part of a biker. Every inch of his face had been covered in ink. There were images of skulls, eagles, crucifixes, snakes devouring mythical beasts. He had more art on his face than the fucking Tate, one of his buddies had once remarked.

Ward had been a gang prospect for more than a year. Twelve months of his life working as a glorified dogsbody for the Blood Kings, running around and doing all the menial jobs for the badged veterans. Cleaning their bikes, scrubbing down the toilets in the chapter clubhouse in Liverpool. Now he had a chance to finally earn his own patch. Become a fully fledged member of the Blood King family.

He was determined to seize the moment.

The plan was simple. They had taken up their position shortly after the target had left his house ahead of the meeting, parking fifteen metres downstream from the pub, at the corner of a T-junction, with the pub entrance at their eleven o'clock. There had been some heated debate about whether to use bikes, or a van. In the end, heads won over hearts, and they went with the four-wheeler option. Purely because it was the more practical method. Two guys sitting on a stationary bike in a sleepy Herefordshire village would draw attention from the natives. But no one would notice a couple of blokes in a delivery van.

Now all they had to do was wait for the heads-up from their friend.

Ward was the trigger man. That had been decided back at the clubhouse. The chapter president had taken him to one side and given him The Talk. The one all prospects dreamed of hearing.

It's time, lad, the president had said. *Are you ready to swear the oath?*

The Blood Kings required prospective members to demonstrate their absolute loyalty to their brethren by committing an act of murder. Usually that involved plugging someone in a rival gang trying to muscle in on their turf. Or a revenge killing. Eye for an eye. Old Testament shit. But this was something entirely different. Ward and Naismith suddenly found themselves in uncharted territory. They were out of their depth, in many ways. A lot of things could go wrong.

Don't fail, the president had warned them both. *Don't even think about it.*

We can't fuck this one up.

The burner phone resting on the dash trilled. Naismith swiped it up and answered on the second ring.

The third man on the team was the chapter treasurer, McAteer. He had the surveillance job.

Naismith, aka Big Daddy, spoke to him for several seconds. He tapped to end the call, set down the phone, and said, 'Target heading for the exit. Any moment now. Get ready.'

Ward hitched up the black gaiter collaring his neck so that it covered the lower half of his face and reached for the shotgun stowed in the footwell. Ready to pounce.

Thirty metres away, the target emerged from the pub.

* * *

The sun had begun to sink below the horizon as Carter emerged from the King's Arms. Six o'clock in the evening on a Thursday night. The pub car park was half full now. Or half empty, depending on how you looked at it. The two fake-tanned women stood near the entrance, sucking on their menthol cigarettes. Further away an old man in a waxed jacket waited for his golden retriever to finish sniffing a lamppost splashed with fresh piss. On the other side of the road, a woman in black joggers and a sweater was out for a late run. The Indian takeaway was empty. The white Sprinter van still hadn't moved.

Carter breezed past the two perma-tanned women and made for his Volvo. He stopped beside the driver's side door, fumbled in his pocket for his keys, depressed the unlock button.

He was reaching for the chrome handle when he heard a scream at his six o'clock.

Carter stopped.

He whipped round.

Then he saw the gunman.

The primitive threat detector in Carter's temporal lobes registered several things at once. The gunman was dressed like a biker; his neck gaiter had been pulled up over the lower half of his face, obscuring his features. Like a cowboy sticking up a bank in the Wild West. The top half of his shaven head was stencilled with tattoos. He was half a dozen paces from Carter, roughly midway between the car park and the Sprinter van. Wielding a pump-action shotgun in a two-handed grip. A sawn-off model, with a shortened chokeless barrel, to generate a wider dispersal of lead pellets.

The shooter raised his boomstick.

Black mouth of the muzzle pointing directly at Carter's mid-section.

The two women outside the pub had dashed their cancer sticks and taken cover in the porch, shrinking their profiles, as if trying to make themselves invisible.

Fifteen metres away, the Sprinter van engine snarled into life.

Carter had less than a second to react. The decision-making part of his brain told him that there was no time to race for cover. No time to dive into the car. He considered it highly unlikely that the shooter would miss. Not with a sawn-off, not at such close range. Wishful thinking.

Only one thing you can do.

Get down.

Carter threw himself to the ground.

In the same breath, the shotgun boomed. The driver's side window exploded inches above Carter's head, showering him in tiny glass fragments, and he felt a searing pain in his arm. The car alarm wailed. The women kept screaming. From the same direction came the thud of footsteps pounding across the blacktop, interspersed with panicked voices.

Carter looked up as the Sprinter catapulted forward. It screeching to a halt in front of the pub.

The tattoo-faced shooter about-turned and leaped into the passenger seat. The side door slammed shut as the van raced away from the scene, hurtling past the garage and the takeaway and the red-brick terraces. A few seconds later, it was out of sight.

Carter scraped himself uneasily off the ground. The dog walker stood stock-still, his golden retriever barking in alarm. Across the road, the jogger had dropped to a crouch beside a van parked at the side of the road, hoping to shield herself from the attack.

Carter looked round as a throng of drinkers rushed outside. The old-timers hung back, rubbernecking the scene. Maitland, Greening and Sutton ran over, the Six officer shouting for someone to call the police.

'Are you hurt?' she asked anxiously as she dropped down beside Carter. She caught sight of the blood on his jacket, the shallow cuts to his face and hands.

'Don't try to move. We'll get you an ambulance.'

'No,' Carter said between draws of breath. 'I'm . . . OK.'

There was a shrill ringing noise in his ears, and the pain on his left side throbbed dully. He glanced at his arm. A couple of lead pellets had peppered his upper arm, tearing through the fabric of his Belstaff jacket. His professional eye told him that the wound wasn't serious – he'd suffered more serious injuries in training over the years – but it still hurt like fuck.

'What happened?' Sutton asked.

'Bastard had a sawn-off,' Carter replied groggily. 'Took a pop at me. Legged it in a van.'

Maitland glanced round, taking in the scene. The scattered glass shards. The blown-out car window. The terrified pedestrians. The panicked dog, still barking wildly beside its owner. By now several people had emerged from the nearest houses, alerted by the commotion outside.

A question flashed in Maitland's eyes. 'But . . . how did they know you'd be here?'

No one answered.

'Get him into my car,' Greening said to the others. Look of quiet fury in his eyes. 'Let's get you to the camp medical centre. Have someone clean you up. Then we'll figure out what the hell just happened.'

Ten

The medical centre at Hereford was situated in a blandly furnished building, next to the sorely overworked physio department. Like a doctor's surgery, minus the glossy magazines and the thousand-year wait for an appointment. The duty medic, Katie, was a kind-faced woman with heart-shaped lips. She gave Carter a shot of lignocaine to numb the pain in his left arm, picked out a couple of lead pellets, cleaned and dressed the wound. Handed him a bottle of prescription painkillers and told him that the injury should heal in the next few days. He was lucky, Katie said. His leather jacket had absorbed most of the kinetic energy. The biggest casualty of the attack, from Carter's point of view. Two thousand pounds of designer clothing down the pan. Plus the damage to his Volvo.

Could have been worse, he reminded himself.

If I'd spotted the shooter a second later, I would have taken the full blast in the chest. And I wouldn't be sitting here complaining about a few holes in my jacket.

Katie stepped outside the room and ushered in a couple of plainclothed police officers. A short woman in her forties introduced herself as Detective Chief Inspector Zaynab Rahman; her partner, DI Bobby Galvin, was an out-of-shape guy with skin as pale as the Dover cliffs, hair like a bed of straw and freckled cheeks. They took him into a separate room and Rahman fired off a series of questions while Galvin stayed mute and scribbled notes.

Carter played dumb. Always the best option, in his experience. Safer than cooking up some elaborate story. Less chance of getting tripped up on the details.

'Tell me about the shooter,' Rahman said. 'What did he look like?'

'He was medium height, I guess. Medium build. I didn't really get a good look at him. His face was covered up.'

'Do you remember what he was wearing, at least? Any distinguishing marks? Anything will help us.'

'He had dark clothes, I think.' Carter shrugged an apology. 'Sorry. It all happened so fast, like.'

'What about the driver?' asked Galvin.

'No. Too far away.' Carter canted his head to one side. 'What about the van? Any sign of that?'

Rahman nodded. 'Officers located it half an hour ago. Dumped in a lay-by half a mile from the scene. Forensics will take a look, but we think it's a dead end.'

Galvin said, 'They poured bleach over the interior. Crime scene contamination.'

'Nothing else?'

'We found a pair of ratchet straps in the back. Front wheel chock fixed to the floor. We're working on the assumption that they had a motorcycle in the rear of the van and made their getaway on that.'

Carter thought: *Motorbike. Neck gaiter. Leather jacket. Tattoos all over the shooter's face.*

'As you can see,' Galvin went on, 'it looks like we're dealing with professionals here. Serious players.'

'Is there anyone who might have a grudge against you?' Rahman asked.

'Not as far as I know.'

'That seems hard to believe, given what just happened.'

'Believe what you want. I'm just telling you the truth.'

'Perhaps there's a long-standing feud, or a petty quarrel. Someone in your family, maybe.'

'Most of my family's dead. There's my brother, but he's been out of the country for several months.'

'What about your friends?'

'I don't have many. Prefer my own company. I'm not really a big people person.'

'Do you owe money to anyone?'

'No.' Carter fumed through his nostrils. 'Look, I told you already, it's a case of mistaken identity. Whoever did this had me mixed up with someone else.'

'Have you seen anyone following you lately? Someone watching your house or acting suspiciously? Anything at all?'

Carter shook his head and sighed in frustration. 'All I know is that I had a chat with a couple of old colleagues at the pub. We said goodbye, I left and the next thing I know some idiot is having a pop at me. That's it.'

'Why were you at the pub?'

'Social gathering. Shooting the shit with some workmates.'

'What were you talking about? Out of interest.'

Carter threw up his hands. 'Reminiscing about past ops. Joking about the latest cuts to the Regiment. That good enough for you?'

'You seem quite relaxed about the situation.'

'I'm a soldier. People have been shooting at me one way or another for the past fifteen years. If you want the truth, I'm more pissed off with the damage to my car.'

The interview ended a short while later. Rahman gave Carter her card and told him he'd have to pop down to the station in Hereford to give an official statement. She promised to get in touch if she had any further developments and said they would check for CCTV footage and speak to witnesses. See if anyone could shed some light on the identity of the attackers. But she didn't sound overly optimistic. They had no motive, no suspects, no compelling evidence left at the crime scene. The odds of making an arrest were presumably low.

The two detectives told Carter to wait in the treatment room. They left, and then Maitland, Sutton and Greening trooped inside. Sutton took the medic's chair. Greening parked himself on the edge of the examination couch. Maitland stood. She closed the door and subjected Carter to his second interview of the evening. Except this time he didn't play dumb. He told them what he knew. The bullshit-free version of events.

'Did you get a good look at the shooter?' Maitland asked after he'd finished.

Carter nodded. Said, 'He was a biker.'

'How can you be sure?'

'He had tattoos on his face. Wore a neck gaiter. Had the look. Leather jacket, desert boots.' He told them about the van, and the ratchet straps, and the bike they had escaped on.

'From the Blood Kings?'

'Who else?'

'And the guy in the van?'

'Him I didn't see.' Carter smiled weakly. 'I was kind of distracted at the time.'

Sutton said, 'We'll have to take some time to look into this thing. See if it's connected.'

Carter laughed bitterly. 'I'm nobody's fool, mate. Of course, it's bloody connected. I'd bet my right bollock on it.'

Sutton held up his hands. 'Hey, let's not jump to any conclusions here.'

'No,' Greening cut in. 'Geordie's right. This has to be related. It's too much of a coincidence.'

'Do the police know anything?' asked Maitland.

Carter shook his head and said, 'They asked the usual stuff, but I just fobbed them off.'

'Good. The last thing we need is the cops all over this. That would be bad for all concerned.'

Greening said, 'The question is, what do we do now?'

'We'll have to put the operation on hold,' Sutton announced bluntly. 'At least until we've completed our preliminary investigation into the shooting. Find out what's going on.'

'I agree,' Maitland said. 'It's too risky to continue. In light of what we know.'

Greening drew his eyebrows together. 'What do you mean?'

'We're not dealing with an opportunistic hit. This was obviously planned in advance. Which means someone has been leaking information to whoever was behind the attack.'

'Maybe one of your new friends sussed out what was going on and decided to silence you,' Sutton suggested.

Greening choked in outrage. 'Ridiculous. I know those boys. They might have fallen in with the wrong crowd, but they wouldn't do that, not to one of their own.'

'They would,' Carter said, 'if it meant saving their own arses.'

'You really think your colleagues would try to kill you?' asked Maitland.

'Maybe not directly. They'd want clean hands. If it was me, I would have farmed out the hit to a third party. Put some distance between myself and the killing.'

'The Blood Kings?'

Carter nodded again. 'That's my guess. But Duncan and his mates wouldn't have sanctioned it unless they were a hundred per cent sure I was a plant. Someone must have given them the heads-up.'

Maitland said, 'Whether that's the case or not, we'll have to suspend the operation for the time being. We'll be in touch through the usual channels, once we know more.'

'What am I supposed to do until then?' Carter asked.

'Give your statement and lie low. If anyone asks, tell them what you told the cops. You were at the pub meeting friends, there was an attack in the car park, the cops think it's a clear case of mistaken identity.'

'What about the police investigation?' asked Greening.

'We'll take care of it,' Sutton said. 'Make sure it goes nowhere. From what you've told us it'll hit a brick wall anyway. We can be thankful for that, if nothing else.'

'In the meantime, I suggest you go home,' Greening said. 'Get some rest. Take a few days off.'

Carter stood up and reached for the door handle.

'One more thing,' Maitland said.

'Yes?' Carter looked back at her.

'Be careful. I mean it.'

'You think they'll try again?' Greening asked.

'Someone wants him dead,' Maitland said. 'Bad enough to risk an attack in broad daylight. We have to assume they'll make a second attempt, once they realise the first one has failed.' She fixed her gaze on Carter. 'You're a marked man. Watch your back from now on.'

That won't be a problem, Carter thought as he breezed out of the room and headed for the exit.

I've been doing that most of my fucking life.

Eleven

Two days after the shooting, Carter found himself sitting in a windowless briefing room in the headquarters block at Credenhill. Two figures sat facing him on the other side of the conference table. Peter Hardcastle, the CO of 22 SAS, was a stern-looking man in his late forties, though he looked about a decade older. His bushy eyebrows were perched above small dark eyes set deep into their sockets. His nose looked like a crow's beak; his lips were so thin you could have sliced onions with them. Next to him was Christopher Smallwood, the ops officer, his slight paunch visible beneath his uniform.

Geordie Carter sat opposite the two senior officers, waiting for them to administer the last rites to his career as a Blade.

He'd received the phone call at home earlier that morning. Smallwood's clipped voice travelling down the line, ordering him to report to the camp at eleven o'clock sharp for a meeting with the big boss man. Carter hadn't bothered to ask why he was being called in at such short notice. Didn't need to. He could think of only one good reason why the CO would want to speak with him.

This is about the shooting.

They were going to stick him back on gardening leave. No doubt about it. The logical option, in Carter's mind. Termination of his short-lived stint in G Squadron. No way he could continue serving in Air Troop. Not after his near-death experience outside the King's Arms. He was looking at another stint on the sidelines, winding down his time in the Regiment with bullshit duties. He'd driven up to the camp gates with a leaden feeling in his chest, steeling himself for the bad news.

'How are you, Geordie?' Smallwood asked. Smiling and putting on the chummy act, as if he and Carter were besties. 'How's the arm, mate?'

'Fine,' Carter replied.

'Water? Coffee?'

'Thanks, but no.'

Smallwood reached for a jug of water and poured himself a glass while Hardcastle coughed to clear his throat.

'Let's get straight to it, shall we?' he began in his public schoolboy accent. 'No point beating about the bush. We've been fully briefed on the . . . incident the other day. I must say, this is a terrible disappointment. I expected better from you, Geordie.'

Carter didn't rise to the bait. He'd spent most of his career taking shit from guys like Hardcastle and knew how to handle them. The guy came from old money, like most of the COs who passed through Hereford. Private school, Oxbridge, Sandhurst. The opposite end of the social spectrum from his men.

Hardcastle also had a reputation as a sneaky fucker. Slippery as an eel, they said. The kind of guy who never committed himself to anything. More interested in his career progression than the nuts and bolts of soldiering. A year from now, he'd finish his two-year post at Hereford and make Director Special Forces – providing he didn't drop a bollock before then. From there he'd have a clear path to general. Then head of the British Army, perhaps Deputy Supreme Allied Commander of NATO. Later on, if he played his cards right, he'd have a lucrative post-army career. Knighthood, OBE, a position on the board of one of the big defence contractors. A life trajectory only available to those born into inherited wealth. His experience was so alien to Carter he might as well have belonged to another species.

'The whole thing's a clusterfuck,' Hardcastle ranted. He sounded like a British officer in a Second World War movie. 'Bloody nightmare. Local hacks are all over it, as you can imagine. Damn swarm. Poking their noses where they're not wanted.'

Carter flinched. 'Do they know about my involvement?'

'Thankfully, no. We're trying our best to keep it that way.'

'All they know is that there was a shooting in Madley,' Small-wood said. 'Victim was an unidentified male who suffered light injuries. Potentially gang related. But we could have done without the attention.'

'I was just doing my job,' Carter replied defensively. 'It's not my fault some greasy fucker took a crack at me.'

Hardcastle made a face as if he was chewing on a mouthful of lemons.

'If you were doing your job, Geordie, we wouldn't be sitting here right now. All you had to do was keep your head down, gather evidence and then we could have dealt with the matter quietly, in-house. Instead, I've got DSF on the phone, demanding to know what's going on. We look like a bunch of amateurs, for God's sake.'

Carter tensed his muscles and resisted a compulsive urge to rearrange Hardcastle's mug.

'Do we have any idea who tipped off the Reapers about the investigation?'

'That's not our main concern right now,' Hardcastle replied.

'What's that supposed to mean?'

'This business with the bikers – the Reapers, or whatever they call themselves. We're putting it on the back-burner for the time being. I've instructed Six and the NCA to suspend the investigation indefinitely. DSF agrees. So does the chief of staff.'

Carter looked at him in dismay. 'You're killing the investigation?'

'I didn't say that. We'll revisit the issue once things have calmed down somewhat.'

'Someone fixed it to get me killed. Someone in this fucking camp. And you're just gonna let it slide?'

'You're not looking at the big picture, Geordie.' Hardcastle's voice was dripping with condescension. 'This is a PR disaster for the Regiment. We don't need any more bad headlines. Not after everything else that's happened. I don't need to remind you of the scandals regarding this unit recently. All before my time, of course.'

'What about Duncan? The rest of the Reapers?'

'They'll continue in their duties.' Hardcastle raised a hand, cutting Carter short. 'I understand your displeasure, I really do. But the reality is that we're badly stretched. Oh, you know how it is, Geordie. Never enough men – not that our friends in Whitehall give a fig about such matters, sadly.' He exhaled. 'The truth is, I simply can't afford to lose so many good soldiers. If it was only one or two chaps . . .'

He smiled apologetically.

'Rest assured, we will revisit this matter at a more . . . appropriate time,' he went on. 'But for now, the reputation of the Regiment must take precedence. You understand, Geordie. Don't you? Good man such as yourself. Sure you do.'

He smiled again, but the look in his eyes was so cold it could freeze an embryo.

'Yes, boss,' he muttered.

Carter knew how it would play out. The investigation would be shelved. Hardcastle wouldn't want anything to tarnish his record as CO. Later on, one or two of the guys in the Reapers might be quietly offered early retirement, maybe a promise of security contracts on the Circuit to sweeten the deal. Everyone would come out of it smelling of roses.

It's a cover-up.

'Of course, this does leave us with one loose end.' Hardcastle locked eyes on Carter.

'Me?' Carter squished his eyebrows together.

'Yes,' Hardcastle said smoothly. 'You see, we're juggling rather a lot of balls at the moment, what with our efforts to keep the lid on the goings-on in Air Troop. Not to mention the situation with DSF. Crisis management. Your presence here could, ah, complicate things.'

Carter said, flatly, 'You want me out of Hereford.'

'We're thinking of your safety, man. You were fortunate not to have been badly wounded – or worse, God forbid. Next time, you might not be so lucky. One can easily imagine how that would go down. A serving SAS man shot dead in broad daylight. The media would have a bloody field day.'

'I'm touched by your concerns for my welfare, boss. Really.'

Hardcastle pressed his lips together in a hard line.

Smallwood spread his hands. 'Bottom line, Geordie, we need you out of the way.'

'You're sacking me?'

'No, nothing like that. We just think it's best if you avoid the camp until this situation has been dealt with.'

'I'm with you on that,' Carter said. 'But I can't just go home and lie low. No fucking way. The lads already know I'm the plant. They know where I live. I'll be badly exposed.'

'We know,' Smallwood said. 'That's why we're going to send you overseas. Somewhere nobody from G Squadron can get to you.'

'There's a job,' Hardcastle explained. 'One that requires your particular talents.'

That caught Carter's interest. He sat up straight. 'Where?'

'Ukraine. Christopher tells me you've been on operations there in the past. Before my time, of course.'

Carter nodded stiffly. 'I did a rotation after the Russians rolled into the Donbas. Two years training up the local SF.'

It wasn't public knowledge, but the SAS had been involved in operations in Ukraine since early 2014. The Crimea invasion. Back then, the Ukrainian SF teams had been poorly equipped, demotivated and lacking in specialist training. Carter had been part of the group running the initial courses, and he had been far from impressed.

Poor quality. Couldn't organise a piss-up in a brewery, one of his fellow Blades had complained at the time.

But the Regiment excelled at training foreign troops. They had deep experience, honed over decades of instruction in every corner of the world. They knew what they were doing. It had taken a lot of hard work, but over time Carter and his colleagues had helped transform the Ukrainians into elite SF operators, skilled at sabotage, ambush, reconnaissance, building assaults and counter-insurgency warfare.

When the Russians had rolled across the border, the Ukrainians had been ready for them.

'Speak the local lingo?' Hardcastle asked.

'Enough to get by. I picked up a little Russian too, boss.'

'Russian?' Hardcastle looked impressed. 'How did that happen?'

'Most of the locals spoke it, or a mixture of the two. What they call Surzhyk. I couldn't hold a conversation in Russian, but I could order a drink in Moscow if I had to.'

'Well. I thought you northern types weren't any good at languages. But that may come in handy, on this occasion.'

Carter was growing tired of the CO's bullshit. 'What's the mission?'

'Christopher will brief you on the details.'

Carter tilted his head towards Smallwood. The ops officer. Hardcastle's yes man, and arse-kisser in chief. Who said, 'The operation concerns Viktor Koltrov.'

'I've heard of him. One of their generals.'

Carter recalled the face he'd seen on TV back at Ramstein. The ramrod-straight man with the leather eyepatch, receiving the medal from the Ukrainian president.

'Koltrov is more than just a general. He's Ukraine's most famous soldier. Highly decorated. Which makes him a celebrity in his own right. Second only to the president himself, in fact. Downing Street and Washington both consider him indispensable.'

'Chap thinks he's a damn war hero,' Hardcastle said, a scintilla of contempt in his voice. 'Reckless glory-seeker, more like. His admirers call him the Lion of Ukraine.'

'What's our involvement?'

'As you are no doubt aware,' Hardcastle said, 'the Regiment has been providing support for Ukrainian officials for some time. Training up and advising local bodyguard teams.'

'A detachment from A Squadron has been in-country for several months,' Smallwood explained. 'Providing close protection for the general. The usual drill. Four-man team, working on a two-year posting.'

Smallwood corrected himself.

'It *was* a four-man team. However, one of the lads was injured in a rocket attack in Kyiv last week.'

'Who?'

'Johnny Longstaff. He was running the BG team. Got caught up during a raid on the capital while he was off-duty. Visiting someone he shouldn't have.'

He looked at Carter for a long beat. The latter threw back his head and laughed.

'That sounds like Longstaff all right. Thinking with his small head instead of his big one.'

'In any case, Longstaff is off the team. Convalescing, pending further inquiries into his conduct. Which means the general's BG team is a man down.'

'That's where you come in, Geordie.' Hardcastle spread his thin lips into a wicked smile. 'You're going to take his place.'

Carter paused to digest this. 'You really think this Koltrov bloke is a target for assassination?'

Smallwood said, 'It's a reasonable assumption. Given the state of play.'

'Meaning?'

'The Russians are getting desperate. They're racking up losses at a frightening rate. Retreating from captured cities and towns. Abandoning key strategic positions. Their soldiers are exhausted, and there's no one to train up the new recruits, since many of the

155

most experienced officers are either dead or bogged down with their troops on the frontline. In any normal country, the president would have fallen on his sword by now. Except, Russia isn't a normal country.'

'That's one way of putting it.'

'Quite.' Smallwood took a swig of water. 'Moscow is having to resort to other means to stop the bleeding. Mass artillery bombardment, destruction of civilian infrastructure to starve or freeze the Ukrainians into submission. World War Two tactics.'

'Like those threats to bomb the plant at Holovika, you mean.'

Hardcastle cocked an eyebrow. 'I had no idea you kept abreast of current affairs, Geordie.'

'Yeah, I'm full of surprises, boss,' Carter replied sarkily. 'I can even write my own name these days, believe it or not.'

Hardcastle glowered at him.

Smallwood said, 'As part of their counteroffensive, the Russians are ramping up efforts to assassinate key Ukrainian officials. We believe Koltrov is high on the list.'

'Very high,' Hardcastle added.

Carter scrunched up his face. 'Why would they bother taking him out? This guy gets knocked on the head, it won't change a thing. We'd still flood the country with hardware, drones, training packages. The Russians would still be on a hiding to nothing.'

'That's not how the Kremlin sees it.'

'Koltrov is the second most popular man in Ukraine,' Smallwood said. 'He might not be a big deal over here, but in their eyes he's Hannibal, Grant and Patton rolled into one. Whenever the president is unavailable for media interviews, they turn to Koltrov. If he's killed, it will deal a serious blow to Ukrainian morale.'

Smallwood shifted uncomfortably and darted a knowing glance at the CO.

'There is,' he went on awkwardly, 'another reason for the increased level of protection around Koltrov.'

156

'What's that?' asked Carter.

'The general has been personally assigned a highly sensitive mission. The president himself has entrusted Koltrov with it.' Smallwood hesitated. 'What we're about to tell you is highly classified.'

That pricked Carter's interest. He waited for the ops officer to continue.

'President Voloshyn has tasked Koltrov with hunting down and eliminating fifth columnists,' Smallwood said. 'Traitors, operating within the Ukrainian political and military establishment.'

Carter looked surprised. 'Are there any left? They can't have many friends in Kyiv, not after what the Russians have done to the place.'

Smallwood grimaced. 'The situation is more complicated than that.'

'In what way?'

'Voloshyn enjoys widespread support across Ukraine, but there are some who have split loyalties. People with family across the border, for example. Some are ideologically opposed to integration with the West. Others have been bribed or blackmailed by the Kremlin into doing their bidding.'

'That's the assessment from our friends at Vauxhall,' Hardcastle put in. 'Langley has reached broadly the same conclusions. They're both working closely with the Ukrainian security service.'

'A few of the suspects were flushed out months ago,' Smallwood said. 'Mainly those whose allegiances were well known prior to the invasion. But the intelligence agencies believe several traitors remain in place within the Ukrainian regime, collating intelligence on suspects.'

Hardcastle shot him a warning look. 'For obvious reasons, Kyiv wants to keep this operation secret. Outside of this room, only eight other people are aware of it.'

'Do the Russians know?'

Smallwood said, 'That's up for debate. We have no conclusive evidence. But without going into specifics, we know that other key information has been leaked to the Russians. Realistically, we have to assume they've been alerted to Koltrov's investigation.'

'Clearly, that poses an additional level of risk,' Hardcastle said. 'The Kremlin will be doubly keen to neutralise Koltrov, if they think their assets are in danger of being exposed.'

Carter shook his head. 'I still don't get why you need me on the team. You've already got the guys from A Squadron on the ground. Why not bring one of their lads in to replace Longstaff?'

'We've suggested that. But General Koltrov wants you. In fact, he has personally requested your presence.'

'But I've never met the bloke. Fuck me, I don't know him from Adam.'

Hardcastle stretched a smile across his face.

'It's all thanks to your brother, actually,' he said. 'Very promising soldier, by the way. Good company man, if you know what I mean. Doesn't have any interest in upsetting the apple cart.'

'Luke?' Carter's frown deepened. 'What has he got to do with any of this?'

'He's part of the team overseeing President Voloshyn's BG detail,' Smallwood explained. 'That information isn't to leave this room, by the way. Strictly speaking, we shouldn't even be telling you this.'

Carter nodded absently. He'd heard that Luke and some of the other guys from The Wing had been dispatched to Ukraine, had guessed that they would be working with the local forces in some capacity, but he knew nothing substantial. The activities of the men who served in The Wing were highly secretive – even the other lads at Credenhill were kept out of the loop.

Smallwood continued, 'There was an assassination attempt. On President Voloshyn. Seven days ago.'

Carter felt his heart skip a beat.

'Luke,' he began. 'Is he—'

'Your brother is fine. Nicks and bruises. Nothing that will keep him out of the game.'

'What happened?'

'We're still piecing the evidence together. But it seems that the Russians left a stay-behind team in one of the towns they'd recently abandoned. Chechens. Suicide bombers.'

'They had constructed an underground shelter. They had cameras, a distraction team,' said Hardcastle. 'Very professional. Lots of planning. Therefore, not an opportunistic hit.'

'Shit.'

'Your brother was the hero of the hour. Saved the president's life, by all accounts. If it wasn't for him, they'd still be bagging up body parts in the town square.'

'But I didn't – there wasn't anything on the news.'

'That's because the camera footage was seized by the Ukrainians immediately after the attack. Phones, laptops. Journalists were ordered not to report on the incident under threat of imprisonment. Total media blackout.'

Carter didn't need to ask why. He could guess at the answer. Even a failed attempt on the Ukrainian president would have been seized on by the Russians and presented as a propaganda victory. It would send a clear signal to the Ukrainians.

No one is safe.

Not even your great leader.

'The point is,' said Hardcastle, 'Voloshyn respects your brother. Admires him. Greatly. One might say that Luke has made quite the impression on the president.'

Smallwood said, 'Somehow – we're not sure how – it came to his attention that Luke has a brother in the Regiment.'

'So?'

'We think Voloshyn must have mentioned this to General Koltrov. Told him about Luke saving his life, and your own involvement in the siege in Mali. Koltrov specifically requested you on the team.'

'When was this?'

'A couple of days ago. Right about the time you were leaving the King's Arms.'

'It seems you have impeccable timing, Geordie,' Hardcastle remarked with a sneer. He snorted contemptuously. 'Either that, or you've got the luck of the Irish.'

An ugly laugh escaped Carter's throat.

'Strange idea of luck, that. Sending me off to a fucking war zone.'

The CO's face hardened like cement. 'We're doing you a favour, you bloody fool. Your brother's heroism has given you a way out of a very sticky situation.'

'Just give me the craic,' Carter replied irritably, his patience wearing thin.

Smallwood resumed the briefing.

'You'll take Longstaff's place with immediate effect. As the ranking officer, you'll be in charge of the other guys. You'll also have responsibility for directing and coordinating the Ukrainian soldiers attached to the general's team.'

'Won't be easy, given our man's personality.'

The observation came from Hardcastle.

'How so?'

'Koltrov is a front-foot guy. Brash. Leads from the front. Likes to put himself about. Share the dangers with his men. Meet the troops, shake hands, tell the boys what a good job they're doing while mortars splash down in the background. You get the picture.'

His withering tone and the disapproving look on his face made it clear that Hardcastle took a dim view of senior officers swaggering about on the frontline. Probably felt they should be safely ensconced behind a desk at HQ, at risk of nothing worse than paper cuts and bad coffee.

'If he's putting himself at risk why doesn't Kyiv tell him to rein it in?'

'They can't.'

Smallwood said, 'Voloshyn has gone underground since the assassination attempt. He won't be doing any more media appearances or public speeches until they flush out the traitors. Which means that Koltrov has got to pick up the slack. Politically, they need him out there, fronting it up. It would be a bad look for them if the two most important national figures vanished from public view at the same time.'

Hardcastle sneered.

'Koltrov would be out there regardless. The man's a bloody narcissist. Treats the war as one big ego trip. Trying to make a name for himself. Get himself killed unless someone knocks some sense into his head.'

Smallwood said, 'You'll be operating as a deniable asset. That means you must remain invisible to the cameras whenever the general makes one of his visits to the front. For that reason, you'll be wearing the same uniforms and carrying the same weaponry as the Ukrainians. All of you will wear face masks whenever you're in public.'

Hardcastle said, 'We don't want to flag your involvement to the Russians. That would be very bad for us – for you.'

'How long's the posting?'

'Eighteen months. But it may be longer. Depending on the threat to Koltrov and your assessment of his BG team in the field.'

Hardcastle leaned forward and said, 'Frankly, Geordie, the longer you're out of my camp, the better. You've been nothing but trouble for this Regiment from the moment I got here. You're arsenic.'

Carter stared at him with gritted teeth. He stayed silent.

Don't rise to the bait.

'What's the itinerary?' he asked.

Smallwood said, 'You'll leave first thing tomorrow, flying from Bristol. Wheels up at six o'clock in the morning. Landing at Rzeszów in south-east Poland, a hundred kilometres from the border with Ukraine. That's as close as we can get you, under the circumstances. Ukraine is currently under martial law. Airspace is closed to civilian traffic. Tickets and travel authorisation have already been sorted. One of the Ukrainians from the diplomatic corps will meet you airside and escort you through immigration, so you shouldn't have any problems getting through. Couple of guys from the A Squadron team will pick you up at the airport.'

'Who?'

'Scott Logan and Billy McVeigh. Billy is a recent transfer from B Squadron.'

'Who's the fourth guy?'

'Patrick Webb.'

Carter rubbed his chin and thought: *Logan. Webb. Good lads. Plenty of combat experience. Had their faults, but they were steady and honest pros. On the level.*

At least I won't have to worry about getting stabbed in the back.

McVeigh he knew less about. One of the new faces around camp. Passed Selection in the spring. Mancunian kid from a rough background.

Decades ago, the veterans in each Troop had been in the habit of intimidating the crows. The onus had been on the younger guys to prove themselves. But times had changed. The demands on the Regiment had increased threefold. The new guys were getting badged and going straight into operations. They didn't take shit from the older lads. Not anymore.

'How many Ukrainians?' Carter asked. 'On the team?'

'Six,' Smallwood replied. 'Handpicked men from the SF units, so they should be capable.'

'I should fucking hope so. After all, we trained them.'

'Quite.'

'Where's the general staying?'

'At Novochanka Air Base, outside Kyiv. Separate accommodation for you and the rest of the team. The other guys will brief you

162

fully on the general's itinerary once you arrive in-country. They'll introduce you to the man himself, too.

'Another thing,' he added. 'You'll be travelling data black. Which means you won't be travelling with any personal phones, tablets, laptops. Anything that could potentially flag up your whereabouts to the Russians.'

'Security protocols.' Hardcastle wrinkled his nose, as if he'd detected an evil smell. 'All this business with the Russians, I'm afraid.'

Carter stared at the two officers and waited for an explanation.

Smallwood said, 'We believe Kremlin spooks are scanning arrivals at all the main airports in Poland. Mining the data of everyone who passes through, then using it to track phone signatures in Ukraine. Allows them to identify SAS operators.'

'This is a serious issue,' Hardcastle said. 'Good men have gotten themselves killed because they got sloppy.'

Carter said, 'If I'm travelling without any devices, it'll look suspicious. I'll stand out like a teetotaller at Oktoberfest.'

'We've already thought of that,' said Smallwood. 'We'll provide you with a clean phone and laptop for the first leg of your journey. Dispose of them once you're across the border. You'll be issued with a new phone with a local SIM card in Ukraine.'

'What about hardware? Uniform?'

'Same deal. That will all be sorted out when you reach the base at Novochanka.'

Hardcastle slapped his palms on the armrests and started to lever himself out of his chair. 'Now, I think that's covered the basics. Unless you have any questions . . . ?'

'No, boss,' he replied quietly.

'Good.' The CO raised himself to his feet. 'This should go without saying, but don't fuck this one up. Don't you bloody dare. Because if you do, God help me, I'll ruin you. I'll make fucking sure of it.'

Twelve

Carter dumped his Volvo in the Credenhill camp car park at two o'clock the next morning and transferred his holdall to the boot of a waiting Audi A3 saloon, driven by a potato-faced guy from the MoD police. The driver nodded a hello at Carter and ferried him south towards Bristol in total silence. The usual friendly MoD reception. Carter was beginning to wonder if muteness was an entry requirement for the police force.

Two hours later, Potato Head dropped him outside the main terminal building. Carter grabbed his leather holdall and paced towards the check-in desk. The Regiment had booked him an economy-class ticket to Rzeszów, with a carrier he'd never heard of. He passed through security, bought an overpriced coffee and a tepid full English breakfast from a garishly lit restaurant, then joined the throng of passengers cattle-herded into the departure gate. The other travellers seemed to be mostly Polish families returning home for one reason or another, along with a handful of businessmen. No tourists, as far as Carter could tell. South-eastern Poland wasn't a big holiday destination. That much was clear.

They boarded the Boeing 737 half an hour behind schedule. Carter crammed himself into his seat, his knees pressed against the back of the seat in front of him, closed his eyes and reflected on the many joys of low-cost air travel. Going in by military aircraft would have been more pleasant, probably.

They touched down at Rzeszów-Jasionka airport two-and-a-half hours later. Ten o'clock in the morning local time. The plane rumbled to a halt, the seatbelt lights pinged off and there was the usual scramble of passengers in the aisles, jostling for space, bumping into one another and hauling luggage out of the overhead compartments.

Carter grabbed his holdall and followed the crowd shuffling out of the aircraft. A sharp wind tugged at his jacket as he descended the air stairs. He immediately spotted a lanky guy in an ill-fitting suit striding towards him from across the apron. The tall man thrust out a meaty paw.

'Mr Carter, yes?'

'That's right.'

The guy flashed his diplomatic ID. 'Eduard Surakov,' he said in broken English. 'I'm from the Ukrainian consulate in Lublin. I was told to expect you this morning.'

'Where are the others?'

'Your friends are inside. This way, please.'

Surakov led him towards a side door, away from the long line of passengers snaking out of the main terminal entrance. They climbed a set of stairs, walked straight through arrivals and strolled past the border guards. The fast-track treatment. No one stopped to challenge them. Guards nodded deferentially and waved them through. Everything had been cleared in advance, Carter assumed. The Ukrainians probably had a standing arrangement with their Polish allies. They had a sizeable number of assets transiting through Poland before making their way across the border. Better to make the process as smooth as possible. A mutual interest thing. If Kyiv fell, the Poles would be next in the Kremlin's cross hairs.

A few minutes after landing, they swept into the arrivals hall. Surakov led him through the bustling crowd, towards a familiar figure standing beside a news kiosk.

'Bloody hell,' Scott Logan said as they approached. 'Geordie fucking Carter, as I live and breathe. Thought you'd be signing on the dole by now, mate.'

Carter grinned. 'Isn't that your family tradition?'

'Claiming benefits? Nah, lad. Popular misconception, that. You're confusing us with them scum up the road in Manchester.'

They shook hands. Scott Logan looked like a boy-band member on steroids. Blond-haired, blue-eyed and lean, with a neat line in banter. The kind of guy who could charm the birds out of the trees. Liverpool born and bred, he had moved south to work for a brokerage firm in the City before chucking it in to become a full-time soldier. He and Carter had done Selection together; Logan's easy-going manner had helped lighten the mood during the grimmest days up on the Brecons.

Logan had a reputation as a serial shagger: the others jokingly referred to him as Sex Machine. It was an open secret around the camp that he was having an affair with the wife of a young captain, but whereas other lads would worry about getting caught, Logan didn't seem fazed. The guy thrived off living dangerously.

'Come on,' he said. 'Car's outside. We'll fill you in on the ride.'

Surakov left them and disappeared through an unmarked door. Carter followed Logan outside, past the taxi rank, across the short-stay car park, towards a big, boxy Chevrolet Suburban at the far end.

As they drew near, the driver's side door flung open and a sinewy bearded guy stepped out.

'Geordie, this is Billy McVeigh,' said Logan. 'Billy, Geordie.'

Carter cast an eye over the younger man. McVeigh had a lean, tightly coiled look about him. His hands looked like they had been cast from concrete. Cold blue eyes peered out from beneath a mop of ginger hair. His thick unkempt beard was the colour of rust; his body language carried a hint of latent violence. As if he might explode into action in the blink of an eye.

He looked aggressive. Motivated. Angry. Ready to fight the world.

Like Carter himself, ten years earlier.

He had heard about McVeigh, had seen him around the camp a few times, but the two had never properly met. By the time the latest batch of students had completed Selection, Carter had already been sent on gardening leave. He knew only two things about McVeigh: he was hard as fuck, and he had quickly gained a reputation as a cocky operator, with a very high opinion of himself.

An amused expression played out on McVeigh's face. 'I didn't know they were sending us another dinosaur.'

'Geordie's a legend of the Regiment,' Logan said. 'One of the best in the business. Me and him have done plenty of ops together. Iraq, Afghanistan. All over. Isn't that right, Geordie?'

'Something like that.'

McVeigh smirked and said, 'As long as you don't bore us to death on the drive back with your old war stories. I've had enough of that shite from Scott to last a lifetime.'

'We're not that old, you little twat.'

McVeigh's eyes glinted a challenge. 'Could have fooled me. From where I'm standing you look fucking prehistoric.'

Carter glared silently at him.

'He's just pulling the piss, Geordie,' Logan said, slapping him on the back. 'You know how it is with the new lads nowadays. Think they're a bunch of comedians.'

'Maybe so,' Carter replied, addressing Logan but keeping his gaze firmly on the younger soldier. 'But he won't be laughing when he's picking his teeth off the fucking floor.'

McVeigh scowled at him. Logan grinned and said, 'Get in, Geordie. We've got a long ride ahead of us.'

Carter popped the rear door, scooched himself into the middle row of seats and dumped the holdall beside him. Logan smuggled into the front passenger seat, while McVeigh took the wheel. The inside of the Suburban had the new-car smell of fresh leather, car polish and some kind of chemical cleaning agent.

McVeigh fired up the engine. He punched in an address on the touchscreen mounted on the dash, turned out of the car park and followed the satnav directions, heading east then south on a half-empty dual carriageway. After several kilometres they took the next slip road, and a few minutes later they were bowling eastward along the motorway towards the Ukrainian border. McVeigh kept the Suburban ticking along at seventy per, ten kilometres below the speed limit.

Logan started to unwrap a chocolate bar and said, 'You hungry, mate? There's some food in the back. Protein bars, snacks, shit like that. Bottled water, too.'

'No, mate. I'm fine.'

Carter had trained himself to survive on very little. In Afghanistan, during the long months he had spent as an embed, directing and fighting alongside SF forces, he had subsisted on a diet of tea, bread and fruit.

Logan, on the other hand, had a monstrous appetite. The guy never stopped eating. On the escape-and-evasion phase of Selection, he had been more worried about his stomach than getting caught. Where it all went – given his honed physique – remained one of the enduring mysteries of Hereford.

Logan tore off a chunk of chocolate and said, 'It's a ten-hour drive to Novochanka from here. Ninety minutes to the border. We should reach the base by nine o'clock tonight, or thereabouts.' He caught Carter's eye in the rear-view mirror. 'How much did Smallwood tell you?'

'The basics. Bare bones of the job. Said you'd brief us on the details.'

'Yeah, well. I don't know what you were expecting, but you're in for a surprise.'

'I've been a Blade for a long time. Nothing surprises me anymore.'

168

Logan grunted. 'That's what I thought when we started the job. But it's turning into a nightmare. More like guarding a Hollywood celebrity than a general.'

'Scott's right,' McVeigh said in his Mancunian accent, eyes pinned to the road. 'Now Voloshyn has gone underground the general has an increased workload. Meet-and-greets all over the fucking shop, showing his mug on the frontline. Pain in the arse.'

'He's mobbed wherever he goes.' Logan was speaking with a mouthful of chocolate. 'The troops love him. Treat him like a superstar. But it makes our jobs ten times as hard.'

'Does he follow your advice?'

McVeigh laughed. 'Does he fuck. We've told him he can't keep exposing himself like this, but he won't listen.'

Logan said, 'It's all that media attention he's been getting lately. Posing for selfies with world leaders. Doing interviews with the big newspapers. Hearing soldiers cheering his name and urging him to run for president. Gone to his head, Geordie. Thinks he's invincible.'

Carter said, 'What's the routine?'

'Depends,' said Logan. 'Sometimes he sticks around in Kyiv to attend meetings, TV interviews and such. On those days, it's a straight drive from the air base to his office at the Ministry of Defence. Back again in the evening.'

'And the rest of the time?'

'That's when it gets dicey. One day he might decide to make a flying visit to one of the army encampments. The next day he's off interrogating some suspected traitor in a police station in the back of beyond. Day after that, he might be sitting down to schnapps with the mayor of a liberated town. Guy barely stops. Got more energy than the National Grid. The only time you can truly relax is when he's on base.'

'Why? What's he doing then?'

'Not what, mate. *Who.*'

'Hookers,' McVeigh explained. 'General Koltrov is a big fan.'

169

Logan said, 'The general gets them in his dorm most evenings. We're practically guaranteed to clock off at nine o'clock on the dot. You can catch your breath, have a brew and a doss, knowing the randy fucker will be occupied until the next morning.'

'What about his family?' Carter asked.

'Wife and two kids,' Logan replied. 'Daughter aged seven, son is twelve. They're safe and sound in Prague. Well out of harm's way.'

'Hence the hookers,' McVeigh said.

Logan glanced at him disapprovingly. 'You know I don't like that word.'

'I don't like your face,' McVeigh retorted. 'Or your accent. But I don't have a go at you for it.'

Logan sighed and said, 'Anyway, yeah, the general gets his girls in. You know how it goes, Geordie. Playing away from home. As long as you're in different countries, it's fair game. Oldest rule in the book, that.'

'What book is that, then?' McVeigh quipped. 'The old farts' guide to dating?'

'Sod off, Billy. Twat.'

'Where are we dossing?' asked Carter, changing the subject.

'Main accommodation block,' Logan said. 'Basic, like, but liveable. One step up from a prison cell. That's where we'll be staying while we're on site.'

'And the other BGs? The Ukrainians?'

'Same location. They tend to keep to themselves. They're friendly enough.'

'Capable?'

Logan paused to consider the question. 'I've seen worse. And I've seen better. But they're keen to learn, and they work hard. Can't ask for much more than that.'

'Where's the general now?'

'At Novochanka. He's hunkered down for the day in his private quarters, running over the plan for tomorrow.'

'Why? What's happening tomorrow?'

McVeigh said, 'There's an operation. In Kyiv. The general's planning an arrest.'

'Who's the target?'

'The current defence minister. Andriy Butko. Rising star of the government, they say.'

Logan let out a belch and said, 'The general's been running surveillance on him for weeks. Intelligence-gathering and what-have-you. But things were ramped up after the Chechens tried to take out Voloshyn last week. That's when Koltrov knew for sure that the Russians had someone close to the president.'

Carter furrowed his brow. He thought about his brother again. Luke. The man who had saved the life of the Ukrainian president. He wondered where he was now, what he was doing.

He said, 'Is the general sure this minister is working for the Russians?'

McVeigh said, 'Looks that way. There's a ton of evidence against him. Bank transfers. Unexplained payments to secret accounts. They think he's been using a go-between to contact his Russian handlers. Some priest in the Orthodox Church. His spiritual advisor.'

Logan said, 'Butko is a senior minister. He wouldn't risk making direct contact with the Russians.'

'Where's the priest now?'

'Russia,' said McVeigh. 'A team was sent in to arrest him three days ago, but he'd already legged it across the border.'

Logan said, 'Butko is our man, all right. He's been under the microscope for a while. The general believes he's been working for the Russians on the sly, feeding them int from cabinet briefings and details of Ukrainian troop deployments. We think he's the one who tipped off the Chechens about the president's movements.'

'What's the plan?' asked Carter.

McVeigh said, 'The general is going to arrest Butko at his office at the defence ministry. We'll be accompanying him.'

'Anyone else in the general's party?'

'Anton Makarenko. That's the general's 2iC. Rank of Colonel. Loyal as a basset hound. Follows Koltrov around everywhere he goes. Along with his press officer, Anna Zinchenko.'

'Now there's a fine woman,' Logan said wistfully. 'Got a figure on her that would put most models to shame, and she's tough to boot. Married, though. Crying shame, that.'

'That hasn't stopped you before,' Carter observed.

'Guilty as charged.' Logan grinned sheepishly, looked round at McVeigh.

'Speaking of which. You could do with a bit of that in your life, Billy. Spend less time beasting yourself in the gym and enjoy a bit of female company instead. Might even remove that giant chip from your shoulder.'

'Fuck off.'

Carter said, 'What happens once the arrest has been made?'

'The minister will be whisked away to a secure location and subjected to hard interrogation. General Koltrov will question the minister personally.'

'If he's guilty?'

'Then he'll disappear, like the others.'

'Others?' Carter repeated.

Logan nodded and said, 'Koltrov has been going after the traitors aggressively. He's a ruthless bastard. I'll give him that,' he added with a hint of admiration.

'What happens to them?'

'Put it this way. They're not being offered tea and biscuits,' McVeigh said.

'Bullet in the back of the head,' Logan said. 'Unmarked grave.'

'Jesus.'

Logan said, 'The Ukrainians are fighting a war for survival. Defending the motherland. Respecting the rights of fifth column-ists isn't at the top of their list of priorities. Besides, it's nothing

compared to what the Russians have been doing to the local popu-
lace. Rape, torture, mass graves. Bombing the country into the
Stone Age. Fucking barbaric. So yeah, I'm not going to lose any
sleep about a few traitors getting the rough treatment. We've got
more important things to worry about.'

'Such as?'

'Keeping the general alive. You'll need to stay fucking sharp,
boy. Once the job starts, you'll see what I mean.'

'Is it really that bad?' Carter said doubtfully.

'No, mate. It's worse.'

Logan twisted in his seat and looked round at Carter, his tanned
face stamped with concern.

'The guy's reckless. Goes around acting like he's fucking bulletproof or something. It's like he doesn't really believe he's in danger
of getting assassinated.'

He looked away with growing anxiety. The smooth brow wrinkled with frown lines.

'Why would he put his life on the line?' Carter wondered. 'He
must know it would be a PR disaster if he got taken out by the
Russians.'

McVeigh snorted. 'He doesn't see it that way.'

'He thinks he knows best,' Logan said. 'Whenever we try to tell
him to slow down, he just ignores us. It took months to get him to
agree just to bolster his vehicles. Until a week ago, we were zipping
around in soft-skinned vehicles. And these Chevys aren't even
armoured.'

Carter shook his head. 'Then they won't be any good. Not if we
run into an ambush. We'd need something more solid to stop a
bullet.'

'That's what we told him.'

'What did he say?'

'The guy didn't give a toss. Said he didn't want to give the impression to his soldiers that he was afraid of being taken out.'

Logan gazed out of the side window, face taut with tension.

'He's going to get himself killed one of these days,' he added quietly. 'Unless we can get him to apply the handbrake, this job is going to go pear-shaped very fast.'

McVeigh grunted with frustration.

'Either that,' he said bitterly, 'or one of us is gonna die taking a bullet for him.'

Thirteen

They hit the Ukrainian border shortly before midday. Carter was surprised to find the area was relatively quiet. He'd expected to see long lines of people fleeing the country on foot, weighed down with their worldly possessions, sprawling tented refugee camps, news crews, reception areas policed by swarms of heavily armed border guards. Instead, the checkpoint looked like any other. There was a long line of articulated lorries and vans waiting to cross into Ukraine, a separate queue of saloons and hatchbacks and motorbikes, the three-lane road flanked by harvested fields on one side and a trash-littered rest stop on the other. Truck drivers stretched their legs and smoked cigarettes while a handful of guards and sniffer dogs searched their cargoes. A handful of people were crossing the border on foot, carrying rucksacks or shopping bags, some pushing along bicycles. Hard to believe there was a war going on to the east.

But then he reminded himself that the conflict had been raging for seven months. That picture – refugee camps, desperate crowds of fleeing civilians, terror stamped on their faces – belonged to an earlier time. The first days of the invasion. Things had dramatically shifted since then. The scores of old Russia hands, think-tank academics and Kremlin-watchers who had predicted a swift and brutal victory for the Russian war machine had been wrong. The defenders had not folded. President Voloshyn and his generals – men like Koltrov – had inspired their fellow citizens to resist the enemy at all costs. Slowly, the picture on the ground had changed. The Russian offensive had faltered, then reversed. The exodus from the cities had dwindled. People were choosing to stay and fight. Or returning home to take up arms.

McVeigh joined the tailback of civilian vehicles slowly crawling towards the checkpoint. After what felt like a long time, they reached the guard post on the Ukrainian side of the border. A couple of guards approached, McVeigh buzzed down the driver's side window and handed over their passports to a surly-looking guy in an olive-green thermal hat, along with their official Ukrainian Ministry of Defence ID cards, issued to all four Blades on Koltrov's BG team.

The guard took a long hard look at their documents while his scrawny mate stood close by, gripping his standard-issue AK-74 assault rifle and giving them his best screw-face. The guard in the thermal hat disappeared into the guardhouse to make a phone call, and there was a short wait before he came back a minute later, dragging on a cigarette. He thrust the documents back at McVeigh and waved the Suburban through. The boom barriers raised, McVeigh started the engine. Two minutes later, they were motoring through western Ukraine.

After five or six kilometres, they stopped again. McVeigh eased into a lay-by and kept the engine running while Carter hopped out, removed the SIM card from his dummy phone, crushed it beneath the heel of his boot, then tossed the handset and laptop into a thicket of gorse and heather. He jumped back into the Suburban, while Logan sprang open the glove box and handed him a cheap handset.

'Here,' he said. 'Clean phone. Local SIM card. Numbers for myself, Billy and Patrick are stored in the address book. Number for the general's 2iC, Makarenko, too. Battery on these models is shite, but there are charging points at the base, and in the wagons, so you shouldn't run out of juice. Portable power station in the boot in case of an emergency.'

'Is it encrypted?'

'Is it fuck. There's better security on the door of my local.'

'So what's the point in us having them?'

'Strictly for emergencies only. In case the comms goes down for whatever reason. Which happens, from time to time. You know what it's like with the kit.'

Carter put away the phone, remembered that Kyiv was an hour ahead of Poland, two hours ahead of London, and adjusted the time on his G-Shock Rangeman.

They rejoined the motorway and carried on in silence. Some minutes later, Logan spoke again. 'Must be a new experience for you, Geordie. Following in your brother's footsteps.'

Carter laughed and said, 'We might be in the same country, doing the same job, but that's where the similarities end.'

'How's that?'

'Luke's an old head on young shoulders. Gets on with the job, stays out of trouble. Me? I've been making enemies my whole fucking life.'

'Are you close?'

Carter nodded. 'Luke's the only family I've got.'

'You must be proud of him. Took some quick thinking to stop those Chechens from killing the president. Got some guts on him, your little brother. Like that incident with the mines in Afghan.'

Carter stared out of the window and said nothing. He knew the story: the guys at Hereford had talked about nothing else for a while.

Seven years ago, during Luke's time as RSM with the Parachute Regiment, a team of guys had been out on patrol when they had stumbled into an IED ambush. One man had been killed instantly. Another soldier had been mortally wounded when he had been sent in to retrieve the metal detectors left behind by the first patrol. His mucker had lost an arm and a leg when he had tried to drag his maimed comrade to safety and stepped off the track, triggering another mine.

All the equipment had eventually been recovered, but the grisly job of collecting the body parts remained to be done: the Taliban were known to collect soldiers' severed limbs and genitalia and display them outside their houses as trophies, which caused the maimed soldiers a great deal of distress. Instead of waiting for the clearance team to show up, Luke had calmly walked into the ambush area and gathered up the body parts, before handing them to the padre to dispose of correctly.

Luke had earned universal respect for his actions, and rightly so. It was a fine example of the Maroon Machine mentality at its finest. Bravery. Thinking of your brothers-in-arms. Putting yourself on the line. Not ordering your subordinates to do something you wouldn't be prepared to do yourself.

'What he did was admirable,' Carter said, after a long pause. 'But he shouldn't have done it.'

'You think he was wrong?' Logan asked, eyes round with surprise.

'He was gambling with his life. Could have lost his legs if he'd stepped on a mine. The sensible thing to do would have been to hold off until the clearance team had arrived. Having said that, I know why Luke did it.'

'Why?'

'He didn't want to shirk the responsibility. Not his style. He's always been the kind of guy who puts himself forward. No one ever had to force him to do anything. He just went and did it. Never questioned the orders. That's the difference between us.'

'What about you?' McVeigh asked. 'What's your deal? I heard you were on long-term leave.'

'Who told you that?'

'It's hardly a big fucking secret, Geordie,' Logan said, lifting his eyes from the road to the rear-view. 'Everyone knows.'

McVeigh said, 'What did you do?'

Carter didn't reply. He cast his mind back eleven months ago. The covert mission to Afghanistan, on the trail of his mentor. He'd discovered that a hero of the Regiment had gone over to the dark side. Opium smuggling. Acquiring nukes on the black market. An operation that resulted in the death of an ex-SAS man, and a CIA officer.

He had no intention of telling McVeigh and Logan about the Afghan op. Or the goings-on in G Squadron. The Liverpudlian had a reputation around the camp as a shameless gossip.

If I fill him in, everyone in Hereford will know about the stories soon enough. Even the camp slop jockeys.

'Ancient history,' he replied tersely. 'I don't want to talk about it.'

McVeigh said, 'Fucking strange, though. The head shed sending you out here like this.'

'Not really,' Carter said, tonelessly. 'Blame your man Longstaff. If that idiot had kept his dick in his pants, he wouldn't have been fragged in that rocket attack. And I wouldn't be here.'

'But why you? Last I heard, you were being transferred to G Squadron. Now you're being cross-decked to our Troop. They could have sent one of our lads out.'

'There's no mystery,' Carter said tonelessly, sticking to the story he'd agreed with the CO beforehand. 'I've made enemies. The head shed was looking for an opportunity to kick me out of Hereford. Then they had one. End of story.'

Logan glanced back at him in amazement. 'Fucking hell, son. Hardcastle must really hate you.'

'Yeah, well. The feeling's mutual.'

'You don't know how to play the game, Geordie. That's your problem.'

Carter chuckled. 'You sound like my brother.'

'Speaking of which. If you're hoping to catch up with Luke for a few beers in Kyiv, you're shit out of luck.'

'Why's that?'

Logan clicked his tongue. He said, 'The president's off the grid. His BG team is hunkering down with him until this business with the fifth columnists is sorted. Even the general can't get hold of him.'

'Sounds like Voloshyn is worried.'

179

'He should be. The Kremlin is desperate to put a bullet between his eyes.'

Carter said, 'Even if they did get him, killing Voloshyn wouldn't change a thing on the ground. Not at this stage. If anything, it would turn him into a martyr. Motivate the Ukrainians to keep on resisting.'

Logan shook his head fiercely. 'The Russians aren't thinking strategically, Geordie. They're getting their arses kicked and thrashing about looking for a way to tip the scales in their favour. Everything's on the table, whether it helps them win or not.'

'Maybe they're not looking that far ahead,' McVeigh mused.

'How d'you mean?' asked Logan.

McVeigh gave a shrug and said, 'If the Russians eliminate the president and his generals, people will start to think they've lost the plot. They'll wonder what else they're prepared to do.'

'So?'

'It might make NATO think twice about the wisdom of helping to fund the war effort. Might even persuade them to bring Ukraine to the negotiating table, if they think the Russians are prepared to do something crazy.'

'Whatever the reason,' Logan said, 'your brother won't be going anywhere. Not while the president's staying out of sight.'

'Shame Koltrov ain't taking the same approach,' McVeigh muttered. 'Would make our lives a lot fucking easier if he stopped popping his head above the parapet every chance he gets.'

'Wishful thinking. The guy's a shameless attention-seeker. More chance of finding a one-ended stick.'

McVeigh grunted. 'I'll be glad when this mission is over. Get back to Hereford and finish my dissertation. Better than nursemaiding this flaming idiot.'

'You're studying?' Carter asked.

'Two-year course at uni. Security management. Cyber. Distance learning. Paid for by the Regiment.'

'Waste of time, if you ask me,' Logan grunted. 'You're supposed to be a soldier. Bloke like you should be practising at the Killing House, not writing essays.'

'You won't be saying that in a few years,' McVeigh said, 'when I'm running my own company on the Circuit and you're begging us for a job.'

'Work for you?' Logan looked horrified. 'Fuck off. Rather take a cheese grater to my balls.'

'He's right, though,' Carter said. 'It's not like it was in our day, mate. You need qualifications now. Degrees and masters. The world's changed. Things have moved on.'

'Have they? Look around you.' Logan indicated the endless flat terrain rushing past. 'We're still fighting wars with bullets and tanks, last time I checked. The Russians are still trying to knock seven shades of shit out of their neighbours. You spend a week here, then tell me the world's any different.'

No one said anything for several beats. Then Logan flashed a grin at McVeigh and said, 'On the bright side, at least I know what to get you for Christmas.'

'Yeah? What's that?'

'Nice shiny briefcase. Carry your papers around.'

McVeigh chortled. 'Everything's digital these days, Grandpa. You'd know that, if you weren't stuck in the past.'

Carter fell silent and stared out of the window. The sky had darkened; a light rain was beginning to fall. He thought about his brother again. Luke Carter. Unquestionably a fine soldier. A leader of men. But Carter worried about how he would fare at Hereford in the long run.

Regiment operators – or some of them – tended to be more snakish than the lads in the green army ranks. The unit attracted the gamblers and the renegades, the loners who had no tolerance level for the yes-sir no-sir bullshit of the parade ground. If Luke had a fault, it was his tendency to trust people, to take them at face value and assume they shared the same moral values. He didn't always see the big picture. Didn't realise that the system was corrupt. In the cut-throat world of 22 SAS, Carter feared he might get chewed up by the big beasts.

I just hope he doesn't make the same mistakes as me.

They motored through a landscape of muted browns and greys. Low hills interrupted the level plains, crowned with thinning clumps of pine and birch. Further on, Carter saw battalions of rolled haystacks and coppiced woods and sprawling fields of rye and barley, their flowery spikes swaying in the afternoon wind.

After ninety minutes, they hit the outskirts of Lviv. They skirted around the depressing fringes of the city, stopped at a petrol station and topped up the Suburban's twenty-eight-gallon tank, then continued eastward. Carter scanned the streets but saw no signs of the recent conflict. No buildings reduced to rubble, or flamed-out tanks, or rocket craters lining the streets. People were sitting in coffee shops, or getting their hair cut, or playing football, or doing any of the multitude of things that constituted normal civilian life.

When he pointed this out to Logan, the Liverpudlian made a pained expression.

'Place was a lot different a few months ago,' he said. 'Back then it was chaos. Air raid sirens, rocket attacks. Crowds of refugees piling in from the east. Everyone in a big flap, trying to get out of the country. Now it's calmed down. You can go out, grab a beer, find a bite to eat at a nice restaurant.'

'What about Kyiv?'

'Same, basically. Everyone is trying to get on with their lives.' Logan's face was a picture of concentration as he tried to find the right words. 'It's weird. The city is almost . . . normal. Apart from the sirens, and the nightly curfew, and the soldiers manning the checkpoints. Different story in the east, though.'

'I can imagine.'

Logan shook his head slowly. 'No, mate. You really can't. Places out there have been wiped off the map by the Russians. Like those photographs of Berlin at the end of the Second World War. Nothing left except bombed-out buildings and rubble. The rebuild will cost a fucking fortune.'

Carter said, 'Do you think they'll lose?'

'Who, the Russians? It's possible. They're definitely getting their arses kicked at the moment. Problem is, the more ground they lose, the more they're likely to lash out. But I'm sure of one thing.'

'What's that?'

'This war is pure fucking hell for the people living in the east. And it's going to get worse. Once the winter sets in, those poor bastards will be freezing cold, with no heating or electricity. God knows how many of them are going to die.'

* * *

The rain became heavier as the afternoon wore on. Needle-sized drops drenched the wheat fields and spattered the windscreen, tracing watery veins down the glass. Logan subjected Carter to a long and rambling commentary on the many charms of Ukrainian women. He was a big fan of them, apparently. Reckoned they knew some tricks that could put a smile on the face of a cleric. And they could drink, too, he said. He'd seen local women knocking back enough vodka to put some of the Regiment drinkers to shame. All in all, he was an enthusiastic convert.

McVeigh said nothing. He fixed his angry gaze on the road, like he had a personal beef with it.

At seven o'clock, they reached Zhytomyr, and Carter figured they were no more than a couple of hours from the old air force base at Novochanka. In the gathering dusk, the gilded onion-shaped domes of Orthodox churches caught the last rays of the autumn light and flamed like torches. Carter saw occasional signs of the missile attacks that had rained down on the city recently: a playground reduced to a tangle of twisted metal and debris, a mountain of rubble from a destroyed housing block, the burned-out carcasses of cars.

Ninety minutes later, they passed the small city of Fastiv and cut north-east for maybe thirty kilometres before they hit a mid-sized town. Soviet-era apartment blocks pierced the gloomy sky-line, foregrounded by pastel-coloured civic buildings, medieval churches and lampposts surmounted with storks' nests. Billboards carried messages of support for the troops on the front.

The road funnelled them north of the town on a two-lane stretch of tree-lined blacktop before they reached a military checkpoint. Half a dozen armed soldiers with AK-74 rifles stood guard in front of a wall of sandbags. Behind them, Carter identified a pair of Spartan armoured personnel carriers, equipped with .50 calibre machine guns and anti-tank missiles on the turrets. A Ukrainian flag hung from a steel pole next to a crude guard post. Concrete barriers had been positioned on alternating sides of the road a hundred metres downstream from the checkpoint, forcing drivers to lower their speed and approach in single file. There was a bat-tered STOP sign staked into the dirt at the side of the road, in case anyone failed to take the hint.

McVeigh eased the Suburban down to twenty per and weaved through the precast barriers before drawing to a halt in front of the two guards manning the checkpoint. The soldiers flashed their Ukrainian ID cards at the nearest guard; she gave each of them a close inspection before shouting an order at her colleagues to step aside and let them through.

'How many guys are living at the base?' Carter asked as they chuntered on past the checkpoint.

'Two hundred all in,' Logan said.

'Security?'

'Dog teams on twenty-four-hour patrol of the perimeter. Soldiers on the inner and outer cordons. No illumination at night, so we're not visible to drones or satellites. Place is as secure as a Chinese city in a pandemic.'

'Anti-aircraft weaponry?'

'Starstreak missile emplacements, guarded by a detachment of soldiers from the 30th Mechanized Brigade. Blastproof shelter beneath the main accommodation blocks.' Logan grinned. 'We're as safe as houses here.'

'What about the staff?'

'All thoroughly vetted. No one is allowed in or out of the base without prior clearance.'

'Not even the general's women?'

'Not even.'

'Who's in charge of vetting them?'

'Makarenko. The general's 2iC. He vets them personally.'

'Is he searching them girls for devices?'

'Far as I know, everyone is checked for electronic footprints before they're allowed on the base.'

'They didn't check us.'

'They didn't need to. We're known to the guards. They see our faces every day. Trust me. The girls are clean. Apart from the obvious.' Logan grinned.

McVeigh didn't join in the laughter. 'Fucking miracle.'

'What's that, son?'

'Your jokes,' McVeigh said. 'They just get more and more shit.'

Carter said, 'Have there been any attacks on the base?'

'Not since we moved in. Once in a blue moon the Russians get frustrated and lob a few rockets at the nearby towns. In the spring, they wiped out the camp to the north, so the general had to shift his operations here. But they haven't laid a glove on the base, not since we've been here.'

'Why not?'

Logan thought about this for a few beats. 'Maybe they don't know we're here. The base is out of commission and has been since the days of the Cold War. No planes take off from here or anything like that. Like we're hiding in plain sight.'

They stuck to the same road for half a kilometre, along a smooth stretch of tarmac fringed with one-storey breeze-block shacks, discount supermarkets and half-finished high-rises. Stray dogs padded along the weed-infested pavement, sniffing at bags of rubbish. After several minutes, McVeigh took a sharp left and pulled up in front of the gate at the main entrance to Novochanka Air Base. Two more soldiers strutted out of the reinforced gatehouse and there was another delay while they checked the Blades' documents. Phone calls were made, orders given, the automated gate whirred open, and then they were arrowing through the grounds of the base.

The access road took them past the main control tower and a row of administrative blocks and parking bays. Then McVeigh turned left again and followed the road as it ran parallel to a row of ugly concrete buildings. He pulled up in front of the nearest structure, next to a couple of identical Suburbans and a muddle of other military vehicles concealed beneath camo nets.

'This is us,' Logan said as McVeigh killed the engine.

They climbed out of the Chevy. Carter lugged out his holdall and took in the view. Which didn't amount to much. Beyond the road, several hundred metres to the north, the main runway ran on a north-west axis for a couple of kilometres. Bomb craters scarred the tarmac in places. There was a helipad close to the hangars, apparently still in use, with the landing spot presently occupied by a British Sea King helicopter. But the rest of the base was in a state of neglect. Weeds poked through the concrete. The rusting hulk of an old Antonov transport aircraft rested in front of a dilapidated hangar, next to an abandoned fire tender.

Logan continued his one-man guided tour.

'Ukrainians are in the same building, but they don't bother us none. Canteen on the ground floor. Food is shite, though. Unless you've got a passion for pork knuckles and borscht.'

186

'Amazing the soldiers here aren't all as fat as fuck,' McVeigh muttered. 'The shit they shove into their pieholes.'

Logan said, 'There's a restaurant in the town. We usually go there whenever we get the chance. Curfew is at eleven o'clock, but the place is dead by then anyway.'

'Where's the general dossing?'

'Separate part of the base. Private dormitory block. We'll introduce you tomorrow. No point disturbing him tonight. He's probably stark bollock naked right now, having fun with one of his regulars. Lucky bugger,' Logan said.

'Who's guarding him now?' asked Carter.

'Ukrainian soldiers,' McVeigh said. He spat on the ground. 'We don't get involved on that front, not while the general is on site. Between them lot and the perimeter defences, he's well covered. Three-sixty protection. We're only needed when the guy is on the move.'

Logan glanced at his watch. 'Let's get you sorted in your digs, then we'll grab some scoff before evening prayers. I'm starving.'

Carter looked at him in disbelief. 'You've been snacking non-stop since we hit the road, you greedy bastard.'

'What can I say? I'm a man with a big appetite.'

'In more ways than one,' McVeigh said under his breath.

Logan didn't appear to have heard the younger Blade. 'Food first,' he said. 'Then we'll go through the plan for the arrest tomorrow.'

Fourteen

They stepped through the entrance, led Carter up a flight of stairs and showed him to his room. Which consisted of a metal-framed single bed with a lumpy mattress, a chair and desk and an old cast-iron radiator, the cream paint flaking in places. There were damp patches on the bare walls, and a chill draught whispered through the gaps in the window frame. Strips of black masking tape formed a 'V' across the pane, to stop the glass from shattering in the event of a rocket attack. But which also reduced the amount of natural light in the room. A naked bulb dangled from the stained ceiling.

Carter wasn't bothered. He had stayed in worse digs. He didn't care where he slept, as long as he had somewhere to get his head down. One of the many things that traditionally distinguished the Regiment from their brother warriors in Delta and the SEALs, in his experience. The Americans were used to getting all the best kit, first-class accommodation, decent food. All the creature comforts. But if they were deprived of them, for whatever reason, they struggled to cope. The guys in the SAS had never suffered the same problem. They learned early on to make do and get on with the job.

'Ukrainian SF clobber,' Logan said, pointing to a bulky kitbag on the floor. 'Everything you'll need to blend into the background. Uniform, boots, gloves, helmet. All in your sizes. Unless you've been piling on the pounds since your last op.'

Carter chuckled. 'I'm not a food monster, mate. That's your party trick.'

'Healthy sex life, Geordie. Best way of keeping off the pounds.'

'Long as you don't have a problem contracting gonorrhoea,' McVeigh joked.

Carter joined in with the laughter. Logan glared at them both with tight-lipped anger. Then he said, 'We wear the uniforms whenever we're off base. Civvies when we're on site.'

Carter dumped his holdall on the mattress, then followed McVeigh and Logan back down to the ground-floor canteen. Whereupon Carter found the fourth member of the team waiting for them.

Patrick Webb sat at the nearest table, four plates of steak and chips in front of him. He wasn't difficult to miss. Firstly, because at nine o'clock in the evening, he was the only person in the canteen. But also because of his bulk.

Webb was the biggest guy in the Regiment. Hands like oar paddles, biceps the size of boulders. His legs were so huge you needed climbing equipment to scale them. He looked like Kimbo Slice on a weight-gain programme. When he stood up to greet the others, Carter half expected the floor to quake beneath them. An M4 carbine rested on the table beside Webb. Obeying the first rule of the Regiment.

Always keep your primary weapon within arm's reach.

'Geordie, you remember Patrick,' Logan began.

Carter extended a hand and hoped it wouldn't be crushed in Webb's grip. 'All right, fella. How's tricks?'

Webb grunted a reply. Carter had worked with the Brummie on several training jobs in the past, but he still knew next to nothing about the guy. He said little, offered up no personal details about himself, his background, his family. Webb had joined the Regiment two years ago, after a stint with the Special Reconnaissance Regiment, one of the newer additions to the UK SF community. He had grown up in Birmingham and had been caught up in some sort of gang trouble in his youth, but beyond that the guy was a closed book.

'Got the chef to rustle us up some scoff,' Webb said, waving a hand at the plates. 'Thought you boys might be hungry.'

'God, yes,' Logan said as he dropped into the seat. 'Starving.'

He reached for the saltshaker, emptied half the contents onto his food and started hacking away at the rump steak with his knife and fork.

Carter popped a chip into his mouth and looked round. 'Where's everyone else?'

'Most of the Ukrainians head into town after tea,' McVeigh said. 'They like to have a few beers, shoot a few rounds of pool in the local joints before hitting the sack. Some of the older guys just stay in their bunks.'

'They're missing out,' Logan said, jaws working furiously as he chewed on a hunk of meat. 'If that was me, I'd be out on the town every night, working the Logan charm on the talent.'

McVeigh said, disapprovingly, 'Don't you ever think about anything other than shagging?'

'I'm a born romantic. Can't help myself.'

'Surprised you can get it up these days. Bloke your age.'

'Piss off, fella. I've had more women than you've had days on earth.'

McVeigh snorted derisively. 'I wouldn't brag about sleeping with a few camp groupies. They'd jump into bed for a packet of crisps and a bottle of cheap voddie.'

Logan tutted and said, 'See, that's your problem, Billy. No respect for the opposite sex.'

'No, mate. I just don't let my dick rule my noggin.'

'You should let me take you for a night out on the tiles when we get back. Teach you a few tricks. You never know, some woman might take pity on your sad arse.'

Carter said, 'Billy's got a point. We're on the job. Focus on that. Leave the other stuff for when we're back home.'

'Tell this moody cunt to stop taking the mick, then,' Logan replied, keeping his gaze trained on McVeigh.

'I'm serious,' Carter snapped. 'Don't make the same mistake as Longstaff. Keep your cock in your pants.'

'Christ, Geordie, calm down.' Logan held up his hands in mock-surrender. 'I was just joking, like.'

'As long as that's all it is.'

They finished up in the canteen, got a brew on, then made their way down the corridor towards a sturdy-looking door at the far end of the building. Logan plucked out a key from his trouser pocket, unlocked the door and motioned for the others to enter. Carter followed them into a small square-shaped room with metal bars on the windows, half a dozen chairs arranged around a scuffed table, and a heavy-duty safe secured to the floor, next to a storage locker the size of a Smeg fridge. Several detailed maps were spread out on the table, along with an array of laptops and tablets housed in military-grade protective cases, and a chunky satellite phone.

Webb gathered up their passports, plodded over to the safe, and worked the mechanical combination, massive hands twisting the metal dial left and right. The safe unlocked with a diplomatic click, the door yawned open, and Webb placed the passports on the top shelf, next to a thick wad of Ukrainian banknotes. There was a separate bundle of US dollars on the top shelf, and a band of euros. Regimental slush fund. Plus a load of SIM cards, a set of replacement phones, a stack of printed documents.

Webb sealed the safe door again, then joined the other guys around the table sipping their brews. The coffee was bitter, and strong. Like getting kicked in the face by a mule.

Logan began the slack briefing.

'The general's scheduled to leave here at 0900 tomorrow morning. It's a straight run from here to Kyiv to make the arrest. Won't be any earlier than that, because we're on a no-move before 0900.'

Carter said, 'That late? Ruperts are usually up at the crack of dawn.'

Logan sniggered. 'Our man Koltrov isn't an early riser. Spends his morning saying his goodbyes to his sweethearts.'

'How far are we from Kyiv?'

'From here to the city centre, it's about forty kilometres. Fifty-minute drive, depending on the route we're taking and the time of day.'

Carter lowered his gaze to the map, familiarising himself with the details. 'How many established routes have we got?'

'Six. We mix it up from day to day. Tomorrow we're on Route Bravo.' McVeigh traced the route on the map with a stubby finger. 'It'll take us direct from Novochanka to Minister Butko's office. That's where the general is planning to make the arrest.'

'Which is where?'

'Ministry of Defence headquarters. Heavily guarded, for obvious reasons. Guard house on the front, manned by Ukrainian SF personnel.'

'Are we sure he's going to be there tomorrow?'

'The general has got access to Butko's calendar,' Logan explained. 'He's due to host a meeting with the head of the SBU – that's the Ukrainians' security service. At nine o'clock in the morning. Lasting ninety minutes.'

'What if the meeting ends early?'

'It won't. The SBU chief has orders to keep him in place until we arrive.'

'He – she? – is in on it?'

'She. Yes. She's been informed of the investigation into Butko. His dealings with the Russians.'

'What if he's spooked and doesn't show?'

'Officers from the SBU are running round-the-clock surveillance on the suspect. If he changes his plans, for whatever reason, they'll sound the alarm and the mission will be aborted.

'The four of us will accompany the general into the building while he makes the arrest.' Logan contorted his features into a scowl. 'We're supposed to have line of sight to him at all times while he's on foot, but it doesn't always work out that way.'

'And the Ukrainians?'

'They'll stay outside, parked in front of the ministry, guarding the vehicles,' McVeigh said.

'Remember, we're under strict orders from the head shed not to get involved politically,' Logan put in. 'They don't want us interfering with the arrest. Our job begins and ends with protecting the general. That's it.'

Carter said, 'What's the routine for everyone leaving the base?'

'There's an RV point in front of Koltrov's digs. We'll collect him from there at 0900 sharp.'

'How many vehicles are we taking?'

'Three. Koltrov will ride in the middle wagon with you and me, Makarenko, and his press officer. Four Ukrainians in the first Suburban. Two more Ukrainians in the rear Chevy with Patrick and Billy.'

Carter said, 'We'll need to check them before we set off. Engine oil, warning lights, fuel tanks. We don't want any problems en route to the arrest.'

'Already sorted. Patrick will take care of that first thing tomorrow.'

'Reminds me,' Webb said. 'Someone needs to tidy the vehicles. Clean up the mess the general left behind last time out. All of those crisp packets and sandwich wrappers.'

Logan said, 'Billy, that's your job. Get on it soon as we've finished here, sunshine.'

'Me?' The Mancunian screwed up his face in disgust. 'Why do I always get the shite tasks?'

'Because you're a gobby twat. Because you're the crow on the team. Because I fucking said so.'

McVeigh stared at the older man, his lips pressed tightly shut.

Carter dropped his gaze to the map. His mind running through scenarios. Choke points. Areas of heightened threat.

'Are we expecting any resistance from the targets?' he asked.

'No,' Logan answered. 'Both targets are unarmed. No security details for either guy. It's just them.'

'Far as we know,' Webb interjected.

'Where are we taking the suspects?'

'Here.' Logan stabbed a finger at a point on the map, three kilometres from the defence ministry.

'Police station on Donetska Street,' he went on. 'It's a ten-minute drive from the target's office.'

'Secure?'

McVeigh nodded. 'Cells have barred windows. Security cameras covering all approaches. Area is grungy, but it serves a purpose, and it's well out of the way of the busiest areas.'

Logan said, 'It's a straightforward job, Geordie. Should be a piece of piss.'

Carter gave a dry chuckle. 'Since when has any op ever been that easy?'

They took a break for another brew and went through the rest of the plan. Logistics, timings, distances. They analysed likely traffic patterns. Checked to see if any streets in the area had been hit in the recent spate of rocket attacks launched across the city. They plotted emergency exfiltration routes from the arrest location and police station. Looked at the layout of the Ministry of Defence building. Studied entry and exit points.

Once they had memorised the details, Logan produced another key and unlocked the fridge-sized storage locker standing flush against the back wall. Inside was a ton of hardware. Carter was looking at more weaponry than a Texas gun shop.

'Not bad, eh?' Logan grinned.

Carter ran his eyes over the equipment: four M4 assault rifles, the same number of Glock semi-automatic pistols, L2 hand grenades and smoke grenades, a dozen of each. Plus four sets of body armour with front and rear plate hangers. Night scopes. Pancake holsters for the Glocks. Personal radio systems. Field dressings. And several boxes of ammunition: 5.56 x 45 mm NATO rounds for the M4, 9 x 19 mm Parabellum for the Glock.

Also inside: an L115A4 sniper rifle, chambered for the 7.62 x 51 mm NATO round. Which was the latest addition to the UKSF sniper armoury. The British Army variant on the Accuracy International AX rifle system, the upgraded version of the company's Arctic Warfare Magnum series of weapons. Fitted with a Schmidt & Bender scope and integrated tactical suppressor. Effective range of at least eight hundred metres. Weapon of choice for the SAS, Delta, and pretty much any discerning SF operator.

Logan, noticing the look on his face, said, 'Rifle was retrieved by the Ukrainians from a dead Russian soldier on an op in the summer. Got their hands on a shit-ton of them. We managed to scrounge one.'

'Scrounging runs in your family, don't it?' said McVeigh.

Logan stared at him with flat eyes. 'Twat.'

He handed Carter one of the M4s and said, 'Look on the bright side, Geordie. At least you won't have to spend time familiarising yourself with the kit on this gig.'

'I thought we were supposed to be carrying the same kit as the Ukrainians.'

'We are.'

Carter frowned. 'But this is all Western weaponry. This isn't what the Ukrainians have been working with.'

'Situation has changed. We had the local stuff until recently,' said Logan. 'All that shitty kit they had been packing before the war. AK-74s and suchlike. But we've been bumped up now, what with the supplies coming across the border.'

Carter remembered reading somewhere about the masses of equipment flowing into the country from abroad. Much of it donated by the US, Britain and other NATO countries. Other stuff had been seized from captured Russian forces. Spoils of war. The country had amassed sizeable stockpiles of grenade launchers, heavy machine guns, sniper rifles, missiles, FIM-92 Stingers, Starstreaks, howitzers, mortars, HIMARs, drones and thermobaric bombs.

Enough kit to start the Third World War. And end it.

'Let's hope this shit never gets turned against us,' he muttered.

'Why would they?' Logan asked. 'We're on the same side. These guys are our friends.'

'So were the Taliban, once upon a time.'

'This is totally different. Jesus, you can't compare this lot to the Afghans.'

'Maybe not. But all I know is, every time we've donated loads of kit to some other country, it's come back to bite us on the arse. You'd realise that, if you spent more time reading up on your history instead of trying to get your end away with the Hereford groupies.'

'That's why I don't read books, see.' Logan tapped the side of his head. 'Put too many grim thoughts in your head. Life's depressing enough as it is. Why make it worse?'

'To educate yourself, mate.'

'Fuck that. Had enough of that shite at school. Give me a pint and a nice woman over reading any day of the week.'

Carter set down his M4 and strapped the pancake holster around his waist. He thumbed the mag release catch on the side of the Glock, checked to make sure there was a full ten-round clip of nine-milli brass inside, slid the clip back into the mag feed on the underside of the moulded polymer grip, secured the semi-automatic in the holster.

'Radios are preset to the same frequency as the Ukrainians,' said McVeigh. 'Secure channel. Voice comms. Got our own private channel, too, so we can chat to one another without them lot listening in.'

'Can they speak English?' asked Carter.

Logan said, 'The colonel, Makarenko, he's up to a good standard. General Koltrov, too.'

'And the others?'

'Passable. Better than my Ukrainian, put it that way.'

Carter stared at him. 'You've been out here six months, and you haven't picked up any of the lingo?'

'Don't give me that look, Geordie. I ain't had the time. Been busy, man.'

'Yeah. You have.' McVeigh's expression relaxed into a dirty smile. 'Failing to chat up the local women.'

The Mancunian's chest started to heave up and down in laughter. Webb and Carter joined in too, while Logan glared at them, his face shading white with anger.

'Get away with you. Fucking idiots.'

Carter stopped smiling and said, 'How do we contact the head shed?'

Webb pointed with his eyes at the satphone on the table. It was mounted on a docking station; a cable ran from the docker towards the ceiling.

'Use that. It's rigged up to an antenna on the roof, so you can use it indoors. Direct line to Hereford. Fully encrypted.'

Carter nodded and said, 'I'll reach out to them once we're done here. Call in a sitrep. Let them know the planning for tomorrow.'

'Tell them to send us some decent beers,' Logan said, half-jokingly. 'Give us a break from that watered-down Polish shite they serve in all the bars in town.'

Carter grinned. 'I'll get them to fly in some Tennent's Super. That's more up your street, isn't it?'

'Prick.'

Carter picked up the satphone and consulted his G-Shock. Eleven o'clock at night.

He said, 'We'll RV back here in a few hours for morning prayers. Seven o'clock sharp. Should give us plenty of time to grab some breakfast, check the radios are working, make sure the Suburbans are ready to roll and load up on smokes and grenades. Meanwhile, get your heads down. Big day ahead of us. We'll need to stay sharp as fuck.'

The other guys trooped out of the room, taking their longs and pistols with them. Webb first, then McVeigh, then Logan. The latter handed over the door key to Carter and paused in the doorway.

'You really think the Russians might have a crack at the general tomorrow?'

'He's going to be in the middle of Kyiv in broad daylight, badly exposed, confronting a known Russian collaborator, less than a week after they tried to kill the president. Anything could happen.'

Logan looked doubtful. 'It's been quiet so far. Not a sniff of trouble in six months.'

'That's what I'm worried about.'

'Maybe the general's not high on their list.' Logan scratched his jaw.

'Or they might just be biding their time. Either way, we'll have to be on top of our game. Especially if this guy is as reckless as you say he is.'

'He is,' Logan insisted. 'That's for sure. You'll see for yourself tomorrow, I guess.' He sniffed and said, 'Looks like they've thrown you in at the deep end here.'

Carter smiled feebly. 'Story of my life, mate. Story of my fucking life.'

Fifteen

Carter rose at six o'clock the next morning. He took a brisk jog around the base perimeter, had a shower and a shave, changed into his Ukrainian army threads and carried his M4 long down to the canteen. Scores of Ukrainians were seated at the tables, forking chunks of greasy sausage and potato into their mouths. They paid Carter no attention as he pulled up a pew at a separate table with Webb, Logan and McVeigh. The four men ate in near silence, their plates stacked high with eggs, bacon and slabs of coarse bread lathered in butter, washed down with mugs of fresh coffee. Like soldiers everywhere, they had learned to eat well, and eat fast.

Could be our last meal for a while, Carter thought, *if this thing goes south.*

They refilled their brews and detoured into the locked office. Webb wrestled open the locker and distributed the hand grenades to the others. Three per man. Each guy was also issued with three smokes, four spare mags of 5.56 x 45 mm rounds for the M4, two extra clips of 9-milli Parabellum for the Glock, an emergency field dressing, tourniquet, two morphine auto-injectors, a camo headlamp, and a personal radio. Carter checked both his weapons again, slipped on his body armour, stashed the grenades, burner phone, ammo and kit in the large utility pouches on the front and sides of his webbing, and tested the preset channel on the radio.

Some time later, Logan left the room. He returned after a couple of minutes followed by two soldiers from the Ukrainian BG team. Captain Yuriy Popov was the officer in charge of the group. He was thick-necked and heavyset, like a boxer gone to seed, with slicked-back hair the colour of urine, and lizard eyes. Popov had managed to squeeze himself into an army uniform. Carter wasn't sure how.

The guy standing next to Captain Popov could have been his twin. The similarity was frightening. He had the same build, the same haircut, same facial features. He was an inch shorter, a little thicker around the chest, maybe. But otherwise they were like clones. Logan introduced the lookalike as Staff Sergeant Davyd Horbach. Popov's deputy.

'How are we looking, Captain?' Carter asked them.

'My men are ready,' Popov said in faintly accented English. 'Tell us the plan.'

Carter walked them through it in English. He had to repeat himself a few times to clarify details, or because Popov and Horbach couldn't understand his Newcastle twang.

'Once we arrive at the target location,' he said, 'we'll accompany the general inside while he makes the arrest. You lot will wait outside and establish a cordon. Got it?'

Popov and Horbach looked at one another. Horbach, eyes pinned to the map, stroked his chin and muttered something to the captain under his breath in his mother tongue.

'What did he say?' Logan asked the captain.

Popov said, 'My sergeant thinks we should be the ones inside the building during the mission. The general is our responsibility. He says you should take the cordon.'

Carter said, 'That's not up for discussion.'

'Why not?'

'You've got the most important job. The likeliest point of attack is from the front of the building. Which means you and your muckers will be the first line of defence between the enemy and the principal. Your guys will be in charge of sounding the alarm and holding any attackers off until we can get your man Koltrov out.'

Logan added helpfully, 'Cordon is the most dangerous job. There won't be a threat from inside.'

It was bullshit, Carter knew. The Ministry of Defence was heavily guarded on all sides. Like a fortress. The chances of a frontal

200

assault were minimal. If there was an attempt on the general's life, Carter figured it would be more likely to happen en route to or from the arrest. But the Ukrainians seemed to buy it.

We're protecting one of the most targeted individuals in the country, he reminded himself. *No point creating bad blood between us and the Ukrainian bodyguards.*

Logan said, 'Routine is the same as always. Your men will ride in the front and rear vehicles in the convoy. Me and Geordie will be travelling with the boss, his 2iC and press officer. Patrick and Billy will accompany your guys in the rear wagon.'

'Keep your eyes peeled,' Carter warned the Ukrainians. 'If anything happens, the priority is to get away from the threat as quickly as possible and return to base.'

'No problem. We understand.'

'What's the deal with the ribbons today?' Logan asked.

'Left arm,' said Popov. 'Yellow and blue ribbon.'

'Any issues with the route to Kyiv? Any rocket attacks in the area overnight?'

'Negative. We checked in this morning. Route is clear.'

They hadn't heard any air raid sirens during the dead hours, but Carter wanted to be doubly certain. An old Regiment habit, engraved deep into his bones.

They inspected their radios and kit one last time. Logan contacted Hereford on the satphone, letting them know they were about to leave the base, checking to see if there were any further intelligence updates on the situation in Kyiv. Carter glanced again at his G-Shock: 0845 hours. He told Webb to get the Suburbans up and running and instructed Popov and Horbach to assemble their men in front of the main block in ten minutes.

Webb came back nine minutes later.

'Wagons are running,' he said. 'Full tanks. Everything's good to go.'

The four Blades slipped on their tactical gloves, helmets and ski masks. They rigged up their tactical radios, tied the blue-and-yellow strips of cloth around their left biceps, identifying them to Ukrainians as friendly forces. Snatched up their M4s.

'It's time,' Carter said. 'Let's get moving.'

*　*　*

They emerged from the barracks block to a crisp autumn morning, the clear sky the colour of a naked gas flame. A chill wind lashed across the base; the air was so cold you could almost snap it. Popov, Horbach and the rest of the Ukrainian bodyguard team stood waiting beside the three Suburbans, primary weapons hanging from their rifle slings, some smoking cigarettes or rubbing their hands in an effort to work some warmth into them. The SAS men greeted their Ukrainian colleagues with curt nods but kept a discreet distance.

Just as it should be, thought Carter.

We're not here to be their mates. We've got a job to do.

Popov stood close by, jabbering into his phone. Too quickly for Carter to understand what he was saying. He hung up as Carter approached and said, 'Principal is almost ready. Two minutes.'

'Tell your men to get in the wagons,' said Carter. 'We'll swing round to the RV point at the front of the general's dorm block and wait for him there.'

Popov relayed the order to his men. They split into groups, two of them diving into the rear Suburban with McVeigh and Webb, while Popov, Horbach and the remaining soldiers took the lead wagon. Carter and Logan made their way over to the middle vehicle, Logan tucking himself behind the wheel, Carter easing into the passenger seat.

Doors thunked shut. Engines revved. Lights beamed. The front Suburban steered away from the parking area, the other vehicles following close behind, cantering past the accommodation blocks.

They hooked a right at the far end of the tarmacked area and drove south for two hundred metres, heading towards the control tower and the front of the air base, until they pulled up in front of a two-storey concrete-faced building set apart from the rest of the admin blocks.

A pair of soldiers stood guard in front of the entrance. A short distance away, Carter spotted a dark grey Volkswagen Touareg in one of the parking bays. Tinted windows, Ukrainian plates. Engine running.

'Who's that?' he asked.

Logan squinted at the Touareg and said, 'Staff car. One of the general's lackeys uses it to ferry the girls to and from the base. Their own private taxi service.'

'Are they local?'

'The girls?' Logan nodded. 'They're staying in a hotel outside the town. Long-term residency. The general pays for their keep.'

Carter lifted his eyebrows. 'Must be costing him a small fortune. How the fuck does he afford that?'

'He's a three-star general. I imagine he's on a tidy income. Probably has a nice side hustle, too. The Ruperts have had their noses in the trough for years in this country.'

'So have ours, mate. They just do a better job of hiding it.'

Logan laughed cynically. 'Guess some things never change.'

'No.'

As they looked on, two women strolled out of the building. A well-upholstered brunette, her shapely frame squeezed into a red plunge dress, and a slender blonde in a black leather mini-dress and a matching pair of platform heels. They stopped outside the entrance, cigarettes in hand, bummed a lighter from one of the guards, then sauntered over to the Touareg, puffing on their smokes and giggling.

Logan looked on greedily as they climbed into the back of the Volkswagen with some difficulty in their high heels.

'Sweet Jesus. The general might be a wanker, but he's got good taste in women. I'll give him that.'

The Touareg reversed out of the parking bay and continued south towards the main entrance to the base. Carter and Logan sat in the middle Suburban and waited.

Ninety seconds later, General Viktor Koltrov stepped outside.

The Lion of Ukraine looked shorter than he had appeared on TV. But he had the same stern-faced look Carter remembered from the medal ceremony, the same arrogant manner. He strode confidently towards the middle Suburban, ramrod straight and square-jawed, wearing his distinctive leather eyepatch. A man marching towards his destiny.

Two more figures hastened out of the building after him. A tall, gangly guy with dark greasy hair and ferret-like features, and an elfin red-headed woman. Both wore body armour over their military uniform; both were armed with belt-holstered pistols. The woman stared at her phone as she walked, dainty fingers dancing over the screen.

Carter swung out of the wagon, trotted round to the passenger side door and popped it open. Koltrov halted in front of Carter, a small groove notching his forehead. His good eye, peering out from beneath its heavy lid, sized up the SAS man the way a wolf studies its prey.

'You're new.'

A statement, not a question.

'Yes, sir,' Carter said.

He had been told to address the general as 'sir'. An ego thing. The general was a stickler for formality, despite his man-of-the-people shtick. Whitehall mandarins, with one eye on the future, had been only too happy to agree. They were dealing with a potential future presidential candidate. They felt it was important to curry favour with the coming man, while staying close to the current power on the throne.

The groove deepened. 'What happened to the other man. Longstaff?'

'Returned home, sir. Injuries. They sent me out to replace him.'

'Then you must be – the Carter brother?'

'Yes, sir.'

Koltrov's good eye lit up like a headlamp. 'This is truly a great honour. I know all about your brother. A fine man. A great soldier. Credit to his country.'

'Thank you, sir.'

'I, too, come from a family of great warriors,' the general said in flawless English.

'Yes, sir.'

'My grandfather was a hero of the Second World War. He fought against the Nazis at the Battle of the Dnieper. They made him Hero of the Soviet Union for his part in the battle. Do you know how they rewarded him after the fighting? The cowards in Moscow?'

'No, sir.'

'They sentenced him to the gulag. Twelve years of hell in the Arctic Circle. Now I find myself fighting against the sons and daughters of Stalin the butcher. History has a sick sense of humour.'

'I guess so, sir.'

Koltrov gestured towards the two uniformed figures at his side.

'My deputy, Colonel Makarenko,' he said, indicating the ferret-faced man.

'Anna Zinchenko,' the general added, nodding at the petite redhead. 'My press officer.'

Zinchenko stopped typing and glanced up from her screen at Carter. Intense moss-green eyes scrutinised him. The bow-shaped lips spread into a businesslike smile, before she dropped her gaze back to her phone again.

Carter stepped aside, giving the general and his staff space. The three Ukrainians ducked into the back of the Suburban; Carter closed the door, scurried round the front of the wagon, dropped back into the passenger seat and reached out to Popov on the comms channel.

'We're all set, Captain. Ready when you are.'

'OK.'

The Suburban directly in front of Carter and Logan steered back onto the access road. Two minutes later, the convoy exited the air base and turned north, joining the three-lane stretch of motorway leading towards Kyiv. Carter settled back to enjoy the view. Which didn't amount to much. Belts of woodland and scrub straddled the roadside, interspersed with gutted buildings and the rusted shells of destroyed vehicles.

In the back, Koltrov said, 'You are carrying M4s?'

'Yes, sir,' Logan said. 'This is all new kit. Just arrived.'

'An excellent weapon. Much better than the AK-74, in my opinion. More accurate. I have used it myself, you know.'

'Is that so, sir?' Carter asked, more out of politeness than any genuine interest in Koltrov's career. He thought: *indulging the principal. One of the key jobs for any self-respecting bodyguard team.*

'Oh, yes,' said Koltrov. 'Many times. At Fort Bragg, when I was given a personal tour by Delta Force. At your camp, too.'

'You've been to Hereford?'

The general nodded. 'I am afraid it was only a short visit. I was in the country to deliver a lecture on urban warfare. At your famous Sandhurst academy.'

Carter said nothing.

'I am in big demand nowadays,' Koltrov went on. 'Always I am giving interviews to the newspapers, the TV stations. Especially the Americans. They are very keen to speak to me. They want to understand how I brought the Russian scum to their knees. I am loved as much in America, I think, as my own country.'

'Yes, sir.'

'My people, they worship me. You will see.'

'I'm sure they do, sir.'

'It is a special thing, to be loved by your own people. They know, you see. They know only I can lead them to victory. Under my command, we shall break the Russian vermin.

'Your leaders, they thought we would lose in a matter of days. They thought they were so clever. They were ready to mourn the death of Ukraine before the first shot had been fired. But they did not understand the hatred we have for the invaders.'

'Yes, sir.'

'I give you an example, OK?' Koltrov was warming to his theme now. 'Because of our shared history, many people here are fluent in Russian. Always, you could hear Russian in the streets. But most people have vowed never to speak the language again. They would rather lose their tongues than let a Russian word pass their lips.'

'Can't say I blame 'em, sir.'

'We will crush the Russians,' the general added, balling his right hand into a tight fist. His one good eye glinted like ice under the winter sun. 'In the spring, we will drive the enemy back to their miserable land. Those who do not retreat, or surrender, we will shoot dead. Like dogs. It will be a glorious victory. And the people, they will chant my name in the streets.'

'Yes, sir.'

'You in the spineless West—' Koltrov leaned forward, pointing at Carter and Logan in turn '—you in the West think we are only winning because you send us tanks and missiles. But that is an illusion. It is a lie you tell each other, to make yourselves feel better.

'We do not have as many tanks as the enemy. We do not have as many planes or drones. We do not have nuclear bombs, or submarines. But still we beat the enemy, and do you know why?'

'No, sir.'

'It is not tanks or rockets that will decide the outcome of this war. It is the heroic efforts of our men – and women,' Koltrov said, nodding at Zinchenko, 'that will defeat the dictator. It is their blood being spilled, while your leaders sit in their comfortable offices, congratulating themselves on sending us another planeload of bullets.'

He wagged a finger at Carter, like a teacher berating a student, before he continued. 'This is why the soldiers love me. I understand the sacrifices they are making. And yet I must ask them to do it, again and again. Do you know why?'

'No, sir.'

'Because it is necessary – because it is the only way to win.' He thumped his fist into the palm of his other hand. 'That is why I insist on sharing the risks of my men. You see?'

'I think so, sir.'

'It is important you know this now. I will tell you what I have told the others. Do not try to change my mind. I will not be forced to hide in a bunker, like a coward,' Koltrov said, scowling in disgust. 'I will visit my troops. I will stand among them, I will share their deprivations and congratulate them on their bravery, and urge them to keep up their spirits, because without me, they are nothing, they are lost children. My itinerary is not up for debate. Clear?'

'Yes, sir.'

'Very good.' Koltrov nodded and sat back, arms folded, satisfied that he had won the argument.

'How long have you been in the SAS?' he asked after a pause of silence.

'Nine years, sir.'

'Good soldiers. Dedicated. Tough. Almost as good as our own Special Forces.'

'Yes, sir,' Carter bullshitted.

In the rear-view mirror, he caught sight of Zinchenko busily typing out messages, her face lit up by the bluish glow of her phone screen. Makarenko stared out of the side window. No doubt the pair of them had learned to tune out whenever their general went on one of his long rants.

'It is a waste,' Koltrov added, miserably.

'Sorry, sir?'

'Your politicians. They refuse to let you fight with us. You and your comrades, you should be in the east. Helping us to eliminate the Russians. Instead, you must act as my chauffeur.'

'Maybe they're worried about escalation, sir. Nuclear war and all that.'

Koltrov snorted out a laugh. 'The Russians wouldn't dare go down that road.'

'They might. If they're desperate.'

'Never,' the general retorted with feeling. 'Their president hasn't got the guts. He is a strong man, they say, but that is a lie. He is secretly afraid. Like all bullies.'

Carter said, 'Even if he is bluffing, it doesn't matter. The only thing is whether people believe him. Sir.'

The general wrinkled his nose in contempt. 'Your prime minister is not a fool. The leaders of Germany, France, America – these are not stupid people. They know Russia is not serious about using nuclear weapons. That is not the reason they do not allow you to fight. No. The true reason they do not let you take up arms alongside our soldiers is because your leaders do not wish to have their citizens' blood on their hands. That is why we are fighting alone against an enemy with an army ten times the size of ours. Because your politicians have no backbone.'

Carter nodded but stayed quiet. He had wondered why the general had taken a keen interest in him. Senior officers didn't usually pay much attention to their BG details. But now he understood. Koltrov liked the sound of his own voice. He clearly enjoyed lecturing his men, offering his opinions, railing against his perceived enemies. He seemed more like a populist politician than a military commander.

'They celebrate our heroism, even as they buy Russian gas. They tell us to make peace with the invaders, even as they rape our women, torture our soldiers, and send our people to die in their camps. You let them steal our lands, commit genocide, and in return, you send us a few malfunctioning weapons and hang flags outside your houses. It is the sign of a civilisation rotten to the core.

'It makes me sick,' Koltrov carried on. 'Why should we die, while your citizens enjoy their lives as normal, laughing and drinking with families and friends? Ukraine has suffered enough in its past. Why should we not just say to Russia, "OK, Ukraine is yours, take it if you must, but only if you promise to drop your bombs on Munich and Paris and London." Then we make Russia your problem. Why not?'

'Don't know, sir.'

'You have no opinion on this?'

Carter shrugged. 'I try to stay out of politics. Not my bag, sir.'

'Then you are a wise man. I wish I could do the same. I wish to be a simple soldier. Like the old days. But now I am a general fighting to save my people from genocide. In my world, everything is politics.'

A thought prodded at the base of Carter's skull. 'What about that nuclear plant the Russians have attacked? Holovika?'

'What about it?'

'Why bother shelling it? What's the point, unless they're serious about blowing it up?'

The general smiled weakly. 'It is another bluff. The Russians have no interest in destroying Holovika. No. When they shell the complex, they are careful not to damage any of the critical infrastructure.'

'But there must be a reason why they're bombing it.'

'Of course. The Russians want Holovika for the same reason they have captured the other plants. Not to blow them up, but to use them to store their weapons. Artillery, rockets, ammunition. They know that our planes would never bomb these places.'

The general leaned forward.

He went on, 'Tell me this. A man who was willing to risk nuclear catastrophe – would such a man use our plants as warehouses for his most prized weaponry?'

'Guess not, sir.'

'Exactly.'

Koltrov sat back and nodded.

'You see, the Russian president is not as crazy as he looks on the TV. Even he is not mad enough to start a nuclear war.'

Sixteen

They ploughed on towards the city. After a short time, the traffic thickened, and long rows of concrete towers sprouted out of the horizon, like something out of a children's pop-up book. They were barrelling through the fringes of Kyiv now. A place fighting for its existence, thought Carter. Though it didn't much look like it. There were billboards carrying faded posters for Czech beer and South Korean SUVs, bustling cafés and shops, people out riding bicycles, or walking their dogs, or chatting on their phones. Two million citizens, trying to get on with their lives as best they could.

The convoy rolled on for five kilometres, came off the main carriageway, followed the slip road as it looped round, then rattled north for a spell through downtown Kyiv. They passed rows of nineteenth-century apartments, public parks, tired-looking shopping malls, chain coffee shops, lakes glinting like metal beneath the pallid sun. On the surface, the city seemed normal. But look close enough and there were cracks in the facade: the heaps of sandbags stacked around the checkpoints, the monuments encased in wooden boxes to protect them from infrequent bombing, the chunks of concrete gouged out of the side of highrise blocks. In front of one building, a gang of kids played atop an abandoned Russian tank with a white 'Z' painted down the side. Close by, a mechanical digger was backfilling a damaged section of the road.

In the back seats, Zinchenko and Koltrov were having a heated discussion. Something to do with an urgent media request from an American newspaper. That was as much as Carter could understand, given his limited grasp of Ukrainian. They were arguing the pros and cons of accepting the interview. Publicity versus the logistical complications. Zinchenko had her reservations. But the general was adamant. He wanted to do it.

Makarenko repeatedly checked his phone and made calls, coordinating with the surveillance team monitoring the suspect.

Logan stayed close to the Suburban in front, driving almost bumper to bumper as they hugged the outside lane. Behind them, the team in the rearmost wagon stuck to the middle lane, positioning themselves so they could accelerate forward in the event of an ambush and engage the enemy, instead of being trapped at the back of the logjam.

Every time they hit a set of lights they went through the same routine. Carter looked round at the surrounding streets, right hand gripping the M4 trigger mechanism, left hand primed on the door handle, ready to lever it open at the slightest sign of danger. But the area remained mercifully clear of threats.

Logan took another clockwise loop in the road, following the lead wagon as it shuttled south across a traffic-clogged flyover. Zinchenko and the general abruptly halted their conversation, and Carter knew they were no more than a minute out from the target location.

They motored down a wide boulevard – decrepit Soviet blocks on the left, grand neoclassical residences on the right – the brake lights on the front wagon flared as it swiftly dropped its speed, the blinkers signalled a right turn, and then they eased to a halt in front of the heavily guarded entrance to the Ministry of Defence.

Sandbags had been arranged in a horseshoe formation either side of the front gate; a group of soldiers were milling about next to a slate-roofed sentry post. Two of the Ukrainian soldiers cautiously approached the front Suburban, while their mates hung back. Carter swept his eyes left and right, alert to the possibility of an ambush. Specifically, he was looking for anything out of the ordinary. A van or car parked where it shouldn't be. Someone on foot taking an interest in the convoy. Anything at all. But the scene was quiet. Mid-morning traffic rumbled along the road. People were cycling, or waiting for buses, or carrying bags of shopping. An ordinary tableau of city life.

Several moments later, the guards stepped back from the Suburban, the gates groaned open, the boom barriers lifted, and the convoy followed the road as it sheered off to the right towards an immense four-storey building with a pastel-blue facade and long wings projecting from either side of the central structure. Marbled colonnades, fondant white and tall as NASA rockets, ran along the length of the main section, below an ornately decorated pediment. Like a temple in Ancient Greece. On the rooftop, a Ukrainian flag flickered tongue-like in the stiffening breeze.

Another group of soldiers stood guard in front of the building, next to some sort of war monument.

'Reckon we'll be safe enough here,' said Logan as he pulled up behind the first Suburban. 'Looks like we've got half the army to protect us.'

'We'll see.'

The men pulled up their face coverings over their nostrils and exited the Chevy. Carter swung round to the rear passenger door and levered it open. Zinchenko got out first, with Koltrov and Makarenko following close behind.

One of the soldiers recognised the general and called out to his mates. Almost immediately, they crowded round Koltrov, excitedly shouting his name, some reaching out to shake his hand while others took snaps on their phones. More soldiers appeared from inside the building, abandoning their posts to catch a glimpse of the great man himself.

By now McVeigh, Webb, Popov and the rest of the Ukrainian bodyguards had exited their respective vehicles. They swiftly rushed over and tried to form a protective cordon around the principal, but with the tight press of bodies it was impossible to shove their way through. Carter bellowed at the mob, ordering them to get back, but Koltrov shot him a scathing look.

'No, no,' he said. 'It is fine. Let them say hello. These are my boys.'

A wave of anger swept through Carter. He clamped his jaw shut, suppressing an urge to argue with Koltrov as the soldiers swarmed round him. Like fans greeting a celebrity at a film premiere. Koltrov seemed in no hurry to head inside. He shook the hand of each man, laughed at something one of them said, smiled patiently for photos. The guy was in his element.

Koltrov wasn't kidding, he thought. *The guy isn't just a famous general.*

He's a bloody rock star.

'This is a fucking nightmare,' he muttered.

At his side, Logan nodded wearily. 'Told you, mate. Now do you believe me?'

Carter offered no reply. He was trying to get his head around the security risks. Just getting Koltrov from his vehicle to the front of the Ministry of Defence building had descended into chaos. Which prompted a question.

If this is what happens in a heavily defended government HQ, how the fuck are we supposed to protect him in the street?

I don't know, Carter thought grimly. *But if we can't persuade the guy to curb his behaviour, he won't last very long.*

At last the general held up his hands and addressed the gathered soldiers, pointing to the main entrance to the defence ministry, as if to say: *I must attend to business, my friends.* The crowd reluctantly parted. Koltrov scraped a hand through his grey-tinged hair and turned to Carter.

'OK,' he said. 'Now I am ready.'

215

Carter beckoned to Popov. 'We're moving inside with the principal,' he said. 'Stay here with your men. You see or hear anything – anything at all – alert us over the radio.'

Popov nodded and bellowed at his men. Carter and Logan climbed the steps leading to the porticoed entrance, moving alongside the general. Makarenko and Zinchenko fell into step a couple of paces behind, with McVeigh and Webb pulling up the rear.

Two soldiers in ceremonial dress uniform stood washboard-erect either side of a set of tall walnut double doors. Koltrov paused in the doorway and narrowed his eye at one of the guards. He said a few words to the man; the soldier blinked in astonishment, and it took him a moment to compose himself before he replied. The general said something else and smiled paternally, patting the guard on the arm. The latter grinned, beaming from ear to ear as Koltrov moved on.

'What was all that about?' Carter asked.

'That man used to serve under me. Seven years ago, in the war in the Donbas, when I was a colonel. Private Oleksiy Lunin. He has a sister who teaches at the university. I was just telling him what a pleasure it is to see him here.'

'And you remembered his name?'

Koltrov gave a faint smile. 'These men are my boys. They are prepared to lay down their lives for me. For us. The least I can do is remember the names of such brave young men. Your officers in the SAS are the same, no?'

'Not exactly,' Carter muttered.

They swept through the doors and entered a high-ceilinged lobby, the polished marble floor emblazoned with the Ukrainian coat of arms of a trident laid over a shield. Dust motes danced in the shafts of sunlight pouring through the glass-domed rooftop. Important-looking men and women in suits sat on rows of fabric sofas to one side of the reception desk, visitor passes dangling from the lanyards around their necks. Another guard ushered the new arrivals past a bank of metal detectors and security turnstiles and led them towards a set of lifts on the far side of the lobby.

Carter, Logan, Koltrov and the others crammed into the next available lift and rode up to the third floor. The doors opened with a polite ping, and they found themselves in a long corridor that looked like it had been modelled on Versailles. Parquet flooring, gold-leafed cornicing, giltwood side tables and chairs that probably cost more than Carter's life earnings. Row of offices to the left, tall arched windows on the right overlooking the grounds of the ministry building.

They continued until they hit the office at the end of the corridor. Koltrov rapped his knuckles once, thrust the door open without waiting for a response and stepped inside a richly furnished office. Oriental rugs covered much of the floor; there was a plush sofa to one side of the doorway, a built-in bookcase against one wall filled with leatherbound volumes. Framed pictures showed the minister pressing the flesh with various foreign dignitaries. To the right, a separate door led into an adjoining office. Andriy Butko's private quarters.

A platinum-blonde secretary in thick-rimmed glasses sat at a desk at the other end of the room, fielding a phone call on her headset while she tapped away on a keyboard. As the arrest party entered the outer office, the secretary stopped what she was doing and looked up, regarding them suspiciously. Playing the role of gatekeeper, like PAs the world over. She jabbered something at them in Ukrainian.

'What's she saying?' Logan asked.

'She wants to know if we've got an appointment,' Carter said.

McVeigh laughed. 'We're door-kickers, love. We don't need one.'

Although Carter had spent time in Ukraine, training up SF operators, several years had passed since then and he could remember only a handful of words and phrases. He could issue commands to soldiers, order a pint in a bar, or ask a passer-by for directions. Following the thread of the conversation between Koltrov and the secretary, however, was impossible. He recognised a few words in the general's response, and guessed he was telling the secretary, *We are here to speak with the minister. Don't stand in our way.* Or words to that effect. The rest was lost on him.

The secretary started to argue, then closed her mouth again. Reconsidering her position. Reality kicked in. She was up against a three-star general and four British soldiers packing rifles. No contest.

She returned her gaze to her computer screen, pretending to busy herself while the drama unfolded around her.

Koltrov nodded at Carter and said, 'I will go in with Makarenko to make the arrest. You shall wait here with your men and Zinchenko. OK?'

'Yes, sir.'

'This won't take long.'

The general started across the room to the second door, Makarenko following hard on his heels. The 2iC stopped in front of the doorway and crashed the minister's office. From where he was standing, Carter had a direct line of sight to Butko himself. The guy was sitting on a throne-like chair, elbows propped on the leather blotter covering his desk. Sheaf of papers in front of him, a huge image of a golden lion and a Cossack on the wall at his back. A short, squat woman in a black trouser suit and heels sat in the chair to one side of the desk. The SDU chief.

The minister and the chief instantly snapped their gazes towards Koltrov and Makarenko. The general stood just inside the threshold and addressed the SDU chief. *You can leave us now*, he was saying.

She didn't need any further encouragement. She hastily gathered up her belongings and hurried out of the room, brushing past Zinchenko as she headed for the corridor.

The secretary watched the scene with growing anxiety.

In the inner office, Butko rose to his feet. A look of bewilderment on his face. The general announced himself in a calm, measured tone. Asserting his authority. Taking control of the situation.

Makarenko stood next to his boss, his right hand resting on the butt of his holstered pistol.

Butko stammered a reply and shook his head angrily. Koltrov remained zen-calm. He spoke for maybe thirty seconds.

Carter, unable to follow the conversation, leaned towards Zinchenko and said in a low voice, 'What's happening?'

'The general is telling the minister that the game is up. He says he should come quietly, not to make a fuss.'

Zinchenko uttered something at the secretary and jabbed a finger at the door. Her meaning was clear enough. Leave. Now. The secretary glanced tearfully at her boss. Then she logged off her computer, removed the headset, slid out from behind her desk and snatched up her phone and bag and started for the corridor. She paused again in the doorway, looked back at the press officer and said something to her in a distressed voice before she turned on her heels and left.

'Why she was in a flap?' Carter asked.

The corners of Zinchenko's lips curved up into a thin smile. 'She said the minister is the most loyal person she's ever known. She says he would never betray his country. She says he is innocent.'

'Maybe she's right.'

'No. She has been fooled. We have evidence of him stealing money.'

'Doesn't mean he's a traitor.'

Hostility flashed in Zinchenko's eyes. 'You don't understand. This is how these people work. They earn the trust of others by making a great display of their loyalty and affection for their country, so that no one will suspect them of betraying our cause. But in secret, they are selling information to the enemy. Information that kills our soldiers, so that they can buy themselves a luxury villa or a new yacht.'

Carter skimmed his gaze back to the inner office. Butko looked petrified. He backed away from the two officers and retreated towards the wall. Putting physical distance between himself and his accusers. Koltrov took a step towards the minister and spoke softly, holding up his hands in a gesture of peace. He sounded like a guy talking an old friend out of driving home from the pub after one too many pints. Playing the role of the nice cop.

Makarenko stood alongside his boss.

Boxing the minister in.

Koltrov took another half-step towards the man. Still speaking in a measured tone of voice. He sounded rational, Carter thought, even if he couldn't understand what he was saying. Butko shouted at the general, repeating the same word over and over. Carter recognised it.

Innocent.

I'm innocent, Butko was saying.

Then Makarenko sprang forward and threw a punch at him.

The blow struck Butko squarely on the jaw. He let out a pained grunt and stumbled backwards, hands raised in a futile attempt to protect his face as Makarenko lunged forward again, tearing into him with a flurry of vicious digs and jabs. Carter saw him unloading a low punch to the minister's midriff; the guy jackknifed and keeled over, gasping for air, a moment before the colonel rugby-tackled him to the floor.

Both men crash-landed on the silk rug, trading blows. Makarenko managed to roll Butko onto his chest, pinning him down while he cinched his wrists behind his back with a pair of plasticuffs. Butko kicked out wildly, writhing beneath the colonel's weight as he hurled a torrent of abuse at the general. Cursing the man.

Makarenko picked himself off the floor; Koltrov calmly approached the minister and swung a boot, kicking him in the ribs. Butko groaned in agony, begging for mercy.

'Shut up, dog!' the general rasped. 'Traitor!'

Koltrov booted the man repeatedly, striking him in the face and chest, while the colonel filmed the action on his phone. Carter started towards the office, intent on putting a stop to the beating, but Logan grabbed hold of his arm and held him back.

'No, Geordie. Don't.'

Carter relented. In the office, the general gave Butko a final kick to the jaw before he stepped back, shoulders heaving up and down as he caught his breath. Butko lay whimpering at his feet, blood gushing out of his nose and mouth. Koltrov dabbed his sweat-glossed forehead with a handkerchief, while Makarenko whipped out a hood from his jacket pocket and slipped it over Butko's face, muffling his soft cries. The colonel hauled Butko to his feet and promptly marched him out of the office, into the outer room, where Carter, Zinchenko and the others stood waiting.

Koltrov, breathing hard, nodded at Carter. 'OK. It is done.'

Carter stared at him. 'What the fuck just happened?'

'Suspect resisted arrest,' Makarenko said, coolly. 'We gave him the chance to surrender and come with us peacefully, but he refused. So we roughed him up. Encouraged him to cooperate.' He grinned.

'You did more than that. Jesus Christ, you fucking battered him.'

General Koltrov glowered at the Briton. 'This son of a bitch does not deserve your sympathy. Or have you forgotten what the Russians have done to us over the years? The bombs they have dropped? The civilians they have killed?'

Koltrov's cheeks were burning feverishly. Carter could almost feel the anger coming off him in waves.

Carter remembered what Koltrov had told him in the car. The hatred he and his fellow Ukrainians had for the invaders. How they would rather lose their tongues than speak Russian again.

These guys don't mess around, Carter thought.

They must really despise the enemy.

Logan gave the minister a quick pat-down, searching his pockets. 'He's clean,' he said, rising to his feet. 'Nothing on him.'

'You'll have to delete that footage,' Carter said. Addressing himself to Colonel Makarenko.

'What for?'

'You lose your phone, or send that video to someone, and that shite will end up online. Once that happens, you'll lose all credibility.'

Koltrov looked amused. He said, 'You don't know my people very well. They cannot get enough of my videos. They like to see me taking revenge on those who would destroy us.'

'It's not the Ukrainians I'm worried about. It's the people back home. You could land us in a world of shit if this leaks.'

The general stared at him. Carter stared right back. Mexican stand-off. Then Koltrov parted his lips into a curious smile.

'As you wish. I will make sure Anton deletes the footage.' He flashed a strange smile. Then he said, 'We've wasted enough time here. Let's get this piece of shit to the station.'

Voices echoed down the corridor as workers from the surrounding offices wandered over to see what was going on. Webb ducked out of the doorway and shouted at them to stay back, while Carter got on the comms channel to Popov.

He said, 'Arrest has been made, Captain. Repeat, we have the target. We're leaving the building in minutes one.'

'OK.'

'All clear down there?'

'Yes,' came the hesitant reply. 'Just lots of people who wish to meet the general before he leaves.'

'Fuck's sake,' McVeigh groused. 'Just what we need.'

'Tell them to disperse,' Carter said over the net. 'We need a clear path to them wagons when we step outside the building. Got that?'

'Yes. All clear.'

Carter cleared his throat and ordered the team to get moving. McVeigh and Zinchenko led the way out of the room, moving into the corridor, where Webb stood acting as a one-man barricade, blocking the view of the ministerial staff. General Koltrov walked just behind his press officer, Butko staggering along in his wake. His hooded head lowered, shoulders noticeably sagging. The look of a broken man. Then came Makarenko at his six o'clock, one hand resting on his side-holstered weapon, ready to plug the suspect if he tried to make a run for it. Carter and Logan started to follow the colonel, bringing up the rear of the crocodile.

'Let's hope we don't have another scrum on the steps,' Logan muttered as they paced back down the corridor towards the lift. 'I could do without a reunion with the general's fan club on the way out.'

'Same here.' Carter pursed his lips and said, uneasily, 'Are you OK with this, mate?'

Logan chortled. 'This is nothing. Wait till you see the general's famous interrogation techniques.'

Carter said, quietly, 'We shouldn't be endorsing this.'

'This is how these guys roll. Big boys' rules.' Logan flinched and raised his eyebrows in surprise. 'Jesus, don't tell me you actually feel sorry for that cunt, Geordie.'

Carter said nothing.

'Look, this is none of our business,' Logan carried on as they neared the lift. 'We're here to protect the principal. That's all. What he does with the likes of Butko is down to him.'

'It's wrong,' Carter murmured. 'This could backfire on us.'

'Roughing up a few enemies? Who's going to give a shit about that?' Logan sighed and said, 'This is their show, mate. Not ours. They're the ones fighting for their lives. You want my advice, as a friend? Keep your mouth shut and look the other way. Just stay out of it.'

'Fine.'

'I mean it, Geordie. You're in the last-chance saloon here, mate. Try not to fuck it up.'

Seventeen

The police station was situated midway down a side street in a shabby part of town, three kilometres south-east of the Ministry of Defence. The district was tattered and run down. Exactly as McVeigh had described it. *Grungy. Well out of the way of the busiest areas.* Steel-grey apartment blocks rubbed shoulders with boarded-up shopfronts and vacant buildings, the bare concrete walls covered with graffiti. A sad patch of overgrown grass and weeds, enclosed within a chain-link fence, constituted the local greenery.

As they neared the station, Carter remembered what Logan had told him on the drive across the border from Poland. The fate of those guilty of working for Russia.

Bullet in the back of the head.

Unmarked grave.

He thought, *if this is how the general and his men are prepared to act in front of us, what are they getting up to when no one is watching?*

He didn't feel any sympathy for the minister. The guy was a traitor to his own kind. He had it coming. Pure and simple. But if Koltrov and his team were going rogue, torturing their own citizens and committing war crimes, that could cause problems for the Regiment. Not for a while, perhaps not for years; but at some point, once the dust had settled on the conflict, someone would inevitably start asking questions about the conduct of General Koltrov and his quest to eradicate fifth columnists inside Ukraine. His behaviour could become a liability. To the Ukrainians, and the wider war effort. Which could lead to some awkward questions about his British bodyguards.

There were two sides to any war, Carter knew. There was the campaign on the ground, fought with bullets and drones and tanks. But there was also a shadow war, contested online and in the media, a struggle for public opinion. The Ukrainians were winning that fight, but if they vacated the moral high ground, things might change. With the Regiment as collateral damage.

The SAS could easily get caught up in the scandal, as a willing accomplice to politically sanctioned assassination and torture. Tainted by association. There would be double-page reports in the papers. Legal experts interviewed on the evening news, giving their opinions, calling for a public inquiry or a criminal investigation. The head shed wouldn't be able to sweep the story under the rug. Not this time.

The Suburbans arrived in front of a drab four-storey building, opposite a seedy-looking bar. A few old bangers were parked in a rough gravel lot next to the establishment; broken glass sprinkled the asphalt; food wrappers tumbleweeded across the street. Mid-morning, and the neighbourhood was practically deserted.

Logan tailed the lead Suburban as it rolled past the main entrance before easing to a halt in front of a cantilevered gate at the side of the station building. Security cameras had been mounted on the posts either side of the access ramp. Barbed wire ran across the top of the brick wall. Signs warned off would-be trespassers.

Makarenko made a quick call on his phone. They waited. Then the galvanised steel gate slid back on its tracks with a motorised whir, and the convoy steered through the opening and parked in a row of empty spaces next to the liveried cop cars. Boots thudded on the ground as the twelve bodyguards disembarked from their respective wagons. Koltrov emerged from the rear of the Suburban, shoving Butko ahead of him. He staggered out of the vehicle, stumbled on the blacktop and almost fell over before Makarenko grabbed hold of him. The colonel kept a firm hold of the minister while Carter took Popov to one side.

Carter said, through his face covering, 'We'll accompany the principal inside the station. You and Sergeant Horbach will lead the way,' he added, nodding at Popov's deputy. 'Me and the guys will follow behind.'

'And the rest of my men?'

'Tell them to wait here. Cordon duty. Same set-up as before. There won't be any threat to the general, but it's better than having them standing around and getting bored out of their minds.'

'OK.'

Carter held the captain's gaze. 'What's the deal with the plod?'

'Plod?' Popov looked at him blankly.

'Police. Is the general likely to be mobbed once we get inside?'

'I would say so, yes. The police love General Koltrov, almost as much as his own soldiers.'

Popov dished out orders to his guys, then fell into step with Sergeant Horbach and Koltrov as they made for an unmarked metal door at the rear of the station. Makarenko slow-walked the suspect in the same direction, with Carter, Logan, Webb and McVeigh moving line abreast at the colonel's six. They stopped in front of the entrance, waited, looked up at the security cameras mounted to the wall above. There was a brief pause followed by a dull clanking noise from the other side as the door unbolted.

The door swung outwards. A podgy cop with a belt-holstered pistol stood inside the doorway, grinning and staring admiringly at Koltrov. He ushered them inside a dully lit corridor, long and narrow, like a submarine, with a series of reinforced cell doors down either side.

A rancid odour of piss, vomit and antiseptic greeted Carter as he followed the rest of the group into the station. Ahead of him, the beer-bellied cop led Koltrov down the corridor. Makarenko shoved Butko along, hissing at him in Ukrainian.

They stopped in front of one of the cells on the right side of the corridor. The cop opened the door, and Makarenko bundled the minister into an interrogation room with a table in the middle, two rickety chairs arranged either side, harsh ceiling lights and metal bars on the window.

By now, word of Koltrov's arrival had spread through the building. Uniformed cops and plainclothed staff approached the general, pumping his hand or applauding him. Others stood back from the melee, content to take snaps on their phones.

Koltrov took it all in his stride, patiently smiling and joking with the cops, making them feel like they were the most important people in the world. He was about to question a Russian collaborator, but he looked totally at ease, thought Carter. Like a football star parading himself before the fans ahead of a cup final. He had that special mixture of charisma, authority and relatability that politicians spent their entire professional lives trying to learn, but few ever mastered.

'Fuck me,' Carter said quietly as the general posed for a selfie with one of his supporters. 'This is mental.'

Logan chuckled. 'You should see him when he visits an army base on the frontline. Never known anything like it. Everyone loves him. Except the obvious.'

'Who?'

'Who'd you think? The big man. Voloshyn.'

'They don't get on?'

'That's putting it mildly. They can't stand one another. Worst-kept secret in Kyiv. Voloshyn hates the idea of someone else hogging the limelight. This guy—' Logan tipped his head at the general '—this guy might be a razor-sharp commander, but don't be fooled. He's media savvy. He's a potential rival, and the president knows it.'

'You think he's the next leader?'

'For sure. If Voloshyn gets taken out, this guy is claiming the throne. I'd bet my mum's house on it.'

'Can't be worth much,' Carter joked. 'They sell houses for a quid up in Liverpool these days, don't they?'

'Sod off. Geordie bastard.'

As he spoke, a senior officer marched over from the front of the building, bellowing at the assembled throng, and the cops swiftly returned to their duties. The general beckoned to Carter and said, 'You and your men will wait here with Captain Popov and Sergeant Horbach. I will question this treacherous snake myself.'

'How long is this going to take?'

'Depends on the minister. If he is prepared to cooperate, then it will be over quite soon. A few hours, maybe less.'

'What if he refuses?'

'Then we will have to persuade him to talk. But he will tell us what he knows. They always do, in the end. Even the ones who think they are brave end up screaming like children.'

At his side, Popov was grinning wickedly.

Carter said, 'This guy should be tried in court. That's the right way to do this, sir.'

Koltrov laughed absurdly. 'We are fighting a war. The rule of law does not exist, not here. Not anymore. For the Russians also, this is true. They do not respect the right of our people to exist.'

'Doesn't mean you have to be like them.'

A dark look crept across the general's face. Something hard glinted in his good eye, like the tip of a knife catching the light.

'That is easy for you to say – you English, who live on an island. You do not have neighbours who wish to exterminate you. Men such as Butko have betrayed their own blood. Their own people. The only law they understand is the one that comes from the business end of a gun. Do not lecture me on how to handle them.'

He glowered at Carter for a moment longer, barked at Popov in his native Ukrainian. Then he turned and ducked into the room.

Through the opening, Carter caught a glimpse of the defence minister. He sat on the metal chair beneath the window, chest heaving up and down while Makarenko watched over him, arms folded across his chest. Koltrov snapped an order; the colonel produced a box-cutter knife from his side pocket, sliced through the prisoner's plasticuffs and tore off his hood.

Butko squinted under the stark glare of the lighting. He looked anxiously at his interrogators, his forehead glossed with sweat, his eyes wide with terror. He started babbling at Koltrov and Makarenko in a strained voice, talking rapidly. Carter couldn't understand what Butko was saying, but it sounded like he was pleading with them.

Koltrov ignored the minister. He calmly removed his army jacket, draped it over the back of one of the empty chairs and rolled his shirtsleeves up to his elbows, cracking his knuckles. Butko realised what was happening. His eyes darted frantically around the room, as if searching for a way to escape.

The general started to close the door.

Carter jammed his foot against the frame, stopping Koltrov from shutting it. The general's features tightened. 'What the fuck do you think you're doing?'

'This door has to stay open,' Carter said. 'Standard procedure, sir.'

'Absolutely not. This is a private interview. Take your foot away this instant.'

'No, sir.'

Koltrov stepped into his personal space, his face bristling with anger.

'Do you want these people to hear of our shame?' He flapped a hand at a gaggle of cops further down the corridor, wandering in and out of offices. 'This man – Butko – is a disgrace to his fellow countrymen.'

'Sorry, sir. I've got my orders to keep an eye on you at all times.'

'I'm giving you an order, you fucking idiot.' Koltrov looked round and dropped his voice so low it was practically crawling on the floor. 'This man is going to provide us with information. Highly confidential information, related to my investigation. I cannot afford the risk of a leak, do you understand?'

'You don't trust us, sir?'

'In my line of work, I trust no one.'

'At least keep him in cuffs, then.'

'Out of the question. I like the suspects to feel at ease during our – conversations. Make them relax. I find it helps to catch them off-balance when we begin asking them the difficult questions. Now step back and let me do my fucking job.'

Carter hesitated for a moment. Then he admitted defeat and withdrew his foot from the gap. Behind Koltrov, the minister continued to plead in desperation with Makarenko. The front of his shirt was drenched with sweat patches.

'Wait here,' the general said, his voice eerily calm. 'This won't take long, I hope.'

The door slammed shut.

Carter stepped away and took up a position with Logan to the side of the door. Horbach and Popov stood further away, chatting among themselves.

Logan lowered his voice to a hiss. 'Are you fucking stupid, lad? Or are you deliberately trying to sabotage the op?'

Carter stood his ground. 'The guy is out of control. Him and his arse-kissing subordinate.'

'So what? No one's going to be shedding tears over a few traitors getting clipped, for fuck's sake.'

'Not now, maybe. Not while the momentum is with the Ukrainians. But things can change. A few years from now, if this ever comes out, we could end up being charged with war crimes.'

'They can't hang any of that shit on us,' Logan protested. 'We're just in attendance. Overseeing his security. What he gets up to is nothing to do with us.'

'Try telling that to a judge at the Hague.'

Logan stared at him.

'Get away with you. You're fucking paranoid, man.'

'Am I? What about them dinosaurs who operated in Northern Ireland. That was decades ago, and they're being dragged back now. This shit always comes back to haunt you.'

'He's got a point,' McVeigh admitted after a beat.

Carter turned to him. 'How long has this shit been going on, Billy?'

'Since day one.'

'We think,' Webb said. 'We don't know that for sure.'

He looked towards McVeigh. Who said, 'The general and his team kept it on the down-low in the beginning. Last few months, they've upped the ante. Getting more extreme.'

'And careless,' Webb added.

'So what?' Logan said. 'How would anyone even find out what they're doing, for fuck's sake?'

'Loose tongues,' Carter said. 'Or leaked footage. Could be any number of ways.'

He was thinking of Makarenko, filming the defence minister in his office, taking a beating from Koltrov. He wondered how many similar videos the colonel had taken in the past. How many had ended up online, or on the phones of other officers.

'All it takes,' he went on, 'is someone getting caught on camera, giving some suspect the crocodile clip treatment to the balls, and suddenly we're on the front pages for all the wrong reasons.'

'It's not just the general, either,' said Webb.

The others looked towards him. The giant Brummie glanced down the corridor, making sure the Ukrainians were out of earshot before he continued.

'The other day I overheard Popov in the canteen, with his mates. Bragging about how they went to town on the last guy we arrested. Did all kinds of sick shit to him. Said he wished he'd filmed it as a memento.'

'But we haven't done anything,' Logan protested. 'Not personally. We're not even allowed in the room during the interrogations.'

'Do you think the journalists will make that distinction? After all that shit blew up about Afghan?'

Carter had been thinking while he listened to the exchange. Weighing up his options. Trying to figure out how to preserve the Regiment's reputation.

He said, 'We'll have to send a report to the head shed. Soon as we're back at camp. Give them the heads-up.'

'What difference would that make?' Logan threw up his arms. 'It's not going to stop the general from getting medieval on the suspects, is it?'

Carter said, slowly, 'I want it down on paper that we challenged the general and his team and made clear our opposition to his interrogation methods. I want our arses covered, in case we get a knock on the door from the cops ten years from now, wanting to have a quiet word with us.'

'This is bollocks, Geordie. Nothing will happen.'

'Maybe not. But I ain't taking chances. I don't know about you, but I could do without this grief.' He eyeballed Logan. 'This is your fault.'

'Me? What the fuck do you mean?'

'You should have flagged this up the moment you realised something fishy was going on.'

'Get off my back, Geordie.' Logan swiped a hand, as if swatting away a wasp. 'I was just following orders.'

'So were the Germans eighty years ago.' The rage swelled inside Carter's chest. 'It's bad enough having to deal with the system at Hereford. I don't need this hassle in my life as well.'

Logan stared at him. Carter thought the guy might get pissy with him, but then he moved away and took up his position to the right of the door, next to Webb. Carter stood next to McVeigh on the other side of the door, fuming through the material of his face covering.

I'll be glad when this job is finally over.

He was facing the prospect of months operating in the crucible of Ukraine, nursemaiding a politically ambitious general with scant regard for his own life, and a penchant for torture.

It'll be a minor miracle if I get through this mission without giving the bloke a fucking slap.

The station was stifling hot. Someone had cranked the heating up to furnace levels. Carter was sweating hard, entombed inside his ballistic helmet, body armour, face mask and gloves. The cloth material covering his mouth made it hard to breathe, irritating his lungs.

He beckoned to Sergeant Horbach, asked him for a brew in clumsy Ukrainian. The bodyguard looked at him uncomprehendingly. Carter tried again and mimed drinking a mug of tea. Horbach got it on the second attempt, gave a big thumbs up and started down the corridor.

'See if you can get them to turn the temperature down, too,' Logan called out to him. 'We're sweating like scientists at an anti-vaxxer protest over here, like.'

Minutes passed.

The four SAS soldiers hung around outside the room, listening to the muted voices coming from within. Popov stood at a distance, shooting the shit with a police officer. Horbach returned clutching four plastic bottles of water. Not the refreshing brew he had been looking forward to, but better than nothing. He twisted the screw cap, lowered his face covering and took a long pull, relieving his parched throat.

One o'clock.

Four hours since they had left the base at Novochanka. Three hours since they had made the arrest.

Carter resigned himself to a long stretch of doing nothing but standing around and waiting. Bodyguarding duties. The less glamorous side of SAS operations. Hours of boredom, the same daily routine, ferrying the principal from place to place, listening to their bullshit.

Seven minutes later, Carter heard a distinct grating noise coming from the other side of the metal door. What sounded like the scraping of chair legs against the bare cement floor.

The voices grew louder.

There was a chorus of shouts, followed by a stifled cry of despair, and a loud crashing sound.

Then the bark of a gunshot.

Eighteen

Carter reacted in an instant. He lunged for the door, wrenched the stainless-steel handle and plunged headlong into the interrogation room, gripping his rifle at his side, eyes sweeping from left to right, McVeigh, Logan, Webb and the two Ukrainians hard on his heels.

Then he saw the body, and stopped dead.

Andriy Butko lay sprawled on the floor, a hole in the middle of his forehead. Blood and bone fragments and brain matter slicked down the wall behind the lifeless defence minister. In his limp right hand was a compact PSM pistol, easily identifiable owing to its slender profile, stubby barrel and steel-sheathed frame. Chambered for the 5.45 x 18 mm Soviet round. Favoured handgun of high-ranking KGB officers, because its small size made it easy to conceal.

Koltrov and Makarenko were standing over the minister. The colonel held his Glock in a two-handed grip, arms extended. Barrel trained at the suspect slumped on the floor.

'Shit,' McVeigh said as he drew up next to Logan and Carter.

Popov barged inside the cell after the Regiment men. He halted inside the doorway, eyes flitting quickly between Butko and the general.

Carter lowered his M4. 'Are you OK? Sir?'

The general didn't appear to have heard him. He stared at Butko, unblinking, as if transfixed by the blood pulsing out of the exit wound in the back of his head.

'Sir? Are you hurt?'

Koltrov snapped out of his stupor. 'Fine,' he said hoarsely. 'I'm fine.'

In the corridor, the pounding of footsteps grew louder as the police officers rushed over to investigate the commotion. A burly cop hurried inside the interrogation room and dropped to a knee beside the minister. Someone else shouted for an ambulance.

Above the gaggle of voices, Carter heard Sergeant Horbach's booming voice, ordering the cops to stay back. At the same time, Webb was speaking into his radio mic, reporting to the Ukrainian BGs waiting outside the police station.

'Shots fired, shots fired,' he reported. 'Stay where you are. Repeat, stay in your positions. No one moves unless we tell you otherwise.'

'What happened?' Carter demanded.

'It seems,' Koltrov said, without taking his gaze off Butko, 'it seems we underestimated the minister.'

Makarenko reholstered his Glock. He said, coolly, 'Suspect had a weapon concealed on his person. He was going to shoot the general, so I engaged. Neutralised the threat.'

'Shit.'

Koltrov was still gazing at the corpse. 'It is fortunate that the colonel was in the room with me just now. He saved my life. Otherwise . . .'

His voice trailed. He turned towards Carter with barely suppressed rage.

'This was your fuck-up,' he said.

Carter jerked his head back. 'Fuck off.'

Koltrov stepped towards him and snorted through flared nostrils. 'Your men had the responsibility for searching the suspect. If they had been doing their jobs properly, they would have found the pistol.'

'No way.' Logan shook his head furiously. 'Geordie, I swear to God I checked that guy twice over before we bugged out of his office. He didn't have fuck all on him.'

'Then how do you explain this?' Koltrov gestured to the PSM in Butko's hand.

'I don't . . . I don't know.'

Carter glared at the general. 'You can't pin this on us. You should have taken our advice. If you had listened to us, he wouldn't be lying there with a hole in his fucking head.'

'And I expect my men to do their jobs, instead of complaining like little bitches.'

Carter drew in a sharp breath. It took every fibre of his being to control his temper.

Last-chance saloon, Geordie.

Don't do anything to piss him off.

Koltrov closed his good eye for a beat and exhaled. 'It does not matter. What is done is done. Besides, the minister told us everything we needed to know. He sang like a canary. That is the expression, yes?'

'He spilled his guts? Already?'

Koltrov smiled cruelly. 'Like I said, my interrogation techniques never fail.'

'What did he tell you?' asked McVeigh.

Carter interrupted the general and said, 'There's no time for that. We'll discuss everything later. The priority is getting you back safe and sound to the camp, sir.'

'What about him?' asked Logan.

He indicated the defence minister. The blood had formed a gleaming puddle beneath his body, oozing outwards. Like an oil spill. Carter said, 'Not our problem. The cops can deal with it.'

The well-built officer who had been inspecting Butko's wounds stood upright and addressed himself to Popov, firing off a machine-gun burst of Ukrainian.

'What did he say?' McVeigh asked the captain.

'He says they will need statements. From the general, and from everyone else present at the scene. Including us. He says there will need to be a full investigation.'

Carter said, 'Tell him to arrange it with the general's people. We can return and make statements on another day.'

Popov translated again. He waited for the officer's response, then said to Carter, 'He is afraid he cannot let us leave. He says it is unfortunate, but they must follow procedure.'

'I don't give a fuck. Someone just tried to execute the general. We're leaving now. Unless this bloke wants to be accountable for putting his life at risk.'

Carter didn't wait for the officer's response. He wasn't about to let some jumped-up Ukrainian copper dictate SOPs to him. He turned and swept into the corridor, gesturing for Popov and Horbach to lead the way, Koltrov, Makarenko and Zinchenko at their backs, Carter and the SAS men to the rear. The same formation they had used when entering the station. Meanwhile, Logan got on the net to the team outside, letting them know that they were about to exit the station.

'Heading straight back to base,' he said. 'Repeat, principal is heading back to base on Route Charlie. Suspect is dead, but principal is unharmed.'

A gaggle of policemen and women had gathered in the corridor. Captain Popov hollered at them in Ukrainian, ordering them to make way for the general.

'Doesn't make any sense,' Logan muttered through his face covering. 'I searched him thoroughly. The minister. The guy wasn't packing, Geordie. I'm fucking sure of it.'

'So how did he get hold of the gun?' Carter asked.

'I don't know.' Logan shook his head again. 'All I know is, this gig just got even tougher.'

'Too fucking right.' Carter exhaled bitterly. He lowered his voice. 'Between you and me, I'm starting to think that keeping this guy out of harm's way is an impossible job.'

* * *

They returned to Novochanka Air Base at two o'clock in the afternoon. The three-vehicle convoy took a different route out of Kyiv, winding this way and that, but the scenery remained broadly the same. Carter and Logan said little during the ride. Koltrov spent most of the journey in a private conference with Makarenko, while Zinchenko sat hunched over her phone, fingers speedily dashing off messages. Carter wondered if she ever went more than five minutes without checking her phone.

They hit the sandbagged checkpoint outside of Novochanka and went through the same routine they had followed that morning, but in reverse. Showed their ID cards to the soldiers guarding the approach to the town, carried on through Novochanka and stopped again at the gatehouse in front of the air base. There was another cursory examination of their ID cards. The convoy rolled on down the access road for half a kilometre before hitting the brakes outside Koltrov's private quarters. Logan kept the motor running while the general, Makarenko and Zinchenko disgorged themselves from the back of the Suburban.

Once they were safely inside the building, the convoy pulled away again. They carried on for two hundred metres towards the tarmacked area fronting the main accommodation block and parked up under the camo nets. The soldiers on both bodyguard teams debussed from the Suburbans and trooped towards the dosshouse.

Carter tore off his face covering and said, 'Sort out your kit. I'll meet you in the canteen in twenty.'

He started down the corridor.

'Where are you going?' Logan asked.

'I need to brief Hereford. Update them on the situation.'

The others headed upstairs while Carter made for the small locked room with the fridge-sized safe and the weapons locker. He snatched up the satphone from the docking station, punched in the number for the ops room at camp, and filed a report with the head shed. Gave them the lowdown on the arrest of the defence minister. The interrogation. The attempt on the general's life. He made a special point of detailing the treatment of the suspect.

He told them about the stories of torture and extrajudicial treatment. An arse-covering exercise. Carter had eighteen months left in the Regiment. He didn't plan on anything coming back to bite him in his retirement.

He dumped his kit upstairs, kept hold of his M4, and joined the rest of the team in the canteen. They sat at a separate table from the Ukrainians, tucking into portions of lukewarm sausages, eggs, chips and sauerkraut. Logan wiped his plate clean, let out a satisfying belch and slid out from behind the table, leaving his rifle propped against his chair.

'The fuck are you doing?' asked McVeigh.

'Second helping,' Logan replied. 'No point seeing all this grub go to waste.'

'You're still hungry?'

'Starving, son.' Logan patted his stomach and grinned. 'I could eat a bloody horse.'

'No change there, then,' Webb cracked.

He shared an easy laugh with McVeigh.

'Brummie bastard.'

'Seriously, though, you should watch your diet.' McVeigh popped a chunk of sausage into his mouth and pointed his fork at Logan. 'Particularly someone at your age.'

'My age?' Logan repeated. He wrinkled his face. 'Fuck off. I'm not that old, you cheeky bastard.'

'Not on Civvy Street, perhaps. But this is the Regiment. Different rules. Best days are behind you.'

Logan pointed his fork at the younger man. 'Are you angling for a fucking slap, son?'

'Just saying. You're getting long in the tooth. Stands to reason you should take better care of yourself. Supplements, diet, all that stuff. Help to keep you sharp.'

'I ain't taking advice from a Manc. Rather peel me own fucking eyelids off with a rusty blade.'

'Suit yourself.'

McVeigh returned to attacking his food.

'We've still got what it takes,' Logan said after a pause of silence. 'Me and Geordie have been doing the business for years. We were cutting around Iraq while you were still in nappies.'

'Yeah, but that was then. This is now, Grandad. You'll be doing ops in Zimmer frames at this rate.'

Webb burst into laughter. Logan stood up and left to reload his plate. Carter ate distractedly. He thought about Koltrov, and Butko, and his younger brother. The attempts on the lives of the president and the general. The two most popular figures in the country. Both the subject of assassination plots within the space of a few days. Which could only mean one thing. The Russians were ramping up their efforts.

Something else bothered him, too. Something that had been scratching at the base of his skull since they had departed the police station earlier that afternoon. He looked up from his food as Logan returned to the table, his plate loaded with carbs and meat.

Carter said, 'Are you definitely sure the minister wasn't carrying? Back when you searched him.'

'Positive.' Logan slathered butter over a thick slice of bread.

Carter said, 'The PSM is small. Easy to conceal. You might have missed it.'

'Not a chance.' Logan set down his knife and fork. Stared hard at Carter. 'The guy had nothing on him in his office. Honest to God.'

'So how do you explain how he had the gun on him at the station?'

Webb stroked his chin thoughtfully. 'Maybe he got hold of the weapon after his arrest.'

'How? He was in cuffs. We had eyes on him in the back of the car, all the way to the station.'

McVeigh had stopped chewing. He looked intently at Carter. 'What are you getting at?'

Carter cast his mind back to the scene in the interrogation room. He thought about Koltrov removing the plasticuffs. Demanding that the cell door remain shut throughout the interview.

'Nothing,' he replied after a pause. 'It's probably nothing.'

They polished off their grub and helped themselves to slices of apple sponge cake and brews. Black coffee for Carter, tea and milk for McVeigh, water for Webb. Who never seemed to drink anything stronger. Logan devoured another massive wedge of cake. He was contemplating a third helping when a podgy-faced officer in fatigues entered the canteen and made a beeline for the SAS men. He stopped in front of their table, cleared his throat. One of the general's flunkeys, Carter supposed.

'Help you, mate?' Carter asked.

He said, in smooth English, 'General Koltrov wants to see you.'

'All of us?'

'Yes.'

'Where?'

'The operations room. General's private quarters.'

'Now? Right now?'

'Yes,' the flunkey said.

'Why?' asked McVeigh. 'What's this about?'

The flunkey shrugged.

'Fucking talkative, this one, ain't he?' Logan quipped. 'He makes you look like a chatterbox, Patrick.'

Webb stared daggers at the Liverpudlian. 'Funny. Very funny,' he deadpanned. 'You've got us all in stitches.'

'Fucking do one.'

Carter necked the gritty dregs of his coffee and stood up.

'Lead the way, mate. Let's see what the general wants.'

* * *

243

They left the dosshouse and followed the flunkey across the base. Three o'clock in the afternoon. Thick grey clouds pressed low in the sky, heavy with the threat of rain. A brutal wind cut knife-like across the base. Carter figured the temperature had to be in the low single digits. Four or five degrees. He remembered what Logan had said about the coming winter. Sub-zero temperatures. No hot water or electricity. People freezing to death in their unheated homes. The moment of truth for Ukraine, and its ability to withstand the aggressors from the east.

After two hundred metres they reached the dormitory block housing the general and his staff. The flunkey nodded at the two guards on duty at the entrance, swiped a security card against the reader next to the main door, then led the four Blades down a long corridor and up a flight of stairs. They hooked a right on the first floor and carried on until they stopped outside a room midway down the landing.

They waited while the flunkey fiddled with a set of keys. At the end of the corridor, Carter spied an open door leading to the general's sleeping quarters. Inside, a woman sat perched on the edge of an unmade bed.

Carter recognised her at once. One of the general's girls. The brunette he'd seen leaving the building that morning. She sat with her long legs crossed, staring at her face in a pocket mirror while she fussed with her hair.

'They're in early today,' McVeigh commented.

Logan said, admiringly, 'The big man must feel like celebrating. Good on him. I'd be doing the same, if I was in his boots.'

The brunette raised her gaze from the mirror to the soldiers outside the room. Carter briefly locked eyes with her, before unseen hands slammed the door shut.

The flunkey unlocked the operations room door and showed them into a cramped space with the same Soviet-prison decor as the main accommodation block. Technically an ops room, in the same way that a Trabant was technically a car. There was a table. There were chairs. A barred window overlooked the row of crumbling admin buildings and derelict hangars. The walls were cracked and in places the paint had peeled away, revealing exposed chunks of brickwork. In the corner, a bin overflowed with chocolate wrappers and coffee cups.

'Wait here. General Koltrov will join you in a minute,' the flunkey said before he left the room.

'Probably getting in a quickie first,' Logan said, a trace of envy in his voice. 'Wouldn't say no to a bit of that myself. Curves in all the right places. My kind of woman.'

'Who isn't?' McVeigh asked rhetorically. 'You'd shag a lamppost if it gave you the eye.'

Logan looked hurt. 'Didn't your parents teach you to respect your elders?'

McVeigh laughed cynically. 'No chance. They were too busy getting hammered.'

They waited.

Two minutes later, the door flung open again, and General Koltrov entered the room, Colonel Makarenko and Zinchenko dutifully following him inside. They took the seats on the other side of the table from Carter and his colleagues. Zinchenko finished tapping out a message on her phone and put it to sleep. Logan winked at her and grinned slyly. Zinchenko didn't look impressed.

Koltrov steepled his fingers on the table and said, 'There's been a development. Something we need to share with you. But first, we need certain . . . assurances.'

Carter said, 'What assurances?'

Makarenko said, carefully, 'What you're about to hear must not be repeated outside this room. This information is highly sensitive. A matter of grave importance to the state.'

Carter spread his hands. 'Fine. You've got our word. What's the craic?'

'Craic?'

'What is it you want to tell us?'

Koltrov exchanged a look with Makarenko and said, 'Before that piece of shit Butko pulled a gun on me, he confirmed something we had heard before. From other collaborators we had questioned.'

'Tortured, you mean.'

'It is the same thing, no? Your American friends share the same opinion, I believe. Given what I have heard about the techniques they have used against terrorists in the past.'

The Ukrainians laughed among themselves. Carter glared drearily at the general. He was tired after the journey into Kyiv, the arrest and the fallout from the shooting. 'Just tell us why we're here.'

Koltrov dropped his smile and looked steadily at him.

Said, 'There is a high-level traitor in Ukraine. Someone at the very top of the pyramid. The identity of this person is known only to four people in the Kremlin, including the president himself.'

'How high are we talking?' Logan asked. 'Because I'd say defence minister is pretty fucking high up the food chain.'

'Much higher.' Koltrov smirked. 'Ministers, they come and go. Mouthpieces. The individual in question is one of the most powerful figures in the country.'

'Who is he?'

'Or she,' Carter pointed out.

'I am afraid I cannot share that information.'

Makarenko cleared his throat and said, 'We have known of the existence of this person for some time, but we did not have a name. Only suspicions. Now, thanks to the traitorous dog Andriy Butko, we are certain of their identity.'

'Why are you telling us this?' asked Carter.

'We need to arrange a meeting with the president. Face to face. As a matter of urgency. He must be told what is going on.'

'Can't you just reach him on a secure line instead?'

'No line is absolutely secure,' Koltrov said. 'There is always the chance that the Russians might be listening in. It would give them the chance to spirit away the traitor before we could arrest him. No. This has to be done in person. It is the only way.'

'But Voloshyn's off the grid,' McVeigh pointed out. 'We were told he wasn't planning on showing his face until them traitors had been flushed out.'

'We have discussed this. He is prepared to make an exception on this occasion. Given the stakes.'

'You've spoken with him?' asked Carter.

Koltrov nodded. 'An hour ago. We had a . . . productive conversation. The president understands the situation. He agrees that this is too sensitive to discuss over the phone. He has agreed to meet with us at short notice.'

'Where is he now?'

'At a residence somewhere in the countryside. Mykolaiv Oblast. The precise location is top secret.'

Logan inclined his head to one side. 'But that's not far from the frontline.'

'Your point?'

'Why would your man Voloshyn be hiding out there? If he's worried about getting bumped, surely he should be tucked up in Kyiv, where no fucker can get to him.'

Zinchenko had been silent so far. Now she said, 'The president is planning a surprise visit to the troops on the frontline in the south.'

'Bad idea,' Webb said. 'That whole area is a meat grinder.'

The press officer said, 'That is why his visit is so important. As you must know, the south has become the focus of our counteroffensive operations. The Russians are holding on, for now. But if our troops succeed in pushing the enemy back across to the eastern side of the Dnieper River before the winter, it will represent a great victory.'

'I love it when you talk dirty,' Logan said.

Zinchenko shot him a frosty glare.

Carter glanced sideways at Webb. The man mountain wore an anxious expression.

'That's why he's in the area?' Carter asked. 'To boost morale?'

Zinchenko nodded slightly. 'The soldiers in the area have endured some of the worst fighting in the war. A visit from the president will help to keep up their spirits ahead of a renewed push for Kherson.'

'Must be a big deal, if Voloshyn is prepared to risk showing his face. Considering the threats against him.'

'His staff are against the idea,' Makarenko admitted. 'But the president is determined to make the visit. If he can make even one per cent difference to the outcome, he believes it is worth the risk.'

'This hideout,' Carter said, 'how safe is it?'

Koltrov smiled slightly. 'You are worried about your brother?'

'I'm not thinking about Luke. I'm just wondering why we can't meet the president at his gaff. Got to be easier than sending in an advanced party to secure some other site.'

'We have suggested this already. The president has refused.'

'Why?'

Koltrov and Makarenko glance askance at one another. The colonel said, 'Voloshyn does not permit visitors to his residence. His advisors worry that the location might become public knowledge and expose him to a potential attack. Even we do not know where it is.'

'This is also why we cannot disclose our intelligence over the phone,' Koltrov said. 'We think the Russians have hidden direction-finding equipment along the frontline. It's possible they might geo-locate any call to the residence. Send in rockets.'

'Where and when is the meeting?' asked McVeigh.

'Tomorrow,' Koltrov replied. 'Somewhere in Mykolaiv Oblast. Not far from the frontline, at a rendezvous to be determined by your colleagues on Voloshyn's bodyguard team. I leave the details to you to sort out.'

'What's the plan? Once we hit the RV?' Carter said.

'I will meet with the president and tell him what we know. Then we shall make plans to arrest the individual in question – the traitor who has brought so much grief and shame to our nation.'

'Can we trust the int?'

'I believe so, yes. We are still verifying the details, but so far, Butko's information checks out. There is no reason to doubt his claims.'

'Who's attending the meet from our side?'

Makarenko said, 'The usual arrangement. Everyone in this room, plus Captain Popov and his team. You'll have to brief them separately, following this meeting.'

Webb had been silent throughout. Now he said, 'This is a bad fucking idea, sir. It's not safe.'

'Nonsense. I will be well protected. I shall have my full bodyguard detail, and the president will have his. Or do you not have confidence in your own abilities?'

Webb ignored the question. 'Perhaps we should wait until the president is back in Kyiv.'

'No,' Koltrov snapped. 'I must meet with him at once. This information is too important to wait for his return. It cannot wait.' The general frowned at his watch. 'Any more questions?'

'No, sir.'

'Then I suggest you liaise with your friends. They're expecting your call. In the meantime, I have other business to attend to.'

'Business, my arse,' Logan said as they paced back down the stairs and headed for the main entrance. 'Having himself a party with Miss Ukraine more like.'

Webb said, guardedly, 'We've got bigger problems than the general's sex life.'

Carter looked round at him. 'What are you thinking, Patrick?'

Webb looked hesitant. He said, 'The southern front is meant to be hell on earth. Rockets, drones, artillery. We're going to be spitting distance from some of the heaviest fighting in the country.'

'What's your point?' asked McVeigh.

'This meeting is asking for trouble. We shouldn't be going ahead with it.'

Carter said, 'We can't worry about that now. All we can do is crack on and get the job done. In and out, fast as we can. Lightning visit. That's the way to do it.'

'And hope for some good luck for a change,' Logan added grimly. 'Because we're sure as fuck going to need it.'

* * *

They made the short walk back across the base to the doss-house, fixed more industrial-strength brews and regrouped in the office. Carter got on the antenna-rigged satphone to Hereford while the others checked their various items of kit, charged their phones and studied maps of Mykolaiv and Kherson Oblasts. Familiarising themselves with the main roads, cities, and other points of strategic interest.

Carter dialled the number for the ops room at Hereford and asked the duty officer to patch him through to his brother's satphone. Like an operating service, but with added military-grade encryption. The officer put him on hold while the sigs team connected him, and there was a short sequence of clicks before a voice said, 'Jamie? Hello?'

'Surprised to hear from me, mate?'

A familiar laugh travelled down the line. 'Not at all. Typical big brother behaviour, this. Stealing my thunder.'

'Yeah. That's exactly why I came out to this shithole. To stop you from getting all the glory.'

'Bastard.'

Carter smiled warmly to himself. 'It's good to hear your voice, Luke.'

'Likewise.'

'Who told you I was in-country?'

Luke said, 'Head shed. Yesterday at evening prayers. Said you were looking after one of our friends in the army. BG duties.' He paused, and Carter could almost see him grinning on the other end of the line. 'Copying me again, I see. Can't even come up with an original mission for yourself these days, can you?'

'But doing a better job of it than you. Obviously.'

Luke burst into laughter again. Several hundred kilometres away, but the distance between them melted into nothing.

Carter said, 'I hear you've been making a name for yourself with the principal.'

'Yes.' Luke's tone became strained. 'Not that I'm happy about it, like. Fuck me, I'd prefer to keep a low profile if it meant the guy stopped taking stupid risks.'

That sounded just like his brother, Carter reflected. Luke had never had any interest in citations or gongs or praise from his superiors. He just stayed in the background and got on with the business of soldiering. Warrior to his core. Go in hard, do the best job possible, and forget about the noise. That was Luke's motto.

Maybe I should have tried that approach myself.

'I know the feeling,' Carter replied glumly. 'Our guy thinks he's channelling the spirit of Napoleon.'

'Probably why he's so popular. He's even threatening to over-shadow our man with his antics. You can imagine how that's gone down.'

'Like a cup of cold sick, I bet.'

'That's about right.' Luke grunted. 'Between you and me, the president is worried that Koltrov is hogging the limelight. He wants to put himself out there again. It's going to be a ball-ache keeping him safe, and that's without having to set up this meeting with your man.'

'We're in the same boat, mate. Dealing with a pair of alpha males. Egos the size of solar systems.'

Luke was silent for a beat. 'Voloshyn is wondering why the general won't discuss his findings over the phone,' he said.

'I've asked myself the same question.'

'They could chat on this line,' Luke suggested. 'If he's worried about the Russians listening in.'

'No use. He wants to do it face to face. He's insistent.'

'We're on the doorstep of the Russian frontline, mate.'

'Is it that bad?'

'Worse. Like, a million times. The Russians have flooded the frontline with drones and mobile anti-aircraft launchers. Flying to the RV from our location is a no-go. We'll have to drive to the meet. You'll need to confirm with the ops desk, but I reckon you guys will have to do the same.'

Carter said, 'Where's the RV?'

'Mayor's office in Zolodyansk. Forty kilometres north of the frontline. I'll send you the coordinates. We'll meet there tomorrow afternoon. Four o'clock. Twenty-four hours from now.'

Carter frowned. 'Is it safe?'

Luke said, 'Only safe place in the vicinity. The mayor's office doubles up as the town's air-raid shelter. Loads of civilians are bunkered down in the basement at the moment.'

'How many people are we talking about?'

'Four hundred or so. Everyone who hasn't fled the town. Women and children. Old men not fit for military service. People with nowhere else to go.'

'Guards?'

'Local militia. Volunteers. They're honest lads, as far as I know, but they're only kitted out with the basics. AK-74s and that shit.'

'Let's hope we don't have to rely on them in a firefight then.'

'One more thing,' Luke said. He paused. 'We'll need to arrange a dummy RV.'

Carter considered. Dummy RVs were used by the Regiment to avoid the chances of the meeting being compromised. BG teams identified and marked out a fake RV point, several kilometres from the real location. Attendees were kept in the dark about the plan, to prevent a security leak. Once they neared the fake site, the bodyguard teams would change direction and head for the actual RV.

'You think there's a risk the Russians might find out?'

'I don't know,' Luke replied. 'But they found out about the president's visit to Balanivka.'

They spent a long time on the mission planning. They discussed modes of transport. Routes to and from the mayor's office. Call-off signs, in case one of the teams ran into an enemy ambush or one of the vehicles went technical en route. If either side encountered a problem and needed to abort the meeting, they would get on the channel to the other team, alert them to the call-off and abandon the RV.

They also discussed the order of arrival. Whoever showed up first would sponsor the location. Which meant throwing up a security cordon, checking the area for threats, and establishing a reception party ahead of the other side's approach.

Carter said, 'We'll take charge of the sponsoring. I'll send one of our guys forward with the Ukrainians, make sure the building is clear before we give you the green light.'

'Negative. The president wants to be the first person on the ground.'

'But that's against Regiment protocol. The president is the number-one priority. We should be the ones sponsoring the RV.'

'It's not my decision,' Luke said, moodily. 'The president wants to meet with the mayor of Zolodyansk before the meeting with your man. Then it's straight back to the president's hideout.'

'It's risky, Luke. Your man will be exposed for a long time. He should be meeting the mayor after our visit.'

'Jamie, I've tried. It's no good. He won't listen.'

'Fuck's sake. What difference does it make?'

'Between you and me, I think it's an ego thing. He wants to establish dominance over Koltrov. Like a king welcoming one of his barons to his court. Make a point.'

Carter chewed on a thought. There was obviously a lot of friction between Voloshyn and Koltrov. They had seemed like best mates in public, slapping each other on the back and smiling for the cameras, but there was no doubt that the president saw the general as a genuine threat. Which could be problematic. Bad decisions happened when people allowed their judgement to be clouded by personal agendas. That was how mistakes got made. How people ended up getting killed.

'Who are the other lads on your team?' he asked.

Luke said, 'Taff Hedges. Tyler Dunk. And Josh Bowman.'

'Bowman?' Carter kneaded his brow. 'I thought he was out of the Regiment these days.'

He didn't mention the stories that had done the rounds at Credenhill. The ones implying that Bowman had a drug problem. Opioids, they had said. A couple of years ago he had disappeared from the camp without explanation. Most of the lads had naturally assumed his departure had something to do with the drug rumours.

'He's been on rotation with the Cell,' Luke said. 'Two years. Came back a few months ago. You two were on ops together, weren't you?'

'Iraq,' Carter said. 'Feels like a lifetime ago.'

They spoke for a while longer. Clarifying details. Checking all the pre-mission boxes. The how, why and when. They agreed to speak again, once Carter had briefed the Ukrainians and checked in with the Regimental ops room. They talked briefly about the general's routine, and the shooting at the police station. Listening to his voice, Carter suddenly realised how much he missed his brother.

'Listen,' he said, 'we'll catch up after the meeting. Have a good chat. Like old times.'

'You're on.'

'And Luke?'

'Yes?'

'Be careful tomorrow.'

Luke chuckled. 'That's rich, coming from you. I seem to remember you were the one always getting into trouble when we was kids.'

'I'm serious. If the general's int is accurate, we've got a high-ranking official spying for the Russians. Could be anyone. Could be one of the guys around your principal, for all we know.'

'I doubt it. No one gets within ten kilometres of the president without being fully vetted.'

'Just do me a favour and make sure you have eyes on Voloshyn's aides from now on.'

Carter remembered the promise he'd made to their mother on her deathbed. How he'd taken her clammy hand in his and vowed to always look out for Luke, no matter what.

'I'm a big boy. I can take care of myself, believe it or not.' The tone was friendly, casual, but there was an edge to it as well. That hint of sibling rivalry that had always bubbled beneath the surface between the two of them, even though they shared an unbreakable bond.

'I know, Luke.'

'Don't worry about me. Just focus on keeping your man in check. If we stick to the plan, everything will be fine.'

'I hope you're right. For both our sakes.'

* * *

Carter clicked off the satphone and filled in Webb, Logan and McVeigh on the plan for the following day. He told them about

255

the dummy RV, the call-off signs, the meeting point at the mayor's office in the small city of Zolodyansk, Mykolaiv Oblast. Voloshyn's stubborn insistence on having his side sponsor the RV, in breach of Regiment SOPs.

He put another call into Hereford and asked the ops desk for an int report on the southern front. A short time later they came back and confirmed what he'd already suspected. Flying to the RV was a no-go. GCHQ had been informed that the Americans had detected a Krug surface-to-air mobile missile launcher south of Zolodyansk. Effective range of up to fifty kilometres. They had been unable to pinpoint an exact location and suspected that there might be further enemy SAMs concealed in close proximity. Furthermore, drones armed with high-explosive warheads had carried out strikes on Ukrainian targets in several neighbouring districts, knocking out armoured vehicles and artillery batteries in an attempt to deny them air superiority. Until further notice, a no-fly order was in effect around the RV.

At six o'clock, they sent for Popov and Horbach. Carter ordered more coffee and brought them up to date on the meeting with Voloshyn. Then they studied the route in detail.

'Distance to the RV from our position is five hundred kilometres,' Carter said. 'Journey time of approximately seven hours.'

He scrutinised the map again. Zolodyansk. A small conurbation of some fifteen thousand citizens, set in a sparsely populated plain. Forty kilometres to the south was the frontline, although the intelligence picture seemed to change every time Carter made a brew. Troops on both sides were moving back and forth, retaking obliterated villages, abandoning defensive positions. The Ukrainian counteroffensive in the south was in full swing, but the Russians were putting up a fierce fight as they desperately fought to maintain a toehold on the western bank of the Dnieper. They had even made gains in some places, recapturing villages previously liberated by the Ukrainians.

Ten kilometres south-east of the RV was the nuclear power plant at Holovika. Still under Ukrainian control, as far as the ops desk knew, although the Russians had been aggressively shelling the area in previous days.

Carter said, 'We'll stop along the way at secure sites. Refuel the wagons, grab a bite to eat and stretch our legs.'

'Why don't we just drive straight there?'

'We need the breaks. Got a long journey ahead of us. It's important we're sharp when we hit Zolodyansk. If we're tired, there's a risk of someone making a mistake or getting sloppy.'

'Where are the stopping points?' Popov asked.

Carter pointed out a pair of small urban enclaves circled on the map. 'First one is a militia camp in an old Soviet army base. Second post is a laager point. Forward mounting base for Ukrainian forces. From there it's a straight journey to the RV.'

'We'll have to have eyes on the general when he's out of the vehicle,' Logan mused, rubbing his chin. 'Knowing how fond the guy is of meeting his diehard fans.'

'Any Russian attacks in the area?' Popov asked.

'We've got reports of shelling in the nearby towns. Russian howitzers. Mainly targeting Ukrainian defensive positions and civilian infrastructure.'

Carter told them about the Russian SAM batteries and the no-fly order.

'Drones?'

'Plenty of them along the frontline,' said Logan. 'Hence the no-fly order. But the route itself should be safe enough by car, according to the Americans.'

Carter looked up from the map.

'We'll need to put together an advance party. Four-man reception team.' He nodded at Horbach. 'Sergeant, you're in charge of the team. You'll proceed along this route, twenty kilometres ahead of the convoy,' he added, tracing a finger over the route marked on the map.

'Your orders are to scope out the ground for threats and secure each stopping point ahead of our arrival. That means maintaining radio contact and having eyes in the backs of your heads at all times. If you spot anything dicey – anything at all – I want to hear about it.'

'No problem, boss,' Horbach said.

'Once we reach each stopping point, we'll take over responsibility for the security and you'll frog-leap onto the next point.'

Popov said, 'Tell me about this dummy RV.'

'Fake site is here.' Carter indicated a point on the map, north-east of the actual RV. 'Industrial estate on the outskirts of the town of Pokrozirka. There's a T-junction on the main road. Fifteen kilometres from the meeting point. East, the road runs straight to Pokrozirka. West takes us to Zolodyansk. Once we hit the T, we'll take the right turn and drive towards the actual RV.'

'Does the general know about this plan?'

'No,' Logan said. 'Outside of this room, the only people aware of the true RV are the lads on Voloshyn's BG team. Everyone else will find out only when we reach the T-junction.'

Popov made a pained face and clicked his tongue ruefully. He said, 'The general will not be happy about this. He does not like information being kept from him.'

'Tough shit. This is how we're doing it.' Carter stared firmly at the captain. 'You are not to tell anyone else about the real RV. Anyone at all. That information is for the BG teams only.'

Popov stiffened. 'I understand.'

'Do you? Because we're taking a serious gamble here. We're going to be danger-close to the frontline. If there's a leak to the other side – if the Russians know about the real RV – we'll be driving into an ambush.'

Horbach held up his hands. 'Don't worry. We will keep this information secret. You can rely on us, boss.'

Carter eyed them for a moment longer, then resumed the briefing. 'Have your guys bring their doss bags with them. Ration packs too, enough for twenty-four hours. We'll be stopping overnight at the laager point once the meeting is over. Safer than trying to drive back after curfew.'

They spent the next few hours fine-tuning the plan. Throughout the evening more int flowed through from the Regiment ops desk. Updates on enemy troop dispositions. Satellite imagery of Zolodyansk and the surrounding area. Architectural diagrams of the mayor's office on Radzenskiy Street.

A network of underground passages ran from the basement level to other local government buildings. Standard requirement for local Communist Party chiefs, Popov explained. Most of the tunnels dated back to the days of the Cold War. The chiefs had built them in preparation for nuclear war. Relics of a bygone era. Or so the world had thought.

At around eight o'clock, Webb and McVeigh left to sort out the wagons, checking the tyres and oil levels and brake fluid, loading the boots with jerry cans of diesel fuel, and blankets, bottles of water, high-calorie snacks, spare batteries. Nothing was left to chance.

Carter called Makarenko, summoned him to the briefing room and brought him up to speed on the plan. Minus the stuff about the dummy RV. The colonel expressed his unhappiness at having to sit in a car for seven hours, and pushed for a helicopter flight instead, but Carter stood firm and ordered Makarenko to be ready at eight o'clock the next morning. The guy wasn't pleased with that news, either. Probably dreaded having to tell the general he'd have to cut short his time with his girls.

A short time later, Makarenko left the doss block. Carter and his colleagues decamped to the canteen for a quick bite to eat before tending to their kit. Weaponry, ammunition, ballistic helmets, armour. They entered the preset frequency for Luke's team into their personal radio systems so they could dial in and communicate with the other SAS lads during the journey south.

Carter also saved his brother's encrypted phone number to his burner, made sure the battery was full. Worst-case scenario stuff. If the comms proved unreliable, he needed a way of reaching the other BG team. But he hoped it wouldn't come to that. Using an un-encrypted device in a hostile environment was seriously risky.

At eleven o'clock, he signalled the end of the briefing. As they slid out from behind the table, he noticed Webb staring at the map with a look of concern.

'Let's hope the Russians aren't raining down artillery on the mayor's office tomorrow,' he muttered. 'Ops desk reckons the area has been getting hammered for weeks now.'

'If there's any heavy stuff coming in,' Carter said, 'Hereford will let us know in advance, and we'll call off the meeting. They'll be keeping us posted throughout the road trip.'

Webb gave the slightest nod and made a noise deep in his throat. 'Still, it would be better if it wasn't going ahead at all.'

'What's your fucking problem?' Logan responded irritably. 'It's a routine visit to the frontline, fella. We've done this shitloads of times over the past six months.'

'Not to anywhere as dicey as this place.' Webb looked up. 'We've got two of the most wanted targets in the country, in one location, pissing distance from the frontline. Pair of sitting ducks. It'll be a miracle if we can get through this without anything going wrong.'

'Cheer up, fella,' McVeigh said. 'Look at it this way. If this thing does go tits up, at least you won't have to listen to any more of Logan's crap jokes.'

Logan stared at him. 'That's not even funny, mate.'

'You're right. I've seen your tragic attempts to charm the local talent. That shite is hilarious.'

Carter stood up and said, 'Get some kip, lads. Clear heads for tomorrow. Meet here at seven o'clock sharp for a final briefing and hardware check. We leave at eight.'

* * *

Nine hours later, as the pale dawn sun lifted into the sky, the four soldiers from A Squadron, 22 SAS emerged from the accommodation block and paced towards the row of Suburbans parked across the tarmac. Each man carried his M4 rifle, Glock 17 semi-automatic pistol and a small daysack filled with provisions and essential kit for the long journey to the frontline. In addition, Patrick Webb, the team's designated sniper specialist, carried the bolt-action L115A4 rifle in a weapon sleeve, plus two ten-round magazines of 7.62 x 51 mm NATO brass.

Captain Popov stood waiting for the Regiment men beside the wagons, along with another guy from the Ukrainian BG team. Junior Sergeant Marko Syrota was a lanky streak of piss, acne scarred and youthful looking, but a competent soldier. Sergeant Horbach and the three other lads on the advance party had departed from the base fifteen minutes earlier in a soft-skinned Land Rover borrowed from the general's staff. They would clear the ground ahead, reporting any potential threats and feeding back information to the rest of the convoy.

The two Ukrainians bundled into one of the Suburbans. Carter and Logan made for the middle vehicle in the convoy. Webb and McVeigh took the rearmost wagon. They went through the same drill as the previous morning. Drove south and stopped in front of the general's quarters. Kept the engines ticking over and waited outside.

Thirty seconds later, the two girls stepped outside, as if on cue, clutching leopard-print purses and fur coats. They climbed in the silver-grey Touareg, and after a short time General Koltrov came out of the building. Then came Makarenko, then Zinchenko.

The press officer joined Makarenko and Koltrov in the middle wagon, taking the seats behind Carter and Logan. Carter gave the all-clear to Popov over the net, and the convoy set off again.

Two minutes later, they left the base and motored south on the main thoroughfare.

Heading for the frontline.

Nineteen

The route took them out of Novochanka on a south-eastern trajectory, roughly following the course of the Dnieper River. Soon they had left the town behind, and the depressing rows of housing blocks were replaced by tree-lined corridors of tarmac. Through the gaps in the woodland Carter saw vast plains stretching towards the horizon, studded with power lines and the occasional huddle of farm buildings.

General Koltrov was in a foul mood. He snapped irritably at Zinchenko when she tried to speak to him and spent the thirty minutes or so glaring out of the tinted window.

'It makes no sense,' he said at last.

'Sir?' asked Carter.

'Driving to the meeting. Why couldn't we just take a helicopter? It would have taken a fraction of the time.'

'As I'm sure Captain Popov said, sir,' Carter said, restraining his voice, 'there's a no-fly order in place around the RV. Going in by car is the only safe option.'

'But I have always flown to the frontline to see my boys. Sometimes the Russians were so close you could almost spit on them. I don't see why anything should be different now.'

'We're just following the advice given to us by the Americans, sir.'

'I am a busy man. Tens of thousands of soldiers depend on me to help defeat the enemy. I cannot afford to spend my days rattling the roads like some fucking delivery driver.'

'Yes, sir. Sorry, sir.'

Carter didn't know what else to say.

Koltrov frowned at the landscape blurring past. 'I don't understand. Why would Voloshyn insist on meeting at an industrial estate?'

'Maybe he wanted to stay away from any built-up environments. Make it harder for anyone to set up an ambush.'

The general snorted angrily. 'How long will this journey take us?'

'Seven hours, sir. Eight, including the stopovers. We'll arrive at four o'clock, bang on time for the meeting.'

'I would not be surprised if Voloshyn is late to the meeting so he can take pleasure for making me wait like some worthless idiot. It would not be the first time.'

'My brother is in charge of the BG team, sir. He wouldn't let that happen.'

Koltrov sat back and resumed his staring contest with the bleak countryside.

Probably pissed off he's not going to spend the night with his girls, Carter thought to himself.

Makarenko kept checking his watch. He looked fidgety. Impatient. Like a businessman on a train, worried he might be late for a meeting with an important client.

On they rolled through the featureless landscape. Mile after mile of the same scenery, as if the terrain was on some sort of a loop. Carter saw oceans of sugar beet fields, the brilliant green rosettes arranged in neat rows. They skated past a sequence of dirt-poor settlements, scattered across the billiard-table-flat countryside. Clusters of single-storey homes, all exposed brickwork and corrugated tin roofs, screened by corroded metal gates and crumbling perimeter walls, linked by a network of unmetalled tracks.

Once in a while Horbach checked in with Carter, updating him on the advance team's progress. The guys were following their orders, maintaining a distance of twenty kilometres between themselves and the main convoy at all times.

After two more hours, Horbach came back over the channel to report that they had reached the first watering hole. The militia camp.

'All clear here,' he replied. 'No sign of trouble. Security cordon established. Ready and waiting for you.'

'Roger that,' Carter said. 'We're fifteen mikes out.'

'Mikes?'

'Minutes,' Carter said. Clearly the Ukrainians hadn't yet picked up the lingo used by American SF operators. 'We're there in fifteen minutes.'

They linked up with the advance party at a tented encampment on the outskirts of a dilapidated town in Cherasky Oblast. Then Horbach and the other three Ukrainians formally handed over control of the post, remounted the Land Rover and took off again.

The general and Zinchenko took the opportunity to stretch their legs and greet the local militia chief, watched over by Popov, Junior Sergeant Syrota, Webb and McVeigh. Carter checked in with the ops desk at Hereford, asking for an update on the situation in and around Zolodyansk. No news, came the reply.

No sign of the hidden SAM. But we're still looking.

Twenty minutes later they were back on the road again. The three-vehicle convoy quickly picked up speed once more. The general and his staff had a furtive discussion in the back, Carter switched channels on his tactical radio and hopped onto the frequency reserved for his brother's team.

'Luke, you there?'

'Here, mate,' came the reply. 'What's your situation?'

'We're en route now,' Carter reported. He dropped his eyes to the dashboard clock: 10.59. 'Five hours out.'

'Roger that. We'll be mounting up in an hour or so. Any problems at your end?'

'None,' Carter said. 'It's all fine.'

So far.

'Good. We'll check in again once we're on site.'

'See you soon, Luke.'

'A reunion with your ugly arse. Just what I wanted for Christmas.'

'Cheeky bastard.'

He clicked off the line, hopped back onto the channel for the general's BG team and focused on the road again.

Logan said, in an undertone, 'Bet you didn't think you'd be heading into a war zone this time last week, Geordie.'

'This time last week, I was wondering if I had a future in the Regiment.'

Logan glanced at him. 'How long have you got left?'

'Eighteen months. I'll finish this job, then I'm done. That's me.'

They were talking quietly. Their voices were almost lost to the machine drone of the Suburban engine; the general and his 2iC were arguing about something in the local tongue and paid no attention to the two Blades up front.

'What will you do?' Logan asked. 'Once this is over?'

Carter wondered why Logan was interested in his retirement plans. Figured he was just passing the time with small talk.

Then he thought: *We're the same age. Part of the same intake into the Regiment. Passed Selection together. He'll be coming up to the end of his time at Credenhill too. Probably wondering what the fuck he's going to do with the rest of his life.*

Same as me.

The question every Blade must confront sooner or later.

'Well, I ain't doing a masters. That's for sure. Not like Billy.'

'You think he's wasting his time?'

Carter thought, then shook his head firmly. 'No, that's the future for them lads. My brother – Luke – he's got the same mindset. Keen as mustard to get himself enrolled on one of those management programmes.'

Logan grunted disapprovingly. 'He needs his head examined. I'd sooner pull my teeth out than spend time in some classroom, taking notes and shit. Fuck that.'

'They don't have a choice, mate. You can't get ahead without this stuff nowadays.'

'Bollocks. Certificates, qualifications – they're like gongs, Geordie. Just for show. Experience is what really matters. Always has, when you get down to it. Knowing how to soldier.'

Carter smiled bitterly. 'It's not like that anymore. Employers – they want more than a reference from the head shed and a few battle scars to show off.'

'World has gone mad, son.'

'You might be right.' Carter fell quiet for a few minutes. Then he said, 'What about you? Got big retirement plans?'

Logan nodded eagerly, his eyes lighting up. 'Gonna open up a boozer in Hereford with a couple of the other lads. Spend my days behind the bar, listening to old war stories and eyeing up the local talent. Fucking paradise, boy.'

'That's it? That's what you're gonna spend the rest of your days doing? Pulling pints and breaking up fights?'

'I don't need nothing else. I ain't interested in making a fortune or running a business like some of the guys. All I need is enough to keep me in women and beer, in that order.'

Carter grinned. 'You're a man of simple pleasures, Scott.'

'That's because they're the best kind. A beautiful woman, a nice cold pint, money in your pocket. What more could you want?'

'I'll drink to that. Long as you're offering free rounds.'

Logan wrinkled up his nose. 'Bollocks to that. You come to my joint, you pay for your drinks. I ain't planning on running a charity, you tight-fisted bastard.'

They both laughed, but when Carter looked ahead again, he felt that familiar pang of unease in his guts.

Time to face facts. He was on the downward slope of his life. *Best days behind him,* McVeigh had said, caustically, but Carter knew there was a kernel of truth to that statement. The prospects for a veteran warrior with a handful of GCSEs and an honours degree from the University of Life were limited. The thought of seeing out his days in some corporate gig, bored out of his mind, filled him with dread.

Soldiering had given him a purpose. Injected meaning into his life. The Regiment had been his calling.

He had no desire to stay in Hereford in the long term. Too many bad memories. Too many ghosts. That might work for a laid-back guy like Logan, but not for Carter. He had a vision of himself sitting in the corner of his local boozer, drinking alone, while the young bucks glanced in his direction and whispered to their muckers.

'That's Geordie Carter. Yeah, used to be a tough Blade back in the day. Did that business in Mali. Hard to believe now though, ain't it? Let himself go. Fucking tragic.'

No, Carter thought. *Better to get as far away from Hereford as possible. Start over.*

And do what? He didn't know. Carter had a talent for killing. He'd found a way to put his skills to use in the Regiment, but there was nothing left for men like him on Civvy Street. Not in the new world.

He closed his mind to his dark thoughts and forced himself to concentrate as they shuttled south-east through the outskirts of Kryvyi Rih.

A hundred and twenty kilometres to the RV, he reminded himself.

Not far to go.

They got the all-clear from the advance party and halted at a laager point in one of the city's western districts. Carter repeated the handover process with Horbach, and the advance party moved on again towards their final destination. Logan, Webb and Syrota lugged the jerry cans out of the backs of the three Suburbans and topped up the depleted fuel tanks. McVeigh and Carter helped themselves to piss-weak brews from a makeshift tented canteen. Koltrov gave an impromptu speech to the soldiers, which drew a round of hearty cheers.

Carter checked in again with the ops desk, three thousand kilo-metres away. *Unverified reports of gunfire and shelling*, came the reply. *South of the RV at Zolodyansk. Vicinity of Holovika nuclear power station. Awaiting more details. Proceed as usual for now.*

He switched channels and reached out to his brother. Luke confirmed that the president and his BG team were on their way to the true RV at Zolodyansk. ETA 1500, he said. Which would give them an hour to establish the cordon and assess the threat level prior to Koltrov's arrival. He promised to check in again once they had arrived at the mayor's office.

They left the laager point shortly after two o'clock, carried on west out of Kryvyi Rih for forty kilometres, then cut south past fields of grazing cattle, coppiced woods and ramshackle barns strewn with rusted farming equipment. A hunchbacked old woman in a headscarf and thick winter coat shuffled down the street carrying a sack of potatoes. Tough folk, Carter thought. Hardened by eighty years of war and famine and tyranny. But unbowed. Going about their daily business. Doing whatever it took to survive.

His kind of people.

Maybe more so than his own tribe, Carter reflected. He barely recognised the country of his birth these days. People talked of sensitivity, and privilege, and micro-aggressions. But here was macro-aggression on a grand scale. Carnage and slaughter and mass graves. The bloodiest conflict in Europe since the Second World War. Not a culture war, but a real one. Men and women fighting and dying in their thousands to preserve an idea. The most important one of all, perhaps. That people had the right to determine their own future.

At exactly three o'clock his brother's voice crackled in his earpiece. Letting him know that they had safely arrived at the mayor's office. A few kilometres further on, the convoy ran into traffic at the next small town. Long lines of battered cars and wagons were heading in the opposite direction. Dozens of people trudged along the roadside, weighed down with their worldly possessions.

'Where are this lot coming from?' Logan asked.

'Beryansk,' Koltrov said. 'Next village to the west. Everyone is leaving. To escape the shelling.'

'Russians must be hitting them hard,' Carter said.

'Like you would not believe. Most of the areas close to the frontline have been shelled non-stop for the past two weeks. Hardly anyone is left behind. Ghost towns.'

'Let's hope they don't start dropping any stuff near the RV. Otherwise we'll be seriously fucked.'

Koltrov smirked. 'There is no need to worry. We shall be quite safe.'

Carter glanced quizzically at the general in the rear-view.

We're entering an area dangerously exposed to attack from enemy artillery, he reminded himself. *Drones, mobile SAM launchers. All kinds of potential threats.* And yet the guy's face didn't betray the slightest flicker of concern.

Then he recalled what Logan had told him on the drive across the border from Poland a couple of days earlier.

Guy goes around acting like he's fucking bulletproof.

Like he doesn't believe he's in danger of getting plugged.

At the time, Carter had assumed it was just a front. A performance. The general playing the role of the fearless warrior to inspire the troops to heroic efforts on the battlefield. But now he was having to reconsider.

Koltrov actually believes this shit.

As they neared the frontline, Horbach came back over the net, reporting that the advance party had reached Zolodyansk and linked up with Luke and the others. Five minutes later, the convoy hit the T-junction, marked by a dented road sign. Left would take them east towards the dummy RV at Pokrozirka. Right would lead to the actual RV at Zolodyansk, fifteen kilometres away. A twenty-minute drive from their position.

Carter glanced at the dash clock again: 15.39.

The road was empty. Ahead of them, Popov and Syrota eased the front Suburban down to a slow crawl at the T-junction, took the right

270

turn towards Zolodyansk and quickly picked up speed again. Logan took the same turn, sticking close to the guys in front, the speedometer clocking up towards the seventy kilometres per hour mark.

Koltrov's expression went tight with rage.

'Idiots!' he rasped. 'You're going the wrong way. Turn around!'

Logan said nothing. He stared dead ahead, concentrating on the road, following the front vehicle as it bombed west. At their six o'clock Webb and McVeigh were bringing up the rear of the convoy in the third Suburban.

'What the fuck are you doing?' Koltrov thundered. He waved a hand at the rear windshield. 'Didn't you hear? Pokrozirka is that way, you fool!'

Carter said, 'The RV isn't at Pokrozirka, sir.'

The general stared at the back of Carter's head. The look on his face alternating between shock and indignation.

'Where?' he demanded icily.

'Zolodyansk. Mayor's office, sir. Radzenskiy Street. That's the real RV.'

Koltrov glowered at him in the rear-view mirror, his cheeks shading crimson. His jaw was clenched so hard you'd need a crowbar to prise it open.

'You lied to me,' he said.

'Protocol, sir. We had no choice. In light of the threat to yourself and the president.'

Koltrov started to say something in response. Then he sat back in silence, anger spreading like cancer across his face.

Carter switched frequencies to update his brother on their progress, but the channel kept dropping. He gave it thirty seconds, tried again. This time he got nothing but dead noise. He jumped back onto his own team's channel and managed to raise Popov, but a few seconds later the net abruptly went silent again.

He turned to Logan. 'Is your radio working? I'm having problems connecting to the lads.'

'Same here.' Logan shrugged. 'Maybe them other lads changed frequencies.'

Carter shook his head. 'Car radio's not working, either,' he added as he tested the entertainment system.

'Could be a signal jammer in the area. One of ours. To disrupt the Russians.'

'No. Can't be. The ops desk would have given us the heads-up.'

'Then what the fuck is it?'

Carter didn't answer. He turned off the radio and stared out of the side window. They were speeding through the village of Beryansk now. A scattering of half-ruined flats and abandoned buildings either side of a bumpy main thoroughfare, surrounded by stubbled fields pocked with artillery craters and the rusted tails of Russian missiles. No signs of habitation except for a few feral dogs and the occasional old man picking through rubbish.

Ten kilometres to the RV, Carter reminded himself.

Nearly there.

15.49.

To the south, several kilometres away, beyond the fields, loomed the concrete cooling towers of the nuclear power plant at Holovika. Giant grey cones, churning out whitish columns of water vapour into the late-afternoon sky.

Koltrov pulled out his phone and stared at the screen for a long beat, anxiety registering on his face.

'Shit,' he said.

Carter uplifted his gaze to the rear-view mirror. 'What's going on, sir?'

'I have a message. From the president. I must call him back at once.'

'Now?' Carter twisted round in his seat. 'But we're almost at the RV.'

'He says it is urgent. Critical situation.'

'So call him back.'

He wasn't thrilled about the general using a poorly encrypted phone, in an area vulnerable to Russian missile attacks, but it was too late to do anything about that now.

Koltrov gestured towards his phone. 'I don't have a signal. No reception.'

'Same here,' Makarenko said. He cursed and held his phone up towards the window, like a surveyor searching for damp with a moisture detector. 'I have nothing. Not even one bar. Zero.'

Carter attempted to raise his colleagues once more. Comms were intermittent. He could hear fragments of the chatter for a few seconds before the channel abruptly cut out. He tried contacting Hereford, to see if the signallers could tell him what was going on, but he ran into the same difficulties when he tried patching through to the ops desk. His radio was malfunctioning. So was Logan's.

Shit.

He was still puzzling over what to do when Koltrov leaned forward and pointed at the horizon.

'There!' He indicated a garage on the other side of the road. The only building anywhere in sight. A workshop and reception office abutted the shop fronting a petrol station forecourt.

'Stop there!' Koltrov ordered. 'They will have a landline. I will use that.'

Logan glanced questioningly at Carter.

Theoretically, an unauthorised stop was against Regiment SOPs. But in reality, overruling a Ukrainian general, the second most powerful man in the country, was career suicide. So he gritted his teeth, made a heroic attempt to mask his frustration, and said to Logan, 'You heard the man. Pull over at the garage.'

'But, Jesus. Geordie—'

'Do it,' Carter muttered. 'Stop the car.'

The comms came back to life, briefly; Carter had just enough time to update the lads in the other two wagons before the line went dead once more.

Logan came off the main road, tapped the brakes and parked up behind Popov and Syrota on the garage forecourt. McVeigh and Webb pulled up two metres to the rear. Both front and rear teams hurried to establish a defensive formation, Popov and McVeigh exiting their vehicles and hefting up their front-slung rifles as they took up firing positions to cover the main approaches, while Syrota and Webb remained behind the wheels, ready to make a swift escape if necessary.

'Place looks empty,' Logan said as he ran his eyes over the site.

Carter nodded absently and looked round. The steel roller shutter had been lowered over the ramped vehicular entrance to the workshop; the garage reception and the shopfront were both dark. Further away was a scrap-metal yard. In the distance, fields of wheat swayed in the susurrant wind.

Two hundred metres to the west, a separate road led south towards the nuclear plant. The faint grey stacks on the horizon broke up the otherwise dull landscape.

Carter turned to Logan and said, 'Wait here. Keep the engine running. I'll accompany the general inside. If it looks clear, I'll stay close and cover the rear of the building.'

'One of us should stay with the principal,' Logan said. 'While he's inside the building.'

'Absolutely not,' Koltrov snarled. 'This is a private conversation. Confidential.'

Carter said, testily, 'We can't let you out of our sight, sir. That's non-negotiable.'

Koltrov gestured towards his subordinate. 'Anton will accompany me into the office. He is more than capable of dealing with any trouble.'

Carter weighed up the wisdom of arguing with a three-star general. Then he said, 'Keep it quick. We're in and out of here in five minutes.'

'I will do my best.'

Koltrov and Makarenko clambered out of the wagon. Carter left Logan and Zinchenko in the Suburban and caught up with the general and his 2iC as they walked across the forecourt towards the garage building. A door on the right led into the station shop; through the dirt-smeared glass he spied a cash register behind an acrylic screen, refrigeration units, shelves of car-cleaning products and junk food.

He made for the other door, to the left of the shop. The garage reception. Carter levered the handle, the door opened with a musical beep, and he stepped into a small office with a waiting area to one side. Ancient-looking computer on the desk, with a landline next to it, amid a clutter of paperwork and tools. Frayed posters of classic cars and swimwear models hung from the walls.

To the left, a crude partition separated the office from the main workshop space; the glass screen had been blown inwards, scattering shards across the worn carpet. Carter approached the partition, glass crunching underfoot, and scanned the workshop area. There was a ramped vehicle bay in the centre of the space with a subterranean inspection pit, six metres long and a metre wide. Like a grave, waiting for a coffin to be lowered into it. Carter saw a load of tyre-changing equipment, wheel alignment systems, brake testers and headlamp testing kit. But no people. No mechanics or customers. *Safe enough.*

'Well?' Koltrov asked impatiently.

Carter said, 'Remember. Make it quick. We can't hang around here for long. I'll be round the back watching the fire door, so we've got you covered from every side.'

'Yes, yes, OK.'

The general barged past him, snatched the receiver, looked at Carter. Waited for him to remove himself from earshot.

Carter took the hint. He walked over to the fire door at the rear of the office, depressed the push bar and stepped outside. Found himself at the edge of a wide parking lot built at the back

275

of the garage, with a row of oil drums, a mound of spare bits of machinery and several stacks of car tyres worn down to the nub. Close by, flies buzzed around a dumpster stuffed full of stinking rubbish.

He visually swept the ground, found a brick next to the dumpster and wedged it in the gap between the fire door and the frame. The stopwatch in his head began ticking as he surveyed the terrain from left to right. He was alert to the slightest hint of a threat. A passer-by, or the distant sound of an approaching drone or vehicle. But the area was utterly deserted.

Ghost town.

From within the office, he heard General Koltrov talking on the phone in his familiar gravelly voice. There was a clearly identifiable pattern to the conversation. From the sound of it, Koltrov was doing most of the talking. Carter was too far away to properly understand what he was saying. But he recognised the language in a heartbeat.

Not Ukrainian.

But Russian.

Carter stepped closer to the door, pricking his ears.

He had spent enough time on ops in Ukraine to distinguish between the two languages. A young officer he'd trained up in the local SF force had explained it to him over a few beers. Russian and Ukrainian were broadly similar, in some ways, but also distinctive. A product of their shared cultural history, and their differences too. Carter could understand maybe two-thirds of what Koltrov was saying.

Enough to grasp his meaning.

The target isn't heading for Pokrozirka, the general said to the person on the other end of the line.

Look for a two-vehicle convoy approaching Zolodyansk on the T1508. Heading for the mayor's office on Radzenskiy Street.

Target is driving in that direction.

Carter stood very still and felt a chill of cold dread trickle down his spine. For a moment he wondered if he had misheard the general. But then Koltrov spoke again, repeating the same words in a slower, louder tone, spelling them out to the person on the other end of the call, and then Carter knew for sure. He hadn't been mistaken.

I know what I just heard.

The general is telling someone where to find the president.

He's just blown the fucking op.

He reacted at once. He tugged open the heavy fire door and moved briskly through the office, his gloved right hand clasped around the M4 rifle grip, the barrel pointing down at an angle.

General Koltrov was standing behind the desk next to the partition screen, talking on the phone in quick-fire Russian. Makarenko stood close by, his arms folded across his chest.

At the sound of Carter's approaching footsteps both men drew sharply upright. Koltrov looked up at him with a startled expression.

'What are you doing?' he hissed. 'I told you to wait outside. Don't you know a fucking order when you hear one?'

Carter ignored the question.

'Who are you talking to?' he demanded.

'The president. I told you.'

'Bullshit.' Carter pointed at the phone. 'I just heard you speaking Russian.'

Koltrov stood very still. Makarenko dropped his arms to his sides and took a half-step towards the cluttered desk.

Carter kept his gaze centred on the general.

'Tell me,' he said. 'Tell me what the fuck is going on.'

Koltrov said nothing. He stole a quick glance at Makarenko. The two men traded a knowing look, and a sudden movement flashed in the tail of Carter's eye. Coming from his three o'clock.

He spun round.

He saw the colonel seizing a heavy-duty pipe wrench from the desk. Carter started to bring up his rifle in response, but even as he lifted the weapon he knew he had been too slow to react. The Ukrainian had time and speed and physics on his side. He had already drawn his right arm back; in the next beat he brought the pipe wrench crashing down on Carter in a vicious chopping motion.

The cast-steel tool struck him on the jaw. A jarring pain flared in Carter's cheekbone and shot up into his skull. Like a dentist, drilling into all his teeth simultaneously. He sagged helplessly to the floor, the taste of blood in his mouth. Makarenko snatched the rifle away from him, yanking it from the three-point sling, and when he looked up, he saw the colonel standing over him, his right hand wrapped tightly around his deholstered Glock.

Black mouth of the muzzle dead-centred on a point between Carter's eyes.

Twenty

Carter didn't move.

Nobody said anything for several beats. Makarenko kept the Glock nine-milli trained on Carter. Ready to redecorate the office with his brains. Koltrov manoeuvred round to the side of the desk and slowly replaced the receiver on the corded telephone. On the desk, the blood-slicked pipe wrench gleamed beneath the anaemic panel lights.

Grogginess settled like a cloud behind Carter's pupils. He shook his head in a futile attempt to clear it and pulled himself up to his knees. Pain stabbed the sides of his skull with every movement. Something felt loose in the back of his mouth; he coughed and spat out a shard of broken tooth coated in slimy blood. His eyes drifted towards the M4 rifle a couple of metres away. Out of arm's reach, but only just.

Koltrov smiled.

'Don't,' he said, 'don't even think about it.'

He snapped an order at Makarenko. The colonel moved away from the desk and side-footed the rifle, kicking it away from Carter. He kept pointing his weapon at Carter while the general knelt down and tore the Glock from his side-holster. He slid back the receiver to eject the chambered round from the snout, released the clip, pocketed the full magazine and the empty piece. Then he straightened up and backed away from Carter until he was level with Makarenko.

Carter hack-coughed violently. He wiped the blood from his mouth, tried to gather his thoughts. Which wasn't easy. Not after getting clobbered in the face with a wrench. Slowly, the cloud lifted. Something clicked into place in his head.

There is a high-level traitor in Ukraine, the general had told him back at Novochanka Air Base.

Someone at the very top of the pyramid.

'You,' he gasped between ragged draws of breath. 'You're working for . . . the Russians.'

Koltrov made a small laugh the back of his throat.

'Yes,' he said.

The cold feeling spread through Carter's guts, turning his blood to ice.

'How long?'

'Many years. Since my days as a young officer.'

Carter nodded groggily. The professional part of his mind was working at quantum speed, crunching data. Processing angles and distances and a multitude of other factors.

He couldn't disable Makarenko. As soon as he made his move, the colonel would open fire at point-blank range. A non-starter. He couldn't seize the M4, either. Out of reach. Even if he somehow managed to lunge for the rifle, it would take him two or three seconds to snatch it up, spin round, take aim at Makarenko and fire. An epoch, in firefight terms. The colonel would drill him before he could get a shot away.

Snookered.

You'd better think, the voice in the limbic part of his brain told him.

Think of something, fast.

Or you're going to die here.

'Why?' he asked.

'You mean, why pledge myself to Moscow?'

Carter managed a weak nod.

He thought: *Buy yourself some time. Keep him talking.*

Focus on surviving.

One second to the next.

'Was it . . . money?'

Koltrov chuckled. 'Only an Englishman would ask such a question. Money had nothing to do with it. It was a patriotic decision. A question of doing what is right for my country.

'Some of us in the army, we did not like what was happening to Ukraine after the Cold War. We witnessed the protests in Kyiv. The talk of friendship with the EU. With NATO. We became disillusioned. Some of us met – in private. Small groups of like-minded soldiers. That was when the Russians approached me through one of their agents. An officer in our security services. They knew of my sympathies. They told me of their plans for Ukraine. For me. They made me understand that the real threat was not from Russia, but from NATO.'

'You're betraying your own tribe.'

The general smiled coldly. 'If you want to talk of traitors, you should start with Voloshyn. He is the one who has betrayed our people, by selling his soul to the parasites of the West.'

The veins pulsed savagely between Carter's temples. 'Bullshit. You're working for a fucking tyrant.'

Koltrov stared at him.

'It is not the Russian president who is leading us to destruction. That is Voloshyn. He thinks the West has his back, but he is deluded. The fascists in NATO do not care about Ukraine. They seek to destabilise us with empty promises. Then they sell us weapons and encourage us to kill our brothers from the east.

'The Russians, at least, are our brother Slavs. We have a shared history – a shared culture. What do we have in common with your leaders in Britain and America? Nothing, that is what.

'The president thinks he has the support of all Ukrainians. But it is an illusion. There are those of us who still have our country's best interests at heart,' Koltrov bragged. 'In the intelligence services, in the Church. Other places, too. There are many more of us than Voloshyn – or anyone else – would believe. And now the time has come for us to seize control. To save our nation from disaster.'

'By working for the enemy?'

Koltrov shook his head. 'By restoring the land to Russia.'

The general caught sight of the incredulous look on Carter's face and tilted his head to one side. His unpatched eye narrowed to a slit.

'You doubt that we will win?'

'Your mates are on the back foot. Feeding conscripts into the meat grinder. They'll raise the white flag eventually.'

Koltrov smiled condescendingly. 'You are a good soldier. Like that brother of yours. But you are killers, not strategists. You do not see the bigger picture. I do.'

The guy was boasting now. Carter could see the fire blazing in his good eye. Like a preacher addressing a crowd of believers. He waited for the general to go on.

Keep him talking.

Keep buying time.

'Ukraine will lose this war. Not for a while, maybe. But in the end, Russia will win, because your friends will lose the will to fight. Just like they did in Afghanistan, and Iraq.'

Carter said, 'You're wrong.'

'Am I?' Koltrov gave a cynical laugh. 'Look at the news. Already public opinion is turning. I have seen the stories. People angry about the cost of filling up their car or heating their home. Politicians across Europe protesting about the money spent on the war in Ukraine. In another year or two, they will grow tired of footing the bill. As they always do. The supply of weapons will dry up. And what will happen then? Our soldiers will be on our own against Russia. That is a fight Ukraine cannot win.

'The truth is, we are safer under Moscow's wing. Russia is our true friend, not NATO, or the EU, or anyone else. It is in our interests to join forces, to form a new alliance. A Greater Russia – an empire of Slavs – opposed to the fascism and disorder and hypocrisy of the West. Then we shall be strong. Stronger than we have ever been before. The rest of the world will tremble before the new Slavic empire.'

'Fucking pipe dream,' Carter said. 'La-la land. You'll be under the boot of the Kremlin.'

'It is preferable to being a puppet of America. That path leads to humiliation. But together, Ukraine and Russia will achieve great things – many great things.'

'Won't happen. Not in a million fucking years. Voloshyn would never agree to a deal.'

'Of course not,' said Koltrov. 'That is why we must get rid of him.'

Carter looked at him in disbelief.

'The phone call,' he said.

Koltrov broke into a chilling smile; his face glowed with triumph.

He said, 'A few minutes from now, once our Russian friends have got a bead on the president's convoy, a pair of Tornado rocket launchers will strike the vehicle before they arrive at the rendezvous. And Voloshyn will die.'

Carter kept staring at the general. He hoped to fuck his face didn't betray the slightest flicker of emotion. Because he suddenly understood. Koltrov had made a fatal miscalculation.

He doesn't know, Carter told himself.

He thinks the president is still en route to the mayor's office.

He doesn't know that they're already at the RV.

A logical assumption. Koltrov would naturally suppose that his team would arrive first to sponsor the RV. Normal procedure dictated that the more important target would arrive second, to limit the time they were exposed to enemy attack.

Koltrov smiled again.

He said, 'Once the president's death has been announced, an emergency cabinet meeting will be convened. After an appropriate period of mourning, of course, I will be sworn in as the new president. A foregone conclusion, given my standing with the people.

No one will dare to challenge me. The nation will look to me for guidance. Then, at last, we can begin the work of restoring Ukraine to Mother Russia.'

'It'll never work,' Carter said. 'The people will support you to begin with. Christ, they might even accept peace talks. But the moment you start getting chummy with Russia, they'll turn on you.'

Koltrov's smile widened. 'Perceptions can change. Do you think the German people universally loathed the Jews before the Nazis came to power?'

Carter made no reply.

'The Kremlin has a plan. To change popular opinion is not an easy thing, but it can be done. They will push stories in the media. Discredit my opponents. Launch smear campaigns. Crush those who defy me. It will be done quietly, at first. So quietly, no one will even notice. But over time, we will turn Ukrainians against the West. And when I speak, the people will follow me, because they know I am a true patriot.

'As for my political enemies – Russia is already helping to eliminate those who might threaten me.'

Carter felt a terrible weight press down on him. He forgot about the dull throbbing pain in his jaw. His shattered tooth.

He said, 'The fifth columnists. The traitors you've been hunting.'

'Loyalists,' said Koltrov. 'People who could not be trusted to support the new regime. My handler supplied me with their names.'

'They were innocent.'

'Not all of them. Some were guilty of corruption. Siphoning money from budgets, securing government contracts for family and friends, that kind of thing. What is the English saying? No smoke without fire.'

Carter thought about the defence minister. Gears turning in his head. He recalled Butko's despairing pleas of innocence at the time of his arrest. Koltrov's puzzling decision to remove the suspect's plasticuffs moments before the interrogation. The PSM pistol.

'He wasn't armed, was he? Butko. When you arrested him. You fucking murdered him, then planted the piece on him to make it look like an act of self-defence.'

'Yes.'

'And . . . the others?'

'The ones we could blackmail, or bribe into working for the Kremlin – they were released. As for the others, those who refused to serve Moscow's interests? We put them to death.'

'You're fucking insane.'

'No.' A look of steely determination flashed in Koltrov's eye. 'I am merely doing what is necessary, to ensure my country survives. If there are casualties, then so be it.

'Of course, I could not believe my good fortune when Voloshyn asked me to personally lead the effort to root out dissidents in the establishment. It gave me an unbelievable opportunity. I could eliminate my enemies, kill anyone who might suspect me of disloyalty to the fascist regime. But then, as they say, fortune favours the brave.'

Carter glanced instinctively at Makarenko. Koltrov read his expression and made a playful grin.

'Yes, Anton is working for us, too. He has been with us from the very beginning. I personally recruited him, in fact.' The grin stretched across the general's weathered face. He added, proudly, 'You are looking at Ukraine's next chief of staff.'

'Who else?' Carter asked. 'Who else is in on it?'

Keep him talking.

'A few others. High ranking officers. You do not know them. And that is just in the military. There are many more, ready to serve once Voloshyn has been taken out. We have a whole shadow government in waiting.'

The clock in Carter's head kept ticking.

He figured five or six minutes had passed since Koltrov had alerted his Russian mates. He clung to the hope that one of the lads on the forecourt might start to get pissed off with the delay. Someone might wander over to the garage to see what was going on, interrupt them.

Think.

There has to be a way out.

Has to be.

'But there are eyes on you constantly,' Carter said. 'Round-the-clock protection. I'm betting the intelligence services have got you under surveillance as well. Them lot are watching everybody.'

'This is true. So?'

'How the fuck have you been contacting your Russian mates? Someone would have noticed by now, surely.'

'I have an interlink,' Koltrov said. 'A go-between. One of the girls. Irina. She supplies information back to Moscow.'

Something else clicked into place in Carter's head.

The brunette.

The general glanced at his watch. 'We have wasted too much time here.'

He snapped an order at Makarenko in Ukrainian. *Do it.* Getting his 2iC to do the dirty work.

Carter swallowed. Hard.

Endgame.

As the two men spoke, he edged a hand down towards the pressel switch on his webbing. Desperately hoping that the comms might be working again, so he could raise the other lads. Then the general read his intentions and smiled in amusement, sharing a laugh with Makarenko.

'I wouldn't bother,' Koltrov said. 'It won't work. Electronic countermeasures. High-intensity warfare system. Jams everything. Radio signals. Satellites. GPS devices. Even mobile phone masts.'

So that's why the general wanted to stop here, he thought. *Because he needed to alert the Russians to the real target location, and he had to find a landline. He knew his mobile phone wouldn't work.*

Makarenko's fingers tightened around the pistol grip.

'Time to die,' he said.

Carter tensed. Fear percolated into his bowels. Not the black terror of death. But something worse. He was afraid of losing.

He stared levelly at the colonel. Eyeballed the Glock.

Don't look afraid, the voice in his head told him. *Don't give the fucker the satisfaction.*

Carter waited.

Then he heard a loud clattering noise at his nine o'clock.

Coming from beyond the office.

His gaze skittered towards the partition window.

Through the gap, he saw a pot-bellied mechanic in tattered overalls crawling out of the inspection pit. A few paces away, a rake-thin guy in matching clobber had frozen mid-stride next to a workbench. Toolbox at his feet, the contents scattered across the resin floor. Spanners and screwdrivers and hammers.

Koltrov and Makarenko simultaneously whipped round, directing their attention towards the disturbance in the workshop, the colonel aiming his Glock in the same direction. The skinny mechanic caught sight of the pistol and thrust his arms into the air in terror. His podgy mate had finished sneaking out of the pit and went statue-rigid.

Carter figured the mechanics had heard the entire conversation in the office. The general's confession. Russia's plan to kill Voloshyn and install Koltrov as a puppet ruler. He guessed they had reached a collective decision: sneak outside while their attention was on Carter. Sound the alarm. Then the thin guy had gotten clumsy, knocking over the box of tools.

Distracting Koltrov and Makarenko.

Both men had turned away from Carter. They were laser-focused on the mechanics.

Carter had a second to act.

Which was all he needed.

He launched himself at Makarenko, slamming into the colonel a split second before he could loose off a shot. The Ukrainian gasped as he stumbled backwards, the impact driving the air from his lungs, the Glock tumbling from his stunned grip. He crashed against the desk and sent the clutter crashing to the floor before he fell away. Carter landed on top of the colonel; the two men rolled on the carpet, trading blows. Makarenko fought wildly, his strength taking Carter by surprise. In the next moment, he kicked out, throwing Carter bodily off him, and suddenly he was on top of his opponent, pinning him down, stinking hands clawing at his throat. Strangling him.

In the corner of his eye, Carter spotted the pipe wrench lying on the floor. He reached desperately for it, straining every sinew in his body. Failed. Makarenko squeezed harder. Carter couldn't breathe; he could feel the blood swelling inside his head, pressing behind his eyeballs. He tried for the wrench again. Fingertips brushed against the cold metal, dragged the wrench towards him. He summoned one last effort, closed his fist around the handle and swung hard, striking Makarenko on the side of the head with a dull thunk.

The colonel flopped to one side, groaning in pain. Carter instantly scrambled to his feet, tossed the wrench aside and dived for the Glock. He swiped up the pistol, whipped round, saw the Ukrainian lunging at him again, drew the semi-automatic level with the man's central mass.

Fired.

The Glock was a marvel of human engineering. There was no safety switch on the side of the weapon. Instead, the operator simply disengaged the safety by applying deliberate pressure to the trigger mechanism, thereby saving valuable seconds in a firefight. All you had to do was take aim, pull the trigger all the way back, and let the gun do the work.

Which Carter duly did.

The muzzle flared.

A round spat out of the snout and slammed into the colonel's midriff at extreme close range. An easy shot, for a Regiment man. At a distance of two metres, it would have been harder to miss.

The discharge sounded deafening in the close confines of the office. Makarenko jerked and toppled backwards, his legs folding beneath him. He landed in a heap on the carpet, like a boxer hitting the canvas after a knockout punch.

The pounding of boots on the ground reached Carter's ears. The reception door chimed, and then Logan burst into the office and looked round, taking in the scene: the smashed computer screen. The bloodied wrench. The Glock in Carter's right hand. Makarenko lying sprawled on the carpet, pawing at his gut wound. Blood staining his army jacket.

In the workshop, the two mechanics climbed to their feet and bolted for the rear exit.

General Koltrov was nowhere to be seen.

Webb, McVeigh and Popov joined Logan in the office. M4s raised. Ready to engage.

Webb dropped to a knee beside Makarenko, inspecting his injuries. Logan was blinking rapidly. 'What the fuck is going on?'

'The general . . .' Carter began. 'Where is he?'

'Outside. He came running out of here in a flap,' McVeigh said. 'Screaming for help. Said something about an attack.'

Carter said, 'It's Koltrov. He's the traitor. He's—'

The bark of a pistol interrupted him. From outside the building. There was the throated rev of a car engine, the high-pitched screech of car tyres skidding across asphalt.

Carter climbed off the canvas and seized his M4. 'Stop him!'

The five soldiers raced for the entrance. Carter crashed through the door and snapped his attention towards the forecourt. Syrota lay slumped on the ground, his limbs twisted at unnatural angles, blood pooling beneath him. The lead Suburban was missing.

'There!' McVeigh yelled.

A hundred metres away, the stolen vehicle raced west down the main road. Rapidly picking up speed.

Carter jerked up his M4, thumbed the fire selector to fully automatic. Right hand clenched around the pistol grip, left hand clasping the vertical foregrip mounted on the underside of the handguard. He lined up the telescopic sights with the rear tyres and squeezed off a four-round burst.

The rounds struck high, glancing off the boot and starring the rear windscreen. Logan and McVeigh had also brought up their rifles and took aim in the same direction, following Carter's lead as they peppered the back of the Suburban with bursts of hot lead.

The brake lights glowed before the wagon slewed hard to the left, tyres squealing, burning rubber as it took the turn off the main road. Then it straightened out and careened south, shrinking from view, the engine roar growing ever fainter.

Heading away from Zolodyansk.

'Fuck is he going?' Logan asked between snatched draws of breath.

'Frontline,' McVeigh said. He cursed filthily. 'Fucker's making a run for it.'

Carter wheeled away from the road. His mind was spinning. His heart beating frantically. Popov was kneeling beside Syrota. He looked up, gave a slight shake of his head.

'He's dead.'

'Zinchenko?' Carter glanced across the forecourt. 'Where is she?'

Webb flung open the doors on the other two wagons. Checking the interiors.

'Not here,' he called out. 'No sign of her. She's gone too.'

'Must be with the general,' Logan mused.

'Shit,' Carter said.

'Hostage?' McVeigh wondered.

'Maybe.'

He started back towards the office at a quick march. Logan was shouting after him, demanding to know what was going on. Carter gave no response. He was thinking about the president. His brother. The RV. The imminent threat to their lives.

He barged back into the office, hastened over to the desk, set down his M4 and reached for the landline. In the corner, Makarenko made some sort of wet sucking noise. Dark, oily blood pumped steadily out of his gut wound.

The door chimed again. Logan stormed into the office. Popov, McVeigh and Webb hurrying after him. Carter fished out his burner, brought up the number for his brother's cell, picked up the receiver and stabbed the digits into the corded phone.

Logan said, 'What the fuck is happening? *Mate?*'

'Koltrov is working for the Russians,' Carter said. 'They set the whole thing up. The meeting with Voloshyn. It's a trap.'

Logan looked dumbfounded. He momentarily lost the power of speech.

'Are you sure? But how—'

'I overheard him talking to the Russians on the phone. Spilling the beans on the RV. The Russians are plotting to kill Voloshyn today. Rocket attack. Replace him with Koltrov. I've got to warn the others.'

'Shit.'

'What about him?'

McVeigh nodded at the wounded colonel. The guy was writhing on the floor, clutching his guts. His breathing was shallow and wheezy, as if he was breathing through a straw.

'He's in on it too,' Carter said.

'Jesus fuck.'

Carter finished punching in the number and prayed that the range on the enemy's electronic countermeasures systems didn't extend all the way to Volodyansk.

291

There was an agonising wait while the line tried to establish a connection with Luke's mobile five kilometres away in Zolodyansk. Then came the familiar bleat of a ringing tone.

Luke picked up on the third ring.

'Hello?'

'Luke, listen to me,' Carter said, breathlessly.

'Jamie?' Luke asked. He sounded surprised. 'That you?'

The line crackled and hissed. A repetitive clicking noise travelled down the phone, faintly audible in the background. Carter figured the reception must be poor at the mayor's office.

'The RV has been blown,' he said. 'You need to get the president out of that location, right fucking now.'

'What are you talking about? Where are you?'

'There's no time to explain. You've just got to trust me. There are Russians in your area, actively scanning for your coordinates as we speak. Get Voloshyn out of that location and head out of the city. Stay on radio silence, if you can. Whatever you do, don't stay where you are.'

Before Carter could continue he heard a strange noise on the line. It took him a few moments to recognise it as a muffled voice, rough and fuzzy. Indistinct. He couldn't make out what they were saying. But it sounded like Russian.

'Who's there with you?' he asked.

'Nobody.'

'You're alone?'

'I'm in the corridor, outside the mayor's office. Principal is waiting with the mayor for you lot to show up. There's no one here, mate.'

The voice faded, then the clicking sound came back again, louder this time.

Carter said, 'Did you hear that?'

'Hear what?'

'That noise.'

'Nothing at my end. It's all quiet here.'

'But—oh, fuck.'

Carter felt his pulse quickening. His bowels clenched with cold dread.

On the other end of the call, Luke reached the same conclusion.

'Shit,' he whispered. 'Jamie, this is an open line. Jesus.'

The Russians, Carter realised.

They've been listening in.

They know the president is at the RV.

Nausea rose in his throat, mingling with the taste of blood in his mouth.

He knew a little of the Tornado-S rocket system. The latest Russian technology. An upgrade on the old Red Army launchers. Half a dozen launcher tubes per truck. Recently the Russians had started using them to fire precision-guided rockets. Hundreds of kilograms of high-explosive per warhead, with a maximum effective range of 120 kilometres. Packing enough of a punch to flatten a building, and everyone inside it.

Including the president.

And his brother.

He had been on the call for maybe forty seconds. It would take another forty to prepare the Tornado launchers. Maybe less. The fire team wouldn't want to hang around a moment longer than necessary. Once they broke cover, they were going to flag their position to every Ukrainian asset in the immediate vicinity. Ten seconds after unleashing the rockets, they would have a ton of ordnance coming their way.

'Get out of there!' he thundered. 'Luke! Move it! NOW!'

Twenty-One

There was a sudden eruption of noise on the other end of the line.

Carter heard a clamour of panicked shouts and screams. Bedlam. Above the noise, his brother bellowed an order at someone. There was a muffled thump, what sounded like a chair scraping on the floor, and then the call abruptly cut out.

In the reception office, Carter stood rooted to the spot, still holding the receiver. Listening to the dead air.

The pressure in his chest intensified. It became intolerable. He couldn't breathe. Couldn't think.

Logan stared at him.

'What?' he asked. 'What is it, mate? What did he say?'

Carter shook his head. He felt sick.

He thought about the civilians sheltered in the basement of the mayor's office. The makeshift bunker.

'Geordie?'

Four hundred people, Carter thought.

Women, children, old men.

People with nowhere else to go.

He said, 'We need to warn the mayor. Get them people out of the basement immediately.'

Webb tapped his pressel switch, testing his tactical radio. 'Comms are still down. We don't have a phone number for the mayor's office, either. No way of contacting them.'

'Fuck's sake.'

'What's going on?' McVeigh asked.

'The Russians,' Carter said, 'they've got a bead on the RV.'

And I'm the one who directed them.

'How?' Popov asked.

'The call. They . . . they must have traced it.'

Open line.

'My God.'

In the next moment, a chorus of low rumbling booms erupted in the distance, and something shifted inside Carter, bayoneting his guts. Because then he knew.

The rockets.

They've struck the target.

The colour plunged from Logan's face. 'Jesus. Jesus fucking Christ.'

Carter tried his brother again.

No answer.

Out of desperation, he tried Sergeant Horbach's mobile phone, fighting the rising sense of dread brewing in his chest. His hands were shaking as he dialled the number.

The phone rang and rang.

No answer.

He clung desperately to the hope that the rockets had somehow missed their targets. But he knew it was unlikely. The Tornadoes were far more accurate than the old Soviet machinery. They were kitted out with direction correcting equipment, satellite-guidance systems. All kinds of cutting-edge technology. Accurate to within a few metres of the target.

He tried to console himself with the thought that the air-raid shelter might have shielded some of the occupants from the impact. Some, perhaps. But not all. Many more would have been killed. Vaporised in the blast, or crushed to death beneath the rubble.

His fault.

Blood on his hands.

Four hundred lives.

He replaced the receiver.

Carter tried to put himself in Koltrov's boots. *You're on the run. You've been exposed as a traitor.*

What's your next move?

A plan began to take shape.

He nodded at Popov and said, 'How far to the frontline from here?'

'Fifty kilometres or so. No more than that.'

Logan stared at him. 'You think that's where the general is going?'

'Wouldn't you?'

'I agree,' Popov said. 'He's blown. Nowhere else for him to go.'

'Even if that's the case,' McVeigh said, 'we'd never catch up with the fucker in time.'

'There might be a way,' Popov said, tentatively.

Carter turned back to the Ukrainian captain. 'How?'

'South of the Holovika plant. Back roads. Through the country-side. Faster than the motorway. No army checkpoints. None that I know of, anyway,' he added.

'You know the route?'

'I have relatives. In Kherson. I have taken that route many times.'

'Will the general know? Them back roads?'

Popov shook his head. 'He is a Kyiv man. Born and raised. An outsider. Only locals know the way.'

'He won't be able to rely on GPS, either,' Webb pointed out. 'Systems are down.'

Carter grabbed his M4, clipped it to his weapon sling. He snatched up the burner, stuffed it into one of the pouches on the side of his webbing and said, 'Come on. We're leaving.'

'What do you want to do with this one?' Webb asked.

Pointing with his eyes at Makarenko.

Carter stepped towards the colonel, drew the M4 level with his head.

'No,' Makarenko croaked.

'Yes.'

The colonel bared his blood-smeared teeth in a look of defiance. 'You're all dead. You're all going to—'

The rifle double-barked. Two rounds erupted out of the M4, drilling a pair of holes in his forehead, painting the carpet with his brains. His mouth went slack. His eyes rolled back. Like someone had disconnected him from the mains.

'What did he mean?' Logan asked warily.

'Fuck knows,' Carter said. 'Let's go.'

He sprinted outside.

The clock ticking in his head told him that Koltrov had a four-minute head start on the team. He figured an hour's drive to the frontline. But there would be delays. Military checkpoints. Shelled vehicles obstructing the roads. Carter felt certain that the general's progress wouldn't be smooth. Not in the middle of a war zone.

It's gonna be fucking close.

We'll have to floor it all the way. And hope the shortcuts aren't closed off.

Carter jogged towards the nearest Suburban.

'Take the other wagon,' he ordered Webb and McVeigh. 'Stay right behind us. We'll lead the way.' He stopped next to the driver's side door, glanced at Popov and Logan in turn. 'You two. Ride with me.'

Webb and McVeigh dashed over to the second vehicle while Carter tugged on the driver's side handle and deposited himself behind the wheel. Popov swung into the front passenger seat; Logan jumped into the back. Both men buckled up as Carter tapped the stop-start button and kick-started the Chevrolet's V8 engine.

He pulled out of the forecourt, blatted west for a couple of hundred metres, then steered hard to the left. The Suburban shuddered as it skidded into the turn at speed, Carter's hands vice-clamped around the wheel as he fought to maintain control. The wagon made the turn, fishtailed for a fifty-metre stretch before straightening out, and then Carter mashed the accelerator. Behind them, McVeigh and Webb took the same turn at speed, staying bumper-close to their colleagues.

'You sure about this, Geordie?' Logan asked as they roared south.

'Can't stay in this area. Compromised. Can't head to the RV, not now. And we've got no way of alerting the ops desk. Russians have been flooding the area with ECM. Everything's fried. It's up to us.'

Logan said, hesitantly, 'We'll be danger close to the enemy. I ain't getting myself killed because you've got a fucking death wish.'

Carter said, 'That bastard knows the names of every fifth columnist in the country. I'm not letting that int slip through our fingers.'

They drove on.

Carter told them about the sham investigations into traitors in the government. Koltrov's ruthless elimination of anyone who suspected him, or who might prove disloyal to the new regime. The ECM jammers. The Tornado rocket launchers. The Kremlin's plan to lean on his popularity to turn Ukraine eastwards again.

'Fucking hell,' Logan said.

'Bastard's thought of everything,' Popov said, bitterly. 'Must have been planning this for many months.'

'Wasted effort. The general's shafted now. His big secret is out. Best he can hope for is to live out his days in some dacha in Moscow.'

'Not necessarily,' Carter said.

Logan frowned. 'What d'you mean by that?'

'The guy's got a talent for spin and bullshit. You've seen how people react when they see him. He's got millions of supporters in the army. He could denounce the allegations as lies. Turn himself into a martyr. Undermine the president.'

'Assuming he is still alive,' Popov reminded them.

'Yes,' Carter said grimly.

They raced on. Logan kept trying Luke's burner phone, without success. He guesstimated eighty or ninety seconds had passed, from the time he'd ended the call to his brother to the rocket strikes. Enough time to exit the building? He didn't know. But as they raced south he felt a compulsive desire for revenge flaring in his veins. Burning like hot coals in his chest.

Koltrov is going to suffer for this.

I'm going to make sure of it.

After a few kilometres Popov suddenly leaned forward and pointed out a Ukrainian military camp situated at the side of the road, in a small clearing shielded by a copse of pine trees.

A loose throng of soldiers hung around a huddle of make-shift tents. A handful of guys poked at a smouldering log fire in a futile attempt to fend off the damp cold; others puffed cigarettes or cleaned their weaponry. There was a stack of RPG-7 grenade launchers next to a dilapidated shack, Carter noticed, along with several canvas backpacks, each one containing three rockets. Close by, a pair of guys checked over a quadcopter drone with an optical camera attached to the airframe.

At the sight of the approaching vehicles two of the soldiers stepped into the road and started waving energetically. Making the universal sign for them to stop.

Carter pulled over and dropped out of the Suburban with Logan and Popov. McVeigh and Webb parked up behind them and joined their muckers while the Ukrainian soldiers trudged over, boots squelching on the thickly muddied ground.

The men were in a rag-order state, Carter noted. Their uniforms were torn and frayed; their faces were caked in layers of dirt. One of the guys had a bloodstained field dressing swathed around his head. His mucker was six or seven inches taller, thin and gaunt-faced, with a thick moustache. Neither man looked like they'd had a wash or eaten a hot meal in months.

Popov addressed the soldiers in his mother tongue. At some point they must have realised that they were talking to a superior officer, and both men pulled themselves up straight and puffed out their chests. The moustached guy gave a long reply and thrust an arm towards the power station. As he spoke, a grim look crept across Popov's face.

'What did he say?' asked Carter when the two men had finished talking.

Popov licked his lips. He said, falteringly, 'The Russian pigdogs have attacked the frontline. Surprise offensive. Our forces have been forced to pull back from their positions.'

'Fuck,' McVeigh said.

'When?' Carter asked.

'Several hours ago. This morning,' Popov said.

'Explains them updates we got from the ops desk,' Logan said. 'On the way down here.'

Carter nodded.

Unconfirmed reports of gunfire and shelling, Hereford had warned them.

Vicinity of Holovika nuclear power station.

He said, 'How far are the Russians from here?'

Popov relayed the question to Moustache.

'Two kilometres,' the captain said, translating the man's reply. 'This is the last friendly position before the frontline. That is why these men have stopped us. They say it is too dangerous to proceed.'

As if to emphasise his point, Moustache traced a finger across his neck in a throat-slitting gesture.

'Two klicks?' McVeigh frowned heavily. 'That means the Russians must be at the plant.'

'Yes.' Popov grimaced; his face went pale. 'They captured Holovika some hours ago. Heavy shelling. The defenders had orders to fall back to this post. Most escaped. A few of their brothers did not. The Russians hit them very hard, these men say. They even knocked out the power lines.'

'There's no juice to the plant?' Carter asked.

Popov shook his head. 'There are backup diesel generators on the site. Should be capable of keeping the reactors running safely

300

until a team can be sent out to restore the electricity.' He added, by way of explanation, 'This is not the first time this has happened. We are familiar with such incidents. The Russians, they are animals. They don't give a shit.'

The moustached soldier spoke again. Popov questioned the man, then addressed his wounded colleague. Carter listened to their exchange with growing impatience. Every second they wasted at the camp gave Koltrov more time to pull clear of his pursuers.

'What?' Carter demanded. 'What did he say?'

Popov translated.

'He says they saw another car coming this way a short time ago. Same model as this one. Same colour.'

'Koltrov,' Logan said, slapping a hand against his thigh. 'Has to be.'

Popov shifted warily.

'What is it?' Carter asked. 'Captain?'

Popov looked him dead in the eye. 'They say he was driving towards Holovika.'

'They're sure?'

'Yes. They saw the car approaching and tried to warn the driver not to go any further, but he did not listen.' Popov indicated a right turn two hundred metres downwind of the camp. 'They headed that way, the man says.'

'Where does that lead?'

'It is the access road. It goes directly to the plant.'

'Does it lead anywhere else? Anywhere at all?'

'No. Only the plant. They are certain of this.'

'What's beyond it? Anything?'

Popov gave a quick shake of his head. 'Holovika is in the middle of nowhere. Around it only fields and the river. There is nowhere else to go from there. It is – what is the saying in your language?'

'Dead end?'

'Yes.' Popov snapped his fingers. 'Dead end. The general is at Holovika. No doubt about it.'

'What the fuck would he be doing there?' Logan asked.

'Nearest safe location, maybe,' Popov said. 'If he drives towards the frontline, the Russians could mistake him for an enemy. Kill him before he had a chance to identify himself.'

Carter said, 'Do we know how many Russians are at the plant? What hardware they've got? Ask them.'

Carter waited while the captain quizzed the soldiers.

'They think only a scratch force,' Popov said. 'Enough to hold the plant until reinforcements arrive.'

'Any other enemy assets in the area? Anti-aircraft defences? Tanks?'

'No. They do not think so. All the Russian heavy firepower is needed elsewhere.'

'If the place is so poorly defended, why haven't these lads retaken it?' Logan wondered.

'They don't have the vehicles for an assault. They had to send their armoured carriers and tanks across to a village to the east. Their comrades are in danger of being encircled and need fire support. These men have been told to hold their position and watch the enemy until they have the capability to retake the plant.'

Carter looked at the soldiers checking the drone. Looked back at Popov.

He said, 'Get them to stick a drone over the plant. We need eyes on the Russian positions. If we're going in, we've got to know exactly what we're up against.'

Popov stared at him with bulging eyes. 'You want to push on? Are you crazy?'

'We're no more than two klicks from the plant. We've got a responsibility to capture the general if possible.' He dead-eyed Popov. 'Give the fucking order, Captain.'

He addressed the soldiers. The guy with the field dressing gave a big thumbs up and grinned.

Popov said, 'OK. They will put the drone over.'

'Tell them to hand over a few of their RPGs, too,' Carter said. 'Couple of them should do the trick. As many rockets as they can spare.'

'OK.'

The order was relayed to the soldiers. One of the guys on the drone team readied the craft for take-off while his mucker operated a touchscreen tablet, working the control pads with his thumbs. The four propellors on the drone buzzed, the unit lifted into the sky, rising above the canopy of the pine trees. It hovered there for several seconds, buffeted by the slight wind, then pitched forward and glided smoothly in the direction of the plant. Then disappeared from sight.

While they waited for news from the drone, McVeigh and Webb hustled over to the stack of RPGs next to the shack and carted the two tube launchers and ammo backpacks over to the front vehicle. The Ukrainians seemed happy to hand over their spare equipment. Although they had orders not to abandon their post, they were clearly frustrated at having to pull back from the plant and the prospect of contributing to the deaths of Russian soldiers outweighed any discomfort about donating their weaponry to the SAS men.

Carter noticed the guy with the moustache chatting away on his personal radio. He looked towards Popov and said, 'Have these lads got comms?'

The captain translated the question. Then he said, 'Yes. They say everything was down for a while. Signals returned a few minutes ago.'

'Russians must have dropped the ECM systems once they loosed off them rockets,' Logan speculated.

Carter hastily fumbled for the pressel swich and tried raising his brother on the tactical radio. Still no response. Just a long stretch of dead air.

He started to fear the worst.

A shout went up from the drone team. Carter hurried over with Logan and Popov and the three men crowded around the operator, staring at the high-res video feed on the tablet screen.

There was no need for a translation this time. Carter instantly knew what he was looking at: an aerial shot of the nuclear power plant. A sprawling complex of cooling towers, electricity pylons, spent fuel dumps, substations and warehouses, bordered on the western side by a winding river and hemmed in behind a security fence topped with razor wire. Half a dozen reactor buildings dominated the centre of the facility, each one housed inside a giant concrete can. A metalled road ran in a straight line from east to west, leading to the front gate. There was a guardhouse to the side of the gate, manned by a pair of Russian soldiers. Carter noted a building site on the left side of the road, six hundred metres due east of the gate, filled with heavy duty machinery and mountains of gravel and sand.

Beyond the gate a large car park fronted a four-storey office block. A distance of perhaps five hundred metres from the gate to the entrance. A cluster of civilian motors were parked close to the building. Employees, Carter deduced. Working to keep the plant running in the midst of a war. He spotted two armoured mobility vehicles to the south of the block. On the northern side stood a row of maintenance units and storage sheds.

Three sangars constructed from sandbags had been positioned in a defensive line a hundred metres or so in front of the main building. A dozen Russian soldiers were milling about the area, warming their hands over the flames from an oil-drum fire, smoking cigarettes, drinking brews or staring at their phones. One look at them told Carter that these guys were poor quality. The dregs of the Russian military. A consequence of the crippling losses their commanders had suffered in the past few months. Now they were having to replenish their depleted units with raw recruits and prisoners.

'Any more enemy positions around the plant?' he asked.

Popov put the question to the drone operator. The soldier wiggled the joysticks, and the view on the tablet shifted as the quadcopter dipped forward and circled over the plant. Like a plane in a holding pattern, waiting for permission to land.

'No,' Popov said. 'There is no one else. Like I said. Scratch force.'

'Until the reinforcements rock up,' Logan reminded him.

Popov shrugged. 'This is true.'

Twelve enemies, thought Carter.

Plus the two soldiers at the guardhouse.

Assume a few more inside the buildings. In the control room and other critical infrastructure, guarding the employees. Four to six guys, perhaps.

We might be looking at anything up to twenty defenders.

Not the best odds in the world.

But not the worst, either.

'Any sign of the general among those guards?' Logan asked.

Carter leaned in closer, squinting at the camera as the drone completed another low sweep of the facility.

'Negative,' Popov said. 'He's not in sight. We don't have visual confirmation. Only soldiers in Russian uniform. No officers.'

'So where is he?'

Carter's eye was drawn to a one-storey structure shaped like a shipping container. South-east of the office block. A car had parked up a couple of metres from the structure.

A black SUV.

The stolen Suburban.

'There,' Carter said, pointing it out to the others. 'That's your proof. The general is definitely there.'

'Must be in that building,' Logan observed. 'Door on the side appears open. He's inside.'

'Why? What's in there?'

'Fuck knows, Geordie. Your guess is as good as mine. At least we know he's there. That's something.'

Carter made a mental note of the enemy positions. The layout of the plant. Protected areas. Blind spots. Obstructions. He looked at the gate. The car park. Lines of sight. Hastily sketching out a plan in his head. Not a sophisticated one. It wouldn't win any prizes for originality. But there wasn't time for anything elaborate. They needed to move in, fast. Before the Russians could boost their defences.

We're on the clock.

He said to Popov, 'Tell your mates we're going in to take the plant right now. They need to get on their comms and alert any friendlies in the area. Let them know we're moving forward. Keep that surveillance drone airborne too. Watch out for any possible incoming Russian forces.'

Popov switched languages and outlined the plan to the soldiers. Then Carter briefed his team.

'This is what we're going to do,' he told them. 'We'll approach the plant entrance in both wagons. Patrick, Billy, you'll stop on the access road here.' He pointed to the building site downwind of the front gate. 'Start putting down rounds on the sentries with the sniper rifle, while we go forward and ram the front gate. You'll be six hundred metres from the gate, so you're well out of range of the guards.

'Once we've broken through, we'll set up a firing position on the left side of the car park, using the wagon as cover. Should give us a direct line of sight to the enemy targets. Then you'll move forward to join us while we hit the fuckers with RPGs and scatter them. Mop up any survivors.'

Logan said, 'Maybe it would be better if we call it in, Geordie. Wait until the Ukrainians are up to strength and ready to hit the plant.'

Carter shook his head. 'It'll take a while to run the request up the chain of command. By which time the Russians will have bolstered their defences, and the general will be tucked up safely behind enemy lines. We've got to go in now.'

'What about rules of engagement? We're not supposed to get involved.'

'Fuck that,' Carter snapped. 'We're too close now. We've still got a chance to nab the prick.'

He gave Logan a flinty look.

'The general's up to something shifty at that plant,' he continued. 'I'm going to find out what. Unless you've got a better idea?'

'Fuck it, then,' said Logan. 'Let's do this.'

Twenty-Two

They piled back into the wagons in the same order as before. Carter, Logan and Popov in the lead Suburban, McVeigh and Webb in the second vehicle. Webb had his sniper rifle assembled, loaded and ready to engage as soon as they neared the target. Then the two SUVs pulled away from the Ukrainian camp and bombed down the road, making the right turn the moustached guy had indicated. Following in Koltrov's footsteps as they raced towards the power station two kilometres away.

While Popov and Logan checked their weapons, Carter jumped frequencies, tapped the pressel switch and tested his brother's channel again.

He waited. And prayed.

There was the world's longest pause. Then a hoarse voice in his ear said, 'Jamie? You there?'

An indescribable wave of relief swept through Carter. The appalling tension he had been feeling in his muscles began to relax slightly.

'Luke. Thank Christ. Are you OK?'

'I'm . . . I'm fine, mate.'

'The president?'

'He's right here.'

'Is he hurt?'

'A few nicks and cuts, but otherwise he's unharmed. The other lads are here too. Your guys, and mine. Fucking close, but we made it out in the nick of time.'

Carter said, 'How?'

'Tunnel. In the basement. Leads to an admin block across the street.'

Luke broke off and coughed violently. Carter heard a faint chorus of distressed voices in the background. People were spluttering and screaming, calling out to one another. He heard something else too. The shriek of ambulance sirens.

'Luke, the civilians. In the basement. Are they . . . ?'

He couldn't bring himself to finish the sentence.

'Don't, Jamie. Just leave it.'

'Tell me.'

His brother sighed.

'There was no time.' Luke's voice was choked with emotion. 'We had to get the principal to safety. Priority number one. You understand. We planned to go back and get the others out, before the rockets hit, but then . . . I'm sorry, mate.'

Carter swallowed thickly. 'How bad is it?'

'Emergency services are here,' Luke said, sidestepping the question. 'Doing what they can. It wasn't your fault. Nobody's to blame.'

'Luke. How fucking bad?'

There was a pause of numb silence. 'It doesn't look good. Building was flattened. Fires everywhere. Rubble. There was no time,' Luke repeated, like a mantra.

Something inside Carter cracked. The relief he'd felt instantly vanished, replaced by a sick feeling of guilt that lodged like a hard lump in the back of his throat. The grim thought played over and over in his head, like a track on loop.

My fault.

I'm culpable.

People had died. Hundreds, maybe.

He fought back against the voice. Tried to counter it with cold logic.

You had to make that call, he told himself.

Had to warn your brother about the compromised location.

Which was true, on one level. Protecting the life of Ukraine's leader outweighed every other consideration. An ugly truth, perhaps. But they were fighting an ugly war. Voloshyn's loss would have been an incalculable blow to national morale.

But the argument foundered against the rocks of his overwhelming guilt. He had flagged the president's location to the Russians. Now hundreds of civilians were dead.

Because of me.

There was nothing in his mental locker to help him process what he had done. He felt consumed by a bottomless pit of guilt – one he knew even then he would never escape from, no matter how hard he fought. Life in the Regiment prepared you for hardship and danger, and the stress of combat, and a million other things. But there was no Selection course on how to deal with having innocent blood on your hands.

You're responsible, the voice in his head said. *You're responsible for the deaths of maybe hundreds of people.*

There's no coming back from that.

'Jamie?' his brother asked. 'You there?'

'Yes,' Carter managed. His mouth was dry. 'I'm . . . here.'

'Where are you now?'

'We're pursuing the general. He gave us the slip, but we've got a bead on his location. Heading there now.'

'Are you close by? I could send some of the lads your way. Get them to RV with you en route.'

'No time. Just focus on keeping the president safe. I'll let you know once we've apprehended the general.'

'Roger that.'

'Can you do something for me, Luke?'

'Yes?'

'Tell the families I'm sorry. Tell them . . . I hope they can forgive me.'

A long silence played out on the channel. For a moment Carter wondered if the Russian ECMs were back and up and running again. Then his brother's voice sounded in his ear.

'Jamie, it wasn't your fault. You know that, right?'

'I know.' Carter paused. 'Watch yourself, Luke.'

'Yeah. You too.'

Carter ended the chat and refocused on the road.

They were closing in on the plant now. Less than two kilometres to go. Popov stayed on the net, communicating with the Ukrainians back at the camp. The drone would stay airborne throughout the attack, watching for any reinforcements heading in their direction.

'No sign yet of any more targets,' the captain reported. 'No further defensive positions around the complex.'

'Let's hope it fucking stays that way,' Logan said.

They travelled on for half a klick, past the shattered remnants of a Ukrainian column caught up in the recent artillery bombardment around Holovika. Discarded army equipment. Tourniquets and canteens, rucksacks and weaponry and helmets. Spent rounds and the shattered remains of a pair of infantry mobility vehicles. In among them, the tangled corpses of four dead Ukrainian soldiers. Carter looked round but there was no sign of any Russian forces lingering in the area.

Directly ahead stood the nuclear power plant at Holovika.

Carter slowed the wagon to sub-thirty kilometres per hour, moving cautiously towards the target, eyes flicking left and right, alert to any potential threats that might be lurking in the vicinity, but the coast seemed clear.

The nuclear plant itself was massive. Bigger than it had appeared from the drone camera. A hundred hectares, perhaps. The size of a large out-of-town shopping complex. Bordered to the north and south by a patchwork of uncultivated fields.

Potentially twenty defenders, Carter reminded himself.

Poor odds, on paper. But skill was a great force leveller. Against the SAS, a group of poorly trained recruits stood no chance. Once the rounds started flying, they would quickly turn and run for their lives.

He hoped.

One kilometre to the target now.

Carter said over the comms to Webb and McVeigh, 'Making final approach to the target. Get ready to pull over on my signal.'

'Ready when you are,' McVeigh responded. 'Just say the fucking word.'

As they rolled down the road, Carter wondered again why the general had fled to Holovika.

The guy could have easily continued south. The nearest Russian encampment couldn't be very far from here. Fifteen or twenty kilometres at most. Instead, Koltrov had deliberately detoured to a poorly defended nuclear plant, surrounded by Ukrainian forces and guarded by a handful of crap quality Russians.

But why?

And what was Zinchenko doing in all of this? Had she been taken hostage? Or was she conspiring with Koltrov?

I don't know, Carter thought.

But one thing's for sure.

I'm going to get some fucking answers.

Seven hundred metres to the target.

At the guardhouse the two Russian soldiers spotted the Suburbans speeding down the access road and turned towards them.

'Two targets in sight at the front gate,' Carter confirmed to McVeigh and Webb over the comms.

'Roger,' McVeigh said.

The guards were equipped with AK-74 assault rifles. Standard-issue kit for Russian grunts. Decent weapons, but useless at anything beyond five hundred metres. Whereas the L115A4 carried by Webb could nail a target at more than twice that distance.

Carter kept rolling forward. Lining up the front bumper with the gate.

'Pulling over now,' McVeigh said.

Carter lifted his eyes to the rear-view mirror. Behind them the second wagon swerved off the road towards the construction site and skidded to a halt side-on to the road, next to a backhoe, the driver's side door facing the distant guardhouse.

In the next moment, the side doors flipped open. McVeigh and Webb jumped down to the asphalt, the Brummie lugging the sniper rifle. Both men knelt down behind the front fender, putting the wheelbase between themselves and any stray incoming. Webb propped the rifle legs on top of the bonnet, head resting against the cheek guard; McVeigh had the spotter's role, peering through the Trijicon scope mounted on his M4 and directing his colleague to targets. If Webb's initial shot missed, McVeigh would look for the fall of the bullet and instruct Webb to adjust his aim accordingly to compensate for the wind or other factors.

Carter kept driving.

Five hundred metres from the entrance now.

The two Russians stepped forward from the gate.

AK-74s raised at the vehicle hurtling towards them.

At four hundred metres flames spewed out of their muzzles.

'Get down!' Carter shouted as he dropped his head.

Logan and Popov both ducked down, assuming the brace position, as a volley of bullets hailstoned against the bonnet. One round struck the windscreen and winged past Carter, several inches above his head; another slapped into the headrest.

Carter kept his head below the wheel, almost driving blind. He didn't hear the report of the suppressed L115A4 as Webb cracked off his first shot at the Russians. But he saw the impact.

Three hundred metres due west, the guard on the left tumbled away, dropping to the ground like a sack of hot bricks. His mate gave up spraying bullets and started running for cover inside the guardhouse. The right decision. But taken too late. He had made it halfway when Webb took his head clean off. Carter glimpsed the mist of blood spurting out of his head, a moment before the Russian bellyflopped to the ground.

Two hundred metres from the gate now.

Across the car park, the gunshots had alerted the Russians scattered around the sangars. They were slow to react to the threat, retrieving helmets and weapons, running around like headless chickens. Slack soldiers. Thrown into the fighting after a few weeks of basic training. They were about to pay for their lack of professionalism.

Carter stamped hard on the accelerator.

The wagon shot forward. Speedometer clocking up towards ninety per.

A hundred metres to go.

Carter put the distance between the gate and the sangars at four hundred metres. The sangars were sixty or seventy metres or so from the main admin block. The south side of the car park was empty; from that position Carter and his muckers would have an unobstructed line of sight to all three sangars ranged across the front of the admin building. But which also meant they would be sitting ducks once they crashed through the gate. They would have to get themselves behind the wagon and let rip with their RPGs before the enemy could put the drop on them.

His mind registered these details a second before the Suburban bounced and shuddered over the slotted Russians.

Then rammed into the gate.

The front bumper struck the entrance; sparks flew; the shriek of metal scraping against metal split the air. More rounds glanced off the Chevrolet, hammering off the grille and spiderwebbing the windscreen, as a couple of the more organised Russian defenders started putting down rounds on the vehicle rushing towards them. Carter held on tightly to the wheel, and suddenly they were through the gate and bolting across the tarmac. He angled towards a point fifty metres south-west of the gate, then stomped the brakes, wrested the wheel in the other direction and skidded to a halt. Another bullet punched through the driver's side window, narrowly missing him before it embedded itself in the car roof.

'Out!' he bellowed at the others. 'Move!'

Popov and Logan dived out of the back seats. Carter circled round to join them behind the SUV, staying in a low crouch while another volley of 5.45 x 39 mm gunfire clanged against the opposite side of the SUV, piercing holes in the bonnet and bursting one of the tyres.

Logan handed him one of the RPGs and a backpack, took the other for himself and scurried over to the rear wheelbase. Carter took up his position behind the bonnet, Popov to his right, the Ukrainian captain resting his weapon on the bonnet, ready to brass up any Russian targets once they popped into view. Their vantage point gave the three soldiers an unimpeded view of the sangars.

A high-explosive anti-tank grenade had been pre-loaded into the launcher. Carter set down the backpack, flipped up the iron sights on top of the barrel, removed the safety cap from the breech end of the steel tube, tore off the safety pin and the fuse cover and took up a kneeling firing stance. He rested the wooden section of the barrel on his shoulder, his left hand clasped around the shorter rear grip, his right wrapped around the pistol grip located further forward.

Carter cocked the hammer on the side of the receiver, curled his index finger around the trigger, lined up the leftmost sangar.

Fired.

The grenade hissed out of the launcher. Smoke swept over Carter, suffocating him. The acrid odour of gunpowder choked his throat. His eyes began to sting.

Three hundred and fifty metres away, the sangar disappeared behind a belching swirl of orange flame as the grenade found its target, shredding the sandbags.

The explosion didn't wipe out the soldiers. But it had the intended effect. It got them moving. The four Russians broke to their right and sprinted towards the armoured vehicles to the south.

They didn't get far.

Popov had already zeroed in on the figures. He unleashed a couple of three-round bursts, killing one of them while Carter chucked aside the spent RPG launcher and hefted up his front-slung M4 rifle, giving the other two Russians the good news with aimed shots. Popov plugged the last guy through the neck; he crumpled to a heap a few metres from his slotted mates, his left leg twitching erratically.

Carter looked round as Logan fired a grenade at the rightmost sangar and scored a direct hit. A cloud of smoke spewed upwards, flinging a ton of flaming material into the air. The smoke drifted skyward, the veil cleared, and Carter saw two of the Russians scrambling for cover behind the maintenance units thirty metres to the north.

A third man staggered senselessly away from the sangar, his guts hanging out of his stomach. Carter put him out of his misery with a quick burst to the head, then shrank behind the Suburban as one of the Russians in the middle sangar opened fire. Bullets scarred the ground to the left and right of the vehicle. Another flurry of rounds blew out one of the side windows, showering Carter in tiny shards of broken glass.

As the firefight progressed, he kept a running tally of enemy kills in his head. Seven defenders had been dropped in the initial onslaught. Which left six Russians to deal with. Four in the middle sangar. Two behind the maintenance sheds.

Plus any soldiers guarding the workforce inside the buildings.

He glanced over his shoulder. Looked beyond the gap where the front gate had been. Next to the building site, seven hundred metres away, Webb and McVeigh hurried into the Suburban and pulled clear of the backhoe, remounting the access road as they raced to catch up with their mates.

Logan eased out another HEAT grenade from the pouch. He inserted the booster end into the front end of the launcher tube, screwed it into place. Shouldered the RPG and centred the sights on the middle sangar. Squeezed the trigger.

Flames hissed out of the breech end of the RPG.

The grenade whizzed across the car park.

Exploded.

A ball of fiery smoke engulfed the sangar.

Men screamed and fled in every direction.

A maimed Russian crawled away from the carnage, half his face hanging off. Carter plugged him in the head, turning his skull into red pulp.

By now Webb and McVeigh had pulled up next to the three attackers in the second Suburban. They positioned themselves behind the engine block and started putting down rounds on the three fleeing Russians, picking them off as they ditched their weapons and bolted for safety. Determination giving way to out-right panic.

One of them went down, nailed in the guts by a burst from McVeigh's rifle. A second Russian ran in the opposite direction from the firefight. Carter nailing the guy three times in the spinal region. The man fell forward as if he'd tripped and landed on his front. Carter emptied another two rounds at him for good measure. The third Russian threw himself behind one of the armoured vehicles, the ground sparking up behind him as Popov narrowly missed his target.

A moment later, a pair of soldiers stormed out of the front of the building, spraying wild bursts at the Suburbans. Two men decked out in workers' overalls and hard hats sprinted past the Russians, blocking Carter's line of sight, and the Russians dived behind the armoured wagons before he could get a bead on them.

The workers hurried on towards the nearest motors as the battle continued raging around them. The Russians kept firing unaimed shots at the vehicles; one of the workers screamed as a stray bullet caught him in the leg. The other man turned to help his stricken friend and took a couple of rounds to the chest, flopping to the ground beside a clapped-out Skoda.

Carter thought: *Three enemies behind the vehicles.*

Two behind the maintenance sheds.

We're winning.

The last defenders were putting up a hard fight, popping out of cover to shoot at the wagons before shrinking from view again. Rounds slapped into the ground half a metre to Carter's left.

Logan slid another grenade into the launcher. Popov and McVeigh were targeting the surviving Russians with short bursts. Webb had his sniper rifle trained on the sheds, ready to put holes in the enemy as soon as Logan flushed them out with the RPG.

Carter cupped his hands and shouted to his colleagues, 'Cover me! I need covering fire!'

Logan looked round at him. 'Where are you going?'

'To find the general.'

He couldn't wait for the lads to finish off the remaining soldiers. The general would have heard the shooting at the front of the plant; Carter figured there was a good chance Koltrov might have fled as soon as the bullets started flying.

No more time.

I've got to move now.

He paused beside the wheel. Waited for Logan to switch to his M4 and bring up his weapon. Then they started putting down rounds on the few remaining defenders, working in pairs. Logan and McVeigh fired first, keeping the Russians pinned down behind cover; once they had emptied their mags, Webb and Popov would take over, maintaining a consistent rate of fire. Between them, they would stop the Russians from taking potshots at Carter while he was exposed.

As soon as Logan and McVeigh started letting rip, Carter sprang out from behind the Suburban and broke into a sprint, chopping his stride as he made for the shipping-container-shaped building two hundred metres away at his eleven o'clock. Running across the vacant car park as fast as his weary legs could carry him.

A cry went up to the north as the Russians spotted Carter and started directing sporadic bursts of gunfire at him, the cracks of their AK-74s splitting the air. He heard the dull thwack of rounds splashing against the tarmac; another bullet whipcracked past him. They were getting closer, he realised. Then the M4s barked in reply as Logan, McVeigh and the others kept up their furious rate of suppressive fire.

Carter ran on. Willed his body to move faster.

Keep going.

Don't lose now. You've come too far.

He pushed on, passed the stolen Suburban and reached the single-storey building in another three ragged strides. Stopped outside and looked cautiously round. There was nothing to indicate the building's purpose. Just a windowless structure with reinforced metal walls and a half-open door at one end of it. Harsh light spilled through the slender gap. From within, the mechanical hum of generators reached Carter's ears.

No sign of the general. Or Zinchenko.

Carter raised his M4 and stepped towards the door.

Eased it open.

Plunged inside.

Twenty-Three

He swept through the door into a long and narrow space, brightly lit beneath the glare of a string of overhead fluorescent tube lights. A steel gangway ran down the length of the main room, past a bank of diesel generators, each one set on a raised metal bed. Carter counted twelve of them, arranged in a long line. At the far end of the walkway, beyond the last generator, there was a separate smaller room housing some sort of big electrical units. Fuses and circuit breakers.

It was furnace-hot in the room. A deafening motorised thrum filled the air. A/C generators whirring away, accompanied by the noise of the generators working to keep the plant operational. Backup power systems, Carter reminded himself. Designed to keep Holovika operating safely until the electrical grid could be restored.

Above the mechanical hum, he heard another sound.

A thick, grating voice speaking in Russian.

General Koltrov.

The voice came from the smaller room.

A terrible feeling swelled up in Carter.

He moved cautiously down the walkway, clearing the space between each generator, the sound of his boots on the metallic surface drowned out by the machine noise reverberating throughout the building.

As he neared the smaller room, the general's voice became clearer. Koltrov sounded like he was projecting his voice. Like a politician addressing a crowd of devoted fans at a campaign rally.

From outside the building came a rumbling boom as Logan unleashed another RPG at the enemy. The firefight would be over soon, Carter knew. The last few Russians would either surrender or make a run for it, once they realised the game was up.

Another two or three minutes, and we'll have regained control of the plant.

He stopped again at the threshold. Pricked his ears. Koltrov was still talking in his booming voice. With his flimsy grasp of Russian, Carter could only pick up on the occasional word or phrase. The general name-checked the Russian president. He spoke of victory, and enemies, and total sacrifice.

Carter pushed through the opening, sweeping his weapon sights from side to side in a broad arc.

There were several colossal metal-cased units lined up on the left side of the room, each one housing an array of buttons and dials and control panels. Like something out of a server farm. Or a prototype computer laboratory in the 1950s. Emergency switchgear equipment, he supposed. For supplying juice to critical power plant systems in the event of an unexpected loss of power. Such as when Russian artillery shells knocked out the electrical power supply.

In the middle of the room, no more than four or five paces away, was General Koltrov.

Zinchenko stood in front of the general, filming him on her smartphone. Koltrov was addressing himself directly to the press officer's handset, delivering a thunderous speech in Russian as he pointed accusingly at the lens.

Koltrov stopped talking as soon as Carter entered the room. He spun round, started to reach for his belt-holstered pistol. Then he caught sight of the M4 trained at the broad mass of his chest and stopped.

Very slowly, Zinchenko lowered her phone.

General Koltrov stared at the SAS soldier. His cheeks were burning with rage and indignation.

'You,' he spat. 'How did you . . . but it doesn't matter. It is done.' He smiled, but there was an eerie calmness in Koltrov's expression that unnerved Carter. 'I am ready.'

'Ready for what?' Carter growled.

Koltrov sidestepped the question. He said with a sneer, 'You shouldn't have followed me here. This is not your fight. It never was. But you will pay now, with your life. All of you will pay.'

'The fuck does that mean?'

'The Russians are afraid to do what is necessary to win. They do not understand that if we wish to defeat the fascists, we must be prepared to take the ultimate step. Make the ultimate sacrifice. Only then can we secure total victory over the west.

'Others are afraid of the consequences. But I am not. I am willing to do what must be done to destroy our enemies. Even if it costs my life.'

The general darted a glance towards the rear of the room.

Which was when Carter noticed the device.

There was an emergency exit door a few paces behind Zinchenko. Beside it, resting on the floor, was a cylindrical unit, no bigger than a piece of carry-on luggage, sheathed inside a foam-insulated canvas carry case. The lid had been removed. There was a mechanical timer on the exposed top of the aluminium drum, along with several switches and dials.

Carter stared at it.

Felt his guts turn to ice.

He was looking at a bomb.

Specifically, a low-yield man-portable tactical nuclear weapon. At least, Carter assumed it was a tactical nuke. It looked similar to the ones he'd seen in Tajikistan, and he'd heard rumours that the Russians had been covertly transferring hundreds of such devices to secure locations across occupied Ukraine. The smallest ones had a yield somewhere in the region of a kiloton. Equivalent to a thousand tons of TNT. A fraction of the destructive force of Hiroshima, say. But capable of obliterating a strategic target such as a dam, or a bridge.

Or destroy a nuclear power plant.

He kept staring at the bomb. He recalled Makarenko's dying words. Right before Carter had blown his brains out.

You're all dead.

All of you.

Now he understood.

'In a few minutes, that bomb will detonate.' Koltrov puffed out his chest in a show of pride and defiance. 'I shall die with honour; I will be remembered as a hero of Greater Russia. The man who brought the West to its knees. And I shall take you all down with me.'

Carter swiftly grasped the general's plan. Once detonated, the man-portable bomb would destroy the backup generators and the rest of the plant's critical infrastructure, cutting the power to the cooling systems and causing the reactors to overheat. Triggering a catastrophic nuclear meltdown.

The resultant explosion would disperse vast clouds of radioactive material. Prevailing winds would push them across much of eastern and northern Europe, exposing the Baltic states, Poland, Hungary and the Czech Republic, Austria – NATO member countries – to potentially fatal levels of radiation. The fallout would be devastating. Untold casualties. It would make Chernobyl look like a minor fuck-up.

Moreover, he realised grimly, the Alliance would be compelled to react to a deliberate attack. Carter cast his mind back to the report he'd seen on the news several days earlier. He remembered the veiled threat from the US Secretary of State to punish Russia if it crossed the nuclear red lines.

Swift and firm retaliation, the secretary had vowed.

The likes of which the world will not have seen before.

Which could mean any number of things. But at the very least it would provoke a strong military response. The US might obliterate the Black Sea fleet. Or start actively targeting assets inside Russia.

Escalation would be unavoidable.

World War Three.

Nuclear annihilation.

323

Outside, the shooting had reduced to sporadic bursts of gunfire, and Carter knew that the fight for the plant must almost be over. Right now McVeigh, Webb, Popov and Logan would be going through the remaining enemies like a dose of salts. The Regiment way.

Oblivious to the imminent threat of nuclear Armageddon.

Carter kept his weapon pointed at Koltrov.

'Disarm it,' he said.

Koltrov smiled but said nothing.

Carter felt the muscles on his neck cording like tensed ropes.

'Disarm the bomb, or you're fucking dead.'

'I cannot. The firing device has been activated. Too late.'

'Bullshit.'

Koltrov gave a nasty laugh. 'You think I am bluffing? Idiot. Whatever I do, I am a dead man. Moscow will not forgive me, not after this. They would leave me to perish in some camp in Siberia. There is no dignity in that death. Here, at least, I can die as a martyr.'

He laughed. Carter felt the pressure building inside his skull. The pounding was relentless now. Incessant.

'You lose, English.'

Koltrov glanced meaningfully at the press officer. Something unspoken passed between the general and Zinchenko. Then Koltrov uttered a command at her in Russian. A single word. Carter understood it at once.

Run.

Zinchenko spun round and ran towards the emergency exit.

Carter automatically swung his rifle towards her.

A momentary distraction. Instinctive. But it took Carter's attention away from Koltrov for a split second. Which was a mistake. Because then he glimpsed a fleeting movement at the fringes of his vision as the general ripped his Glock pistol from his side holster and brought it up to shoulder height.

There was a loud bang as Carter swivelled back towards the general. A sharp pain flared up on the right side of his trunk. Like getting punched in the ribs by a heavyweight boxer. Carter drew his M4 level with Koltrov and shot him twice, drilling him in the upper chest, holing his vital plumbing.

The general collapsed.

Carter looked round, but Zinchenko was nowhere to be seen.

The rear door yawned open. He staggered forward, started to give chase, then heard the small voice in the back of his head.

Let her go, the voice told him.

The bomb. Deal with the bomb.

He stumbled towards the tactical nuke. It took a great effort to put one foot in front of the other. The simple act of walking left him gasping for breath. The pain in his side was excruciating. As if someone had buried a spear in his ribs. He almost lost his balance, released his grip on his M4, steadied himself against the switchgear unit, looked down at his jacket.

Blood.

It was covered in fresh blood.

His own.

Carter struggled out of his webbing, plate armour and jacket, then crooked his head to get a better look at the wounds. Two bullets had bored themselves into the side of his chest cavity, an inch or two above the lower ribs. Both entry holes were deep. He figured a bunch of shit had been sucked into the penetration sites. Bits of fabric, dirt and fuck knows what else. And he was bleeding heavily.

The basic knowledge Carter had gleaned from the SAS medics' course told him that he was in serious trouble. Perforation of the liver, maybe the bile duct too. Massive internal blood loss. High mortality rate.

He took a field dressing from one of the pouches on his webbing, ripped open the foil packaging, applied the dressing directly to the wounds and wrapped the bandage around his chest. Within moments the surgical material was soaked through.

The pain dialled up a notch. Worse than he'd ever felt before. The invisible spear twisting, lacerating his vitals. Carter was flagging badly. Nausea surged in his throat, like a bout of travel sickness, but a million times more crippling. He thought he might retch. The effort of standing upright required every last ounce of his remaining strength.

He struggled over to the general. Sank to his knees beside the man and grabbed him by the collar. Koltrov was drowning in his own blood.

'How do I stop the bomb?' Carter demanded.

Koltrov convulsed as pain wracked his body. He coughed up blood and made a soft gurgling noise. Carter shook him violently.

'Tell me!'

The general parted his cracked lips slightly. Blood leaked out of the corners of his mouth. He couldn't speak. The light was going out in his right eye. Carter had seen it happen before, to mates and hostiles on the battlefield. The body recognising its own limitations. Raising the white flag.

Carter released his grip on the man's collar. Left him on the floor, choking to death on his own blood, and staggered over to the tactical nuke. The gunfire outside had ceased, and Carter figured that his colleagues had wiped out the Russian guards.

He knelt beside the bomb, inspected the fuse on top. The arming switch had been set to the engaged position; a red light glowed to indicate that the device had been armed. A line of rotating digits counted down the time to detonation in hours, minutes and seconds.

Carter peered at the display.

00 06 23

He had less than seven minutes.

Enough time.

Maybe.

There was no chance of getting a medevac. Not in the middle of a war zone. Any friendly chopper would be at risk of getting blown out of the sky by Russian anti-aircraft systems, and in the cold, brutal logic of Carter's mind, the threat to their lives outweighed any slim chances of preserving his own.

He was bleeding out.

Dying, he thought.

I'm dying.

He was done. Carter knew it. He was more certain of it than he had been about anything else in his life. The blood loss. The depth of penetration. The nausea rising into the back of his throat. The truth was inescapable. He had only minutes left. Fifteen, perhaps less.

He had to hope that he stayed alive long enough to get the bomb out of range of the plant, and any nearby civilians or military personnel.

He reached for his pressel switch with a bloodstained hand. Spoke into the comms.

'Lads, I've been hit. Repeat, I've been hit.'

'Shit,' came Logan's reply in his earpiece. 'Where are you, mate? Stay put and we'll come get you. We're just about done here. Checking the bodies now.'

'Leave them,' Carter said. 'Get the fuck out of here. Head back to the Ukrainian camp. Now.'

'What about the general?'

'He's rigged up a bomb. I think . . . I think it's a man-portable nuke. He's planning to blow up the whole plant. Cause a meltdown. You need to get clear of this place.'

'But . . . what about you?'

'I'm hit bad. Liver's fucked. I'm not going to make it.'

'Sod that, you daft cunt. We're not leaving you here. Forget it.'

Carter breathed in painfully and said, 'You're not hearing me, mate. Someone has got to take the bomb and get it as far away from this place as possible.'

'But ... there has to be another way. There must be,' Logan repeated, as if he was trying to persuade himself.

'There isn't. It can't be defused. Now get moving. I'll deal with the bomb.'

Carter didn't wait for a reply. He clicked off again, dropped to his haunches, slid his arms through the straps attached to the olive-green canvas case and lifted up the bomb. It was heavier than he had expected. Thirty kilograms or so. Like carrying a weighted Bergen at the end of Test Week.

He stumbled through the emergency exit, willing his tired body to move faster. Every footstep sent a fresh wave of searing pain running up his side.

Carter grimaced through the agony as he rounded the building and limped towards the stolen Suburban parked twenty metres away. In the distance, he caught sight of McVeigh, Webb, Logan and Popov bundling into one of the wagons. The vehicle swerved clockwise on the asphalt, nosed through the gate and took off back down the access road. A few moments later it was lost to view.

He set the nuclear device down next to the passenger side of the Suburban, leaned inside and raked his eyes over the interior. He found the key fob in one of the cup holders, and offered up a silent thank-you to the God he had never believed in.

Carter humped the bomb into the front passenger seat. The timer dial indicated five minutes until detonation.

He unclipped the toughened nylon sling from his rifle, looped it round the seat and the nuke and pulled it tight, securing the device in place. The roads on the approach to the plant had been riddled with potholes: he didn't want the thing shaking around while he was driving away from civilisation. He chucked the deslung M4 into the back seat, somehow made it over to the driver's side door, had to rest for a moment as the sickness threatened to overwhelm him. Spots were colouring his vision as he dropped heavily behind the wheel. Every draw of breath triggered a burning pain in his chest.

He fought it. Pushed back against it.

It's only pain, he told himself. *Don't give in to it.*

Get moving.

He started the engine. Navigated out of the plant. Drove at full pelt down the access road and hung a right at the road, taking him further south, closer to the Russian frontline. Away from the Ukrainian military camp, and his SAS muckers. Away from the nuclear plant, and the spectre of radioactive clouds sweeping over the continent.

He drove hard. Foot to the pedal. Engine snarling with the strain. There were no other cars on the road in this area. Contested territory. The Russians were pouring their scant resources into the Ukrainian fighters defending the nearby villages. They couldn't spare the manpower to establish checkpoints or set up camps along the roadheads.

It became increasingly difficult to stay focused on the road. Black waves were creeping in at the edges of his vision. His eyelids felt heavy, as if they had lead weights sewn into them. Carter felt himself in danger of slipping out of consciousness. He wanted more than anything to stop the vehicle and close his eyes.

No.

Not yet.

Just a little further.

After five kilometres he reached a clearing at the edge of a wooded area. A desolate area. No buildings in sight. No farmhouses or shacks or signs of human occupation. Just fields and woods, the autumn leaves glowing in the light of the day. Beautiful, in its own way. There were worse places for a man to die. He figured this was as good a place as any.

Carter stopped the car. Engaged the handbrake.

The timer on the bomb ticked down to twenty seconds.

The blackness spread outwards, crowding the centre of his eyesight. His mouth was sandpaper-dry. The sickness faded. He could no longer feel his fingers or toes. His chest and legs were soaked in his own blood. Pints of the stuff.

He felt so tired. So very tired.

He stared out of the window, but he couldn't see much. Not anymore. The darkness enveloped his vision, like a dark veil had been drawn over the world. The pain had numbed. He felt light-headed.

If this is death, he thought, *it isn't so bad. There's nothing to be afraid of. Nothing at all.*

He closed his eyes. Counted down the last seconds of his life. He thought of his brother. He thought of the dead bodies lying amid the rubble of the mayor's office. He thought about the Lion of Ukraine, drowning in his own blood, and a promise he made a lifetime ago to a mother he no longer had.

Five seconds.

Four.

Three.

Two.

One.

Twenty-Four

Credenhill. Twelve days later.

A sombre mood hung over the group of mourners gathered in the sergeants' mess. The Regiment NCOs, and the men of D Squadron had come to pay their quiet respects to their fallen comrade, drinking beers and trading stories about Jamie Carter. A good turnout, Luke thought. All things considered. Even the CO, a man who famously disliked his brother, had put in an appearance. Jamie had been an abrasive character, never been the most popular guy in the camp, but every Blade respected him for his ability to soldier. That mattered more than winning any popularity contest.

They had buried him earlier that afternoon, beneath the pale grey sky, in the cemetery at the Regimental church at Credenhill. The service had been simple, and short. Apart from Luke, there had been no family members to mourn Jamie, no wife or children, and an outsider might have concluded that the dead man had lived a tragic and isolated existence. But they would have been mistaken. Jamie had been part of the brotherhood of the Regiment.

Scott Logan walked over to him and smiled awkwardly. Logan, McVeigh and Webb had been called back to Hereford after Koltrov's death, placed back on standby with the rest of A Squadron until further notice.

'How are you holding up, lad?' he asked.

Luke shrugged. 'You know.'

'I'm sorry, like.'

'Thanks, mate.'

Logan scratched the back of his neck and fumbled for the right words. 'Had some balls on him, your brother. He could be difficult. But you knew that already, I guess.'

'Yeah. I did.'

Logan hesitated. 'I . . . I was the last person to speak to him. Before . . . it happened.'

Luke looked up from his beer. 'What did he say?'

'He wasn't thinking about himself. Even then, at the very end, he was only concerned about us getting to safety.'

Luke half smiled. 'That sounds like Jamie all right.'

Logan stared at his drink, as if searching for inspiration in a can of Polish lager.

'He was a hero,' he said. 'I want you to know that. A fucking legend of the Regiment. What he did took courage. There's not many who would have done the same.'

'I know.'

They lapsed into silence, sipping their beers.

Luke had been called back to Hereford in the aftermath of the attack. He'd wanted to stay on in Ukraine and continue his duties, but the head shed had overruled him. They wanted to give him time to mourn his brother, they said. Get his head clear. Decompress. He had been coming up to the end of his rotation anyway. Someone else could fill his spot on the team.

The day before he'd left, President Voloshyn had taken him to one side and privately expressed his gratitude. He knew only a few details about the attack on Holovika, but enough to grasp the enormity of the sacrifice his brother had made, and the crisis that he'd helped avert. He'd added that Luke would always have a friend in Kyiv. If there was anything he could do . . . ?

The president was a good man, Luke thought. Honest. True to his word. The rarest of qualities among politicians these days. He hoped the guy would stay out of harm's way. With Voloshyn running the show, backed up by NATO training, support and hardware, the Ukrainians would stand a fighting chance of defeating the invaders in the long run.

There had been a post-op debrief on Luke's return to camp. Hardcastle had been present, along with the OC of A Squadron, and a corporate-looking woman he didn't recognise. Hardcastle had introduced her as Ellen Kendall and said she was from Vauxhall. One of the higher-ups at Six, Luke had surmised.

Over coffee they had laid bare the circumstances surrounding his brother's death. Luke had picked up bits and pieces of it from the other lads in A Squadron, but he hadn't known the full story. Reports of the plant assault and the bomb had been ruthlessly suppressed. Likewise the president's presence during the rocket attack on the mayor's office. They didn't want to hand the Russians a PR victory by showing how close they had come to causing a nuclear disaster. Or killing the president.

For the same reason, Koltrov's treachery had been withheld from the media. The official line was that the general had been courageously killed leading a counter-attack against Russian forces around Holovika. In recognition of his actions, he had been posthumously awarded the Hero of Ukraine – the highest title a citizen could receive.

According to testimony from Logan and the other men on Koltrov's security detail, Jamie had believed that the general had emplaced a low-yield tactical nuke at the plant. But investigators from the MoD had ruled out the possibility of a man-portable nuclear device. Based on the force of the explosion and the recovery of components from the blast site, they concluded that Carter had been killed by a high-grade conventional bomb. Similar devices had been recovered by Ukrainian forces at several nuclear sites recaptured from the enemy in recent weeks. The bombs had been emplaced to demonstrate their willingness to blow up the plants, but Six believed the Kremlin had never intended to actually use them. They were there for show, they explained.

Although less powerful than a nuke, the device would still have packed enough of a punch to destroy the generator room and inflict serious damage on the rest of the plant. By removing it to a safe distance from Holovika, Jamie Carter had narrowly averted the nightmare scenario of radioactive fallout; detonation on-site would have almost certainly prompted an aggressive response from a US president desperate to flex his military muscles. Instead, the bomb had harmlessly exploded in a depopulated swathe of Ukrainian countryside.

Two days after his brother's death, the news had carried stories of a rocket attack on a Russian military base near Donetsk. Hundreds of soldiers had been killed, among them a two-star general and several high-ranking FSB officers. Unofficial reports claimed that the operation had been carried out in retaliation for a Russian attack on the mayor's office in Zolodyansk. Two hundred and eighty civilians had died, many crushed to death in the basement.

'It's a crying shame Koltrov wasn't taken alive,' Hardcastle had said during the debrief. 'We would have liked to have a conversation with him. Find out the names of those other traitors inside Ukraine. But it won't make much of a difference.'

Kendall had explained that Six would work backwards. They would reopen investigations into potential suspects Koltrov had deliberately avoided arresting. Working on the assumption that at least some of them were Russian agents the general had been trying to protect. It would take some time, Kendall said. But they would tease the remaining traitors out of the woodwork eventually. Those who had not already fled to Russia.

'Any word on that press officer who was with Koltrov?' Luke had asked.

'Zinchenko?' Hardcastle had looked briefly ruffled. 'Afraid not. Vanished into thin air, as far as we can tell.'

Kendall had said, 'We believe she escaped across the frontline to the Russians. If she was on the Ukrainian side of the battlefield she would have been picked up a long time ago. I doubt we'll ever hear from her again.'

They had smiled diplomatically and fed Luke the usual spiel about not discussing his brother's death with anyone else. The facts would remain known to only a handful of people inside the Regiment and at Whitehall. Officially, Jamie Carter had been accidentally killed by a stray Russian shot while on protection duties in southern Ukraine.

'Obviously,' said Hardcastle, 'we can't mention your brother engaging in direct combat with Russian troops. That would be tantamount to admitting full involvement in the conflict. We'd be facing a political shitstorm. Downing Street and the White House are in full agreement on that point.'

'Fine,' Luke had said. He didn't have the desire to lock horns with the head shed over his brother's death.

Then Hardcastle had leaned forward and looked him in the eye.

'I hope I shouldn't have to say this, Luke. You're a good soldier, so I know we can trust you. But if you spill a word of this to anyone, we'll skin you alive. Your career will be the least of your worries. I'll make damn sure of it. Am I making myself clear?'

'Yes, boss.'

At the end of the meeting, Hardcastle had ordered him to go on leave for a while.

'Take a couple of weeks off,' he'd said. 'Go on holiday, decompress. Catch up with your mates. Mourn your brother. But stay sharp, mind. Once you're back on duty you'll report to me.' He added, with a slight flicker of a smile, 'We got a job for you, Luke.'

'Job, boss?'

Kendall nodded. 'I understand you ride a motorbike?'

'Yes, boss.'

'A passion of yours, is it?'

'You might say that.' Luke pulled his chin. 'What's the mission?'

'We'll discuss that later. Let's just say that it's a highly confidential assignment. One that is perfectly suited for someone with your particular . . . interests.'

In the sergeants' mess, the crowd of mourners was beginning to thin out. People returned to their duties, leaving the wake as soon as it was polite to do so. As if Luke was contagious. As if grief was a virus you could catch. That was fine by him. He had a bunch of stuff to deal with anyway. His brother's cottage needed to be cleared out. Banks and credit card providers and a hundred other companies needed to be notified of his death. Some of the lads had arranged to meet up later in Hereford and drink a toast to their dead colleague, but Luke declined to join them. For once in his life, he wanted to be alone.

He was finishing his beer when Logan's phone buzzed.

The Liverpudlian unlocked the handset. He opened the new message. Read it. Tapped a link. Watched.

Frowned.

'Fuck,' he whispered.

'What?' Luke asked. 'What is it?'

Logan handed him the phone.

On the screen was a breaking story on the Sky News website. There was a video at the top of the article. A short clip showing the late General Koltrov standing in some sort of generator room, delivering a long and angry tirade to the screen in what sounded like Russian, wearing his trademark leather eyepatch. The subtitles suggested that the general was preparing to martyr himself.

Below it, a short article claimed that the video had been mysteriously uploaded to social media several hours ago. Irrefutable proof, it said, that General Koltrov had been working for the Kremlin all along. The clip had been widely circulated in Russia, the story added. The most popular video ever shared in the country. Forty million views and counting.

The new hero of Russia.

If you enjoyed *Cold Red*,
why not join the
CHRIS RYAN READERS' CLUB?

When you sign up, you'll receive an exclusive Q & A
with Chris Ryan, plus information about upcoming
books and access to exclusive material.
To join, simply visit:
bit.ly/ChrisRyanClub

Keep reading for a letter from the author . . .

Hello!

Thank you for picking up COLD RED.

In early 2022, Russia began its invasion of Ukraine – triggering a brutal war that has shocked and appalled the watching world.

Back then, plenty of experts confidently predicted that the Russian military machine would seize Kyiv in a matter of days or weeks. But through a mixture of bravery and self-sacrifice, NATO and EU support and the ineptitude of Russian forces, Ukraine refused to roll over. Key to their success in defying the aggressors has been the courage shown by their civil and military leaders.

Such high-profile figures are inevitably targets for an increasingly desperate enemy. As Russia seeks to regain the initiative, it's easy to imagine the Kremlin ramping up efforts to assassinate top public officials. With that in mind, there's only one team in the world capable of keeping Ukraine's leaders safe: the SAS. Their unique training and specialist skillsets make the Regiment the best-in-class when it comes to close-protection ops. From this initial idea, the story for COLD RED was born.

This is my most topical book yet. Writing about the conflict wasn't a decision I took lightly – but I felt it was important to describe the horrors of a conflict that has, at times, resembled the battlefields of WWI. We have seen humanity at its worst – torture, rape and murder on an unimaginable scale, the indiscriminate bombing of schools and hospitals. But we've also witnessed the remarkable heroism of Ukraine's defenders, in their struggle against a corrupt and despotic foreign power. A struggle that has, I hope, reminded us of the importance of defending our hard-won freedoms.

If you would like to hear more about my books, you can visit **bit.ly/ChrisRyanClub** where you can become part of the Chris

Ryan Readers' Club. It only takes a few moments to sign up, and there are no catches or costs.

Bonnier Books UK will keep your data private and confidential, and it will never be passed on to a third party. We won't spam you with loads of emails, just get in touch now and again with news about my books, and you can unsubscribe any time you want.

And if you would like to get involved in a wider conversation about my books, please do review COLD RED on Amazon, on GoodReads, on any other e-store, on your own blog and social media accounts, or talk about it with friends, family or reader groups! Sharing your thoughts helps other readers, and I always enjoy hearing about what people experience from my writing.

Thank you again for reading COLD RED.

All the best,

Chris Ryan

B.